YANKEES UNDER SAIL

YANKEES UNDER SAIL

EDITED BY
RICHARD HECKMAN

FOREWORD BY
ROBB SAGENDORPH

*A Collection of the Best Sea Stories
From* Yankee *Magazine with Rare
Photographs Taken During The
Age of Sail*

DESIGNED BY
AUSTIN N. STEVENS

FROM YANKEE BOOKS, A DIVISION OF
YANKEE PUBLISHING INCORPORATED
DUBLIN, NEW HAMPSHIRE

Yankee Publishing Incorporated
Dublin, New Hampshire 03444
First Edition
Copyright 1968, Yankee Publishing Incorporated
Fourth Printing, 1983
Printed in the United States of America

Library of Congress Catalog Card No. 68-31685
ISBN: 0-911658-58-0

FOREWORD

Cohasset, Massachusetts, about halfway along the South Shore of Massachusetts Bay from Boston to Plymouth, is the port from which I experienced my first real voyage under sail. It was in the fifteen-foot sloop, the *Kestrel*. My destination was Boston. My companion, as in every other adventure at that age (12), was "Beaut," a handsome, huge Newfoundland dog. All went well until off Nantasket; the wire from the nose of the bowsprit to the waterline of the bow parted. Despite a strong offshore breeze, I made it to the beach, repaired the damage, and completed my voyage.

I mention this incident here only because I feel some two-thirds of the individuals who live along the coastlines of America can quote "fun" experiences in or on or by the sea. Joseph Lee, for example, a Cohasset neighbor, took off for Labrador in his Manchester seventeen-footer, and Charles Higginson used to sail us across Massachusetts Bay in the moonlight in his Marblehead eighteen-footer. (I never can remember about those Marblehead and Manchester "footers"—were they seventeen or eighteen?)

In the pleasure of reading YANKEES UNDER SAIL, I am certain some of the enjoyment will be, as it was for me, in recalling your own personal adventures. We are not all ocean racers, ship designers, or anything else nautically great. But—shall we say—we just might have been? This book brings together a number of people who, over the years, did take to the sea—and what happened to them. Would you exchange your career for theirs? If yours is or has been employment or existence chiefly on the land, would you now wish to go back and live it over again on the sea? Only you can answer such a question. For my part, the majesty of the sea seems somehow greater and less manageable-by-man than does that of the land. When one embarks on a sea voyage, there is no getting off at Albany or Chicago or St. Louis!

There is no getting off this book either until this reading voyage is over. Welcome aboard!

Robb Sagendorph

TABLE
OF
CONTENTS

YANKEES UNDER SAIL

They were a bold breed, the Yankees in Section **I**   And indeed they surely had to be;

survival was a concern for these **Seamen** from their very first day aboard.

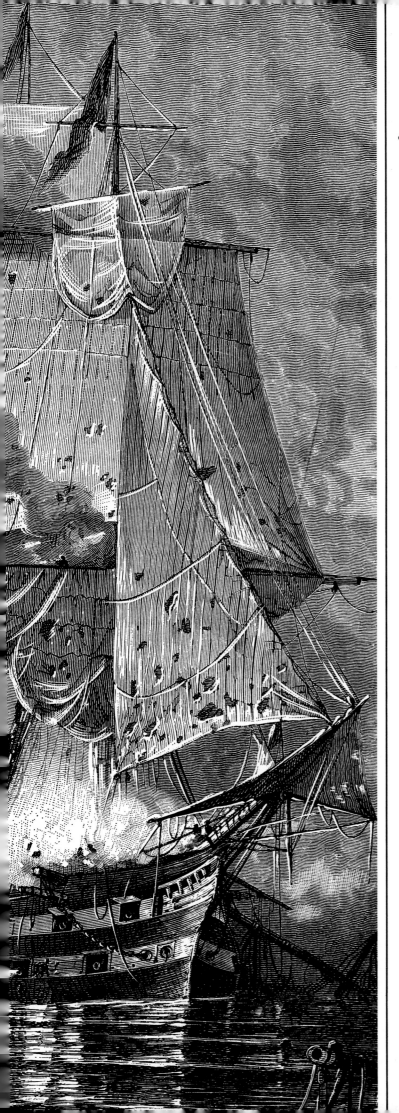

MAD JACK PERCIVAL

by Alton Blackington

A WEATHER-BEATEN SIGN SWINGS ABOVE THE STONE wall that separates the ancient burial ground from the main highway in the historic township of Barnstable, Massachusetts. It is at the junction of Routes 6 and 149 and proclaims:

> Here lies Captain John Percival
> who served in the War of 1812
> and at one time commanded the
> Frigate Constitution

Scores of people walk by this grave every day and thousands of others can see it from their automobiles. However, not one in ten thousand ever heard of Captain John

As Master of the man-of-war Peacock *during the War of 1812, Mad Jack Percival captured seventeen enemy vessels worth more than a million dollars.*

11

Deceptively affable in appearance, Percival was known from Boston to Calcutta as "that cantankerous cuss from Cape Cod." Today, however, this hero of the War of 1812 who saved "Old Ironsides" from the scrapheap and sailed her around the world is seldom mentioned.

Percival brought this old pistol back from his round-the-world cruise on the Constitution *and gave it to the Peabody Museum, Salem, Massachusetts.*

"Get me some rotten fruit and a crate of ducks!"

Percival, or knows how he saved "Old Ironsides" from the scrap heap and then sailed her around the world.

I first heard of John Percival one spring day in 1945 from Alfred Weeks of Barnstable.

"Everybody knows," he told me, "that John Percival was born here on Scorton Hill and is buried down at the corner, but very few realize that he lived in a house that stood over there by that bare spot. Father filled up that cellar hole and planted grass seed, but 'twould never grow. Too gravelly, I guess. Some say that Percival put a curse on this place after his house was flaked and he moved down to the village; but I don't put any more stock in that story than I do in all the other legends about John."

He filled his pipe, lighted up and went on. "Johnnie Percival was a good little tyke when he was a kid, but he was as contrary as a hog on ice. Independent, too. There was the time his ma served him corn-meal mush for supper while she and his pa had fish and taters. He pushed his plate away in disgust and his dad said, 'You eat that hasty puddin' now, John Percival, or you'll find it on your plate every meal until you do.'

" 'I don't want that damned stuff,' Johnnie said, and he dashed out of the house and climbed up on that rock which

was his favorite sulking place. He told old Mr. Bodfish, who lived up the road a-piece, 'Some day I'll get so damned mad I'll get up here and spin 'round until I'm dizzy and fall off; and whichever way I'm facing when I come to, that's the way I'm going.' "

Mr. Weeks scratched another match, puffed and went on.

"Well, next morning, Pa Percival had eggs and bacon for breakfast, but on Johnnie's plate there was the same old soggy mess of hasty puddin'. Johnnie ran down to that boulder, climbed up and spun around until he was so dizzy he couldn't stand. He did fall off and when he come to, in them blueberry bushes, he was facing the road that goes to Plymouth and Boston. He ran back to the house, put on a clean shirt, and, with a handful of his mother's biscuits and some apples, he struck out for Boston, madder'n a wet hen. He got a job as cabin boy, ran away to sea, and ever since then us Scorton Hill folks have called that hunk of granite 'Hasty Puddin' Rock.' "

"When did he come back?" I asked.

"Not until he was a grizzled old sea dog, years after he had saved the *Constitution* and had sailed her 'round the world. He was a cantankerous old cuss then and was known

12

from Cape Cod to Calcutta as 'Mad Jack'!" Mr. Weeks hesitated, "But, at heart, John Percival was one of the kindest men that ever lived."

Naturally I wanted to know more about this forgotten figure of American history, so I looked him up in several well-known libraries. There was very little to be found. The few crumbs of information that I did manage to salvage whetted my appetite to search further.

Finally I found, in the March, 1935, issue of the *United States Naval Institute Proceedings,* an article prepared by Professor Allan Wescott that gave a few highlights of Percival's career.

"With only nine months' schooling and a clean shirt," he says, "Percival ran away from home and went to sea as a cabin boy and cook. He rose quickly to officer's rating, but while second mate of the *Thetis,* out of Boston, the vessel was seized by a British warship. Percival was impressed and sent to the *H.M.S. Victory,* the flagship of Sir John Jervis who had just won the famous battle of Cape St. Vincent. While serving aboard the *Victory,* Percival formed a lifelong friendship with another youth of American parentage, Midshipman Isaac Coffin, who later became an admiral in the Royal Navy.

"Percival was soon shifted to an eighteen gun brig, and from her, as one of the prize crew, to a captured vessel laden with wheat which was taken to Madeira. There the American merchant brig *Washington* was lying at anchor. Percival determined to escape. Waiting until the portly prizemaster dozed off after a heavy lunch, Percival grabbed him by the throat and hissed, 'Silence—or death.' The Britisher was so surprised and scared that he kept still as Johnnie leaped over the side, jumped into a boat and rowed miles to climb aboard the *Washington.*

"After a long voyage to Batavia by way of Rio and Goa, he sailed back to England in the East India Company's ship *Rose.* After crossing the Atlantic to New York, he immediately enlisted in the American Navy as a master's mate. This plucky lad from West Barnstable, Massachusetts, was not yet twenty-one, but he had seen more action than most Cape Codders do in a life time."

After he had been in the American Navy for a while, the War of 1812 broke out. It was on July 4th, 1813, while Percival was stationed in New York, that he gained distinction with a trick that enraged the British, delighted the Americans, and won him a promotion.

New York harbor was blockaded at that time by the British, but a good-sized crowd of Americans had gathered at the Battery to hear a band concert. While roaming around the waterfront, young Percival saw a waterlogged fishing smack named the *Yankee* tied up to the wharf. Her rigging was in sad shape and her sails in shreds, but this suited John Percival to a "T." Quickly he rounded up thirty-two navy men who were on shore leave and sent them to gather all the stale fruit and vegetables they could find in the old Fly Market district.

Locating a smelly billy goat and two ragged sheep, Percival chained them to the foremast and later added a crate of quacking ducks and one grey goose. All of this colorful cargo was arranged topside, in full view, but below decks Percival secreted his thirty-two sailor friends, fully armed with weapons obtained from an American naval vessel at a nearby pier.

When all was ready, Percival, clad in a loose duster, wearing a straw hat, and looking for all the world like a farmer from Long Island, hoisted the *Yankee*'s shredded sail, the innocent-looking "bumboat" eased out into New York harbor.

He had gone but three miles when he was overtaken by the British tender *Beagle* with thirteen Red Coats on board. Her commander, on the lookout for fresh vegetables, took one whiff of the lumbering "bumboat" and ordered Percival to bring his craft about and follow the tender to the flagship. With a knowing smirk on his face, Percival spun the wheel over hard, the ships came together, and, as they bumped, Johnnie shouted the watchword, "LAWRENCE! LAWRENCE!"

Instantly his musket-bearing sailors came tumbling from the *Yankee*'s hold, firing as they came. They poured over the Britisher's bulwarks; a short, sharp fight followed and the enemy vessel surrendered.

Two hours later, the old fishing smack *Yankee,* with Percival at the helm and his British prize in tow, sailed up to the Battery to the cheers of an admiring crowd. As an American naval officer jumped forward to grasp Percival's hand and congratulate him, he explained, "Shucks, we was just having a little fun. We ought to do something to celebrate the Fourth of July besides listening to a band concert."

Percival was quickly promoted and, as sailing master of the sloop of war *Peacock,* he participated in three successful cruises that resulted in the capture of seventeen enemy ships worth more than a million dollars.

A year later he was put in command of the 88-foot, 12-gun schooner *Dolphin.*

The *Dolphin* then sailed for the Sandwich Islands where she remained until May 1826, being the first American man-of-war to visit Hawaii. Percival rendered valuable service in protecting American interests, and helped salvage cargo and specie from the ship *London* wrecked on Renai Island.

There had been much ill feeling between American sailors and the missionaries who had instituted a taboo on native women who frequently visited the ships. Early that year, a group of American sailors, including several from the *Dolphin,* made a murderous attack upon the missionary headquarters. This fracas was finally subdued by Percival himself who, cane in hand, came ashore. With several well-directed blows and much violent language, he succeeded in breaking up the brawl. He ordered the sailors from the *Dolphin* put in irons and, next day, invited missionary Bingham to come aboard to witness the floggings which were meted out as punishment.

Shortly afterward the taboo on native women being allowed aboard American ships was discontinued. It had never been popular or practical.

13

Clad only in red underwear, Percival dove into the ocean

For his outstanding achievements in the Sandwich Islands, particularly in rendering assistance to the American whaling fleet, Percival was advanced to the rank of Captain. He was given command of the new sloop *Cyane,* and served under Commodore Isaac Hull who was only six years his senior.

We were having a great deal of trouble with West Indian pirates at this time and the big brass in Washington thought that if anybody could make these pirates behave it would be "Mad Jack" Percival. Captain Percival immediately received orders and sailed for the West Indies aboard the *Cyane.*

On the pretext of taking on wood and water, he dropped anchor at the island of St. Thomas. He warped the *Cyane* so that her guns pointed directly at the Governor's estate, and then he hastily scribbled a message to the pirate chieftain who lived there, saying:

Dear Governor;

I am writing this note on the breach of a 32 pounder which, with other guns, is pointed directly at your residence. There is a lighted match at each of the guns which I fear will not burn more than 30 minutes. If the money which you took from the American brig *Reliance* and other American ships is not turned over to me within the hour, I will send you more bunches of grape than you can digest.

J. Percival.

The terrified Governor wanted to "negotiate," but, seeing the snouts of all those cannon pointed at his windows, he reluctantly gave in. He ordered his slaves and soldiers to dump the coins in bags and boxes and cart them to the wharf where the gold was speedily stowed aboard the *Cyane.* Later it was taken back to the United States.

Without firing a single shot, Percival had accomplished results where months of government letter writing and shilly-shallying had failed. He was hailed as a hero, and overnight new legends and stories sprang up about "Mad Jack" Percival.

I picked up the best story of "Mad Jack" from a retired naval officer who, like myself, prefers the little-known human interest yarns not commonly found in naval reports, books, and magazines.

We were enjoying a noonday snack of clam chowder, pickles, and crackers at a restaurant in Fairhaven, and somehow the conversation drifted to the colorful careers of such navy heroes as Isaac Hull, Edward Preble, and John Paul Jones.

"And," I added, "Don't forget 'Mad Jack' Percival from West Barnstable. I have heard how he sailed 'Old Ironsides' around the world, but I don't know the story of how he saved the *Constitution.* Do you?"

The navy man's eyes sparkled and his thin face broke into a smile. "Indeed I do," he said, "and its a corker. I can't be sure of my dates or names, but the essential facts are these."

I ordered another cup of coffee and opened my note book.

He began, "It was while 'Old Ironsides' was in Norfolk Navy Yard between 1841 and 1844, about the time she was flagship of the Home Squadron and Charlie Stewart was Commodore.

"The question arose, 'Can "Old Ironsides" be put in suitable shape to make another world cruise? If so, how much will it cost?' A committee was appointed to investigate. They went all over "Old Ironsides" and came back to the yard. It may have been pure coincidence, but the very day they made their report who should be poking about but old 'Mad Jack' Percival.

"Just as he walked into the conference room, he heard the Secretary of the Navy, David Henshaw, say, 'It's too bad, gentlemen, but I fear that this time "Old Ironsides" will have to be scrapped. I'm told that her hull is badly rotted and that she needs new rigging and sails. The board estimates it will cost $150,000 to put her in shape. You know as well as I do that we haven't that much money.'

"Percival strode forward, eyes blazing. 'Who told you that rot?' he roared. '$150,000! Bah!' and he pounded the table with his fist. 'Do you mind if I take a good close look at her hull and spars?'

"So, to humor the hot-tempered Percival, they told him to go ahead and look all he wanted to, and then come back and report."

The admiral poured himself another cup of tea and continued.

"Know what Percival did? He peeled off his jacket and trousers and, clad only in a suit of red underwear, dived into that cold water. He swam all 'round the *Constitution,* poking and punching her timbers with an awl. Then he shook himself like a dog, put on his pants, and climbed into the rigging to look at shrouds, stays, lifts, and braces. Took him four hours and, when he came down, he was pretty shaky. But he brushed himself off and went right back to the Secretary's office and said, 'I'm glad to report, sir, that the *Constitution* needs only a few repairs. Give me a crew of real ship riggers and $10,000 and I'll put her in shape to sail 'round the world.'"

My guest drained his tea cup and smiled. "They gave 'Mad Jack' the $10,000 he wanted and he came up to New England. From Boston, Salem, New Bedford, and Portsmouth he got enough old-time ship riggers to do the job right. It was a mighty proud Percival who finally turned "Old Ironsides" over to the Navy Department instead of sending her to the scrap pile. And, 'Mad Jack' was made even more proud when Secretary Henshaw said, 'Captain Percival, you have saved "Old Ironsides"; now sail her to the China Seas.'

"By golly, he did. He sailed on a voyage of 55,000

miles that took him two years. Mind you, 'Mad Jack' was then sixty-seven years old."

Captain Percival's clerk, on this memorable voyage around the world, was Benjamin F. Stevens who faithfully kept a diary of all that happened, and he gives a picturesque description of the 26 ports the *Constitution* visited. The account was first published in *The United Service Magazine*. Later it was brought out in book form. I located a copy in the Lynn, Massachusetts, Public Library and I found it very interesting.

"Mad Jack's" name was placed on the reserve list on September 13th, 1855 and, thus relieved of sea duty, he took up residence in Dorchester, Massachusetts.

Whenever I see that yellow and black sign board swinging over the granite tablet that marks "Mad Jack's" grave in West Barnstable, I think it is a shame that more people never heard of him. He was a Yankee of whom we can all be proud.

Mad Jack Percival as he looked a few months before his death. This picture now hangs in the Navy Building, Washington, D.C.

Every so often there pops up in the newspapers a story about some man or woman who dreamed that something terrible was going to happen—and a few days later it did.

I couldn't begin to count the number of people who have had just such experiences with hunches, dreams and prophecies; and I'll bet you that you can't beat the yarn I'm going to spin for you now about Captain Joe Mesquita who was known and loved by all the fishermen from Provincetown to Portugal.

In Gloucester, Massachusetts, each Trinity Sunday, more than 10,000 people pay tribute to his memory as the Portuguese population observes an old, old ceremony inaugurated in the fifteenth century by Queen Isabella of Spain.

The streets are draped with the national colors. Foreign flags flutter, bands play and banners are lifted high as a colorful procession starts from D.E.S. Hall.

Dark-eyed senoritas, dressed in white with red capes, march behind the handsomely uniformed members of the patriotic societies, and ALL of them pay tribute to the "Captain Courageous" who made possible by his generosity this glorious pageant of color and romance, a pageant as vivid and impressive as any of the similar ceremonies that are held on Trinity Sunday in the cities of the Old World.

The picturesque parade wends its way through the narrow streets of Gloucester to the home of a fisherman who appears holding a dazzling crown of solid silver. Four young ladies carrying red and gold "varda sticks" form a protecting square for the crown as it is carried through the streets to the Cathedral of Our Lady of Good Voyage.

Waiting for the appearance of the Crown at the portico of the Cathedral of Our Lady of Good Voyage in Gloucester, Mass. This photograph was taken on May 27, 1934—the first year that "Cap'n Joe" Mesquita was not present to participate in the ceremony.

THE CROWN

by John Mason

Brown had a feeling that something terrible was going to happen . . .

Participating in the 1934 Trinity celebration are (left) flower girls Mary Fernands, Mary Gasper, and Mary Silveira. Above, a portion of the parade that year, led by a contingent from the Gloucester Police Department.

As this impressive ceremony takes place at the altar of the Cathedral, little flower girls scatter pink and purple petals over the bowed heads of a score of fishermen kneeling at the foot of the altar reaffirming the secret, sacred vows they have recently made to God. High in the towers of the Cathedral of Our Lady of Good Voyage, a young lady plays "Ave Maria" and the "Rosary" on the famous carillon chimes. After the service, the procession winds its way back to the D.E.S. Hall where there is a roast beef dinner—a la Portugal—followed by an auction.

If you have no particular place to go on Trinity Sunday and would like to combine the beauty of Massachusetts' North Shore scenery with a bit of Old World pageantry, drive down to Gloucester and see this "crowning" ceremony. And you'll appreciate the beauty and solemnity of this occasion more fully when you know the dramatic story behind it all.

Captain Joe Mesquita was born in Portugal. When he was 19 years old, he ran away and landed in Gloucester with 49¢ in his pocket. He got a job on a fishing boat, and after working hard for 20 years, he owned several fishing smacks of his own.

The apple of his eye was a handsome, new, two-masted

schooner—the *Mary P. Mesquita*—named for his wife, and it was upon this vessel that a strange and horrible event occurred on the night of October 10, 1894.

The schooner had sailed from Gloucester, bound for the Grand Banks with a crew of 16 men and Cap'n Joe at the wheel. The first night out, one of the crew, a man named Alfred Brown, had a dream that he was being choked to death. He awoke in a cold sweat and rushed to the Captain telling him it was a bad omen. All fishermen are superstitious, but Cap'n Joe was a level-headed fellow and told Brown to forget it and go back to bed.

Well, by jingos, Brown had the same dream at the same time the next night—only the second dream was more terrible than the first. He came rushing to Cap'n Joe, warning him that something terrible was going to happen.

Cap'n Joe was a little scared himself, but he didn't admit it (well, not then, that is—he did admit it to Mrs. Roosevelt and the President when he told them the story I'm telling you—but we'll come to that later). Cap'n Joe

18

Captain Joe Mesquita, who had a solid silver crown custom-made in Spain. The crown and the colorful Gloucester Trinity Sunday ceremony all came about because of a promise kept.

took the terrified sailor to his cabin, and there before the little altar, where the Patron Saint of "Our Lady of Good Voyage" stood in the flickering candlelight, the two men implored the protection of the Virgin Mary.

All the next day Cap'n Joe kept wondering if Brown would have a third nightmare. He didn't have to wait long. After the crew turned in, the air was suddenly filled with screams from below. Brown came tearing up on deck, yelling that someone was trying to choke him. "Cap'n Joe, I'm gonna die—I know I'm gonna die!"

With kind and sympathetic understanding and the tenderness of a mother with a frightened child, Cap'n Joe took the terrified fisherman back to his bunk, put him in bed, and sat by his side for a long time, talking about this, that, and other things until he fell asleep.

The schooner was about 40 miles off Thatcher's Light, when without warning a thick, wet fog rolled in and a feeling of uneasiness came over the Captain and crew. Lookouts were posted and the vessel crept slowly through the fog.

At 11 o'clock Cap'n Joe went below to see if Brown was still asleep; but before he reached the companionway, he heard a sharp cry from the forward lookout—"All hands on deck!" Rushing to the rail, he was horrified to see the sharp steel prow of an ocean liner looming above his tiny schooner. It was the steamship *Saxonia,* and before the helpless men could make a move, the liner struck the little fishing smack and cut it clean in two.

The first thing Cap'n Joe thought of was the sleeping sailor. He grabbed a lantern and, wading knee-deep in water, he went below; but there was no sign of Brown. With superhuman strength, the Cap'n fought his way up against the onrushing torrent. Just as he reached the deck, it slid from under him and sank.

The *Saxonia*—her searchlights trying to pierce the fog and her lifeboats already lowered—was standing by. One by one the injured sailors were picked up and taken aboard the liner. When Cap'n Joe gathered them about him on the forward deck, he found they were all there—except Alfred Brown. He was never seen again.

Then the passengers of the *Saxonia* witnessed as dramatic a scene as ever took place on the deck of a liner.

Standing in the midst of his shipwrecked crew, Cap'n Joe raised his arms to heaven and lifted his voice in prayer. Then he knelt on the deck with his men around him and made a vow that, if he and his companions survived the ordeal and reached Gloucester safely, he would devote his entire life to helping unfortunate fishermen.

"I will send to Portugal for a special good-luck crown," he shouted, "that the fishermen can keep in their homes, and I will see to it that no fisherman or his family will ever go hungry."

Back in Gloucester, no one worried about Cap'n Joe's boat until several days had passed. Then came word that the wreckage of the *Mary P. Mesquita* and two dories had been found near Highland Light. Flags were hung at half mast in Gloucester, and all New England mourned the loss of another brave crew of fishermen—all except Captain Joe's wife, Mary, who steadfastly refused to believe that her husband was dead.

Then, one happy day, a cable from Liverpool announced that Cap'n Joe had arrived on the *Saxonia,* alive and well, with all of his crew except Alfred Brown. Needless to say, there was great rejoicing when the men came back to Gloucester.

Cap'n Joe went at once to his old friend Father De-Bem, the parish priest of the Portuguese church. "Father," he said, "I want you to send to Portugal and get the finest silver crown that can be made. I don't care how long it takes, I don't care how much it costs—I want the best."

The order was placed in Lisbon and for months the silversmiths toiled on the intricate design of the crown that for years was to bring good luck to the fishermen of Gloucester: the same sparkling, silver crown that is carried through the streets of the old seaport city every Trinity Sunday.

When the crown arrived, it was given a royal reception, taken to the church, blessed by Father DeBem, and placed in front of the altar, where all might gaze upon its hand-wrought beauty.

For many years, the crown reposed on the family altar in Cap'n Joe's own home. From time to time he loaned it to the original members of his shipwrecked crew to bring them good luck, but as the men were changing from one vessel to another, he decided to give it to all the fishermen; and so, with great formality, it was presented to "Our Lady of Good Voyage."

Years later when a group of famous skippers sailed into Washington, D.C. on the *Gertrude Thebaud,* the Gloucestermen were invited to call on President and Mrs. Franklin Roosevelt at the White House.

Mrs. Roosevelt, much impressed by Cap'n Joe's story, handed him her autograph album.

Cap'n Joe was a little fussed. He fumbled for a pen and then drew from his pocket a little pad. From his overcoat he took a rubber stamp and, after inking it on the pad, he stamped on a clean white page of Mrs. Roosevelt's album his name—"Captain Joe Mesquita—Gloucester, Massachusetts"; and when the ink was dry he made a big cross over the signature.

Turning to the President and Mrs. Roosevelt he said, "This is the best I can do." Mrs. Roosevelt replied, "There will never be any signature in this book more valuable than the one you have just placed there."

It wasn't long after that Cap'n Joe passed away. All Gloucester mourned his passing. There were humble fishermen and millionaires at his funeral. The Coast Guard of Base Seven made a 12-foot replica of his fishing boat out of roses, and with green garlands they fashioned these words—

"A fair wind on your homeward run, Cap'n Joe—we rise to our feet as you pass by."

WHEN MARY MET THE "CAPE HORN GREYBEARDS"

by Wanda Webb

ONE OF THE MOST HEART-STIRRING STORIES OF THE sea is Mary Patten's Cape Horn voyage in the clipper *Neptune's Car*.

The story begins in Boston, in the Old North Church of Paul Revere fame. Here, on an April day in 1853, a wedding took place. The bride was Mary Ann Brown of Boston. Daughter of English-born parents, George and Elizabeth Brown, she was one of a large family living on Salutation Street. Slender, with delicate features, dark hair, and large, dark eyes, she had an "air of feminine softness" strangely at variance with the role she was destined to play. She was only 16 years old when she spoke the fateful words: "I, Mary, take thee, Joshua, . . . to love, cherish and obey."

For better, for worse, the marriage joined her life to the sea. Her husband was Capt. Joshua A. Patten of Rockland, Maine. He had followed the sea from his boyhood and had struggled up from the forecastle to become one of the youngest captains on the coast. At age 26, he already had a reputation for fine character—and *fast voyages*.

By a strange coincidence, at the very time of Mary Patten's marriage, the *Neptune's Car* was about to become a bride of the sea. Her oaken frame lay cradled in the shipyards of Page & Allen of Portsmouth, Virginia. And, on the

16th of April, 1853, she slid off the ways.

She was a large ship of 1,616 tons, 216 feet long, with a depth of 23½ feet, and a beam of 40. Her dimensions were close to those of the *Flying Cloud*. And, like her, she was a splendid ship, and a fast one.

Young Joshua Patten was offered command of the *Car* following the sudden illness of her first captain on the eve of a voyage around the world. It was a great honor to be chosen, for only to men of superior seamanship came the chance to command these costly, capricious speed-ships. Yet he hesitated, so the story goes, for he was deeply in love and did not wish to leave his young bride. So the clipper's owners, Messrs. Foster & Nickerson of New York, gave Patten permission to take his wife with him. And "within twelve hours after they had been notified" according to one account, Mary and Joshua were aboard the *Neptune's Car*.

On their first voyage "the wind shifted suddenly to SE and squalls which carried away jiboom . . . and split royals, blowed away flying jib outer jib and light staysails," reads the log. "*Neptune*'s doing her best." Her best was so fine that she was one of three clippers to make a record passage around the Horn that season. Also, she almost beat the clipper *Westward Ho* to Frisco. So close was the race—the *Westward Ho* making the passage in 100 days, 18 hours, and the *Neptune's Car* coming in only 5½ hours later—that the famous Captain Hussey of the *Westward Ho* offered to race Patten to Hong Kong, since both their ships were loading for China.

So Joshua and Mary Patten began a second honeymoon aboard the *Neptune's Car.* Perhaps it was during this voyage, under the starry skies of the wide Pacific, that Mary began learning navigation from her skillful husband. The voyage was a long and a difficult one. Misfortunes befell their crew of "14 white Seamen and 18 Lascars . . . Sinbad, one of the sailors, fell from the upper deck . . . and was badly Injured . . . Manlias, one of the Lascars, . . . fell overboard . . . and was Drowned. Brought the ship to the wind and Sent a Life Boat in Serch." The seaman was never found, and hours were lost. The winds died, and the *Neptune's Car* had to crawl across the Pacific. Even so, she beat the *Westward Ho* to Hong Kong by 11 days.

The young Captain was now given a London charter and sailed with Mary from Foochow to London, back to New York, and so around the world.

Then, for the last time, Mary and Joshua boarded the *Neptune's Car.*

The ship cleared from New York on the first day of July, 1856, heavily laden with a valuable cargo for the West Coast. She carried everything from wine to sheetlead and iron.

Two other fast clippers, the *Intrepid* and the *Romance of the Seas,* sailed about the same time as the *Neptune's Car,* and it was doubtless Patten's aim to beat them to the West Coast. But the race course was the roughest in the world—around the Horn.

Neptune's Car must have been a beautiful sight as she came down the river—"her masts and spars they shine like silver!" Towed to sea, she passed Sandy Hook, discharged her pilot, and spread her wings.

And such wings they were! For clippers generally carried more than an acre of canvas when all outspread—mainsails, topsails, topgallants, royals, and skysails, sometimes moonsails so high they seemed a part of heaven.

Proud of his ship, and supremely confident of her fast-sailing ability, Patten probably planned to carry all the canvas possible to make a record passage.

The trade winds came from the east-northeast and blew the *Neptune's Car* towards the equator. Flying fish leaped in rainbow colors as the ship flashed her way through the blue waters. White sea birds flew in the dazzling light. And the white wings of the royals sped the ship onward like some great oceanic bird.

Patten was eager to let his ship drive. But there was one man aboard who was strangely indifferent to his Captain's wish for speed. He was the First Mate. "He's a rocket from hell," says the chantey; but this man was more like some ever-growing barnacle of trouble that had fastened itself upon the ship to slow her speed. "He reefed the courses while his Captain slept," and this happened more than once —the Mate putting the ship under shortened sail when wind and weather proclaimed full speed ahead.

Neptune's Car crossed the 45th parallel, and the cold began to grow. Colder, too, grew the relations between Mate and Captain. Several times the Mate was discovered asleep on watch. Reprimanded, he grew sullen.

The cold increased. The sea became grey-green. Stormy petrels rode in the wake of the *Car* and the white albatross spread his 12-foot wings and flew near the ship as darkness fell. The brilliant stars of the Southern Cross rose later as the *Neptune's Car* drew nearer to the Horn. Somewhere, in this cold corner of the world, something happened; some final action of the Mate cracked Patten's patience, and he deposed the Mate for insubordination.

Now, night after night, the young Captain stayed awake, his heavy load doubled by the failure of his first officer. He could not replace him, for the Second Mate was almost as ignorant of navigation as any member of the crew.

Strain and fatigue began to tell on Joshua Patten. And, when the ship was passing through the Straits of Le Maire, he fell ill with "brain-fever." He grew delirious, and unable to command his ship.

Now, when the worst waters of the world were upon her, the great clipper held no man qualified for her command. Terrible westerly gales began to blow, and mile-long waves, "Cape Horn Greybeards," rushed up from the Antarctic.

Mary Patten, now 19, faced this black crisis at a time when she was least fitted to cope with its darkness—for she was expecting a child.

One star shone faintly in this night of foreboding. It was her knowledge of navigation. Once it had been only a hobby to while away the long hours at sea. Now it was a matter on which many lives depended.

Quietly, Mary Patten took charge of the great clipper. And, though the longing to run for the nearest port must have been very strong, she knew her husband's orders that "under no circumstances was the ship to be taken into any other port than San Francisco." So, with that devotion which shines through all her story, the young wife prepared to obey her beloved husband's command.

When the disgraced Mate heard that the Captain's wife had taken charge and would attempt to navigate the *Neptune's Car* to San Francisco, he is reported to have written her a letter of warning, pointing out the dangers of the coast, and the fearful responsibility she had assumed, and ending with the statement that he would relieve her of her post and take command himself.

To this proposal Mary Patten is said to have replied, with spirit, that since her husband had considered him unfit for *Mate,* she could not consider him qualified for *Captain.*

Many a bride left her home to join her husband at sea, but few could duplicate Mary Patten's experience. With her husband, the Captain, suddenly rendered deaf and blind, and with the First Mate having been locked up for insubordination, this 19-year-old girl assumed command of the giant clipper ship as she was rounding the Horn's raging seas.

Then the Mate "sought to excite mutiny among the crew, insisting upon carrying the ship into Valparaiso," according to several accounts. Mutiny is perhaps too strong a term for the Mate's action; but it is probable that he wanted to run for Valparaiso, perhaps honestly believing that the safety of the ship depended upon making for that port. Whatever his actions, it is reasonably certain that Mary Patten had to summon the crew and appeal her case to them.

To this young girl it must have been a fearful ordeal. Clipper crews were a wild lot—from the waterfronts of the world. Alarmed now, over the turn of the voyage, they were perhaps openly hostile.

What Mary Patten said to them we shall never know. Perhaps she told them frankly of her husband's helplessness, of his plea to her to take the ship to San Francisco, not putting into any foreign port where delay would prove so costly. Perhaps she reassured them on her navigation knowledge, told them how her husband had taught her to "box the compass," "shoot the sun," and use the tables in Sam Bowditch's book.

Perhaps it was her spirit and courage, more than any words she spoke, that overcame the crew. "To a man," wrote one reporter, "they resolved to stand by her and the ship, *come what might.*"

What came was terrible. For 18 days the *Neptune's Car* was off the Horn. It was 18 days of cold and howling gales.

Before the raging of the gale, the *Car*'s great masts became like matchsticks—her giant sails like ribbons. The wind snatched off the towering white crests of the waves and hurled them over the decks. It lashed the men fast against the rigging.

"Each man vied with his fellows in the performance of his duty," said a reporter. They risked their lives out on the great yards which bent like birches in the gale. The huge blocks beat about like whips, and the sails could flatten out a man's life with the violence of their lashing.

The sea brought up its 60-foot waves and sent them crashing against the clipper. It burst foaming cataracts over her bows, and formed a mountainous range of peaks and precipices over which the *Neptune's Car* plunged and struggled.

"How Mrs. Patten fought that ship to the westward," says Carl Cutler in his book, *Greyhounds of the Sea* . . . "is a story that has no parallel in fiction."

For 50 days and nights Mary Patten was on duty constantly. When she was not on deck, she was hard at work in the cabin. "Her time was divided," so someone wrote, "between the bedside of her delirious husband and the writing desk, working up the intricate calculations incident to nautical observations, making entries in the log book in her own delicate penmanship, and tracing with accuracy the position of the ship from the charts in the cabin."

The rough sailors all obeyed the little woman, as they called her, "with a will." And, in the intervals of calm, "eyed her curiously and affectionately through the cabin windows while deep in the calculations on which her life and theirs depended."

So, with her navigation knowledge, and the response of the crew, *Neptune's Car* fought her way northward.

During the long voyage Mary kept her husband alive by her devoted care, tending him with skill and tenderness, studying books of medicine to learn what she could do for him. "She shaved his head," says one account, "and devised every means in her power to soothe and restore him." The "brain-fever" from which he suffered is described in one of the journals of the day as "The New Epidemic . . . which baffles the skill of physicians . . . Persons are attacked very suddenly, soon become insane."

For a time Captain Patten seemed to rally. Then he

They called her the Florence Nightingale of the ocean

had a relapse. His hearing and sight began to fail. He became deaf and totally blind!

This happened just two days before the ship crossed the equator in the Pacific, October 17, longitude 115. How interminable the rest of the voyage must have seemed to his wife!

One more trial awaited them. To 30 North the ship had "light NE winds; thence to 36 N had strong NE winds." But then came fog, thick as brown blankets. And for days, off the heads of San Francisco, the *Neptune's Car* was fogbound.

When the fog finally lifted, and the ship approached the harbor of San Francisco, Mary Patten "was warned of the danger she would encounter in passing in," wrote one reporter, "and was advised to lay off until they could secure a pilot. This she refused to do; presuming upon her acquired knowledge, she took the helm herself and steered the vessel safely into port."

Neptune's Car docked on November 15, 1856, after a voyage of 136 days. She had beaten one of the two clippers that sailed with her, the *Intrepid,* by 11 days.

She was a proud-looking ship as she came to rest at her wharf, for her crew had expressed their affection for "Mrs. Captain Patten" by making her ship a shining one from deck to skypole. "Both vessel and cargo," it was said, "were in better trim than any of her competitors."

After debarking in San Francisco, Mary and Joshua were helped by the Masons, for Joshua Patten was a member of the Polar Star Lodge. One of his brother Masons, a Dr. Harris, was delegated to watch over him on the voyage home. The Pattens were put aboard the *Golden Gate* steamship, then transferred at Panama to the steamer *George Law,* bound for New York.

"One day last month," according to the *London Daily News,* "the people in the streets of New York observed a litter, evidently containing a sick person, carried from the shipping to the Battery Hotel. Beside the litter walked a young creature, who, but for her careworn countenance and her being near her confinement, might have been taken for a little school girl. Her story soon became known, and it has presently reached all hearts."

Their Odyssey finally ended in Boston. Here, on the 10th of March, their child was born, a boy, named for his father. "My husband," wrote Mary, "takes great delight in our little boy."

One thousand dollars came to Mary from the underwriters of the *Neptune's Car,* accompanied by a beautifully written letter of praise and thanks.

Mary replied that she was "seriously embarrassed by the fear that you may have overestimated the value of those services, because I feel that without the services of Mr. Hare, the second officer, a good seaman, and of the hearty cooperation of the crew to aid our endeavors, the ship would not have arrived safely at her destined port."

However, as people were quick to point out, "considering that the ship and cargo were worth nearly $350,000 and that to her (Mary Patten's) skill and decision they are mainly indebted for its safety, under most adverse circumstances—for the weather was unusually severe . . . the least they should have done would have been to give her a check of $5,000."

". . . It was not to be supposed," observed a New York paper, "that the sum bestowed upon her would last long, and it did not. It was soon exhausted, and the heroic young creature, who . . . assumed and accomplished a task from which the stalwart sailors shrank with dread, is now lying impoverished and sick of typhoid fever. . . ."

The ladies of Boston came to her aid, raising a fund of $1,399 for her benefit; and admiring strangers from other places sent her gifts. A blind gentleman in London wrote her a check for a hundred dollars with a letter saying, "Your own noble conduct must be to strangers an excuse for addressing you. Our journals have made all Europe acquainted with deeds which are appreciated as much in the Old World as in your native country."

A long, purple-passaged poem was written about her in England. And over here she was hailed as a Woman's Rights heroine—a role she disliked intensely. Ministers held her up as an example of wifely devotion and referred to her in their sermons as the "Heroine of Cape Horn." And Edward Everett, the foremost orator of the day, called her the "Florence Nightingale of the Ocean."

Honor and glory were hers for a while. But the ending of the story is sad. Before the year was out, Captain Patten died, in the Somerville Lunatic Asylum. His funeral was in Old North, with the flags of Boston harbor flying at half mast in his honor.

Mary followed him a few years later, dying of tuberculosis in her 24th year.

The *Neptune's Car* which was so closely woven into her life passed from our shores and was sold to the British only a year after her death.

Today, two plain white headstones stand in Woodlawn Cemetery in Everett, near Boston. No legend is on them to tell the story of love and heroism aboard the *Neptune's Car.*

They stand side by side:

Mary Ann Patten	Joshua A. Patten
Born	Born
April 6, 1837	April 20, 1827
Died	Died
March 17, 1861	July 26, 1857

TWILIGHT OF A MERCHANT HOUSE

by James A. Finn

CHARLES BREWER & COMPANY, SHIPPING AND COMmission Merchants, 27 Kilby Street, Boston, Mass. That was the legend at the head of the handwritten letter I received in October 1901, asking me to call with reference to their office boy ad in the *Boston Transcript*.

A greenhorn in downtown Boston, I walked up and down State Street until a friendly lettercarrier pointed across to Kilby Street and along down to the ancient narrow building—long since torn down—on the corner of Exchange Place. Scarily I climbed No. 27's stone steps, took a creepy ride up in the pull-rope elevator and stood, just turned eighteen, before the door of Charles Brewer & Company's top floor office. A thump at my midriff to banish the butterflies, a resolute twist to the doorknob—and I was inside.

A barrier railing with a latched gate at its far end confronted me. Across it I swept a glance at this strange house of business, and knew that I had been romancing. For those words "Shipping" and "Merchant" on the letterhead had set me to picturing a museum of a room filled with antique furniture brought home by merchant princes from voyages to the Far East, to England and the Continent; with time-mellowed paintings of the sea hanging on the walls; with rugs and curios picked up in the bazaars of the Indies carelessly strewn about. But before me of elegance and ease there was nothing, not a thing to soften and charm away long workaday hours. Everything was solid, Spartan. The floor was bare; heavy roll-top desks were that and nothing more; a ceiling-high cabinet was crammed with filing boxes, yellowing records, old account books, dusty trade papers brown with age. A formidable-looking letter press which

well might be a torture wheel—and it was—weighed down a stand which had seen years of hard usage. Along the windows stood a tall bookkeeper's desk, its two work surfaces sloping down from a centered book rack, and two high stools, on one of which was perched a clerk poring over an account book from which he did not raise his head to favor me with a glance. On the wall above a battened fireplace, there at last my eye lit on one bit of the other-world atmosphere I had been expecting to find. A huge pair of walrus tusks, thrusting themselves menacingly out from the skull, were keeping watch over a room-high office safe with open door. Long years later, when I read in *Anthony Adverse* the description of the Casa Bonnyfeather counting house in Leghorn, I said to myself, "There is the Brewer office, transported to the Mediterranean."

I was roving a still hopeful eye farther along the walls; at an aged map of the Sandwich Islands, the largest of which looked like the mummified head of a monk with a cowl, his deeply wrinkled nose pointing northwest; at faded photographs of ships, and of oldtime waterfront buildings which I learned later were early Honolulu, when in from what evidently was a private office stepped a courtly, white-bearded gentleman. "I am Edward M. Brewer," he told me, and unlatching the gate, he escorted me in to meet his equally white-bearded brother and partner Joseph Brewer. And while they were examining me and my credentials my inspecting eye was taking in a set of wicker chairs brought

Whaling Captain Charles Brewer who in 1826 founded Charles Brewer & Company, Shipping and Commission Merchants.

back, no doubt, from a voyage to the Orient; a mid-Victorian revolving bookcase loaded with cable codes, Lloyd's Registers, atlases, catalogs, reference books. And most of all, full length on top of Edward Brewer's roll-top, a big half-model of a ship's hull in a glass case with a mirror set at each end, at an angle, so that anyone looking into either mirror saw the ship full beam. According to the legend plate, the ship was built in Scotland, and I conceded that the half-model was a tribute to Scottish craftsmanship—and thrift.

To Mr. J. B.'s query as to whether I had had any business experience, I answered, altogether convincingly I thought, that as manager of the baseball team at Boston Latin School I had kept a cash book to record receipts and disbursements. That brought forth the first smile of the day from the brothers; they retired to the wicker chair compound to confer, and Edward Brewer, returning, made me a formal little bow and announced that I was hired—at three dollars a week. Incredible in these openhanded prodigal days? I didn't blink, for I knew from office boy acquaintances that three dollars was the going rate; in fact one boy told me he was required to take home the office towels to be washed. Also I knew that in some of the oldtime banking

houses a boy not only got no pay at all, his fond parent was required to put up a training fee of $150, which was the cost then of one-year's tuition at Harvard (to whose freshman class I had in my pocket a certificate of admission, to be flashed if needed as a clincher. Later I learned that the brothers' nephews, Charlie and Arthur Brewer, made Harvard football history against Yale in what were known as the "slaughter days" at Springfield, 1890s).

The partners thereupon briefed their new employee on the history of the firm. It was founded in 1826 by their father, Charles Brewer, a whaling Captain, whose long-deserted mansion I often saw standing across from Jamaica Pond in the midst of its acres, now solidly built with fine homes along the Jamaica Way. Captain Brewer, they told me, made Honolulu his base of operations and his second home, also founding C. Brewer & Co. Ltd., still one of the Big Five Honolulu sugar factors and plantation owners. I was informed that the firm's business was primarily ship-owning, carrying cargoes of general merchandise to Hono-

The Nuuanu, *iron bark built in Scotland in 1882. The Brewers finally sold her in Honolulu after she had been repaired following a severe battering during a storm off the Strait of Magellan. Her final fate is not known.*

lulu, and bringing back sugar in their ships, of which they then owned three: *Helen Brewer,* a full-rigged ship, a model of which stood there before me, and the barks *Nuuanu* and *Foohng Suey* (the latter name being Chinese for Good Luck). Also they acted as purchasing agent— that was the Commission Merchant end of the business— for several Honolulu firms. They bought and shipped everything, it seemed to me as they reeled off the list, from a toothpick to a baby elephant, the buying being done at their New York office.

Thus briefed, I was escorted back to the outer office, presented to the clerk, who now climbed down from his high stool to greet me, and I was told to report next morning. So at 9 A.M. on October 9, 1901, I became a wage earner in the employ of Charles Brewer & Company, Shipping and Commission Merchants.

My job was to do all the leg work, errand running, bank messenger, picking up railroad bills of lading for goods shipped overland to Frisco, thence by steamer to the

Joseph Brewer (right) and Edward May Brewer, sons of the founder and partners of C. Brewer & Company. They hired the author as "office boy" in 1901 at the going rate of three dollars a week.

Islands, making up the mail and depositing it in the Post Office. Also I had to check Indents, as orders from the Honolulu clients were called, mark on invoices the date for payment (we were required to take all discounts possible), houseclean the partners' desks, learn to type on the old Hammond machine with its interchangeable slots of type and its one-of-a-kind keyboard. And worst of all, copy the letters, handwritten or typewritten, into bound books with paper that was impossible stuff. If the blankets weren't damp enough, the copy was so faint you could hardly read it; if too damp, the copy was a smear. Many a copy I made a mess of, and it wasn't until books made of Japanese paper came on the market that my problem was licked.

Mail took a minimum of ten days to reach the Islands, by rail and steamer from Frisco. There was no cable until I had been in the employ for several years. When the cable was being laid, Mr. J. B. sent me to the office of the Cable Company to file the first message to be sent from Boston, Brewer & Co. being the oldest firm doing business with Honolulu. That message never did reach C. Brewer & Co., Ltd. The Cable Company said they had no record of our message; it was plain that the clerk simply tore it up and pocketed the cost which I had paid to him in cash.

In my time, the shortest passage of a sailing vessel round the Horn to Honolulu was 110 days, the longest 150 days; which meant that a round voyage could easily run a full year, longer when there were disasters and delays. When a ship had discharged its cargo of sugar, or occasionally out of the sugar season it might be nitrate from Iquiqui or Caleta Buenos in Chile, and was loading for a new voyage out, there was one typing job I did enjoy. That was Mr. E. M.'s letter of instructions to the captain; such tang-of-the-sea items as when to keep the hatches open, the port of call on the voyage home (oftenest it was Lewes, Delaware) "for orders." If there was adventure cargo, the captain was told what he would have to sell it for to net a profit for the firm. If there happened to be a passenger booked, the captain was told what the firm knew about him. During my years there were four passengers: one was a nephew of the Brewers, John Nichols, whose knowledge of marine birds gained on that voyage started him on his way to become Curator of Marine Birds at the Natural History Museum in New York.

Those captains, two of them with families at home in New England, away for at least a year on the high seas, were owners' representative with full responsibility for ship, cargo and crew, and had to be not only navigators but doctor, even surgeon if one of the crew fell to the deck out of the rigging. For all that their pay did not exceed $1,500 a year, plus a share in a voyage's profit if the captain happened to own a few 64ths interest in the ship. "Why 64ths?" I asked. And I was told that 64ths were from time immemorial the share division which busy shipowners had never bothered to change.

All goods purchased by the firm were not shipped in Brewer vessels. Drygoods went overland by rail; quick-turnover, light hardware and some soft stuff were shipped by American-Hawaiian Company's steamers down to Tehuantepec, across the narrow isthmus by rail, to be picked up by American-Hawaiian's Pacific fleet. Once the Panama Canal was opened the American-Hawaiian Company lost no time in abandoning the makeshift Tehuantepec route. Only heavy durable goods on which the lower freight rate was a prime factor and delivery date not of importance were shipped in Brewer vessels. Always a large and basic cargo item was case-oil from Standard Oil Company, two five-gallon tins strapped together with slats. There was steaming coal for Honolulu Iron Works, machinery, steel rails which had to be painted to prevent rusting, galvanized iron sheets, wire fencing, nails, building materials such as cement, plantation tools, plumbing supplies, all the myriad items carried by a big general jobbing house. Before my day the ships even carried vats of wine for S. S. Pierce Co., the theory being that the constant lapping of the wine in the vats during a round voyage would age the wine the equivalent of years. I often wondered just how much of that vintage wine would have reached S. S. Pierce's cellars if the crew got wind of those vats sitting down there in the hold.

We had frequent visitors from the Islands. The regulars were students at Harvard, sons of the firm's clients, for whom we acted as banker. On the whole a serious, orderly lot, they got into few scrapes; although once, with cablegrams flying back and forth, we did have to act *in loco parentis*. Gen. Alfred Hartwell, Chief Justice of Hawaii, would stop in when he was in Boston on a visit to his daughters. There came Jimmie (Kimo) Wilder, a Harvard legend, the man who introduced the ukulele to his rollicking classmates. One day appeared a slightly built youth with a thatch of straw-colored hair. He was taken into the private office by Joseph Brewer, who told me later that the man was James Dole, nephew of Sanford B. Dole, the first Governor of Hawaii after its annexation by the United States in 1898; that young Dole had tried—in vain—to sell him stock in a pineapple canning factory he had just started. Mr. J. B. was a shrewd investor who, as the saying goes, bought them when they were coming out of the ground; but he sure missed out on that one. If only he had taken a flyer in Jimmie Dole's venture, what a clean-up he and his heirs would have made. Dole's Hawaiian Pineapple, one of the great industries of the Islands, is still selling its product all over the globe!

In all my years with the firm I never could figure out how marine insurance underwriters managed to stay solvent. For there was hardly a voyage, either of our own or of chartered ships, on which there was not either a partial or a total loss, occasioning what is known as a Particular or a General Average, both highly specialized proceedings. Mr. Joseph Brewer told me once that the word underwriter means just that. In the days before insurance was organized into a business, merchants would meet in a coffee house in London, where a shipowner who wanted insurance wrote on a blackboard the name of his ship, its destination, type of cargo, and the amount of insurance he was seeking. And any of his fellow merchants who liked the risk would step up and, *under* the name of the ship, he would write on the blackboard his name and the amount of insurance he would take. Thus he became an underwriter.

The ship's hulls and freight money were insured with Lloyd's, whose coverage was against loss "by perils of the sea," which included stranding, sinking, burning, or collision with another vessel. In case of a loss, partial or total, each interest, hull, freight money, and cargo bore its share as apportioned by professional Average Adjusters; with us it was Johnson & Higgins, after Theodore Gore of Boston retired from the profession. Every single item of cost, repairs, wages and subsistence of the crew throughout the period of layup, port expenses, fees, every single expense occasioned by the damage, was listed in minutest detail. In one case the Average Adjustment Statement was as bulky as an office dictionary, and many a long hour of intensive checking was put in by Mr. E. M., with me standing by to dig out the vouchers. By that time I had become sole monarch of the outer office, errand boy, typist, bookkeeper and buyer of shoes and leather in the Boston market, and my pay was on its way up to its pinnacle of $1,000 a year.

Helen Brewer

The company's *Helen Brewer* was a full-rigged ship built in 1891 in Scotland, 1,600 tons. She was named for Joseph Brewer's wife, and was commanded by Capt. Daniel Mahany, a resident of Melrose, Massachusetts. Her first involvement in a loss was in the 1890s in Hong Kong harbor, where she was in collision with the French warship *Jean Bart*. There followed a claim-on and a long controversy with the French Government, which finally made a settlement.

In the fall of 1902 there weren't enough cargo offerings for her regular run to Honolulu, and the ship was chartered to Standard Oil Company to carry case-oil to Java, and to a Baltimore firm to load sugar for the voyage home. Three ports were named in the charter: Samarang, Surabaya and Batavia, all of which figured prominently in the Pacific in World War II. Captain Dan was a peppery little bearded man who looked like General Grant; he had no trouble in letting his crew know who was boss of his ship. He came into the Boston office a few days before he was to sail and, in jovial mood, he told me he was giving Mrs. Mahany a treat, her first voyage with him in many years. He handed me his crew list, written in pencil. "Type this for me, Johnnie, and I'll bring you back a monkey from Java," said he. I thanked him and told him I'd have the monkey properly mounted and hang it on the wall alongside the walrus tusks.

A day or two later came a cablegram from nephew Arthur Brewer, who a short time before had sent a bundle of jaguar skins to the uncles from his ranch in Guadalajara, Mexico. "Hold the ship," the message read, "Would like to make the voyage." The uncles were agreeable and the ship

was held for a week, during which, according to our New York office, Arthur Brewer had many comforts, including a piano, loaded on board. Finally the ship sailed away and arrived in due course at Java. There Arthur Brewer, having had his fill of the monotony of long days at sea, decided— fortunately for him—to call it a voyage and left the ship to return home via Honolulu, where he had been born.

Her cargo of case-oil discharged, the ship loaded sugar for the voyage home, and sailing out of Surabaya early in 1903 she grounded on a sand bar. Enough of her cargo was lightered for the ship to be pulled off by tugs, the sugar was reloaded, and she set sail for home. But she never arrived. Neither ship nor Captain Mahany nor his wife ever was heard from. Though the ship was long overdue, the Brewers did not give up hope, not even when the owner of the sugar cargo came up from Baltimore and insisted the ship be posted as missing. This the brothers refused to do; they held out for another week. Finally, almost tearfully, they consented that she be posted. Once that happened, sensing the front-page news value of a Boston ship lost with its Captain and his wife, residents of a nearby suburb, the *Boston Post* scooped the other newspapers by rushing a reporter to our office. I calmed down the breathless chap, anchored him in the outer office, and went in to break the news to Edward Brewer, who flatly refused to see the man.

It happened that I had knocked around with more than one reporter and knew their devious ways. I told Mr. E. M. the man had been sent to get a story and get it he would, or else make up one out of whole cloth. Reluctantly he called the reporter in, told him all he knew about the ship and Captain Dan, got me to reach down from the wall an old photograph of the ship lying at a dock in East Boston, handed him the picture, and begged him to stick to facts in his story. And on the front page of the *Post* next morning the story and the picture of the ship were full spread. Even the Brewer brothers agreed that the story was in the main factual, though the reporter did give rein to his imagination by inventing the stern board of a lifeboat, bearing the ship's name, picked up on the coast of South America.

So ended the gallant ship *Helen Brewer,* and its Capt. Daniel Mahany and his wife.

Early in 1907 there was a rush of freight offerings, and with the *Helen Brewer* gone from the fleet, the firm chartered the ship *Tillie E. Starbuck* for the Honolulu run. She sailed out of New York with a full cargo, rounded the Horn, and somewhere in the Pacific she was lost—"abandoned" was the entry made in Lloyd's Registry. One more total loss for the underwriters to post on the debit side of their ledgers.

Nuuanu

Named for the well-known Honolulu mountain valley, the *Nuuanu* was an iron bark of just over 1,000 tons, built

in Scotland in 1882. Regularly on the Honolulu run under command of Walter L. Josselyn, she had a good, clean record. I never saw the ship, but Captain J. I did see the few times he came into the Boston office. He wasn't an outgoing, expansive soul like the other two captains; he said little about himself. But one thing he did love was to be invited by a Sunday school or a men's club to give his thrilling talk "The Wreck of the Bark Coringa," when he and the one other survivor had to beat their way through the Malay jungle before they finally got through to Singapore.

In 1910, Nuuanu sailed out of New York bound for the Horn and Honolulu, and several weeks later came a cablegram from the Falkland Islands, sent by Captain Josselyn. It was bad news. The ship had run into heavy gales off the Straits of Magellan, her bulwarks were washed away, and the Captain turned back under practically bare poles. He took what sights he could, pored over his charts certain that land was close by, sent up flares, and finally ran up a signal of distress. The signal had hardly been set when out of the storm loomed a launch whose skipper threw him a line, yelled to Josselyn that he was off the mouth of Port Stanley Harbor, and the launch towed the ship in. The launch owner, of course, could claim salvage money, which he did and it was subsequently awarded to him. All this was described in dramatic detail in Josselyn's letter, and as I read it I recalled his confident statement to me when we were discussing the loss of Helen Brewer: "Young man, the safest place in this world is the deck of a ship at sea. You come home from a long voyage, you walk up State Street, and a blind falls off a roof and kills you." In the same letter he wrote that in ahead of him at Port Stanley were two Sewell ships, from Maine, in a similar plight, and that Nuuanu would have to await her turn for repairs in that primitive port. He sent along a snapshot of Port Stanley Harbor, which looked very much like one of the bleak Maine harbors I had put into on a cruise with my good friend Joe Santry of Marblehead, who later won three Astor Cups with his schooner Pleione, now swinging to her last mooring in the basin of the Marine Museum at Mystic, Conn.

In another letter, written when at last repairs were under way, Josselyn wrote that there was no work being done on the ship that day, for the ship's carpenters—there were only three on the Islands—were ashore making a coffin for the minister's wife! Small wonder that the ship was in Port Stanley a full year, and that the bill for repairs and salvage the underwriters were presented with ran close to $25,000. Finally the ship did get away, and when her cargo was discharged at Honolulu, the Brewers sold the patched-up ship for a whole lot less. What became of Nuuanu after that I never did hear. But Captain Josselyn wasn't killed by a falling blind; he died in his bed from pneumonia.

The full-rigged ship Helen Brewer, *built in 1891 is shown top left docked at East Boston. She disappeared in 1903 on her way home from Java. Lost with her were Captain and Mrs. Daniel Mahany of Melrose, Mass. The steel bark* Foohng Suey *was dismantled by a hurricane off Puerto Rico, after which the Brewers sold her and she became a coal barge.*

Foohng Suey

Built in Scotland in 1888, a steel bark slightly larger than Nuuanu, she was christened by Queen Victoria who happened to be in Scotland when she was launched. To truckmen, stevedores, and the waterfront gentry her Chinese name was a tongue twister; they called her every name imaginable, the one oftenest heard being "Fooling Lucy." To me she was the one Brewer ship and the one Brewer Captain, John E. Willett, I really did know. Twice when the ship was loading, a call for help came from our New York office, and I was sent over to give them a hand with the stacks of tally sheets, manifests, bills of lading, paper work of all kinds. The ship's compasses had to be sent to be adjusted, her chronometers rated, long lists of stores ordered for the voyage, the crew's slop chest restocked, and the medicine chest replenished.

On both trips I lived on the ship, once at Erie Basin in Brooklyn, the last time at her berth on the East River at the foot of Wall Street. And I loved it all. The great bowsprit thrusting high out over the waterfront street. The Chinese cook leaning out the galley window, grinning down at the crowd of landlubbers staring up at this out-of-the-past ship they never hoped to see with their own eyes, wondering if she really could sail all those thousands of perilous miles round the Horn. The swarming deck, lighters making fast and casting off, the hooting of craft of every size churning up and down East River, the tangy smells, tar, wet rope, mildewed sails, paint, the rummy odor of raw sugar that still lingered in the hold and wafted up through the open hatches. And most of all the main cabin, beautifully finished in teak and maple, out of which opened the officers' quarters. To me was assigned the cabin of the third mate; but on that voyage there would be no third mate; his cabin would be occupied by a passenger, a Mr. Anderson. Many years later at a Junior Yacht Racing Association dinner at Seawanhaka in Oyster Bay, I was seated next to one of the Club's flag officers who introduced himself as Anderson. "Anderson?" I asked. "You're not by any chance related to an Anderson who made a voyage on the Foohng Suey with Captain Willett?" "Related to him? I am the Anderson —" he exclaimed. And for the rest of that dinner the Juniors played a decidedly second fiddle to Captain Willett and his ship. One thing Anderson told me I could hardly credit; Willett and he were the only navigators on board. If they had been washed overboard, what a nerve-wracking time easy-come easy-go Mate Keegan would have had with nothing but dead reckoning to sail the ship by!

On board I felt as grand as Arthur Curtiss James on his bark Aloha as I stretched my legs under the big dining table and laid into the Chinese cook's tasty dishes brought in from the galley by the Filipino cabin boy. Came a day when everybody but Mate Keegan and the Filipino had gone ashore for their last weekend. They had no sooner gone off the ship when down came pelting a stiff Easterly and I was marooned aboard. On my plate for lunch the Filipino boy placed a slab of tinned beef. One cautious nibble was enough. "Keegan," I asked the Mate, "is this

the kind of food the Brewers serve when the Captain isn't aboard?" "Young feller," said Keegan, wabbling, half-seas over, in his chair, "this is shore food. You ought to see what we get off Cape Horn." That did it! The yen which had been building up inside me to make a voyage, it just oozed away, it wasn't there any more. But ever after I kicked myself for being a softy who hadn't the guts to chuck earthbound clerking and sail away on what would have been the most thrilling adventure of my life.

At eight the next morning into the main cabin walked "the old man," Edward M. Brewer, over for a final check-up of the ship. Hastily downing the Filipino's attempt at a cup of coffee, I did the honors. "Breakfast?" I asked. "Well," said Mr. E. M., almost bashfully, "I would like some rice. Willett's Chinese cook makes the best, every kernel alive, crawling." It had to be me, clerk James, to tell the principal owner of the ship, standing there smacking his lips, that there'd be no rice; the cook was ashore. The old gentleman was game, he took it in stride and fell to yarning with Keegan who, fortunately, was cold sober. He told us he was born in Honolulu, had made several voyages in his father's ships, on one of which they ran out of drinking water and landed on Juan Fernandez, Robinson Crusoe's island, for a fresh supply. On a later voyage they sighted off on the horizon a big bark which kept wearing over to the Brewer ship. When it got within hailing distance, they saw it was flying the Russian flag, and over the side came a blackboard on which was written the heart rending lament, "Je n'ai pas rhum!" Two little yarns, tossed off at random. What full-size *Saturday Evening Post* tales the sea story writers, McFee and Out-o'-Gloucester Connolly, would have woven them into!

Next evening, back from a visit to his home in Dover, New Hampshire, Captain Willett brought to the ship his old pal Captain Pendleton, both of whom had been mates under Captain Mahany before he took command of *Helen Brewer*. After dinner—no tinned beef was served at that one—the two sea dogs decided they would like to take a fling at New York night life. "Where shall we go?" they asked, putting it up to me who knew as much about night spots as I did about navigation. The one spot I had seen, and that from the top of a bus, was Pabst's, a little tucked-away place on Columbus Circle.

So up to Pabst's we went—and got a big jolt when we stepped in to find soft lights on every table, each little nest occupied by a dressy male and a dressier lady bird, every one of them with a frosted champagne bucket moored alongside. Just as frosty was the waiter who finally deigned to saunter over to the three fish-out-of-water who had come floundering into that exotic cabana. And when, finally seated, we gave the order for beer and cheese sandwiches, the waiter hoisted his nose aloft. The two Captains airily brushed off the snooty waiter, lit up their Manila cigars, settled back to enjoy their beer and, as always with men of the sea, they got to spinning yarns of far-flung voyages. When it came time for refills, I looked around for the waiter. He wasn't standing at attention at any of the bubble-water tables; he was nowhere in sight. And why? Because there he was, right behind me listening, all ears, to the yarning. Finally he just had to join in, for he too had been a blue-water sailor, who knew all the ports and many of the ships the Captains were recalling to each other. And not until we had finished our beer and were on our way out to the fresh air of Columbus Circle did our sailor-waiter drift back from the Seven Seas and scull over to the table-pounding winebibbers.

When Willett got back from that voyage, he took a year off to be at home with his wife and young daughters, and the ship was given over to a relief captain who got her safely out to Honolulu; but on the return voyage, almost home, he ran into a hurricane off Puerto Rico and the ship was dismasted, cleaned to the decks. Towed into port, her sugar cargo discharged, the Brewers sold the hulk to a towing company, who made her into a coal barge. And that she remained, a thoroughbred turned into a truck horse, until the outbreak of World War I. Ship bottoms in any state were as scarce as hen's teeth in those early war years, and the towing company sold the hull to Galena Oil Company who spared no expense to refit her as a bark, put Captain Willett back in command, and send her to England to carry war supplies to North Sea ports. Willett made two voyages through the submarine-infested waters, then decided he had

earned time off for a few peaceful weeks ashore. On her first trip under command of a relief captain, the ship was torpedoed, sunk to the bottom of the sea which she had proudly plied for many a long year.

So died *Foohng Suey*. Her passing, almost at the very end of the centuries-long era of wind and sail, came but a short time after Charles Brewer & Company's farewell to the sea. Its fleet gone, its mainstay Honolulu client, Theo. H. Davies & Co. Ltd., about to open its own office in New York, on January 31, 1914, the firm hauled down its house flag in Boston and closed its doors after almost a hundred years of honorable existence in the forefront of Boston's famed old ship-owning companies.

And its sole Boston employee took the midnight train to New York, there to take his turn standing watch over the interests of the Messrs. Davies, now faring forth from the placid waters of the Pacific into the home port of hard-bitten captains—not of ships but of industry.

≈≈≈

The author (left), the late James Anthony Finn, and Edward S. Brewer, son of Joseph Brewer, outside the Brewer home in Milton, Massachusetts.

THE HEART THAT BEAT THE SEA

by William P. Deering

To the Gloucestermen of the morning watch on the deck of the schooner *Fears* that ill-starred Thursday in the last week of January 1883, it seemed as though the day was reluctant in its dawning. At false dawn uneasy, plucking winds, like complaining human voices, went moaning eerily across the water above Newfoundland's Grand Banks. The sun, showing a visage as red and inflamed as congested blood, was immediately forced back below the horizon by the heaping cloud bastions of storm.

But the dories shoved off smartly, the men giving the weather their expert appraisal, and hastening to perform their important tasks before, to use their own expression, "all hell broke loose."

Blackburn and Welch were in the last dory to go—and their lines were farthest removed from the vessel.

Of the two men, Welch, tall, athletic and bold, had an advantage in height of a couple of inches, but the men were well matched for their strenuous calling. Blackburn, also a tall man, was heavy, burly and compact with wide shoulders, deep chest, mighty limbs and heavily muscled torso. His stamina was endless and his courage a flag that had never been struck to any foe. Moreover, he had the endless nervous vigor required to back things up.

Their boat was a craft worthy of such seamen. To this day double dories for the Grand Banks fleet are built to be super-seaworthy. The two knew her quality and had confidence in it.

Laying to their oars, they came out from the poor shelter of the schooner and immediately caught the full force of the wind. It was a sou'easter, blowing across the schooner and, therefore, fair for them at this stage of their operation, helping some to shove them along.

Presently they saw flag buoys, forlorn and lonely, bobbing with the seas. These marked their line and Welch soon picked up the trawl. Bringing it to the dory's gunwale, they began to take off fish. From the bait tub, they rebaited the hooks, many of which hung naked—no fish, no bait, no nothing, but the futile steel.

They worked hard and fast, hoping for a full dory-load and a quick return but results were disappointing. They found a few prime fish and a good many small ones but, on many hooks, little more than fragments remained. Bitterly they cursed the dogfish which a stormy time such as this was bound to attract.

Meanwhile the weather steadily worsened. It grew darker. The southeast gale kept picking up and with it the sea. Phosphorous-maned surges, those wild horses of Poseidon, raced down on them all the time.

Welch spoke anxiously, "Can't hardly see schooner now, Howard. Gettin' awful thick down there."

"Aye," Blackburn agreed, "but wind's still from sou'-east, so, iff'n we lose her, we'll just row up wind till we're somewhere near an' then we'll raise her foghorn."

Danger, increasing steadily, was soon too obvious to be longer ignored and, with unspoken mutual consent, they let go the trawl and sat gazing anxiously toward the schooner. A good half mile away, she was tacking back and forth keeping as near as possible to the dories.

They rowed in dogged silence wasting no strength in words. Soon, however, Blackburn, casting a glance over his shoulder, saw that which caused him to relax in his rowing, as though convinced that their best efforts were in vain.

He had, indeed, seen an appalling thing, a howling northeaster, their traditional foe, quartering across the seas to join the "southeaster" already raging. This new storm folded in between the schooner and the dories and, in a minute the vessel was completely blotted out. As a matter of course it brought a terrific cross-sea. The foghorn kept on blasting futilely.

Welch gasped incredulously, as though unable to believe in the completeness of their catastrophe, "Howard, she's gone!"

Shortly before Blackburn died on Nov. 4, 1932 at the age of 73, he posed for this portrait. The fingerless fisherman finished his days as a proprietor of a saloon; but as long as there are old salts to tell his story he will be remembered as the man with unlimited will power.

All night long they rowed, but no better they were for it

"Aye, she's gone," Blackburn agreed, "no use to pull our guts out now. Maybe the wind'll thin this damned stuff out after while so's we can see her. But jeez, boy, keep her head up. This cross-rip is plain murder. Watch it."

It was a great cross-sea, that hung over the dory for a menacing eternity and then broke partly inboard. Immediately she became sluggish and heavy.

"The scoop! The scoop!" Welch yelled. "Right there foreninst y'r foot!"

"Aye," Blackburn said, unshipping his oars. "Keep her head up, lad."

And, meanwhile, he took to bailing.

Nevertheless, as he again ran out his oars, Blackburn turned to his dorymate a gloomy face.

He said, "I lost me mittens, young-feller-me-lad. As God's my judge, I must have thrown 'em over in the bailin'."

"That's bad," Welch replied. "Oh, man, that's bad, an' the cold really just settin' in."

"Aye," Blackburn said, "that's bad."

It was only mid-afternoon when this happened, and there were still many hours of that dreadful day to struggle through.

Day was done at long last and, with nightfall, the snow ceased. The wind blew harder, though, and the seas became a succession of watery hills. The cold was biting as the skies grew clear and the stars appeared. Then, brightest star in any firmament, they saw the schooner's light.

Surely that meant they were to be saved after all even though it was so far away! They again bent to their oars, giving way right lustily, but, pull as they would, they drew no nearer to that golden beam. All night long they rowed, while the strong hand of nature pushed against them.

Often they lost the light and then they would keep their course by the stars until they again picked up the feeble beacon. Finally came daylight but there was no sign of the vessel. Definitely she was gone, and they were alone on the unstable sea.

Blackburn drew his oars inboard and thrashed his stiffening hands against his shoulders. "Don't seem to help much," he commented. "Well, Tommie, gotta bring her about. Next port's Newfoundland."

Welch said, "Aye, nothing else to do," and added, "that's a main long way."

Blackburn said, "Aye, it's a lot of water, but we'll make it."

They brought the dory round and that was no small miracle. Then they headed nor-west-by-north and again bent to their oars.

Black night after gloomy day, the wild winds, never weakening, howled their hostility while the weather grew colder every hour.

Ice sheathed the inside of the dory and had to be broken up and pitched overboard. A hard routine developed: pound ice, bail, watch the stealthy seas, row, row.

Welch did his part right up to his last gasp and brave men have long paid tribute of sorrow to this humble hero. All the hardships of those sub-Arctic waters could not subdue his manhood. He fought to the very last but the combination of evil things was just too much to bear. He slowly froze to death at his post of duty. He died on the third night and lay, an ice-shrouded passenger, on the dory's bottom. Thereafter, Blackburn fought alone.

By this time, he was conscious that his feet were frozen and that his utmost efforts to keep life in his stiffening hands were unavailing. Then, with a new and desperate emergency, death seemed to tap him on the shoulder. If a man could not close his hands around his oar-handles, how could he row?

His solution of this problem was as characteristic as it was direct.

Gripping the hafts of his oars firmly, while yet his fingers would bend, he sat quietly, keeping the dory's stern to the following seas, and watched his digits turn to marble. Then he continued to row. Here is what he said later about this phase of his martyrdom.

"My fingers are getting whiter and stiffer. I think too late now to stop 'em freezing. I knew that if my fingers froze straight and stiff I couldn't keep on rowing after they froze. So I made up my mind there was nothing else to do. If my fingers were bound to freeze, I'd make 'em freeze in such shape as to be of some use afterwards.

"So I curled 'em around the handles of the oars while yet they wa'nt too stiff and I sat there without moving while they froze that way around the handles of the oars."

And so he rowed—hands frozen, feet frozen, no sleep, no food, no water and with a dead man as his passenger. What of breaking ice? What of bailing? He had to do it all.

He finally raised the Newfoundland coast and landed in a tiny inlet. Most of its margin consisted of ledges and tumbled rocks, surf-lashed and seaweed-covered. At the head of this cove, he found a shingly beach and ran his dory ashore on a pebbly bottom.

The short twilight was swiftly fading as his desperate gaze surveyed the uplands and there, to his infinite relief, he perceived a small house on a ledge above the cove.

The house had been long abandoned and was almost as badly off as its wretched wharf. Windows had been knocked or blown out, doors creaked wearily as the wind blew them about. Snow had drifted in all over. There were no furnishings, no food, no fuel. In a room that still retained its windows he cleared away a space and there he spent the night.

Blackburn found neither comfort nor ease in that night, but the edge of his exhaustion had been dulled by slumber, and, at daylight, he returned to the shore, intent on shoving off and proceeding up the coast.

The day was clear, continued cold, and the water not too rough.

From "Lone Voyager" by Joseph E. Garland

Thomas Welch, Blackburn's dorymate who died during the ordeal and whose frozen body Blackburn kept with him throughout his agonizing journey.

When he reached the shingle, and viewed the lamentable situation, however, his stout heart sank. During the night, wind and sea had torn his dory loose, cast Welch's body from it, and hurled it overboard.

With only ice for feet and chunks of ice for hands, he stumbled along the shore and then out on the rocks, hideously heaped, slippery with ice sheathings and festoonings of kelp. Carefully, carefully, he made his way and once it seemed as though the dory itself would be his destruction. A surge picked her up and hurled her right at him but the wave's volume was soon spent. The dory fell, just short of striking her master and began to drift tantalizingly away.

Then came the moment, which Blackburn, to the day of his death, remembered as the time, the only time in all that voyage when Neptune relaxed his hostility and gave the hero a sporting chance.

Almost at his feet, the free end of the dory's painter, a mooring rope, had become caught between two rocks.

How could the man stand on those frozen feet, much less walk? How could he make his way among the rocks, guiding the dory back to harbor? How could he hold the wet and writhing rope in those stumps of hands? There are no answers except that he did all those things.

Having repaired the dory against the sea, he secured her against all possibility of again going adrift and turned to a sacred task that could not be neglected. The search for his shipmate's body.

He found it floating clear and not too far from shore; not jammed among the rocks as it might so easily have been. A stroke of luck, perhaps.

By means of an oar, he drew it in and then dragged it around to the shingle and to a spot far above the high water mark. There he protected it with a small cairn made of bushes and driftwood weighted down by stones.

Then he launched the dory, shipped his oars and rowed out of the cove, proceeding along the coast to the northward. The weather was even colder but, by this time, a few degrees either way meant very little to this conqueror of the sea. He was prepared to row, if necessary, until the Arctic night again descended, but the end was not that far away.

This was the village of Three Rivers, a metropolis of just three houses.

He was seen from the shore and hardy, but profoundly astonished, men put off to his aid.

They helped, assisting him ashore and up to the nearest house. Quietly he told his story, while men shuddered and women and children wept.

Everything they could do for him was done, but alas that their means were so limited and his needs so great! There was no doctor in the hamlet and mountains of ice and snow shut them off from communication up and down the coast. Such home remedies as could be applied were of practically no help to one so sorely stricken.

For a long time his own case was parlous indeed. It proved impossible to "draw the frost out" of his frozen members and gangrene set in as soon as circulation began to struggle back. One by one his fingers and thumbs dropped off; he lost all his toes and substantial parts of both feet. This torture lasted 51 days.

Nevertheless he lived.

Blackburn returned to Gloucester, but he never went fishing again. His handicaps incapacitated him for that strenuous calling. He entered business on Main Street near the foot of Union Hill and was quite successful. For many years his place was a sailor's rendezvous, where, never despondent, he always had a bluff and friendly greeting for seafaring men.

And he went to sea again, this voyage, also, making marine history. Crippled as he was, he crossed the Atlantic alone in a light sailing dory, made his way up the historic Seine and attended the Paris exposition.

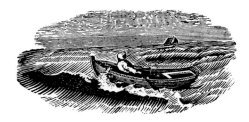

Oᴺᴇ sᴘʀɪɴɢ ᴇᴠᴇɴɪɴɢ ɪɴ 1878, Cᴀᴘᴛᴀɪɴ Bᴀʀɴᴀʙᴜs A. Briggs bent over the table in his New Bedford, Massachusetts, home studying sea charts of the southern reaches of the Pacific Ocean. The tall, trim master of the whaling bark *Tamerlane* ran a fingertip around the outline of New Zealand and nodded with satisfaction.

Now he was ready to sail into what was to become one of the most amazing and unorthodox battles ever recorded in the chronicles of the sea; he would challenge a man who owned an ocean. If Captain Briggs was successful, the supremacy of the Downeasters as whalers would be proved beyond doubt and the nation's economy would get a much-needed boost from a tidy fortune in sperm whale oil.

During the bitter winter months, Captain Briggs had been gathering every fact about Paddy Gilroy, the New Zealand whaling skipper who had staked out a claim over a large part of the Pacific Ocean, including the fabulous Solander Bay whaling grounds where so many big sperm whales sounded that the sky was filled with spray.

There in the storm-lashed waters beyond Foveaux Strait on the southwestern tip of New Zealand, Paddy Gilroy on his ramshackled old windjammer *Chance* had been steadily building up his wealth while the Downeasters were being hard pressed to eke out a slim profit.

Captain Briggs reasoned anything the New Zealander could do, he could do better. Let Paddy Gilroy try and stop him.

And so, a dozen weeks later, the *Tamerlane,* accompanied by the *Matilda Sears,* the *Rainbow,* the *Eliza Adams,* and the *Coral*—all owned by Downeasters—came swooping down on Paddy Gilroy's private pond. Every man was prepared for pea soup weather and sudden howlers that came from nowhere and often lasted for days on end.

As they began cruising west of the grim cliffs guarding the entrance to Foveaux Strait, a weird-looking vessel came before the wind and bore down on the *Tamerlane.* Through his glass Captain Briggs saw the paint peeling letters spelling the word "Chance" and the stocky, red-headed man leaning against the taffrail in a most unskipperly fashion.

Captain Briggs lowered his glass. The sight was almost too much to absorb in one look.

by John Cowe

The Downeaster looked again—trousers made from old sail cloth, frayed frock coat, a battered black bowler hat tipped back. The Captain's eyes had not deceived him the first time. That was just how Paddy Gilroy was dressed.

"Fantastic," said Briggs. "Fantastic!"

If only Captain Briggs could have known what Paddy Gilroy was thinking, he might have chosen some other adjective. For the New Zealander was shrewd enough to see the advantage of appearing ridiculous to those who challenged his kingdom. It set the stage for surprise.

Captain Briggs was too far away to hear the laughter on the *Chance* from a mixed crew of whites, Maoris, and half-breeds as they looked the invaders over. To curses and chuckles, the crew of the *Chance* laid bets on how many days the Yankees would last in the storm-thrashed waters. Sighting an invader was always cause for good humor. It meant bigger profits.

Captain Briggs dismissed Paddy Gilroy and the *Chance* from mind. He was more interested in whales.

Next morning at first light he saw them. Thousands of spouting, thrashing, whales turned the sea white as far as the eye could see. And there was the *Chance,* her men fast into a big bull.

Contrary to usual practice—and unknown to Captain Briggs—Paddy Gilroy had posted lookouts on the mastheads at midnight rather than dawn. While darkness usually covers the movements of whales during the night, the great herd of Solander sperm whales churned the sea into flaming acres of phosphorescence that could be seen on the darkest night.

Captain Briggs quickly ordered his boats away. Harpoons flashed. Blood stained the sparkling sea.

Hours later, his men began the tedious task of towing whales back to the *Tamerlane.* The other vessels in the Yankee flotilla were wresting similar prizes from the sea.

Captain Briggs was surprised to see his adversary sailing away with only one whale in tow, but was too busy with his own preparations for the intricate cutting-in and trying-out operations to give it more than passing thought.

It was way past noon by the time the whales were lashed alongside the *Tamerlane.* The venture into Paddy's

Sighting Yankee whalers was always cause for good humor aboard Paddy Gilroy's Chance. *Paradoxically, it meant bigger profits for Gilroy and his crew.*

Pond had got away to a good start. If their luck held, the *Tamerlane* could return home with the holds filled with the liquid wax-like sperm oil for the leather factories being established on the outskirts of Salem, Massachusetts, and the iron works of Pittsburgh, Pennsylvania.

In the meantime the Yankee fleet had slowly drifted south of the straits. A gentle breeze stiffened to a wind veering several points. Captain Briggs noticed the change. It gave him nothing to worry about until crowding masses of purple-edged clouds began building up on the horizon. A wind suddenly piping up from the northeast placed Foveaux Strait well out of reach to windward.

Captain Briggs sharply ordered the cutting stage taken in and the boats hoisted. The blubber hatch was battened down. The whales were made fast alongside until the cutting-in could begin again as soon as the weather calmed.

The dead whales held the bark heavily in the water. The only way Captain Briggs could control his vessel was to run before the wind. The *Tamerlane* and the other Yankee

ships plunged south into the vast wind-swept wastes of the Antarctic.

By dusk the weather thickened. The bucking fleet scattered. The dead whales seemed to come alive, hammering against the *Tamerlane*'s hull. Seams split under the battering punishment. Captain Briggs had no other choice but to give the order: "Cut the whales loose!"

For five days of wind-driven, watery hell the storm went on battering the *Tamerlane*. Then, as quickly as it had come, the storm blew itself out.

Above. Gilroy's crew were quick to swoop in and pick up whales cut loose from Yankee vessels. Typical of the swift action that must have followed is this rare photo taken during the same period showing the "overboard man" on top of a whale during "cutting in."

Old salts from Camden to Cape Cod knew of the exploits of Paddy Gilroy. Few storytellers were better at recalling Gilroy's daring deeds than Oliver Ingersoll of Lobster Cove, Massachusetts.

The weather thickened and the bucking fleet scattered

The Yankee ships joined up again. Two of the ships, the *Eliza Adams* and the *Coral,* were taking so much water their skippers had to abandon all thoughts of whaling and make for the nearest dry dock. Captain Briggs and the skippers of the *Rainbow* and the *Matilda Sears* were more determined than ever to stick it out.

Entering Foveaux Strait together, the Yankee trio were saluted by a saucy wave from Paddy Gilroy, who had been methodically processing his whale in the sheltered waters of Port William while the Downeasters had been fighting for their lives in the storm.

While repairs were being made, Captain Briggs visited British officials in the port. Mr. Cross, the resident, told him he had heard nothing but praise for Paddy Gilroy. He was jolly, generous to a fault, and greatly admired by the Maoris for his courage and audacity.

A couple of days later, Paddy Gilroy nosed the *Chance* into harbor. There was a whale each side of the vessel. He doffed his bowler to the Yankees as he passed between them —a greeting they did not return. Captain Briggs was appalled by the wretched, poverty-stricken appearance of the *Chance.* She was a shadow out of the past, the sole survivor

of the once great whaling industry of New Zealand.

Paddy Gilroy had nothing personal against the Yankees. But, in trying to live up to his reputation, he found nothing brought more chuckles or won him more laurels than escapades humbling the vaunted Downeasters.

The crew of the *Tamerlane* finished making repairs, but were forced to sit twiddling their thumbs as another storm blew up. There was nothing to do but watch Paddy Gilroy render his blubber.

One morning Captain Briggs awakened to find the *Chance* had slipped out of harbor during the night. It meant fair sailing weather. He rapped out orders, and soon the *Tamerlane* was sailing through the straits to join Paddy Gilroy on his pond. This time Captain Briggs was going to use Paddy Gilroy's weather nose as a weathervane. A foolproof plan. There was just one flaw—it was old stuff to Paddy Gilroy.

Captain Barnabus Briggs' home port of New Bedford, Mass., as it appeared at the time of his "invasion" of Gilroy's waters. The boarded area is a storage bin containing whale oil covered with seaweed.

The sea broke open as hundreds of spouting whales sounded

Soon came the excited shouts from the masthead lookouts: "Thar she blows! Whale."

The sea broke open as hundreds of spouting whales sounded, their single jets rising against the cobalt sky to the west. Captain Briggs ordered two boats away. At any other time he would have used four, but the uncertain weather and a slight dip in the barometer made him cautious. He was taking no chances. As the *Tamerlane* slid into a long green hollow in the sea, Captain Briggs realized another disturbing fact. The seas were not diminishing in size, as they should have done after a storm.

It could be some local peculiarity such as the prevailing western currents; or it could mean another big blow from the west. Paddy Gilroy would know.

"Gilroy's grounds" were rich with whale, too many to kill by himself. With an eye on the weather, he stood by and let the Yankees help themselves, then waited for the wind to shift.

He did. He was sure it would be coming up thick and fast from the west before dusk, and he hoped to be at anchor in Port William by then. But he was much more interested at that moment in watching the Yankee vessels.

"Mastheads, there!" he yelled. "Keep a sharp lookout for them Yankee boats. There's a guinea for every wounded whale they'll be cutting loose."

The words were unnecessary with threatening weather. Every man on the *Chance* had profited in the past and earned guineas by reporting wounded whales Yankees were forced to abandon when a wave-blasted gale hit.

Paddy Gilroy knew where to find the whales along the inlets and coves of South Island once the storm had passed over. It was a simple way of doubling his profits at the expense of the Downeasters.

Just after midday the *Tamerlane*'s boats returned with their prizes in tow. They were not a moment too soon. Already a sticky calm had fallen. The sky turned an ugly gray, making the sun a dull silver circle, like a well-used quarter.

45

"Cutting in"

The wind came in warm puffs and thousands of mutton birds came streaking in for their breeding grounds on Stewart Island.

Captain Briggs saw the *Chance* had already come about with a whale in tow, staggering under a mountain of canvas, burying her bows in the green seas, and wetting her topsails with bursts of flying spray.

It seemed an eternity to Captain Briggs before the *Tamerlane* finally came about and squared her yards to the wind. Hampered by their whales and heavy seas it would take the Yankee fleet better than two hours to reach the coast. Two hours! A lot could happen in that time on the tempestuous fringe of the Antarctic.

Pitching and tossing, the *Tamerlane* shuddered as the frothing combers overtook her and slid under her counter. Alongside, the 60-ton whale was thrown about in erratic jerks and the following seas tore at it and let it go, threatening to tear the fluke chain bitt from the forward deck.

The New England skippers all had their eyes on the *Chance*—their weather gauge. The *Chance* was in an unenviable position, better than 2,000 yards down wind on the port tack and still heading up the straits.

Suddenly the situation changed for the Yankees. About a dozen miles beyond where the *Chance* lay, the towering cliffs of Stewart Island had unexpectedly come under their lee. They were being driven towards the barrier of rock by the lateral thrust of wind and waves. If they insisted upon keeping their whales, they were in a tough spot. They were too far into the mouth of Foveaux Strait to uphelm, go about on another tack, and make a reach for the open sea. And they were not far enough into the straits to reach a safe haven.

If they had been alone, Captain Briggs would have known just what to do—cut the whale loose. The drag of a 60-ton whale was too much of a burden for a vessel riding close to the wind under storm canvas. He knew from long experience that was the only safe way out; but there was the *Chance*, still hanging on to her whale, plunging before the storm. As long as Paddy Gilroy kept his whale, Captain

Briggs was going to keep his.

Paddy Gilroy tenaciously continued his bold course. As Captain Briggs saw it, he had no other chance but to follow Paddy Gilroy's example.

Captain Giles L. Bennett of the *Matilda Sears* and Captain Bernard Cogan of the *Rainbow* shared the same thinking as Captain Briggs. They continued battling up the straits. They all felt some assurance in having Paddy Gilroy far to leeward. Paddy Gilroy was no fool, they reasoned. He would certainly calculate his risks carefully and know when the last clear margin of safety had been reached.

The possibility Paddy Gilroy might not be bothering about a safety margin never crossed Captain Briggs' mind —well, not at first.

But the more Captain Briggs saw of the behavior of the *Chance,* the more he began to wonder, and finally he began to question the sanity of the New Zealander drifting a scant half-dozen miles from the jagged rocks of Stewart Island. Closer and closer the *Chance* drifted towards the crashing breakers. Paddy Gilroy seemed determined to keep the same course.

Captain Briggs measured the distance with his eyes. Each passing second brought them closer to the foaming inferno. He estimated the slow forward movement and the leeward drift. In his head he worked out the time and sea room needed to claw off to another tack.

He applied these calculations to the position of the *Chance* and learned to his horror Paddy Gilroy was passing

Bailing the "case"

The Chance *in pursuit of the "loose ones."*

the point of no return. Nothing could save the *Chance*. The ship was doomed. He had thrown away his last chance.

"Cut the whale loose," cried Captain Briggs.

The *Tamerlane* gradually came about, bracing up on another tack. To windward the *Matilda Sears* and the *Rainbow* had also dropped their whales and were struggling to claw off.

Looking astern Captain Briggs was shocked to see a scene of horror direct from the twilight zone. In a bid for immortality Paddy Gilroy was sailing gallantly on, magnificently playing his part to the bitter end. He was already drifting into the white turbulence.

Fingers of mist plucking at the rigging seemed to draw the *Chance* and her men into eternity. The wreathing mist gathered around the windjammer and the *Chance* faded from sight.

Captain Briggs had won victory over the New Zealander, but at a terrible price.

The winds backed into the west, blowing harder than ever. The Yankee whalers ran before it up Foveaux Straits and dropped their hook in Port William.

The following day Captain Briggs completed the story for his journal. As he was closing the brown leather covers, a cry from the deck echoed into his cabin. Captain Briggs dashed topside.

The *Chance* was sailing towards them towing a whale. And Paddy Gilroy was standing at the wheel, large as life, a grin of triumph on his red, weatherbeaten face.

As a man, the Yankee seamen rushed the rail and rigging and cheered. Paddy Gilroy returned the salutation by raising his bowler.

That evening Captain Briggs learned the explanation of Paddy Gilroy's miraculous return to life from one of the New Zealander's own seamen. Captain Briggs listened as the man told how the *Chance* had been caught in the backlash of the seething seas and hissing breakers. Suddenly the ship's motion stopped. Paddy Gilroy ordered the yards trimmed with a wave of his hand, spinning the *Chance* on her heel, and plunging straight into the maelstrom of blinding spray.

In seconds they were through the mist and slipping through a narrow opening in the rocks. The anchor slid down into the quiet waters of an inlet almost completely enclosed by towering cliffs.

While the storm raged outside the sheltering rocks Paddy Gilroy's crew removed the blubber from the whale and, when the wind dropped, the *Chance* was ready to nose out of the inlet to go searching for a whale cut adrift by the Yankees. As soon as he salvaged one, Paddy Gilroy towed it into Port William. He made a great show of cutting into the whale before their eyes and made no bones about the origin of his extra carcass of blubber.

With the box score reading Paddy Gilroy five whales, Yankees none, Captain Briggs called a conference with his fellow skippers. The terrible weather conditions and the audacious seamanship of Paddy Gilroy were too much for the proud Yankees. Not only that but their men were beginning to worship at Paddy Gilroy's shrine and would willingly join him at a beckon. If the Yankee skippers did not want to sail their ships back to New Bedford single-handed, they had better do as Downeasters had done before them and sail away, leaving Paddy Gilroy in undisputed possession of his watery kingdom.

Next morning on the tide the Yankee ships sailed out of Port William. Paddy Gilroy had scored his greatest success against invading Yankee skippers. After this great victory, he reigned supreme over his private pond until his retirement only a few years before peacefully passing away in bed at the solid age of 84.

And Captain Briggs, his dream of a whaling fortune from Solander shattered, turned his dogged attention to the sperm whales off the coast of Brazil, helping America gain a world-wide monopoly in the industry.

They were schooner-rigged and square, and Section **II** records their outstanding achievements.

Small craft or large, these Yankee **Vessels** were unequaled by any of the era.

FRISCO
IN UNDER
90 DAYS

by Charles H. Jenrich

THERE ARE PROBABLY FEW SHIPS IN THE HISTORY OF sailing vessels that have received more admiration and veneration than Donald McKay's *Flying Cloud*. Recorders of the past have marked her as the high point in the efforts of man to attain greater speed over water by wind power alone. Looking back to her era she was not only a tableau of beauty but also an efficient carrier of men and merchandise. She set the pace for others to follow and was the inspiration for the many fine craft that came off the drawing boards of marine designers.

The gold rush to California in 1849 is credited with giving the greatest impetus to the demand for faster moving ships. In the first year and a half of the stampede to the West Coast more than 700 ships cleared from the ports of the Atlantic seaboard for the Golden Gate. Of these, 224 sailed out of the harbors of Massachusetts. Over 100,000 persons took passage around the Horn preferring to face the hazards of storm-tossed seas rather than endure the long wagon trek overland with the risks involved. Arriving in the gold fields these hordes of people were in desperate need of food, clothing and tools. The railroad did not get to the coast until twenty years later and wagons, the only other

The Flying Cloud *rounding the Horn on her record-breaking trip to California. Her skipper, Captain Josiah P. Creesy of Marblehead, Mass., did not believe in shortening sail until an emergency was critical. This photograph is of a painting by J. E. Buttersworth.*

means of transportation, were too slow to meet the feverish demand for the necessities of life in the mining camps. The only answer was fast ships capable of carrying thousands of tons of food and merchandise.

On April 15, 1851 Donald McKay launched the *Flying Cloud* from his East Boston yard. She was Boston's first "extreme clipper" and, built for Enoch Train, she was purchased by the New York firm of Grinnell, Minturn and Company for $90,000. Her length was 235 feet over all with a beam of forty feet and a tonnage of 1,783. Her main mast, with top mast and sky pole, towered to a height of 200 feet. The main yard measured eighty-two feet and her bowsprit with jib boom reached out fifty-eight feet. A winged angel with a trumpet to her lips graced the bow as a figurehead. Thousands of people cheered from housetop and waterfront while harbor craft whistles screamed a salute to the stately ship. It was June 3, 1851, and the *Flying Cloud* was going down the bay on her maiden voyage to California.

Captain Josiah P. Creesy, of Marblehead, who was in command, held the high esteem of all who knew him. In shipping circles he was rated a top sailor with an uncanny knowledge of men and ships. He believed that nothing made by man had more human qualities than a sailing vessel. To him a ship was the nearest thing inanimate that provoked the best and the worst in mankind. Although he was a stern disciplinarian, he tempered his judgments with a keen understanding and was never at a loss for a full crew on sailing day.

The *Flying Cloud* crossed the Equator when she was twenty-one days out of New York. There were sixty-five persons aboard including the captain's wife, eleven passengers, three mates and the crew. Exasperating days of calm in the doldrums put everyone on edge, particularly the sailors working under a scorching sun as sails were braced and trimmed to the constant changing of light airs. All was well aboard, however, until July 12th when an officer came upon two men boring holes in the vessel to scuttle her. They were promptly put in irons and repairs were made. That day marked the slowest of the entire voyage as the log showed only forty miles.

Gale force winds, drenching rains and swirling tides met the *Flying Cloud* at Cape Horn. Captain Creesy had doubled the Cape in far lesser ships and he did not believe in shortening sail until the emergency was critical. He planned to make the pass on the first tack and drove his ship with lee rails under while her bow plunged through huge rolling seas. Her decks were aslant at an angle that would seem perilous to the landlubber but to the skipper this ship was behaving very well. The screaming demons of wind through the rigging, the drum-beat of hail and rain on taut canvas and the deafening boom of boarding seas were a symphony of music to Captain Creesy. He had three of his huskiest seamen life-lined to the wheel and putting all their weight on it to hold the given course. He stood behind them, roped to a stanchion, and with an eye on the binnacle lamp, calmly said: "Keep her steady as she goes." It was

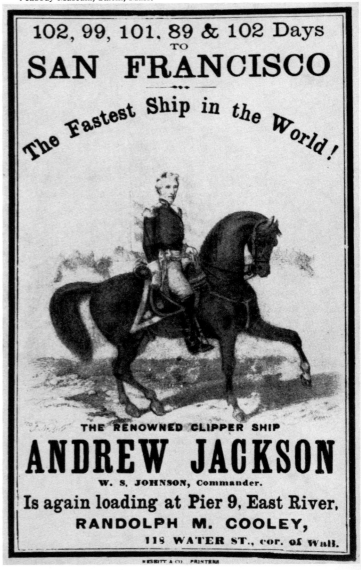

This sailing card of the Andrew Jackson *boasted in 1860 that she was "The Fastest Ship in the World," after bettering the* Flying Cloud's *run from New York to San Francisco. Sailing cards were a means of advertising.*

the voice of confidence and dispelled any fears that might have overcome these sailors.

Rounding the Horn was a trying time for officers and a siege of exhausting hours of labor for the crew of any vessel until she gained the calmer waters of the Pacific. When all danger was passed, Captain Creesy had a kindly word for his crew and looked his ship over with pride; both had met the supreme test to his satisfaction. The hazardous doubling of the Cape had been done in good time, taking but seven days from the crossing of the fifty degree Latitude in the Atlantic to the crossing of the same Latitude in the Pacific.

The clipper sped on to San Francisco averaging better than 200 miles per day and dropped her anchor in the Golden Gate harbor just eighty-nine days and twenty-one hours from the time she left New York. She bettered this record in 1856, on the same voyage, making it in eighty-nine days, eight hours. But in 1860 the clipper *Andrew Jackson* cut the time down by four hours. On a run from

The Andrew Jackson. *Records show that she ran from New York to San Francisco in 89 days, four hours (1860), beating the* Flying Cloud's *time of 89 days, eight hours (1856).*

San Francisco to Hong Kong the *Flying Cloud* made the trip in thirty-six days, a record that any steam ship would have been proud of in those days but one that was never equaled in the clipper ship era.

It was on her homeward passage from the Far East in June 1854 that she struck an uncharted reef which cut deep into her hull below the water line. The cry of "All hands on deck to man the pumps!" rang through the ship. Her hold was filling at the rate of nineteen inches per hour. After working the ship off the reef, jury-rigged patching was applied by the carpenter. The costly cargo of silks, tea and sandalwood was saved and Captain Creesy decided to continue the course rather than put back to China. For the crew it meant many long weeks of manning the pumps, which in those times were hand driven.

The success of the *Flying Cloud* as a fast and able carrier of passengers and freight started similar ships down the ways. Britain had long held a monopoly on the Far East trade but she felt it slipping away as each new Yankee clipper was seen in the ports of the world. They could outfoot Her Majesty's fastest ships, and British merchants, quick to recognize the fact, chartered or purchased outright American vessels to transport their goods.

Although the era of clipper ships lasted for little more than a decade they made a tremendous impact on ocean commerce. Their performance was never equaled by European shipwrights and the merchants abroad sent designers to America for the sole purpose of observing these creations from drawing board to launching. These scouts returned with some pertinent information for the shipping tycoons of Europe and noted also, in their findings, that it was not the vessel alone that was responsible for these fantastic voyages but the quality of the skipper and his crew as well.

During the Civil War the *Flying Cloud* was sold to James Baines and Company, British merchants in Liverpool. She served at one time as a troop ship and at a later date carried immigrants and freight to Australia. By this time her tall spars had been rerigged to shorter heights and her great spread of canvas was sharply reduced. Eventually she was used to carry lumber from Canada to England. It was while on this route that she foundered on a reef off Nova Scotia in 1874. Broken beyond repair, she was put to the torch for what metal could be salvaged.

THE GREAT CLIPPER DEBATE

by Allan Granquist

POISED ON THE STOCKS OF THE SMITH & DIMON SHIP-yard in New York's East River that January morning in 1845, was a daring new concept of what a full-rigged sailing ship should be. She was designed by young John Willis Griffiths for one supreme purpose—speed. As the *Rainbow* slid into the cold waters of the river, the fabulous decade of the clipper ship began, an era when sailing vessels travelled almost as fast as many a modern liner.

The greybeards of ship design looked at the slim hull, with its sharp, concave bow, and declared that she was "turned inside out" and that "she'd do better sailed back-'ards."

In the four years since he had first displayed his model of the ship, and during the two long years when her construction was repeatedly interrupted, Griffiths had argued that such a ship, with its greatest width near the center of the hull, as opposed to the traditional custom of having the buoyancy at the bow, would not only be faster by affording less resistance to the water, but the concavity of the bow, by exerting a gradual braking action against the seas while descending into a trough, would facilitate a steadier passage.

The skeptics were silenced when old Captain Land brought her home from Macao, on September 19, 1845, in 105 days against the seasonal monsoons of the Far East, and beat this time the following year with a 79-day run during a round trip voyage of only six and a half months.

"The ship couldn't be built to beat 'er!" the Captain boasted. The clipper fever had begun.

"The blocks are off," the Far East shipping firm of Howland and Aspinwall told Griffiths. "Design for us another ship like this."

The new ship was 192 feet of lean, lithe beauty, even sharper-lined than her sister, with a red and white stripe along her black hull and a gilded dragon figurehead curling menacingly below her bowsprit. As she nudged her way

The 192-foot Sea Witch, *the ship that many old salts say achieved the greatest sailing record of all time—a 74-day run from Canton, China to New York, March 25, 1849.*

Donald McKay's third clipper, the Flying Fish, *out of Boston. She had some of the decade's most exciting races with New York's* Swordfish.

The launching of the Flying Cloud *at East Boston in 1851. She held, for a time, the record number of miles covered in a single day—427½.*

The Surprise, *which was skippered by Phillip Dumaresq,
who learned fast sailing in the opium traffic.*

Captain Josiah Perkins Creesy of the *Flying Cloud*.

Captain Robert Waterman of the *Sea Witch*.

As she neared the Horn, gale winds screeched through her braces

down the greased rail toward the water, a name was called out in christening which was soon to enthrall the world . . . *Sea Witch!*

Captain Robert Waterman, "Bob" to his admirers, "Bully" to his enemies, was to command. With a picked crew, big Bob blasted out of New York on December 23, 1846, on the wings of a northwest gale, headed for the Cape of Good Hope and the silks, spices and tea of faraway China. In 25 days they were at Rio de Janeiro and in 79 days were slicing between the turquoise hills of Hong Kong harbor. Wherever Waterman was to point the *Witch,* records tumbled in his wake. One of these, a 74-day run from Canton to New York, March 25, 1849, is considered by Carl C. Cutler, eminent marine historian, as the greatest sailing record of all time!

Spurred on by the lucrative China trade and the California Gold Rush of '48, more merchants ordered ships of this New York "clipper" design.

Then twenty-one-year-old Samuel Pook's *Surprise* propelled Boston onto the scene. Skippered by Phillip Dumaresq, who had learned fast sailing in the opium traffic, the Boston clipper ran in October, 1852, from New York to San Francisco in 96 days, trimming a day off the record then held by Waterman and the *Sea Witch.* This passage

signalled the beginning of a rivalry between the cities which was to intensify during the ensuing years and become dramatized most conspicuously by the great California races.

June 3, 1851 . . . the East River, New York City. A clipper sheds her tug and heads seaward with all her canvas drawing. The *Flying Cloud* is her name, fresh from the yards of Donald McKay in Boston . . . Donald McKay, a perfectionist whose name is synonymous with the finest packets on the Atlantic. The *Flying Cloud* is his second clipper—a sleek, but powerful ship, designed to show her speed in heavy weather. A Cape Horn ship . . . a ship meant to be driven. And with Josiah Creesy commanding, everyone knows she will be driven.

Now, to record this voyage of the *Cloud*—the splintering spars, the frozen canvas pregnant with the blast of gale winds which screeched through her straining braces as she neared the Horn, and the mountainous greybeards lunging at her as she passed the bleak and misty hump of "Cape Stiff" itself—is only to capsulize the hardships met by any clipper on the Frisco run.

But the *Cloud,* on this maiden voyage, was travelling faster than any sailing ship had ever done before. She passed the Horn 51 days out of New York and flew up the Pacific, at times logging over eighteen knots and once doing 436 statute miles in twenty-four hours! When she dropped anchor in San Francisco Bay on the first of September, she had made the voyage in 89 days and twenty-one hours, a record which only she and one other clipper were ever to beat.

The *Cloud*'s sensational passage, together with the preceding record run of the *Surprise,* strengthened the New Yorker's resolve to show up their Boston competitors. When McKay's third clipper, the *Flying Fish,* headed down the coast from Boston, New York was ready with the *Swordfish,* just completed at the yards of William Webb, New York's McKay. This was to be the first of the great California races. The ships were about evenly matched as to size and were commanded by two of the greatest competitors in the clipper fleet—Edward Nickels of Boston and David Babcock of New York.

The Boston vessel was some 900 miles south of New York when Captain Babcock, with the shouted order to "Lay 'er on!" tore out past Sandy Hook after her.

As if in confirmation of her name, the *Flying Fish* sped across the Equator in the record time of nineteen days from Boston, thus gaining four more days on the *Swordfish,* which was twenty-three days reaching this point. But on the run down to the Horn, the New Yorkers quickly narrowed the gap and were only three days behind when Nickels pounded into the stormy corner of that turbulent region. Cape Stiff was in one of her angriest moods and as Nickels fought to make headway in the heavy seas, Babcock drew

Donald McKay

closer until they were racing bow to bow as they swung up the Pacific side. Bearing more to Eastward, Babcock got the better of the wind and sprinted ahead, and with a climactic burst of speed arrived in San Francisco, on February 10, 1852, in a time of 90 days, eighteen hours—less than a day behind the mark set by the *Flying Cloud*. While the crew hurried ashore to blow their pay on the bawdy allurements of that city, the Bostonians were still some five or six hundred miles down the coast, fuming in a becalmed sea, finally arriving ten days later.

The following year, 1852, Nickels and the *Fish* were again participants in one of the most thrilling duels in Cape Horn history—this time with a Boston vessel, the *John Gilpin*. After another see-saw battle round the Horn, Nickels was again trapped by calms just as he had been a year before. But he won this one on elapsed time with a passage ending January 31, of 92 days, four hours. On his 88th day, when he was beset by a calm, the Boston skipper was 156 miles nearer port than Creesy had been on his record run with the *Flying Cloud*. With a fair breeze, Nickels could have lowered that mark by a full day. In her last-minute fickleness, Nature had denied him attaining the pinnacle of clipper ship fame.

Going the other way, Pook's *Northern Light* and Webb's *Contest* made sensational runs—Cape Codder Freeman Hatch bringing the Boston clipper into that city on May 28th, 1853, with a time of 76 days, six hours, while Brewster's time to New York was just one hour longer—over-all averages of two hundred miles a day for the entire distance.

In the Far East, the tea races to England introduced another act into the drama. With their fat India merchantmen virtually driven from the seas by these freighter-yachts, the British were soon fielding their own clippers into the contest and driving for the honor of the Queen. But seldom did they flaunt their sterns to an American.

Dewing's time of 86 days from Shanghai to London with the *Golden Gate* in 1854; the 83½-day passage in 1855 from Hong Kong to London by the *Eagle Wing*, Linnel, Master; and Gardiner's run in September, 1854, with the *Comet* of 85 days from London to Hong Kong are some of the outstanding records compiled by Yankee clippers in this deep sea derby.

At home, from stately mansion to waterfront saloon, everyone was talking clipper. Newspapers shoved international news to the rear pages, while their front pages and editorials blazed with the exploits of these vessels and the speed fiends who commanded them. It was speed and more speed. It was captain versus captain, shipowner versus shipowner, Boston versus New York, America versus England.

But smoke, which once belched impudently above the tranquil waters of the Hudson River from the stack of Fulton's river barge, was gradually building into great clouds above the major ports of the world. Already steamships were spanning the Atlantic in nine days. But to predict that these "smoke pots" would ever replace the ship of sail, particularly the clipper, still induced indulgent smiles along the waterfront. Let the mechanic dream of the steamer, but as for the sailor, the future was still one of towering sails taut and white against the skies—and besides, no one knew yet how fast a clipper really could be made to travel.

One answer came on March 18, 1853, when Donald McKay's *Sovereign of the Seas,* commanded by his brother, Laughlin, logged 421 nautical miles—485 statute miles—in one day, while running to New York from Honolulu. And this despite a sprung foretopmast which hindered the Captain from carrying a full press of canvas and a short-handed crew, which numbered only one-third of the original complement. Hanging on to what sail he could, McKay rode a strong quartering wind for subsequent average rates of 378 nautical miles a day for four consecutive days, and 330 miles daily for eleven days.

Enroute to England McKay's *Lightning* bettered even this performance by logging a phenomenal 438 nautical miles in one day. Driving her for all she was worth was James "Bully" Forbes, "a pious, hard-hitting, damn-your-eyes Scotsman," to quote author Helen La Grange. Four months later, September 12, 1854, the *James Baines,* with Captain Charles McDonnell at the reins, continued the record-breaking tradition of McKay ships by crossing from Boston to Liverpool in twelve days, six hours. On a voyage to Melbourne, on February 12, 1855, the *Baines* once clipped off twenty-one knots, the highest speed ever attained by a sailing ship.

Samuel Pook, who always had the habit of designing fast ships, came through again in January 1854 with the *Red Jacket* which drove through wintry North Atlantic seas to establish the record for the course from New York of thirteen days and one hour. Upholding the pride of Baltimore in this Atlantic contest, the *Mary Whitredge* made the best time of all, distance considered, by crossing on August 6, 1855 from Baltimore in less than twelve and a half days.

On the California run, the *Flying Cloud* climbed a rung higher above the crowd by lowering her own mark to 89 days, eight hours. Her time for the 2,100-mile course between Frisco and Honolulu of eight days, eight and one-half hours made in September, 1852, was never equalled.

Suddenly, totally unexpectedly, in 1857, America began slipping into a depression which was to culminate in a debacle. Ships waited in port for weeks, then months at a time, for a cargo. Unable to profit legitimately, many a clipper was reduced to hauling in the opium and coolie traffic. No longer able to afford the spar-smashing voyages of former times, shipowners began trimming down the tall masts to less vulnerable proportions, and built what new ships they could afford, along more conservative lines.

From 1855 on, only a handful of extreme clippers were built, the last one being the *Twilight* of Mystic, Connecticut, in 1857. In March, 1860, the *Andrew Jackson,* another Mystic vessel, broke the seemingly untouchable California record of the *Flying Cloud* by four hours in a hell-driving dash around the Horn . . . then, but for a brief after-glow of glory, the clipper's day had ended.

The sea, which the clipper had mastered in its youth, gradually claimed the aging vessels. The *Sea Witch* dashed herself to death in 1856 on a reef off the Cuban coast while running a cargo of coolies to Havana, and the *Sovereign of the Seas* was wrecked in the Straits of Malacca. The *Flying Cloud* foundered on a reef off Nova Scotia. Fire, always the nemesis of wooden ships, destroyed the *Lightning* and the *James Baines*—the latter suffering the most ignominious fate which any proud clipper could endure, by finishing her days as a landing stage for steamship passengers.

By 1920 only two clippers remained of the 276 which had been built. That year, the *Dashing Wave* went aground while hauling cannery supplies to Alaska, and the *Syren,* rigged as a barque by the Portuguese, drifted into oblivion on some distant sea.

The records they compiled not only testify to the conquering of the Old World by the New but also to the fastest voyages across the seas by vessels under sail which ever will be made.

༺☙❦☙༻

Voyage	Ship	Time	Date
Macao to New York	Rainbow	105 days	Sept. 1845
New York to Rio	Sea Witch	25 days	Jan. 1846
New York to Hong Kong	Sea Witch	79 days	Mar. 12, 1847
Canton to New York	Sea Witch	74 days	Mar. 25, 1849
New York to San Francisco	Surprise	96 days	October 1852
New York to Cape Horn	Flying Cloud	51 days	July 24, 1851
New York to San Francisco	Flying Cloud	89 d. 21 hrs.	Sept. 1, 1851
Boston to Equator	Flying Fish	19 days	1851
New York to San Francisco	Swordfish	90 d. 18 hrs.	Feb. 10, 1852
San Francisco to New York	Northern Light	76 d. 6 hrs.	May 28, 1853
San Francisco to New York	Contest	76 d. 7 hrs.	May 28, 1853
Shanghai to London	Golden Gate	86 days	1854
Hong Kong to London	Eagle Wing	83 d. 12 hrs.	1855
London to Hong Kong	Comet	85 days	Sept. 1854
Boston to Liverpool	James Baines	12 d. 6 hrs.	Feb. 12, 1855
New York to Liverpool	Red Jacket	13 d. 1 hr.	Jan. 1854
Baltimore to Liverpool	Mary Whitredge	12 d. 6 hrs.	Aug. 6, 1855
New York to San Francisco	Flying Cloud	89 d. 8 hrs.	1856
San Francisco to Honolulu	Flying Cloud	8 d. 8½ hrs.	Sept. 1852
New York to San Francisco	Andrew Jackson	89 d. 4 hrs.	March 1860

SOME RUNNING TIME RECORDS

Ship	Knots	Date	Destination
James Baines	21 in one hour	1855	Melbourne
Lightning	438 in one day	1854	England
Sovereign of the Seas	421 in one day	1853	Honolulu
Flying Cloud	436 in one day	1851	San Francisco

Distinctly Yankee in origin, the catboat has had a distinguished career both as a workhorse and a racer. The photo on the right was taken in 1900; the catboat Pilgrim *of Boston is off to the races with two reefs tucked in. A large jib was set from the long-hogged bowsprit. Note the four-master in the background. Below are two "cats" designed for work. Resting is the* Beatrice, *which was often rigged for swordfishing. Without sails is the 20-foot catboat* Vanity *used by Oscar Pease for scalloping. The* Vanity *was worked by the Pease family for thirty-eight years.*

NINE LIVES
OF A
YANKEE CATBOAT

by John M. Leavens

Early in the 1900s a five-masted schooner bound from South America to Boston was beating her way sou'west of Noman's in a northeaster heavy with snow squalls. Her crew spotted a small fishing boat pitching and rolling in the rough waters, her reefed sail slatting to and fro, and in seeming distress. It was the 22-foot Crosby catboat *Goldenrod*. Her owner, Captain Everett A. Poole of Menemsha, was taking in his lobster gear at the end of a successful season.

The schooner stood in close and her skipper sang out: "If you can hold her into the wind, I'll lower a boat and pick you off."

The reply was prompt and crisp: "Well, thank you Captain. I think you better worry about keeping that thing off the beach yourself. We're all right. Your troubles are just beginning!"

A hardy breed of men fished New England waters in those days. The craft they sailed were equally hardy, for commercial fishing in New England in the days of sail gave rise to a wide variety of small sailing craft, distinctive, able, and sturdy, to serve those who made their living exploiting the rich fisheries. Of them all, the catboat is not only the best known but the one most likely still to be encountered under sail in the coastal waters of New England.

Most people are acquainted with the more familiar fishing craft, such as the New England dory, the New Bedford whaler, and the Gloucester fishing smack. In between these extremes one could almost call the roll of New England states by the names of native fishing craft designed for inshore fishing. Maine had the Eastport pinky and the famous Friendship sloop, one of the few types that survives today. New Hampshire's contribution was the Hampton whaler. The Kingston lobster boat and the Noman's Land boat spoke for Massachusetts. The Block Island boat came from Rhode Island and Connecticut's craft was the New Haven oyster sharpy. Each was distinctive. Each was designed to meet local needs and conditions. Moreover, each was successful so long as local conditions remained substantially unchanged. Of them all, the Cape Cod catboat is the most widely distributed and best known.

It is commonly agreed that the catboat is uniquely American. Different localities along the Atlantic seaboard vie for the honor of having originated it. New Jersey produced the Barnegat Bay cat long before the 1870s. New York harbor rests its claim on the Una boat of the 1850s. Newport, Rhode Island, developed a distinctive cat about the same time. But it remained for Cape Cod and the Islands—Martha's Vineyard and Nantucket—to evolve the

Racing catboats became dangerous and tricky vessels

catboat in its finest form, the Cape Cod cat.

The well-known rule that form follows function finds confirmation in the catboat's lines. Practical considerations dictated her draft, her dimensions of length and breadth and her graceful sheer—the profile line of her deck.

The harbors along the south shore of Cape Cod are shoal. Shoal, too, are the waters of Nantucket Sound where the swift-running currents and unpredictable wind often produce a wicked, choppy sea. The catboat designer's task was to build an able, seaworthy boat capable of operating under these conditions. The cat's shoal draft—three feet or less with the centerboard up, seven feet or so with the board down—enables it to go most anywhere.

Broad of beam for stability, high in the bow for protection against breaking seas, the catboat is safe and sea-kindly. Mertie Long of Bourne, Massachusetts, built catboats with W. W. Phinney more than 60 years ago at Monument Beach. Awhile back, he explained the importance of the catboat's dimensions.

"By tradition," he said, "the catboat is a two-beam boat. This means that her length is twice the dimension of her beam. A 24-foot catboat has a beam of 12 feet. That's why she is so roomy. Look at the catboat's sheer. It's strong and graceful. It starts at a high point in the bow, curves down to a low point just aft of amidship and rises gently at the stern. A cat's beam and sheer combine to provide a large, convenient and stable platform for handling gear, or for hauling nets and lobster pots. You get more comfortable and useful working space in a catboat than in any other boat her size."

Forward of the cockpit the catboat has a small cabin house with sitting headroom and two or more transom bunks, a godsend to any crew forced to stay outside overnight. H. Manley Crosby, one of the famous Crosbys of Osterville whose name is synonymous with that of the Cape Cod cat, records the story of his catboat *Mblem*, caught in a southeast storm near Cross Rip in the middle of Nantucket Sound before the days of power.

"The whole gale," Crosby relates, "made it impossible to carry sail and as night came on we anchored in mortal terror of the wildly tossing waters about us. Dawn, however, found *Mblem* still riding safely to her anchor, but the breaking seas had washed the varnish off the sides of the cabin trunk and cockpit coaming."

The late Manuel Swartz Roberts, known to thousands of summer visitors as The Old Sculpin, built catboats for 45

Cats in flight during a race from Fenwick Point, Saybrook, Connecticut to Duck Island in August, 1962.

Foster Nostrand

63

years in Edgartown. He recalled one dimension, speaking of the cats he had built: "From the center of the stem to the center of the mast was 16 inches. That shows how far forward the mast can go in a cat." This is the most distinctive feature of the catboat's rig. The large, single sail, stretched between a high-peaked gaff and a long overhanging boom, assures a minimum of sail handling. At the same time the catboat, on and off the wind, while no America's Cup boat, is nevertheless reasonably fast. Because of her rig the catboat has a notorious weather helm. She tries to meet each puff of wind by turning towards it. To offset this tendency, a huge rudder is hung outboard of the stern. The first of these big rudders prompted some awed wag to remark, "It's big as a barn door," and the name stuck. Holding a cat on

course in a stiff breeze is a real test of "sailmanship."

Working catboats came in a variety of sizes depending upon the use to which they would be put. The smallest, by and large, were the scalloping cats ranging from 16 to 20 feet and designed to dredge bay scallops in sheltered waters. Next larger were the lobster cats generally 22 to 26 feet in length. Cats for swordfishing, trawling and hand-lining ran 24 to 28 feet. Larger still were the packet cats that carried fish from the traps and weirs to market, and the partying cats that congregated at Nantucket or Oak Bluffs and along Cape Cod offering summer visitors day excursions to favorite bluefish and flounder grounds.

Dan Larsen, an old-time catboat fisherman, explained how fish were kept fresh without ice on cats. *Cygnet,* he

Function finds confirmation in the catboat's lines

remarked, "had a compartment set off from the rest of the boat by watertight bulkheads. There were 70 holes in the bottom on each side of the keel for the sea water to circulate. We often carried as many as 300 live codfish, perhaps as much as a ton or more of fish in the well." A live fish well gave a fisherman flexibility in marketing his catch. From the fishing grounds southwest of Noman's, Dan could easily put in to Woods Hole, New Bedford or Newport. He rarely made the same port twice in a row, partly to confuse his competitors and partly to avoid flooding the market in any one port.

Informal contests between fishermen racing to market under sail led to more formal catboat races and the development of the racing catboat. In the 1890s and early 1900s Massachusetts and Narragansett Bays were centers of catboat racing. Interest and stakes ran high. Efforts to increase speed led to the construction of long bowsprits and more and bigger sails. The inevitable result was that the racing catboat became a dangerous and tricky boat. The qualities that made for stability were sacrificed for speed. In the end, other racing types came along and the racing cat disappeared from the scene but not without leaving behind its bad reputation to be attached indiscriminately and undeservedly to all catboats.

Changing cycles of fish, new methods of fishing, but above all, the introduction of the gasoline engine, brought about the decline of the cat as a working boat. The process of change was slow, however, for the decade of the First World War was perhaps the peak period for working catboats and many survived even into the twenties and thirties. New cats became prohibitively expensive and few were built to replace those that, hardy as they were, succumbed to old age.

Some few cats were built as pleasure craft, and as time went by many of the old working cats were converted for cruising. The cat's great adaptability to cruising has encouraged a few designers and builders to help keep the catboat tradition alive in recent years. Fenwick C. Williams of Marblehead has probably designed more catboats than any man now living. Roy Blaney in Boothbay Harbor, the Marstons in Westbrook, Connecticut, and John Little of the Mile Creek Boatyard in Old Lyme have also added to the catboat fleet. Breck Marshall of South Dartmouth has developed fast fiberglass 18- and 22-foot cats of great promise. More recently, some admirers of old wooden catboats have undertaken to make new cats out of old. Tom Hale's yard in Vineyard Haven has turned out several of them. So complete has

Breck Marshall alongside the first fiberglass catboat hull, built in Mattapoisett, Mass., February, 1965.

been the rebuilding that one critic observes, "All they have left of the old boat is the name and the shape."

Reviving interest in cruising cats led to informal races on Long Island Sound in the late 1950s. Sponsored by the Essex (Conn.) Yacht Club, word of these races spread and, in the summer of 1962, some 20 cats rafted together in the Duck Island harbor of refuge after a hard race from the mouth of the Connecticut River. The assembled skippers concluded that the time had come to organize an informal body of owners, sailors and persons interested in catboats. Thus was born The Catboat Association. The name has prompted Joseph Chase Allen of the *Vineyard Gazette* to observe: "Only a few organizations of any variety anywhere on earth are so exclusive, but so far as is known this is the only catboat association on earth."

Whether a cat has nine lives or not is anyone's guess. The fact is that old catboats go on forever and ever. The Catboat Association now numbers among its ranks more than 200 members and more than 125 catboats, many of them 40, 50, and 60 years old. Cats have turned up from Canada to the Gulf of Mexico, from the Atlantic to the Pacific. But most of them happily sail New England waters, reminders both of the Yankee ingenuity of their builders and the fishermen whose courage and skill have added many lustrous pages to New England history.

☙❦❧

When 22 years old, the Iris *won the Massachusetts Bay Championship in 1908. Built in 1886 at Monument Beach, Mass., the vessel is being raced by Frank C. Crane of Quincy, Mass. (1908). He won the "Captain Kidd Plate" for season's races, presented by Charles H. Taylor, Jr. of the* Boston Globe.

SEE HOW SHE SCOONS!

by Loren E. Haskell

THE SAILING SHIP IS SO SYMBOLIC OF THE PAST THAT IT is a little startling to be reminded that such vessels continued to throng the seas into the early part of the twentieth century; and it was the opening of the Panama Canal in 1914 that finished them for good as part of the world's merchant marine.

There were two types of large sailing vessels—the square riggers and the schooners. The square rigger's sails were extended by a yard and hung by the middle and balanced. The schooner's sails were set on a gaff, boom or stay.

For years we have rightfully honored the great square riggers and inadequately praised the famous schooner colliers. Around the early part of the twentieth century these schooners made up the greater portion of the American Merchant Marine.

American schooners were the most weatherly and economical sailing vessels in the world. Their extreme weatherliness made for ease in handling in narrow coastal waters, and rendered them comparatively independent of tugboats in entering and leaving port. They were the hard-working cargo carriers along the Atlantic seacoast, and were to be found in every river, bay, and inlet, from Passamaquoddy to Cape Fear. With a maximum crew of only twelve to eighteen men, most of the schooners paid for themselves from earnings two and three times over.

They delivered the products from New England farms, shores, forests, and local industries to southern ports, and brought back pine, pitch, tar, and turpentine, and many other products to the businesses, trades, and manufacturers of the north.

The majority of the schooners were built in the state of Maine, at Bath, Camden, Rockland, Thomaston and Waldoboro. The building of these schooners provided employment directly and indirectly for so many of the inhabitants of these communities, that launching day was a big event. It was usually proclaimed a holiday and the shipyard workers, farmers and others flocked to these cities and towns with their families and made a gala day of it. Any person owning a share in the vessel was allowed on board while the new ship slid down the ways. Others arrived at the shipyard early in order to have a point of vantage from which to view the launching.

The present day ship owner can reflect with envy on the low cost of marine construction in the days of the

The 4-masted schooner E. Starr Jones *of the Dunn & Elliott fleet. She was built at Thomaston, Maine in 1904, and was of 787 net tons. This photo shows her moments after getting underway, with most of her sails set, and heading south for the Virginia capes to take on a load of coal for Rockland, Maine.*

67

Although the Bradford C. French (*right*) *was the largest 3-master ever built, this photo does not do her justice. She was built in 1884 by David Clark at Kennebunk, Maine.*

This large 2-master, the Harriet C. Whitehead (*below*)*, was built at Waterford, Conn., in 1892. She was of 211 tons and was still working on Chesapeake Bay in the late 1920s. Although of slightly less tonnage than the* Oliver Ames*, she ranked among the largest 2-masters.*

The 6-master George W. Wells (*below*)*, designed by John J. Wardell of Rockland, Maine. She was built in 1900 at the Camden, Maine yard of H. M. Bean.*

schooner. The average cost of the big five- and six-masters ranged from $75,000 to $220,000. The only seven-master, the steel constructed *Thomas W. Lawson,* built at the Fore River Shipyards, Quincy, Massachusetts, cost only $240,000.

Taken from Lloyd's Shipping Register as of 1910, the most important Maine owned and managed fleets of sailing vessels were the J. S. Winslow & Company of Portland; the firm of Percy & Small, shipbuilders of Bath; and the Gardiner G. Deering firm also of Bath. To these might be added the Pendleton Brothers of Islesboro and New York. The other large companies were from Boston, consisting of the Coastwise Transportation Company, managed by the Crowley brothers, John, Arthur and Elmer; the Palmer fleet managed by William F. Palmer; and the firm of Crowell & Thurlow.

One of the most deserving schooners ever to grace the open sea was the 5-masted Cora F. Cressy. *Built in Bath, Maine, in 1902, she is shown here arriving in New Orleans, La., with a cargo of steel rails from Baltimore, Md., under the command of Captain Ellis E. Haskell. The author was aboard as a member of the crew.*

The names of some of these schooners indicate the financial powers which bought into them.

The Coastwise Transportation Company had vessels named for such well-known men as William L. Douglas, former Governor of Massachusetts; Colonel E. B. Haskell, owner and editor of the *Boston Herald;* and Thomas W. Lawson, president of the Bay State Gas Company, financier and author of "Frenzied Finance."

The Percy & Small fleet had an extraordinary six-master *Wyoming,* and a big five-master *Governor Brooks,* named for the Governor of Wyoming, thus reflecting an element of western money in Maine-built vessels.

The carrying capacity of these vessels ranged from 3,000 to 7,000 tons of cargo. However, the first and only seven-master, the *Thomas W. Lawson,* was capable of handling 11,000 tons of coal in one cargo on a draft of twenty-eight feet.

While the transportation of coal was the primary cargo for the schooners, they also found employment in other trades, such as case oil, railway ties, steel rails, phosphate rock, sulphur, quebracho wood, and cargoes of ice from Maine on their southbound summer voyages.

The sailing ability of these schooners was surprising. If their hulls were covered with barnacles they made a poor showing. If not, it was a common occurrence to pass steamers when there was a strong fair wind. The six-master *George W. Wells* was considered the fastest sailing vessel in the fleet of big schooners and her captains reported she frequently made fourteen knots or better.

When World War I commenced, these schooners came into their own. Due to the shortage of vessels, they plied to ports all over the world. The first five-master built, the *Governor Ames,* and the steel constructed five-master *Kineo,* had already sailed around Cape Horn to Asia and Australia. During the period of their greatest use from 1888 to

The second largest 4-master ever constructed was the Governor Powers. *She was launched from the shipyard of Cobb, Butler & Co., at Rockland, Maine in 1905. Here she is at anchor in Boston Harbor as part of the* Crowell & Thurlow *fleet.*

1920, a span of thirty years, there were fifty-four five-masters, ten six-masters, and one seven-master placed in service.

Whereas the carrying capacity of the two-masted schooner around 1865 was only 150 tons, the individual bulk coasting cargoes available were rapidly increasing in volume.

As a result, the two-masters being built were gradually increasing in size to the point where their sails were becoming too cumbersome to handle with convenience and safety.

The largest two-master ever constructed was the *Oliver Ames* of 435 tons, built at Berkley, Mass., in 1866 for the Taunton coal fleet. She was a well-built vessel, and easy to handle. Nevertheless, when caught in a gale at sea, it was a superhuman task to "reef down" on a sailing ship of this type. All too often she ran away with her exhausted crew, and was blown off her course into the Gulf Stream.

The only solution, if the advantages of the schooner rig were to be retained, lay in adding a third mast, thereby dividing the sail area into smaller, more easily handled units.

Just when and where the first three-master was built is likely to remain a mystery. There were several towns along the Maine coast which made claim for the honor of originating the rig once the three-sticker had become popular, and these towns, no doubt, considered themselves quite honest in making this claim.

See How She Scoons!

The startling tones of an excited bystander cleft the air with the above exclamation, as he witnessed the "peculiar skipping motion" of a little fishing vessel that received its baptism in Gloucester harbor. This "ketch" was rigged in a new and remarkable manner, having gaffs to her sails instead of the lateen yards previously in general use, and the luff of the sails bent to hoops on the masts. Her builder, Captain Andrew Robinson, who invented this novel arrangement of spars and sails, was apparently undetermined as to her name up to the moment of launching; for history indicates that he was quick to catch the inspiration of the curious words of the looker-on and, breaking a bottle of rum over her bow, shouted: "A scooner let her be!" Thus the "scooner," or "schooner" was christened; and the word so impulsively uttered and so promptly utilized thenceforth furnished the typical designation of vessels similarly rigged.

Joseph W. Collins

The Charlotte T. Sibley, *launched in 1882 from the yards of Carter Brothers, Belfast, Maine. She was of 358 net tons and was part of the fleet managed by Pendleton Brothers of Isleboro, Maine, and New York.*

The mighty Wyoming, *built at the Bath, Maine yard of Percy & Small in 1909. She was the tenth and last of the 6-masters, and also the largest.*

Ocean freights fell and many schooners went home to stay

From many points of view, the three-master of the '70s and the early '80s compared favorably in appearance with the larger schooners which succeeded them. They were modeled with fine lines, tended as a class to be very handsomely proportioned, and possessed abundant sailing power. The three-masters never attained as much as 1,000 tons carrying capacity. The largest ever constructed was the *Bradford C. French,* built by David Clark, at Kennebunk, Maine, in 1884; it was capable of handling 968 tons of cargo.

The success of the three-masters, coupled with the discovery that the larger hulls could be sailed without any proportional increase in cost, led after 1880 to the building of a four-master named the *W. L. White.* She was launched at Bath, from the yard of Goss, Sawyer & Packard, for Jacob M. Phillips of Taunton, and registered 995 gross tons. At the time, she was the largest of her type in the world. She was soon followed in the New England shipyards by other four-masters of constantly increasing size. In 1882, the B. W. & H. F. Morse firm launched the *Augustus Hunt* of 1,200 tons, a notable vessel that paid large dividends. Four years later the New England Shipbuilding Co. surpassed her with the *Sarah W. Lawrence* of 1,569 tons. Ultimately the four-masters culminated in size when in 1897 Nathaniel T. Palmer put afloat the very pleasing in appearance *Frank A. Palmer* of 2,014 gross tons.

The M.V.B. Chase, *a 3-master similar in size to the* Bradford C. French. *She was built at the shipyard of William Rogers, Bath, Maine, in 1882. This photo shows her with all sails set, including her two stay-sails.*

In 1888, Capt. Cornelius Davis of Somerset, Mass., made the necessary arrangements and plans to build a large four-masted schooner. Mr. Albert Winslow of Taunton designed and built the model. It appeared to Mr. Winslow that this proposed schooner should have one more mast than the usual four masts. After weighing the pros and cons sufficiently, they decided to try the experiment and built the first five-masted schooner on the Atlantic coast. This was the famous Waldoboro-built *Governor Ames.* She had the misfortune to lose her insufficiently-stayed masts while on her maiden voyage so that she was burdened with a $20,000 bill for re-rigging before she delivered a cargo. Consequently, she did not pay a single dividend for more than two-and-a-half years after she had left the hands of the builders. In an effort to find higher freights than prevailed in the coal trade, Capt. Davis took her from Baltimore to San Francisco in 143 days during 1890 and 1891. In the spring of 1892, she sailed from Port Gamble on Puget Sound for Port Pirie, Australia, returning via Honolulu to Port Townsend late in the same year. After another year carrying lumber on the West Coast she sailed from the Puget Sound sawmill town of Port Blakely for Liverpool where she arrived on June 2, 1894, after a passage of 139 days. In August she was back in Norfolk and immediately re-entered the business for which she was originally designed after an absence of nearly four years.

It was ten years before another five-master appeared, but thereafter their popularity grew rapidly; in all, fifty-six were built before the last one left the ways in 1920.

In 1904, from the shipyard of John N. Brooks at East Boston, the five-master *Jane Palmer* was launched. She was the largest five-sticker ever built, and was 308 feet in length, with a net tonnage of 2,825 and a gross of 3,138 tons. She was very unwieldy to handle and was a perfect example of a vessel that should have had that extra mast added while in the process of her construction, and subsequently operated as a six-master. In size she exceeded some of the six-masters.

The pioneer six-master, the *George W. Wells,* built at the Camden yard of H. M. Bean, slid into the waters of the Penobscot on August 4, 1900, a scant two months ahead of her Kennebec rival, the *Eleanor A. Percy.* At the time she was built, the *Wells* created a sensation and was hailed as a symbol of the rebirth of the American Merchant Marine. No sailing ship since the days of the clippers had received more attention. She was modeled by John J. Wardwell, of Rockland, Maine, who ranked with B. B. Crowninshield and Fred W. Rideout as the ablest of the ship designers.

The mighty *Wyoming,* built at the Bath yard of Percy & Small in 1909 at a cost of $190,000 was the tenth and last of the six-masters and also the largest. Her net tonnage measured 3,730; and the length of the vessel from the tip of the jib boom to the tip of the spanker boom was 420 feet. She was longer than the fields upon which football teams play today. Despite her colossal size, she had the reputation of being an unusually easy vessel to handle and a speedy sailer.

The only seven-masted schooner ever to grace the waters of the open sea was the *Thomas W. Lawson,* built in 1902, at Quincy, Mass., by the Fore River Shipbuilding Company. With the exception of topmasts and spars, she was constructed of steel throughout. Thanks to considerable steam equipment used to handle her sails, this gigantic schooner was a magnificent creation under sail, although she was a dismal failure in the coal trade, being too deep to load her full cargo of 11,000 tons at any port but Newport News. She steered by steam, but even so was almost impossible to handle unless there was a gale of wind to give her steerage way. Most of her short career was spent in the oil trade, towing between Texas ports and Philadelphia with her topmasts removed. Late in 1907, the *Lawson* was chartered to carry case oil to Europe, and improperly ballasted, she capsized in a severe storm off the Scilly Islands on Friday, December 13, 1907, taking down all hands with the exception of Captain George Dow and his engineer Edward Rowe.

The fall in ocean freights, beginning in 1920 and continuing in 1921, caused countless sailing vessels to be laid up indefinitely and then permanently.

The only 7-masted schooner ever built was the Thomas W. Lawson. *She was constructed at Quincy, Mass., by the Fore River Shipbuilding Company. Here she has all sails set and is heading out to sea.*

The modern coal-carrying steamers and big oil tankers of today have superseded the great schooners in the transportation of fuel. These efficiently designed vessels are constructed for quick loading and discharging of cargo, and it would be out of the question for the windjammers to try to compete with them.

The big schooners were loved by so many mariners and landsmen alike, that when the huge five-master *Dorothy Palmer,* the last survivor of the Palmer fleet, was lost off the Massachusetts coast in March 1924, there were many wet eyes as the marine brotherhood up and down the coast realized the big schooners were things of the past, never to return.

Largest Fore-and-Afters
(classified by masts)

Vessel	Masts
Oliver Ames	2
Bradford C. French	3
Frank A. Palmer	4
Jane Palmer	5
Wyoming	6
Thomas W. Lawson	7

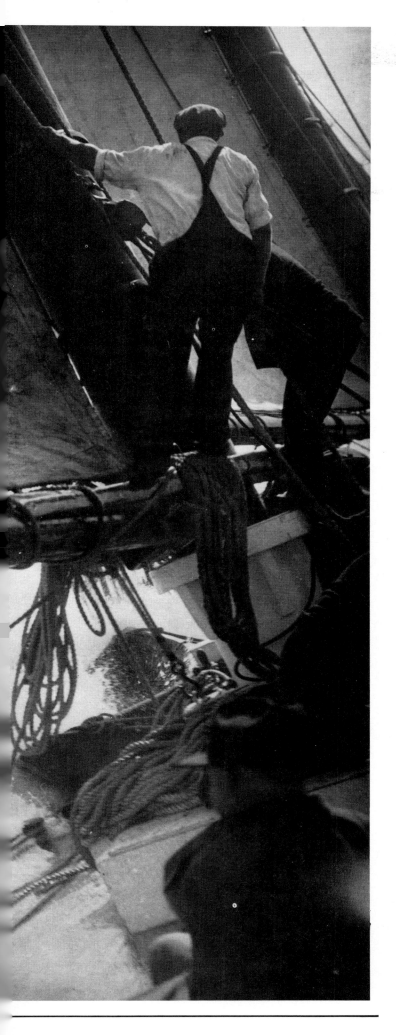

WITH A BONE IN HER TEETH

by Edward F. Moran

Summer, 1948. It has been learned from official and reliable sources that the erstwhile Queen of the Gloucester Fishing Fleet and Last of the Flying Fishermen, has been abandoned as a total loss. The famous craft, the *Gertrude L. Thebaud,* has been shipwrecked on the Venezuelan Coast and all hopes of conducting salvage operations have been given up as too costly.

While at anchor in a storm, the 18-year-old craft was rammed by another vessel, parted her moorings, collided with a seawall and subsequently foundered. She now lies half submerged in a seaport called La Guaira, on the Venezuelan Coast. Very little chance is seen of the black-hulled, magnificent white-winged racer ever again spreading her lofty white wings, as of old, in her glorious racing and fishing days, as a fisherman out of Gloucester, Massachusetts.

At the time of her tragic and untimely loss the craft was owned by Mr. William H. Hoeffner of New York, flew the flag of Venezuela, was equipped with a powerful diesel engine and carried a reduced rig, a three-sailed, stem head rig and a modified top hamper. The magnificent, grand old stager has left her bones on a hard lee shore, on a distant, foreign strand, far from her native Gloucester home.

The *Thebaud* was one of the most famous of all Gloucester fishing schooners, having been in her time a participant in the International Fishermen's Races in 1930, 1931 and 1938 and, in 1933, carried the official representatives of the Gloucester fishing industry to Washington,

With decks awash, she beat the best—to the Banks, and to the finish line

The last of the Flying Fishermen: 1930–1948

D.C., for a meeting with President Roosevelt. In the summer of the same year, the vessel voyaged to the World's Fair at Chicago, as the representative and proud exhibit of the Bay State. In 1937 she voyaged to the far north, under the supervision of Captain Donald B. MacMillan, the arctic explorer, and on this expedition went to Frobisher Bay. During World War II, the *Thebaud* saw active service as flagship of the Corsair Fleet of the United States Coast Guard.

In 1944 the schooner was sold by her first owner, Captain Ben Pine of Gloucester, to William H. Hoeffner of New York. She was converted to freighting and sent to the West Indies waters.

We must now, although reluctantly, set down the final word of the picturesque, historic saga of a famous and deeply mourned sailing craft, which has come and gone in our time. For the beautiful, 18-year-old craft has found her grave in Venezuelan waters. The sea has claimed her. The *Thebaud* has crossed the finish line for the last time; Gloucester's queen will never wet her bobstay again. She was the scion of a once large fleet of splendid, redoubtable American fishing schooners and with her passing we sadly note the absolute vanishing point of a long line of speedy schooners of the engineless era and the T Wharf days; also the end, perforce, of International Fishing Schooner Racing. She represented the last vestiges of the era of the sailing fishermen.

Gloucester Harbor, October 12, 1931. The Gertrude L. Thebaud *is being readied for a race with the* Bluenose *of Lunenburg, Nova Scotia. The* Thebaud *sailed from Gloucester to Halifax, Nova Scotia to challenge the Canadian schooner in her own waters.*

In the spring of the year 1921, the drawing board of Mr. William J. Roue of Halifax, Nova Scotia, produced the phenomenally speedy, extremely able, engineless Canadian fishing schooner *Bluenose*. Lofty and black-hulled, the *Bluenose* was an indescribably handsome craft. From the first day she spread her symmetrical white wings on the waters off her quaint old home port, Lunenburg, Nova Scotia, the *Bluenose* proved herself a world-beater and met and defeated many fine schooners. The rise of her reputation was meteoric and she became known as the Flying Nova Scotiaman and The Pride of Lunenburg.

Yankees decided to build a suitable opponent for the Nova Scotia speed king, and the schooner *Gertrude L. Thebaud* was built. The craft was expressly designed by Frank C. Paine of Boston and constructed from selected material at the Arthur Dana Story Shipyard, Essex, Massachusetts. She bore on her bow, inscribed in golden letters, the name of her sponsor's wife, and across her shapely transom, the name of her home port, Gloucester, Massachusetts.

To those present at her launching, March 17, 1930, the shapely semi-knockabout presented an unforgettable ap-

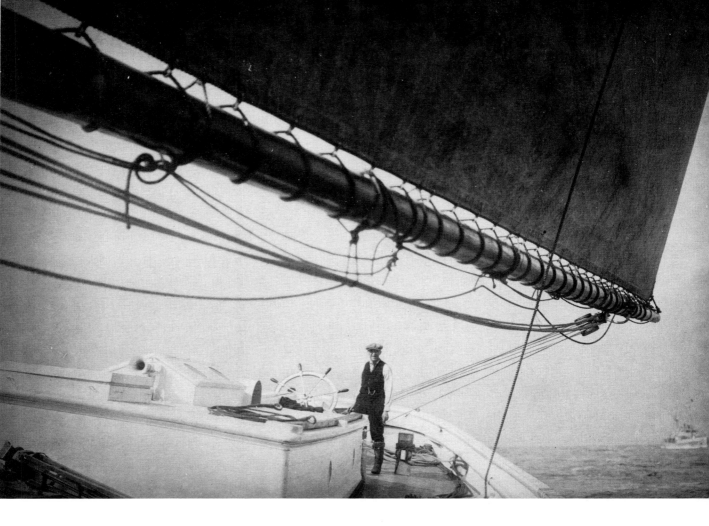

The Thebaud *made the run from Gloucester to Halifax in thirty hours, record-breaking time. Skippered by Ben Pine, her First Mate was John Matheson, shown here at the wheel as she headed out of Gloucester Harbor. The* Thebaud *lost the race to the* Bluenose.

pearance, for the general sharpness of hull design and long, knifelike underbody suggested great potential driving power. She represented an investment of approximately $80,000. The following were her principal measurements: length overall, 135′; length on sailing waterline 98′; beam 25′; and draft 14′-8″.

The vessel proved to be a true sailing champion in her own right as well as a bona fide fishing schooner. She carried a tremendous spread of sail and when in racing ballast hoisted eight sails, namely the four lowers: jib, jumbo fores'l and mains'l, as well as four light sails. These latter were called balloon, fore gaff tops'l, fisherman's flying stays'l and main gaff tops'l. Under a billowing cloud of new, thrumming canvas she flew through the water with the speed of a torpedo and displayed prowess as a prospective challenger for the tall-sparred racer from Lunenberg.

In her many tussles on the open sea, under the command of Captain Ben Pine and against Captain Angus Walter's *Bluenose,* she proved herself a sailing champion in her own right. These two superlative craft staged many a spectacular contest.

The *Thebaud* will be remembered by all who knew her as she appeared in the last of her racing days, sailing a fine race in all weathers from a gentle zephyr to a whole sail breeze and in a four lower breeze and a genuine snorter, real fisherman's weather, as we say. When ghosting in light winds, with the wind dead aft and her fores'l and mains'l swung out, with their sheets out to the knots, she carried her stays'l "scandalized" (changed about throat for clew), and with its sheet led to the end of the long main boom. The tops'ls were "sheeted home" to the gaff ends and the head sheets flowing, the working canvas distributed in a manner reminiscent of the double-jointed wings of an albatross.

When sailing with started sheets and the wind quarterly, *Thebaud* sailed magnificently as this was her best point of sailing. Aye, she carried a bone in her teeth and churned the water at the forefoot to a smother of foam.

The *Thebaud* has tragically terminated her unique, eventful and dramatic 18-year life and has seen the last of her glorious sailing days. Who knows what ghosts of the bygone crews who once manned her may revisit the grand old stager's tradition-shrouded grave, on languorous tropical nights, when gentle zephyrs whisper along the shore and the harbor lights shimmer on the peaceful, starlit waters?

Fast and trim Friendship sloops on the last leg of one of the annual races held at Friendship, Maine.

WﾟHAT WAS IT THAT INSPIRED THE FOLK OF A TINY Maine-coast fishing village to develop a workboat that is acclaimed today as one of the most beautiful sailing vessels afloat?

A good boat doesn't come about overnight. It is seldom, if ever, the brain child of just one man, and it might take decades of experimentation and change to evolve a boat that is able in any weather or sea.

For the professional fisherman, fortune and destiny depend greatly on how well his vessel responds to the capricious moods of the sea. And many a salty gentleman, while wrestling with the helm of a ship engaged by an angry squall, has cursed a presumptuous designer who had thought to tame the titans of nature with a slide rule and mathematical formulas.

By 1850, fishermen in the vicinity of Muscongus Bay, in Maine, were using a centerboard sloop, rigged with a jib and gaffed mainsail, from which they set trawls far off shore and hauled lobster pots among the rocky reefs close to the ledges. Although beautiful and roomy, these craft lacked speed and were hard to handle—as many as three, and sometimes four, men in a crew being necessary. While working, the shoal craft pitched and rolled and occasionally foundered in rough seas. And when work among the ledges demanded clever sailing, they were clumsy and sluggish.

THE ENDURING FRIENDSHIP

by Thomas H. Baldwin III

The records show it was pretty costly for many a man. Too often, a long night's vigil for a late ship had ended in the dawn beside an empty sea.

Recognizing that their shallow-draft centerboarders were just too lightly built and too heavily sparred ever to be safe or comfortable vessels, the fishermen began to talk with their boat carpenters about a new breed of boat. They envisioned a vessel that wouldn't need too much attention while seines or pots were being hauled—something akin to a good drayhorse that would just stand there waiting while the man worked; and then, with the day's catch in the hold, take it upon herself to run home with a burst of exhilaration.

Coming home quickly had become more important. A new phase in commercial fishing had reached the northern villages. Hitherto, the solitude of provincialism had prevailed; but in the wake of the country's growing industrialization, the pressures of competition were increasing in New England. No longer did merchants waiting at the wharves offer a uniform price to all boats with a day's catch; the best price now went to the first vessel home, and the lowest to the last.

It is said that about this time some folk from Bremen, Maine, while visiting in Gloucester, had an opportunity to observe the lines of a Portuguese shallop that was grounded off shore. Noting the touch of stability in the full-bellied mid-section of this foreign craft, made advantageous by the use of a deep keel and inside ballast carried low, they brought the idea home to their local shipbuilders.

As early as 1860, several of the Muscongus Bay builders, notably those of Bremen and Friendship, had been experimenting with keel fishing sloops and schooners. The substitution of a keel for a centerboard gave greater depth in proportion to beam and length, and contributed considerably to the stability of a boat. So it was that, as the midriffs of the sloops were bellied out, and keels became the vogue, centerboard fishing vessels in the deep and often treacherous waters of the Maine coast passed out of existence entirely.

The deep-draft keels made other modifications practicable. The mast could now be stepped well forward so that the boat would handle well among the ledges under mainsail alone. A topmast soon appeared, to which could be set a topsail that would gather in the light upper breezes that escaped boats with lower sail profiles. Such rigs also made the boats easier to handle, safer in heavy weather, and often lessened the time a boat had to sit becalmed.

It was not long before the simple jib-and-mainsail rig was replaced by a highly sophisticated copy of the sail sloop-boats. Double headsails, in place of the old single jib, made their debut, and with these some boats sported a flying jib.

By modern standards, this huge expanse of canvas was nothing short of extravagant. It was not unusual to find a

81

Photographed near the close of his long career, Wilbur Morse in 1939 had no idea that his lobsterman's boat would become a favorite of yachtsmen. Morse built his first Friendship (the world's first) in 1875, and then proceeded to produce hundreds more.

The Black Jack *(right), built by Wilbur Morse in 1900, and owned by William Pendleton of Suffield, Connecticut. Below, the Friendship sloop* Estella A *at Mystic Seaport, Connecticut.*

Mystic Seaport

In the early 1800s, boat carpenters in Muscongus Bay, Maine, began talking about a new breed of boat— the Friendship sloop (drawing), which later replaced its forerunner, the centerboard fishing vessel (silhouette).

Sweeping lines, and a sharply-cleaved clipper bow

sloop no more than 30 feet from stem to stern, whose boom overhung the counter by as much as eight feet, while at the same time having a 10-foot bowsprit to carry the long-footed headsails. But this broad sail plan suited the rugged little hulls, and so successful were the new sloops in meeting the demands of fishermen that they became the predominant workboat along much of the northern coast for nearly 25 years.

The period was one of evolution, and out of it emerged the sturdy, capable, and beautiful craft that in later years came to be known widely as the "Friendship sloop."

The success of the Friendships brought fame and fortune to their builders, and there were many. By 1900, over 25 boat shops lined the shores of Muscongus Bay. One of these belonged to Wilbur Morse, whose fame as a shipwright will survive for as long as there are Friendship sloops.

Wilbur built his first boat in 1874 on Bremen Long Island, not far from Friendship, and in 1882, with his reputation as a craftsman already established, he moved to Friendship. There, in the ensuing years, he brought the sturdy sloops to their high degree of perfection.

The Morses were a family of shipbuilders. Jonah Morse joined his brother at the age of 19, and for 40 years the brothers worked together building boats. By 1904, using a system of mass production, they were able to build as many as six sloops at once, sometimes turning out a finished vessel in less than one month!

Another brother, Albion, built close to 100 sloops in his shop at Cushing, and Charles Morse set up boatworks in Thomaston.

Other builders, too, have their names forever linked to the Friendships. For example, George, Charles, and Abdon Carter operated a shop on Bremen Long Island.

Although only a few of the hundreds that were built between 1890 and 1915 remain in existence today, even this comparatively small number is surprising, for nearly all were constructed of unseasoned, native timber. Keels and framing were invariably of oak, and often this wood was used to plank the hull as well. Fir, pine, and even spruce were also used, and occasionally an experienced fisherman requested the more enduring qualities of a cedar-planked hull. The fastenings were nails, sometimes not even galvanized, and since cost was a large factor, the fastenings were rather sparse.

The hulls lasted well, however, in spite of such drawbacks. The scantlings were massive—unusually heavy framing was used, often set 10 inches on center; and strong, scarfed sheer timbers ran the full length of the boat. But curiously, much of the cause for their long life has been attributed to the apparent neglect of maintenance and care that was given them. The vessels were seldom protected from the weather, even in winter when ice and snow covered them, but air circulated through the hulls and prevented the problem of rotting, faced so often by over-protected modern boats.

About 1915, the gasoline engine began to be adopted by the fishing industry, and the days of working sail came quickly to a close. Although several of the working sloops, equipped with power auxiliaries, continued to appear on the fishing grounds, a few more were built. The boat shops put away their precious molds and trim half-models from which the sloops had been made, and began to build the new designs that typify Maine shipbuilding today.

One by one the displaced sloops were abandoned for the faster and more suitable power craft; nearly all were either burned or just left to rot on the shore. Occasionally, a boat was converted for pleasure cruising; the *Right Bower,* a 40-footer, was acquired by a Rockland hotel and for many years used as a party boat. But an era had ended, and the noble Friendships sailed into history—or so it seemed.

Then, in 1960, Bernard MacKenzie entered his 1904 Morse-built Friendship, *Voyager,* in the Boston Power Squadron Race for auxiliary sloops. The 30-foot workboat looked about as out of place in the company of the sleek racing sloops as a drayhorse at the starting gate of the Kentucky Derby.

But that day the wind blew hard and heavy and drove the fragile racers to leeward, forcing them to shorten sail in order to stand up. The sloop *Voyager,* however, was of a different lineage and, to the astonishment of yachtsmen, came bursting across the finish line with all sails set and all opponents far behind. From this single display of excellence there came a new respect and admiration from discriminating yachtsmen throughout the world.

To preserve the remaining sloops and to foster an interest in Friendships, the Friendship Sloop Society was founded in the fall of 1960. Its membership quickly swelled from a handful to several hundred. Headquartered at Friendship, Maine, the society each summer welcomes sloops and visitors with a colorful festival and regatta. Last year, 26 sloops journeyed to Friendship for the event and nearly 10,000 spectators gathered along the shore.

Nearly all of the remaining original sloops have been restored as magnificent yachts, and many new hulls have been built by families of the original builders. As much as $15,000 and four to five years of labor have gone into some restoration projects. One 30-foot reproduction, carefully copied from the original lines, and constructed of the choicest woods and hardware, cost her owner in excess of $30,000!

Wilbur Morse at one time was able to build a 30-foot sloop for $675!

Out of history they came. The old, rotted hulls that for so long were forgotten are suddenly glittering treasure. Whether under sail or moored or hauled for winter, the Friendship sloop is besieged by spectators. Artists find an easily saleable subject for their easels; landlubbers discover why some people love the sea, and sailors know a deep nostalgia in the graceful, sweeping lines, the sharply-cleaved clipper bow, the long-hogged bowsprit, and gallant rigs of sail. And wherever yachtsmen gather to talk of ships and seas, a mention of the Friendship sloop brings conversation to respectful silence, in general agreement that there is no more beautiful boat afloat.

The granddaddy of the Friendship sloops, the 45-foot Jolly Buccaneer, *the largest of the Friendships in existence. For ballast, she carries thousands of axeheads.*

On a single voyage the seamen in Section **III** experienced more danger and excitement . . .

. . than all the hardship, thrills, and **Adventure** most people know in a lifetime.

FOR
GOD'S SAKE,
WHERE DID
YOU COME FROM

?

by Chester S. Howland

In the Spring of 1897, the 400-ton Yankee whaling bark *Belvedere* had completed her fitting out in San Francisco for another summer season in the Arctic Ocean. Her Master was M. U. B. Millard. George Fred Tilton of Chilmark on Martha's Vineyard, Massachusetts was the Third Mate. The *Belvedere* was a five-boat ship with a total crew of forty-eight men. San Francisco was the active West Coast whaling port for Arctic whalers and the *Karluk*, *Jeanette*, *Marwhal*, *Thrasher*, *Belugo* and *Bowhead* also sailed for a season North.

One thousand miles out of San Francisco a severe gale swept down from the northeast. Sail was shortened and the *Belvedere* hove to. A gigantic sixty-foot sea boarded the vessel smashing the jib boom and the davits on the starboard side of the ship. A seaman was crushed against the bulwarks and was fatally injured. Under difficulties, Captain Millard took the ship to Unalaska.

A new jib boom was set up in that port. After two weeks' delay the *Belvedere* sailed on her course. Good weather favored the passage. Pribilof Island and the first ice was reached in three days. Three weeks later the ship had broken through the ice and entered the Arctic through Bering Straits. Within a few hours a whale was raised and Mate Tilton, heading his boat, captured it.

Fine weather continued as the *Belvedere* and other whaleships cruised between Diomedes and St. Lawrence Island. However, whales were not sighted with the customary frequency at this time of year. No ship had caught more than one whale up to the first of July. This might have been an indication of a severe cold and early ice.

Supply ships with provisions and coal arrived at Unalaska about July 15. The *Belvedere* left the Mud Hole on the Siberian Coast on that date, obtained supplies, and returned to Blossom Point, 200 miles north of the Arctic Circle, on July 23. Pack ice was forming and lay five miles off shore. Captain Tilton (he was later promoted to this rank) years later reported it was the iciest season he had ever seen.

The fleet of whalers anchored inside Point Lay waiting for the ice to move and to sail for Point Barrow.

It was the last of August before the ships sailed for Point Barrow and Herschel Island. The whaler *Navarch* was caught solid in ice and was last seen drifting northwest in pack ice. It was later reported that on July 29 the pack ice, driven by an east wind, went off shore taking the *Navarch* and all on board, helplessly gripped.

September 8, the *Belvedere* was laying in young ice three miles east of Point Barrow and would have been jammed if the *Orca* had not hooked on and towed her into a safe position.

No one believed he'd make it. But with four whaling vessels crushed between floes of arctic ice, stranding 150 crewmen, George Fred Tilton (facing page) knew he had to complete his 3,000-mile walk for help.

After a consultation of captains on September 9, it was decided to blast a path through heavy ridge ice to open water. A thousand pounds of powder and all ships' crews, working day and night for three days, opened a canal a mile and a half long. But young ice began forming immediately. The *Orca* was crushed between two great floes. Two hours later the *Freeman* was crushed, the crew tumbling from the vessel to safety on the ice.

The *Belvedere* rescued the crews of the *Orca* and the *Freeman* and had 150 men aboard. Any moment a shift in the wind might start the ice to piling mountain high; it was decided to build a camp on Sea Horse Island which was accessible at the time. It took eight days of travel over treacherous ice, that might crack or split without warning, to reach Sea Horse Island on September 22. Many of the whalemen aboard the fleet had never been North on whaling voyages and did not know how to travel on Arctic Ocean ice.

After another consultation of captains and officers of the fleet of ships, it was calculated that, if there was no rescue, the ships' provisions and stocks would allow but two scant meals a day from October through the winter until July 1.

It was then that Mate George Fred Tilton suggested his plan.

"Captains, it is my opinion that half of our crews, unaccustomed to winter in the Arctic, will die before July 1 of next year, and there is no guarantee that ships will bring us relief even then.

I'll go south to the State of Washington, and beyond, and once in the United States I shall report our condition and ask for assistance and relief."

The Captains reluctantly agreed to Tilton's offer. A number of men wanted to go with him but were refused.

"I want some good dogs and a well-built sled and a couple of Siberian Indians. The Indian women can make skin clothing and native sleeping bags for the three of us. The dogs will take care of themselves."

The sled was specially fitted, according to Tilton's directions, with a mast and sail to make the journey easier on the dogs. Fifteen days' rations for the men and frozen fish for the dogs were loaded onto the sled.

The first objective was Point Hope where it was expected more provisions would be found.

October 31 at noon the Captain, his eager dogs and native men, with sail set and dogs straining in their harnesses, set off amid the cheering crews and sober countenances of the more experienced masters of the beleaguered Arctic whaling ships.

There was a stop made at the spot where the *Belvedere* was solidly held in the crushing grip of heavy ice. Here a compass, firearms, navigating instruments and a chart were taken and packed aboard the sled. Limitless areas of solitary, barren ice lay around the party. On October the 28th, due to heavy wind and a strong current, an airhole in the ice had opened and it took from early morning until nearly midnight to circuit this danger and gain straightaway progress south a half mile.

On November 1, twenty-five miles were covered with little difficulty; but that night a gale and heavy snow came out of the northeast. No effort to travel could be made until November 3. That morning the Captain and his companions came into a small deserted Indian village. They found an old axe which they took and, thinking the villagers were out on a deer hunt, left two boxes of cartridges in trade.

November 4 and 5 were days of extremely exhausting travel. The country was mountainous, with some places so steep it was necessary to unload the sled and haul it, its equipment and the dogs from level to level with a rope.

As the group traveled on the high land, Captain Tilton decided to get nearer to the shore. The descent was less laborious but far more dangerous than climbing up. Sheeting the sled sail forward against a head wind served as a brake. If the sled had gotten out of control, it would have dropped onto the rocks far below. The men and dogs would have been carried along with it.

It took eight hours to reach the beach. The dogs' feet were bruised and sore and the day was spent in camp to allow the dogs to rest.

The group started off the morning of the 8th of November with a strong fresh northeast wind blowing. When late afternoon came on, a raging blizzard blinded them. The tent could not be pitched and a snow house was built for protection through the night.

Although equipped with an eight-dog sled, Tilton and his two Indian companions walked most of the way.

The snow house was simply made by digging into a snow bank until there was room enough to allow Captain Tilton and his two natives to crawl in. Their eight sled dogs jumped in without invitation, and the opening was closed with a block of snow cut to fit. All hands that night had a comparatively good rest.

Storm conditions had swept to the east through the night. Starting at ten o'clock the next morning, they reached a native village at midnight. The natives accepted cartridges and powder in exchange for a seal which provided supper and breakfast for dogs and men.

The next day, the group encountered fifteen miles of the most difficult travelling they had found. The shelves and ice hummocks were so precipitous that the unloaded sled, packs and dogs had to be hauled up by hand ropes to overcome obstacles that otherwise would have ended the trek, or at least seriously delayed it due to lack of food supplies.

Three days after leaving the Indian village, an open stream of water 150' wide and extending toward the sea so far there was no end visible confronted the travellers. It seemed as though it would be necessary to retrace the journey for miles. There was now no food for either dogs or men.

Captain Tilton made a dangerous investigation, alone, by following the very edge of the land and lying on his stomach looking over into the large body of water. He discovered large cakes of ice under the shelving edge of the floe. Hewing and cutting all day with a snow knife, a cake was cut large enough to take the men and dogs and equipment and serve as an ice raft to span the water. For four days now the men and dogs had been without food and were weakening.

The morning of the fifth day, an air hole was sighted and ducks were swimming in it. A whale's carcass was seen, evidently cast adrift by a whaling ship. The dogs and natives ate the whale meat. The Captain built a fire of driftwood and cooked and ate duck meat.

That night a northwest blizzard struck the tent where the men were in sleeping bags. The tent was blown to tatters and again a snow house was cut. When morning came the gale still raged.

Captain Tilton later described the situation thus: "It was no use to hitch up the dogs, for they won't travel in a northern blizzard. It's hard to do anything with them even after it stops snowing as long as the wind blows, for the snow blows around and around so. But we didn't have anything to eat but that ancient whale and none too much of that, so I decided to leave the dogs and gear and move. I had the ship's mail with me, wrapped in an oilskin sack, so I took that and strapped it on my back and tied myself and the two natives together with a sled line, and we started for Point

This was the situation (right) of the four whaling vessels on November 1, 1897. Most of the seamen had never been to the Arctic Ocean before.

Hope, eighteen miles away, where I knew there was a whaling station and white men.

"We couldn't see a thing, but there was no danger of getting lost, for we followed the beach. It was a great deal longer that way, but I didn't dare to take to the ice. As we went along I would stop and dig through the snow once in a while. If I struck soil I knew I was too far inland, and if I struck ice, too far offshore, and altered my course accordingly. That's the way we worked along from daylight until dark. When the wind squalls struck, there were times when we would all have to lie down, and later in the day, when within a mile of Point Hope, the natives gave up and laid down and I had to force them to get on their feet and go on. You can get an idea how thick it was when I tell you that I ran into the first house at Point Hope before I knew it, or saw it. I knew it was a house, though, and felt my way along the side, looking for an entrance. The barking of a dog helped me to locate it. It was a tunnel, built Eskimo style, and I ducked into it. I crawled over a dog and found the door, and as I did a Norwegian by the name of Anderson, who had started the station, opened it, and said, 'For God's sake, where did you come from?'

"I told him 'Cape Lisburne,' and I had hard work to make him believe it. He didn't think it was possible for men to live in that storm. My natives laid right down on the floor and went to sleep. I sat up and drank the coffee and ate the hard-tack that Anderson gave me and I felt like a new man as soon as I got it down. Grub works mighty quick in the Arctic.

"We stayed with Anderson for two days. The natives had frozen ears and feet and I had a toe frozen which gave me some trouble. Then when we were rested and our frostbites were better we borrowed a dog team and two of Anderson's natives and started back to Cape Lisburne for our own dogs and gear. The sled wasn't hurt a bit and we found all of the dogs but one, underneath the snow. We camped that night in the snow house and the next morning went back to Anderson's. I had to ride, for my toe was paining me badly. On the way back to Anderson's we found the body of a dog we had lost in the storm. He had been blown off a seventy-five foot cliff and killed. That's a sample of just one more kind of death that lays in wait for man and beast in the Arctic."

A complete refitting was required before continuing

91

In 1927, George Tilton was made Captain of the whaler Charles W. Morgan, *and he spent his last days entertaining visitors aboard her. Tilton is the one with the pipe.*

the bleak and hazardous journey. Two new human companions and three new dogs were to accompany Captain Tilton.

On the 29th of November, the new journey began toward the United States and aid for the 200 ice-bound seamen within the Arctic Circle.

They fought mountains, canyons, ice floes, treacherous soft ice over mile-deep streams, the wide open straits of Shelikof where the west wind and terrific tides running against it created a watery hell. At times the weather fell to 57° below zero.

The force that drove the Captain on was the certainty that "if I fail to get help for those men they might never come out of the Arctic."

In early March of 1898, the weather became too warm for further use of dog teams. The rigors of travel lessened and messages sent to ship owners by Tilton on his way to

Left. The famous whaler Charles W. Morgan *as she appeared before she was enshrined on the Colonel Green estate in South Dartmouth, Mass. She was later refloated and taken to Mystic Seaport in Connecticut, where she can be seen today.*

San Francisco began to show results. The U.S. Cutter *Bear* reached Point Barrow July 22, 1898. A merchant ship was fitted and sailed with supplies.

In Captain Tilton's own words, "My shipwrecked companions were rescued, taken to the States and to their homes." Captain Tilton had travelled—mostly by walking—approximately 3,000 miles to save them. Of the original fleet of four vessels, only the *Belvedere* survived. Five years later, Tilton took her back into the Arctic—this time as her Captain.

When, in 1927, Hetty Green's multimillionaire son, Colonel Edward Robinson Howland Green, enshrined the famous whaleship **Charles W. Morgan** on the extensive shore of his 200-acre estate at Round Hill, South Dartmouth, Massachusetts, Captain Tilton was sixty-six years old and his whaling days were over. But the Colonel, aware of Captain Tilton's abilities, selected him as Captain of the **Morgan.** For several years, on the deck of the century-old ship, Captain Tilton captivated the tens of thousands of visitors who came from far and wide to see the **Morgan** and hear the man.

Visitors found Captain Tilton to be a character with powers of expression that immediately commanded attention. His speech was heavy-voiced and plain, without any half measure approach to any subject. He was with you or "agin" you without fear or favor. His big, massive, round face expressed pleasure or wrath in unmistakable muscular variations.

He loved to hold visitors to the **Morgan** spellbound with the tales of his many sea adventures as a whaling captain. But someone would always ask him about that 3,000-mile walk back in 1897 when he was third mate on the **Belvedere.** The feat remains to this day one of the most remarkable in arctic history.

NOT WHALES BUT MEN HE SOUGHT

Captain George S. Anthony of the *Catalpa*

Editor's Note: *After the unsuccessful rebellion against England of William O'Brien and his Young Ireland movement in 1848, a secret organization sprang up in Ireland and America known as the Fenians. This group consisted mostly of Irishmen driven from their land by famine. Their original purpose was to make Ireland a republic independent of England. In Ireland, plots toward this end were created by the Fenians against the British Government. In 1865–67, a number of incidents occurred which resulted in the execution of three Fenians, confinement of many, and the shipment of seven to the English penal colony in Australia. The following is an account of the daring rescue of these men ten years later by a Yankee whaleship out of New Bedford.*

AT 1 P.M. ON THE BALMY AFTERNOON OF APRIL 16, 1876, Captain George S. Anthony of the whaleship *Catalpa* threw a coat into one of the whaleboats, stowed away a bag of hardbread, two kegs of water and half a boiled ham, and ordered the boat lowered. Five men were called and moved quickly to the oars. They must have wondered what was up, for the *Catalpa* lay twenty miles south of Rottnest Lighthouse, off Fremantle on the southwest coast of Australia, and no whale had been sighted.

In fact, this voyage, begun a year before from New Bedford, Mass., ostensibly for whale oil, was bent on more dangerous game—men.

High on a pine-thick hill overlooking the dusty town of Fremantle bulked "The Establishment," the white stone English penal colony in which six stubborn Irishmen marked the tenth year of life imprisonment for their parts in the abortive Fenian uprisings of 1866. A seventh man, John Boyle O'Reilly, had escaped to America with the aid of an Irish priest in the bush country nearby.

And even as the whaleboat bobbed toward the empty strand shining in the distance, two disguised members of the powerful Irish Clan-na-Gael were making the last arrangements onshore for a daring, split-second rescue attempt the next day.

Captain George S. Anthony had fifteen years of whaling behind him when he beached himself at the age of thirty-one to become a mechanic in a machine shop. He wanted to stay at home with his young bride of a year and their three-month-old son, but the sweet smell of the sea and the sour smack of the waterfront loosened his landlubber resolutions.

One day in February 1875, he told his father-in-law, John T. Richardson, of his restlessness. A few days later, Mr. Richardson told Captain Anthony to come to his clothing outfitters shop that night.

He did. Five men were seated around the big potbelly

by Eli Flam

Peabody Museum, Salem, Mass.

this painting depicting the escape, the Fenians are being
wed to the Catalpa. *The police vessel is pressing in on the left,*
d the British steamer Georgette *on the right. The painting*
by E. N. Russell of New Bedford.

stove in the rear. Besides Mr. Richardson, there were Captain Henry C. Hathaway, the burly city marshal, and three strangers, John Devoy, John W. Goff and James Reynolds.

They were Irish refugees and members of a rescue committee of the Clan-na-Gael; they asked Captain Anthony if he would take the *Catalpa* on a whaling voyage with the real—but secret—purpose of arriving off Australia to rescue the prisoners. Captain Anthony thought he was the wrong man for the expedition, but he was won over, and on April 29, the bark *Catalpa* stood to sea from New Bedford.

Of the crew of twenty-three, only Denis Dugan, the carpenter and a Clan member, knew the destination. Aside from the captain's hand-picked first mate, Samuel P. Smith of Martha's Vineyard, most of the others were Malays, Kanakas, and Cape Verdeans, and several were green hands.

The *Catalpa,* bought by the Clan in East Boston, was 202.05 tons net, ninety feet long and twenty-five feet in breadth. She was rigged as a merchant bark, with double topsails and a poop deck.

Following Devoy's written orders, the *Catalpa* went whaling in the North Atlantic until fall. They stopped at Fayal in the Azores to ship home 210 barrels of sperm oil but made a hurried departure because of Thomas Brennan. Brennan, a determined Fenian, wanted to go with the *Catalpa* but was turned down by the Clan-na-Gael for reasons of their own. Now he was on a steamer for Fayal to join up.

Alerted by a letter to Dugan, Captain Anthony left port the day before Brennan was due. Later, working down the west coast of Africa, the Captain explained the secret purpose of the voyage to Samuel Smith, the First Mate. Aside from Dugan, the carpenter, the rest of the crew knew nothing of it.

The *Catalpa* had passed the Cape of Good Hope when she spoke the *Ocean Beauty,* a large English bark. Captain Anthony went on board for a gam and learned, without revealing his own plans, that the *Beauty*'s captain had been master of the convict ship that had carried the Fenians to prison in Fremantle, Australia. Captain Anthony returned to his own ship carrying the very chart used in landing the prisoners.

From February 29 to March 10, a prolonged gale blew dead ahead and only 120 miles easting was made. But fair winds came from the west and then the *Catalpa* sailed along with a bone in her teeth. On March 28, she reached anchorage off Bunbury Harbor, Australia, at the head of Geogrape Bay.

Devoy's orders ended, ". . . You are to go to Bunbury, on the west coast, and there communications will be opened with you from our Australian agent." That agent was John J. Breslin, a Fenian hero who had sailed from San Francisco in September with Captain Thomas Desmond, another key member of Clan-na-Gael. They had separated in Fremantle.

Breslin became a wealthy American gentleman seeking investments. He made a great impression, and was frequently entertained by the governor of Australia, himself. Once, he was given a tour of the prison by the superintendent. Breslin finally contacted the six prisoners through a former inmate.

Captain Desmond went on to Perth to make further arrangements, during which time he worked as a carriage-maker.

John King, a former Dublin man living in New South Wales, collected several thousand dollars for the rescue. Two other Fenians were assigned to cut telegraph wires after the escape.

After three days at Bunbury, Captain Anthony finally met Breslin, who explained the plan after dinner in an elegant hotel. Breslin would bring the escapees to Rockingham Beach, an isolated strip twenty-one miles south of Fremantle and 100 miles north of Bunbury. Captain Anthony would be there with a whaleboat and haul them to the *Catalpa,* anchored at least twelve miles offshore to avoid suspicion.

Boarding the armed mail steamer *Georgette* the next day for a "study" trip, Breslin and Anthony were surprised by Thomas Brennan, who had just arrived on his own.

"They were picked up by two rigs shortly after 8 A.M."

Against their wills, they included him in their plans.

Then from Fremantle the men drove two hours and twenty minutes in rented rigs to Rockingham. On a point covered with tall grass and bush, Captain Anthony stuck an old joist above high-water mark to set the meeting spot.

The rescue try was delayed until April 17, a Monday, by fear of an English gunboat in Fremantle, trouble with the *Catalpa*'s crew, and bad weather. Captain Anthony landed at Rockingham late on April 16, and Desmond arrived in Fremantle with a rig and a pair of horses.

At 6 A.M. April 17, Brennan started for Rockingham with arms and luggage. The six prisoners, because of good behavior, were working on the roads or outside private homes. They were virtually unguarded and knew this was the day.

With precision timing, they were picked up in two rigs shortly after 8 A.M. and given long linen coats and hats to cover their convict clothes. At 10:30, the party clattered up to the beach and saw Brennan making urgent signals to hurry. The *Georgette* was expected at a nearby jetty to pick up a cargo of timber.

The men, two six-shooters strapped to their belts and rifles in their hands, rushed to the whaleboat. It was a half mile offshore when a squad of eight mounted policemen, who'd already missed the prisoners, reined up with a group of "trackers"—bushmen who acted as human bloodhounds—but no shots were fired.

Breslin had prepared a note for his "friend" the governor. He tied it to a float to drift inshore. It concluded, "In taking my leave now, I've only to say/ A few cells I've emptied (a sell in its way);/ I've the honor and pleasure to bid you good-day,/ From all future acquaintance, excuse me, I pray."

The *Catalpa* was still distant when a gale and early darkness came on. The whaleboat's mast broke and went over the side. Soon the men had enough work just bailing the seas they shipped. The rescued men, violently seasick, lay huddled in the bottom.

At sunrise the sea had gone down and the *Catalpa* was seen again. An hour later, the *Georgette* was spotted by the whaleboat. Oars were shipped, a makeshift sail was taken down, and the men lay down on each other. The *Georgette* passed within a half mile but did not see the whaleboat.

Within three miles of the *Catalpa,* the whaleboat was spotted by a guard-boat which was looking for the men. The *Catalpa,* seeing the predicament, immediately put on sail and raced the guard-boat—hauling up to the whaleboat as the guard-boat came abreast.

The escapees crowded to the rail and shouted in high spirits at the thirty or more men in the guard-boat, many of whom they knew by name. The officer in command, apparently a good loser, saluted Captain Anthony, who responded with a greeting.

New Bedford, Mass., September, 1876. The Catalpa *is shown shortly after returning home from Australia with the rescued Fenians.*

The next hour aboard the *Catalpa* was more like a Saturday night in port than a Tuesday morning at sea, especially for the rescued men—Martin J. Hogan, James Wilson, Thomas Hassett, Michael Harrington and Robert Cranston.

The next day, the *Catalpa* was overhauled by the 400-ton *Georgette*. Many soldiers were aboard and a big gun gleamed on her upper deck. She fired a shot across the *Catalpa*'s bow and came abeam. Colonel Harvest, in charge of the deck, ordered Captain Anthony to heave to. He refused.

A faint breeze filled the *Catalpa*'s sails and the two ships moved along with Captain Anthony and Colonel Harvest in spirited contention. The Colonel threatened to shoot at the *Catalpa*'s mast. Captain Anthony's answer was to have Smith pass out cutting spades, whaling guns and heavy pieces of iron. After several hours, the wind freshened. Captain Anthony, by some slick sailing, led the *Georgette* to think the *Catalpa* was going to haul back and the steamer stopped. Then the *Catalpa* fairly leaped away. With the now strong breeze, she simply outsailed the slow steamer which shortly gave up the chase and headed for port.

The *Catalpa* reached New Bedford in September. Captain Hathaway, the city marshal, received a letter from the Perth, Australia, Police Department requesting particulars about the "absconders." The marshal (police chief) of New Bedford had been a crewman aboard the whaleship on which John Boyle O'Reilly escaped to the United States. He filed the letter, one report says, in a wastebasket. The "absconders," the last Irish political prisoners in Fremantle, remained free to their deaths.

After reaching New Bedford, the Fenians remained free to their deaths

Canton, China. Waterfront scene, circa 1860—by an unknown Chinese artist. Canton was the crossroads of commerce, bringing together seamen and merchants from the East and West. In this painting a variety of ships of the day have come from all over the world to gather in this famous harbor.

ON A BRIGHT MAY MORNING OF 1787 THE PEACE OF Salem, Massachusetts, was shattered by a seaward cannon blast that startled housewives in their kitchens, routed the pigeons from the elms, and sent Elias Hasket Derby scurrying to pier's end, glass in hand. He saw what he had hoped to see. Rounding Naugus Head with skysails set and drawing full, billowed the good ship *Grank Turk,* first New England vessel to return from Canton in the opening years of the great China trade.

She had barely dropped anchor when half of Salem's population swarmed aboard her—merchants, farmers, wives, and daughters eager to trade whatever was acceptable for the *Grand Turk*'s cargo of teas, silks, and porcelain.

From that moment on, Salem was never quite the same. Housewives dressed in silk gowns served their neigh-

THE CHINA TRADE

by Samuel Carter III

bors Hyson tea on delicate, exquisitely decorated sets of Canton chinaware. Deborah Fairfax Anderson displayed to envying friends her custom-made cups and saucers etched with pictures of Minerva in the throes of Cupid. Shipmaster Ebenezer West proudly showed his fellow Salem captains the porcelain punch bowl presented by the Chinese merchant Pinqua, which, beneath the glazed surface of its base and sides, depicted the *Grand Turk* itself in glowing oriental colors.

For Elias Hasket Derby—"King Derby" to his followers—the voyage was a thundering success, netting him double the value of New England commodities that Captain West had bartered in Canton. But more than that was its overwhelming influence on tastes and fashions and the foreign commerce of the new American republic. It sharpened the ambition of New England merchants to join the

race for products from the Far East, and created an insatiable market for the radiant, translucent porcelain which the Chinese had excelled in since the 16th century.

True, the *Grand Turk* was not the first American ship to visit Canton—the only port in all of China open to world commerce. Ever since the Revolution, which had closed West Indies ports to Yankee vessels, American merchants had looked desperately for other sources of foreign trade to break the stifling post-war depression. A small sloop named the *Harriet* had sailed from Boston to the Orient in 1783 with a cargo of ginseng root, much prized by the Chinese for its aphrodisiac and therapeutic powers. But a British East-Indiaman, alarmed at this threat of Yankee competition, had bought her before she even unloaded her cargo.

A year later the *Empress of China* had sailed from

Elegant mansions were built in Salem largely from profits earned in the China Trade. The Trade also enabled Salem merchants and masters to furnish their homes with oriental opulence, including prized collections of Chinese porcelain, such as this teapot (below) and tea caddy.

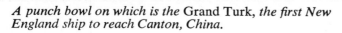

A punch bowl on which is the Grand Turk, *the first New England ship to reach Canton, China.*

This bowl has been described as "the most exquisite man-made product ever to reach the New World in the 19th century."

Photos courtesy of Peabody Museum, Salem, Mass.

Examples of the fine Canton porcelain that changed the face and fortune of New England.

New York with her "supercargo" or business manager, Maj. Samuel Shaw of Boston, and returned with a cargo of six tons of porcelain, plus teas and silks, that brought a 70 per cent profit to her owners. Shaw later returned to Canton as America's first consul in a foreign country.

The *Grand Turk,* however, was New England's own, and she marked the beginning of a good half-century when Yankee ships and Yankee seamen would all but dominate the seas. In fact, New England's maritime history, its progress and prosperity, can be equated with the China trade.

Flushed with success, King Derby sent four more ships in the wake of the *Grand Turk,* among 14 Salem vessels bound for Canton in the next three years. One was the famous *Astrea* whose supercargo was Salem-born Nathaniel Bowditch, destined to make history in navigation. Merchant-shipowners furnished most of the outgoing cargo— ginseng, kitchenware, nails and needles, saddles and bridles, lard and flour. But housewives eagerly participated, bringing to dockside their salted cod and homemade spermaceti candles to be traded, on the best terms possible, for Canton tea sets, serving platters, soup tureens, and custom-decorated punch bowls.

For the proud and practical New Englander, there were very sound reasons why Chinese export porcelain was so desirable, apart from its sheer beauty. Teas and silks, the other principal commodities, were perishable. Tea was consumed; silk fell apart after several seasons' wear. But the chinaware, treasured in cabinets, endured almost forever— to be handed down as family heirlooms from one generation to another.

More than that, it had identity; it could express the owner's personality. A piece of china could be decorated with the family crest or monogram or a design submitted by the purchaser. It could reflect national pride with the Seal of the United States, the American Eagle, or pictures of General Washington, Mount Vernon, or Old Glory. And custom-made punch bowls or platters catered to the spirit of free enterprise by depicting the vessels of New England merchants, somewhat stylized perhaps, but with the ship's name clearly lettered on the bow.

Shipmasters, too, were partial to the porcelain trade, however difficult the product was to handle. Wrapped in "rice paper" (actually wood-fibre tissue: rice was too precious as a food to use for paper), crated, and stowed deep in the hold where other commodities might perish from the dampness, chinaware paid its way as ballast and provided a "flooring" on which other cargo might be placed. Too, almost every captain was allowed some cargo space for private trading ventures. Here he might stow his personal purchases at Canton, such as ornamental tea sets to delight the heart of a wife or sweetheart weary of New England pewter.

But New England traders found themselves abruptly at a disadvantage. What they had to offer at Canton was limited. Ginseng was in short supply, and the Chinese were not drawn to pots and kettles, cod and candles. The competitive British East India Company had the edge with silver dollars, which New Englanders could not supply, along with the much-desired opium smuggled in from India, which was closed to Yankee vessels. Some new medium of exchange would have to be discovered if the promise of the *Grand Turk* was to be fulfilled.

It had already been discovered. A young adventurer, Groton-born John Ledyard, sailing with Captain Cook's third voyage to the Pacific, had noted that Russian sailors were selling Alaskan otter skins to Chinese mandarins. When Cook's own account confirmed this lucrative trade in Northwest furs, a group of Boston merchants met in Charles Bulfinch's mansion to discuss the matter. Putting up $50,000, they purchased the 212-ton ship *Columbia,* with the sloop *Lady Washington* as her escort, and sent the vessels around Cape Horn to the Northwest territories to take a fling at trading furs in Canton.

The *Columbia*'s voyage was even more epoch-making than the *Grand Turk*'s. Stopping at Nootka Sound in Vancouver Island for a load of pelts, she proceeded to the Sandwich, or Hawaiian, Islands for a supplementary load of sandalwood, and traded the lot at a fabulous profit at Canton for teas and silks and tons of porcelain. The *Columbia* then rounded the Cape of Good Hope on her return voyage —41,900 miles in 40 months—becoming the first American ship to circumnavigate the globe.

One year later, on a similarly routed expedition, the *Columbia* discovered the mouth of the salmon-infested river to which she gave her name, laying the groundwork for United States possession of the Northwest territories. As Samuel Eliot Morison writes: "On her first voyage, the *Columbia* had solved the riddle of the China trade. On her second, empire followed in the wake."

The Boston-Canton axis was now solidly established on a three-way pattern: Boston to the Northwest coast with chisels, hatchets, knives, and knickknacks for the Indians; on to Canton via the Hawaiian Islands; and back around Cape Horn to Boston, steadied by tons of Chinese porcelain in the hold. By some silent gentleman's agreement, Salem merchants routed their ships around the Cape of Good Hope, picking up products surreptitiously in the West Indies and stopping at Madeira for wines to exchange for silver on the way to Canton.

Shortly after the turn of the century "the peddling keels of Salem," inspired by the village motto *Ad ultimum sinum*—"To the uttermost gulf"—made it the richest town per capita in the nation. Salem ships outnumbered those of Providence and Boston in Far Eastern ports. Responding to their new-found wealth, successors to King Derby moved from the windy waterfront and built their majestic, square, three-storied homes on Chestnut Street and around the green, making Salem Common the loveliest in America.

Many of these gambrel-roofed brick mansions, with their shining cupolas and captains' walks, were the work of Salem's architect, Samuel McIntire. In simplicity and elegance, they were more than a match for those that Bulfinch built for Boston's merchant princes, and rivaled for magnificence even John Brown's house on Power Street in Providence, hailed by John Quincy Adams as the most impressive dwelling in America.

The China trade which had built these mansions also furnished them with oriental opulence. Each contained its prized collection of Chinese porcelain: tea sets, coffee pots, pitchers, punch bowls, flagons, caddies, hot-water plates, and serving platters, embellished with the family crest or monogram. They were used as much for decoration as for service—notably such treasures as the 22-inch tureens in the shape of geese which Captain Ward Blackler brought home in 1803, and Captain Isaac Smith's flagon depicting in glorious technicolor the battle of the *Guerriere* and *Constitution*.

Homes such as those of the Peabodys, Crowninshields, Pickerings, and Pingrees became virtually museums (as indeed some are at present) of oriental treasures; while the house of Capt. Robert Bennett Forbes in Milton, Massachusetts, displayed not only porcelain but Chinese silver—for today it is being discovered that much of the English-looking silverware which abounds throughout New England was actually another, if subsidiary, product of the China trade.

As the volume of this trade increased, and export china became an enviable status symbol, the market extended to almost every seaport family of modest wealth. New England journals began to print shipmasters' notices of "China, a great variety" arriving on a certain date, along with such advertisements as appeared in the *Providence Gazette* in May of 1804:

Yam Shinqua, Chinaware Merchant at Canton, begs leave respectfully to inform the American Merchants, Supercargoes, and Captains that he procures to be manufactured in the best manner, all sorts of Chinaware with Arms, Cyphers and other Decorations (if required) painted in a very superior style and on the most reasonable Terms. All orders carefully and promptly attended to. Canton (China) Jan. 8, 1804.

The phrase "procures to be manufactured" indicates that the Canton merchant was merely a middleman, and Canton itself not much more than a trading post. Actually "Canton china" came from the potteries of Ching-te Chen, hundreds of miles in the interior. Arriving at Canton in the form of "blanks," undecorated or with stock embellishments and borders, it was farmed out to families on the nearby island of Honam to be painted according to sketches submitted by the purchaser.

The War of 1812, caused partly by English interference with Yankee ships in Chinese waters, brought scarcely a pause in the China trade. If anything, it heightened America's influence and reputation on the high seas, and spurred a shipbuilding boom from Mystic to Penobscot Bay. In contrast to the large ships of the British East India Company, carrying weighty cargoes, the Yankee builders developed a new class of Medford East-Indiamen—small, swift vessels that could carry half the amount of cargo half again as fast.

Their average weight was around 300 tons, and their crews numbered less than 20.

Most of these crews were homogeneously Yankee. They came not from the waterfront saloons, but often from the proudest families in New England—for the sea was an honorable calling, and many an adventurous scion traded a Harvard education for two years before the mast. They were young, ambitious, and they rose fast in their calling. Robert Bennet Forbes, for instance, shipped aboard the *Canton Packet* in 1818 at the age of 13, rose to be master at the age of 20, and commanded his own ship at the age of 26—later to become head of Russell & Company's agency at Canton. John Perkins Cushing started his career in 1803 at 16 to become the wealthiest merchant in the China trade, retiring in 1830 to Boston's Summer Street with a wall of Chinese porcelain screening his house from public gaze.

Many of the great New England family fortunes, and most of the old-time shipping dynasties, were founded on these 40 or more years of Far East commerce. In contrast to the organized companies of the Dutch and English, Yankees took to the China trade as individuals. Such famous merchant-shipping firms as J. & T. H. Perkins of Boston, Russell & Company, Augustine Heard, Brown & Ives of Providence, and Peabody and Crowninshield of Salem actually represented one man willing to risk his fleet of privately owned ships in the hazardous route to China.

And risks there were, in this daredevil, blood-and-thunder trade. Not just from the dangerous weather and treacherous passages around the Cape or Horn. Hardly a voyage was completed without a battle with the Northwest Indians, Chinese pirates, and, later, Fiji Island cannibals. But as Obadiah Brown wrote, in spelling as bad as his grammar: "If I should venter nothing, I should Never have nothing."

Furthermore, the Cantonese, who regarded all Europeans as "foreign devils" and Americans as "flowery-flag devils," were hardly cordial hosts. All foreign ships were obliged to anchor at Whampoa, 12 miles south of Canton, and the cargo had to be lightered upstream to the forbidden city. Here only a narrow strip of waterfront was allotted to the use of foreign merchants, and here each nationality—English, Danish, Dutch, French, American, and half-a-dozen others—built its "Hong," or factory, for unloading goods to trade. When their business was done, all ships and merchants were obliged by law to retreat to the Portuguese enclave of Macao until the next trading season opened.

No foreigner could venture beyond the precincts of the Hongs, or deal with any but the 10 Hong merchants who had charge of the entire foreign trade of China. These were all-powerful, sometimes corrupt, and universally addicted to accepting bribes. In 1816 Benjamin Shreve of Salem began helpfully to circulate among his colleagues a confidential guide, or "Who's Who," of Hong merchants, with such cautionary comments as "So-so rich but a great scoundrel," and "Cannot be depended on at all."

Yet there was exotic color, romance, drama in this epic of the Far East. One can well imagine the reactions of a

fledgling New England cabin boy, just out of school, approaching the harbor of Canton. Before him ranged the stately terraced Hongs with flags of all nations flying above their pillared porticoes. Along the seawall crowded the flowerboats with their superstructures carved in the shapes of birds and blossoms. Beyond them bobbed the floating city of sampans with their teeming families of artisans and tradesmen. To and fro raced the gilt-oared mandarin boats, eyes painted on their prows ("How to see to walk on water without eyes?"). And over it all the haunting san-hsien music, the shouts of peddlers crying their wares, the odor of incense and spiced oriental cooking; and at night the soft glow of paper lanterns suspended from the bamboo mooring poles. Sights, sounds, and scents remote from Beacon Hill and Chestnut Street.

The years from 1800 to 1840, the Golden Age of the China trade, offer no parallel in American maritime history. It was a period that restored prosperity to the New England States and to America at large. In one year straddling 1818–19 the trade totalled $19 million—a tremendous fortune for the times. And while the quality of Chinese porcelain began to vary, its complexity of kind and decoration grew.

It offered infinite variety. In addition to the staple Canton chinaware, there was "nankeen" or Nanking china, mostly burnished blue on white; Fitzhugh porcelain, named probably from a mispronunciation of the Chinese city of Foo Chow (the trade was full of misnomers such as "Lowestoft China," named for a city in England but actually of Chinese derivation); Rose Canton or Rose Medallion with their typically oriental patterns of birds, butterflies, and flowers; purple and gold Mandarin and sea-green Celadon

—types that overlapped with similarities yet somehow kept their individual distinctions.

The decorative themes became more varied, too, as New England families demanded more personal or more original memorials. These now might be a sketch of the family homestead, a portrait, or a bit of homespun verse. Or they might tell simple, sequential stories, depicting a sailor parting from his sweetheart on the village green and later returning to claim her in a fond embrace. As popular as "The Sailor's Return" was another scenario labelled "Fair and Foul," showing a ship in the death throes of a storm and later, on the other side of the receptacle, emerging into quiet seas and sunshine. Some of these oriental bowls were used by Paul Revere as patterns for his silverware.

But the trade was a voracious one. Chinese demand for pelts exhausted the supply of Northwest furs, sending Yankee ships to the Chilean coast for sealskins, which in turn became depleted. The sandalwood, which the Chinese prized for incense and for making ornamental boxes, was shortly stripped from the Hawaiian Islands. Desperate for articles of trade, American supercargoes turned to *beche de mer,* or sea cucumbers, and edible birds' nests from the Fiji Islands, both prized in China as gustatorial delicacies. When these ran out, tortoise shells and pearl shells, used for decoration and for inlays, were seized on as commodities for barter. At one low point, even gravestones were exported,

A nation saved from financial rot

some already engraved with such legends as: "Sacred to the memory of Maria Peabody."

While United States ships at Whampoa were second in number only to the English, the British East India Company had a distinct advantage in its opium from India. Though outlawed by Imperial decree, no Hong merchant would spurn a cargo of opium smuggled up the Pearl, and no shame attached to handling the forbidden drug—it was banned by Chinese, not by Anglo-Saxon law.

Yet few Americans engaged in opium smuggling. For one thing, they had no access to the ports of India, and had to settle for the inferior Turkish product. A handful of freebooters made the run from Smyrna to Canton with cargoes of the "vile dirt"—one of them Capt. John Prescott of New Hampshire who wrote home boasting of tremendous profits and urging his relatives to join him. But this renegade operation hardly qualifies as part of the New England China trade, although a few legitimate operators such as Captain Forbes and even the punctilious Joseph Peabody might add a few chests of Smyrna opium to their cargoes, smuggling it ashore in coffins of "departed shipmates."

The subsequent Opium War (1840–1842) between Great Britain and China, which resulted in the opening of other Chinese ports besides Canton, had little effect on New England's commerce with the Orient. If anything, it favored the Americans, allowing Yankee ships to monopolize the trade which the English were forced to abandon as they stormed Shanghai and hammered at the walls of Nanking.

But already the old China trade was waning. According to Ernest S. Dodge, director of the Peabody Museum and an authority on Chinese art and exports, the inevitable mass production led to a decline in quality which sharp New Englanders were quick to note. On top of that, New England potteries were learning to make porcelain comparing favorably with that of Canton, while England and France were producing equally desirable chinaware. Bit by bit the strangest commercial alliance in history—the mysterious, forbidden East with the vernal, burgeoning seaports of New England—passed into oblivion.

It left behind, however, a rich heritage in Chinese export porcelain, perhaps the most exquisite man-made product ever to reach the New World in the 19th century. Some of these collections remain in the anonymous hands of private families, but many can be seen today, graciously lent for exhibit by their owners. There are excellent sets from the Crowninshield collection in the Peabody Museum of Salem; from the Helena Woolworth McCann collection in the Museum of Art at Rhode Island's School of Design; from the Forbes collection at the Robert Bennet Forbes home in Milton, Mass.; and notable examples of fine export China at the Ropes Mansion and Peirce-Nichols House in Salem, the Museum of Fine Arts in Boston, and New York's Metropolitan Museum of Art.

But the nation profited by much more than this heritage of heirlooms. The China trade saved the young American republic from financial rot, brought it an unforeseen prosperity, and led to events by which the Northwest territories became part of the United States. Moreover, many of the great New England fortunes built throughout this period were later used to finance factories making shoes, tools, fabrics, furniture, and other goods on which the region's economic health depended. While the China trade today is only a colorful chapter in our history, its sequel is still being written in New England industry and craftsmanship.

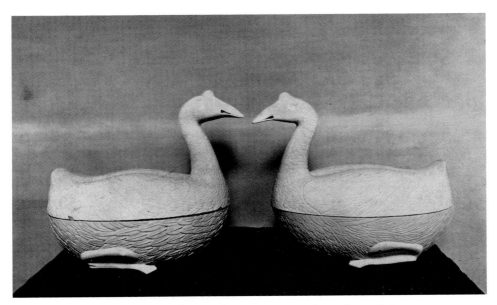

Two 22-inch white geese soup tureens brought to Salem in 1803 from Canton and given by Capt. Ward Blackler to the East India Marine Society, now the Peabody Museum of Salem.

THE GREAT STONE FLEET

by Frank A. Magune

It was about 9:30 on the night of December twentieth that I clambered below decks of the *Rebecca Simms* for the last time. I walked the aisle between the towering cargo, a heavy mallet swinging in my hand. In a small open space between the heaped tiers of stone, I located the first plug. Swinging the mallet from side to side, striking first on the left and again on the right, the huge plug began to loosen, letting in the first seepage of sea water. One final blow and it popped like an enormous cork, and the water gulped into the hold like liquid gurgling from a gallon jug. A sad ending, I thought, for this old whaler that had romanced her way into the far-flung ports of the world. Her final cargo was nothing but stone, and her grave was a Southern harbor far from her home port of New Bedford.

"I scrambled up the ladder to the dry deck above into a scene of orderly confusion. The crew of the *Rebecca Simms* had already begun the task of cutting away her masts, and the night air resounded with the clamor of axes cutting into the tall spars and the sound of rending wood. Other vessels of the Stone Fleet were being stripped of their spars and canvas by the crews of the Union warships. It must have been a strange sight, indeed, to the residents of Charleston. A small armada of ships was lined up bow to stern in the main channel, and a horde of men swarmed about them cutting away the masts. The guns of Fort Sumter finally awakened, and as the masts struck the decks or smacked the water, they were accompanied by the booming challenge from this unconquered stronghold of the South, a requiem that sounded over the fast-settling ships."

A shout from the first mate brought Captain J. M.

106

Willis back to the fate of his own ship. "Cap'n," the mate bellowed, "she's listing to starboard and going down by the stern!"

Captain Willis looked quickly aft. The old whaler was slowly settling, and as the water rose higher toward the taffrail, the prow of the *Simms* pointed upward to the dark skies in rearing dignity. Willis cupped his hands against the growing din of sound. "Cut away those remaining spars," he shouted.

As the last of the tangle was cleared away he ordered the men over the side into the whaleboats. Taking a wide stance against the ever-increasing list, he looked for the last time along the sloping deck. Three hacked stumps were all that remained of the once-proud masts that had bent under wind-filled sails of the whaling voyages of not too many years ago.

Sixteen vessels carrying one of the strangest war-time cargoes ever to be shipped from a Yankee port left New Bedford, Massachusetts under sealed orders on the morning of November 20, 1861.

The Sunbeam *was similar to the type of whaling ship used for the Stone Fleet. Her equally violent end, however, came later, when she was wrecked off the coast of Georgia in 1911.*

...fitted for the strangest cargo ever shipped

As they pulled away from the sinking whaler, Willis surveyed the scene about him. All was confusion and havoc, with the valiant fleet on their beam ends, down by the head or the stern. The dismantled hulks were lying across the channel in every position. The harbor waters swelled over some, others stood upright on their rudders and spouted water over their sides as the rolling ground swell lifted and dropped them on the channel sand. The epoch voyage of the Great Stone Fleet had ended. The mission had been accomplished: blockading Charleston Harbor against the swift Southern blockade runners in their dash to a sympathetic England.

The story of the Great Stone Fleet opened its first page a short month before in the whaling port of New Bedford, Massachusetts, on November 20, 1861. On this Wednesday, at seven in the morning, sixteen vessels sailed under sealed orders bound for Savannah to report to the commodore of the Union blockade squadron.

Birth of the fleet was conceived in the Navy Department in Washington. The Southern blockade runners were a thorn in the side of the Federal government. With every bay and inlet of the three thousand miles of twisting South-ern shoreline offering shelter for the rebel runners, the task of the few serviceable Northern watchdogs seemed insurmountable.

On April 19, 1861, the North announced a blockade from South Carolina to Texas. To combat the steady flow of contraband pouring into the storehouses of the South, the Navy Department unfolded a plan to send down a fleet of stone-laden ships and sink them in the inlets and close the channels.

New Bedford, long the whaling capital of the world, was beginning to decline. Commercial oil was replacing the sperm oil used in the lamps of the day, and steel stays were taking the place of whalebone. The whalers, once known to every land, were lying at idle anchor, tier on tier at the wharves. There was no further need of their services, and their owners were only too eager to sell rather than see them rot where they were berthed.

Assistant Secretary of the Navy Gustavus V. Fox was given the task of raising the Stone Fleet. Twenty-four ships were bought in New Bedford, and this old port became the headquarters for the building of the Stone Squadron. As fast as the old whalers pulled into port from their last voyage, they were purchased, berthed and fitted for their final mission. Gangs of ship's carpenters and riggers kept four leased wharves alive with activity.

Being readied for the secret journey south is the bark Garland. *She was captained by Rodney French, and carried 190 tons of stone.*

The history of the ships would make stories in themselves. The bark *Margaret Scott* had been seized by a United States Marshal on grounds that she had been fitted for a voyage in slave trading. She was outfitted for her first slave voyage September 16, 1857. Of the circumstances and results of such African trips, nothing has ever been written. Her owner, Rodney French, who, a short time later was to be named Commodore of the Stone Fleet, was found guilty of the charge of slave trading. Nevertheless, shortly after his return from the voyage to blockade a Southern harbor, he was elected Mayor of New Bedford.

Many of the old whalers were patched with cement, and the ancient bark *Potomac* was so rotten that she was said to have a hull made of mortar. Nonetheless, she was bought for the fleet, because she was copper fastened, her owners even receiving a thousand dollar bonus in the bargain. Of the twenty-four whalers bought out of New Bedford, the *Valparaiso* brought the highest figure of five-thousand, five-hundred dollars; the *Leonidas* bringing the lowest price of just a bit over three thousand.

Another ship purchased for the fleet was the *Progress,* which whaled for Stonington, Connecticut, for a number of years as the *Charles Phelps*. She was found to be in such good condition that the government decided not to sink her as part of the blockading fleet, and she was returned to New Bedford and re-sold. This same vessel took part in the rescue of 1219 persons shipwrecked ten years later. In September, 1871, thirty-four whalers were caught in the ice of the Arctic Ocean and sunk with the loss of a million, five-hundred-thousand dollars, but not one life was sacrificed. The men, women and children sailed eighty miles in the longboats through the ice floes to the open sea, where they were rescued by seven ships of the whaling fleet that had not been caught in the ice.

Realizing the necessity of speed, gangs of carpenters stepped up the work of refitting and rigging to a continuous pace. In the three week period of "face-lifting," each ship was fitted with just enough quarters for the necessary crew members and officers, a minimum amount of sail to get them to their destination. Just one anchor and chain, and reinforced hulls and bulkheads for the cargo of stone.

About seventy-five-hundred tons of stone was estimated as proper ballast for these old greyhounds, keeping in mind the amount required to sink them in a minimum amount of time. James Duddy, a local teamster, was awarded the contract to furnish the fleet, and he scoured the countryside for this strange New England cargo. He spread the word that he was offering fifty cents a ton, and he ranged about the whaling ports of New England's South Shore, bargaining with the farmers of Dartmouth, Westport, Acushnet, Fairhaven and Mattapoisett.

The first few farmers that Duddy approached soon spread the word that a crazy man was paying good money for old stone. When the teamster approached yet another

BK. GARLAND	SH. MARIA THERESA	SH. REBECCA
Capt. Rodney French	Capt. T. S. Bailey	Capt. J. M.
190 Tons of Stone	320 Tons of Stone	425 Tons of
REVENUE CUTTER VARINA	BK. AMERI
Capt. Sands	Capt. W. A.
	300 Tons of

...under sealed orders and bou

BK. LEONIDAS	SH. SOUTH AMERICA	SH. ARCHER	BK. FRS. HENRIETTA
Capt. J. Howland	Capt. Chadwick	Capt. Worth	Capt. M. Cumiski
200 Tons of Stone	550 Tons of Stone	280 Tons of Stone	381 Tons of Stone

. HARVEST	BK. AMAZON	BK. COSSACK	SH. COURIER
W. W. Taylor	Capt. J. S. Swift	Capt. Childs	Capt. S. Brayton
Tons of Stone	328 Tons of Stone	250 Tons of Stone	350 Tons of Stone

Savannah

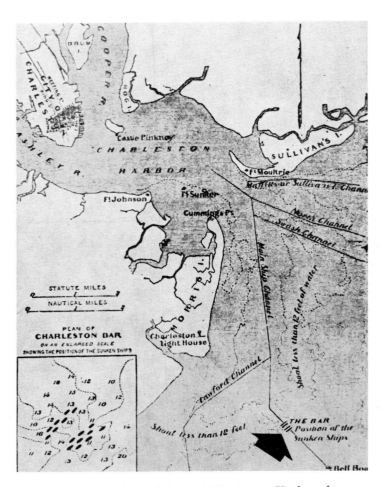

The arrow on this old map of Charleston Harbor shows the position of the sunken ships. The box on the lower left shows exactly where each vessel was placed beneath the main ship channel.

farm, the owner was usually waiting for him, curious to talk to the man who was buying such strange merchandise.

"Morning," said Duddy, climbing down from the wagon seat. "Got any stone I can buy?"

"Stone? What d'you want stone fer?"

"Load the fleet down to New Bedford. Gonna sink 'em in a Southern harbor."

"Seems kinda foolish to sink a ship a-purpose." The farmer spat and queried again. "What's the stone fer?"

"I told yuh," the teamster said. "They load the stone 'board the whalers, sail 'em down South to some harbor and sink 'em. The Rebs bin dodgin' past our Navy and gittin' back with guns and sech. The gov'men's gonna sink the ships and block the harbors!"

The rural looked Duddy up and down, then spat again. "How much you need?"

"All I c'n git my hands on, and more if'n I c'n find it. How 'bout that stone wall over there?"

"Need it. Keeps the cows out'n the corn." He thought a minute, let his gaze rove over his land, then seemed to make up his mind. "Got an old stone silo gotta come down. And there's some big ones in thet field yonder I bin plowin'."

"Good," said Duddy. "I c'n use all you got. Spare it all?"

"I reckon."

The scene was repeated in other towns, at other farms. Stone walls were torn down, and old barns and silos, and

The Masters of the Great Stone Fleet posed for this photograph prior to leaving New Bedford on their top secret mission.

112

for the next few weeks loaded drays and stone drags trundled to the New Bedford docks. The Yankee cargo tumbled into the holds by the tons . . . big boulders and smaller field stones, cobble stones from highways, jagged-edge granite from the refuse heaps of the quarries.

Captains for the fleet were chosen carefully by the government, whaling skippers who knew the ships and knew the sea. They were Captains Bailey, Willis, Chadwick, French, Gifford, Swift, Howland, Worth and Tilton, to name a few. These were the famous men of the old whaling ports, and many of the names can be seen today, commemorating the streets and parks of New Bedford. The captains signed on the crews, efficient men who had chased the Right, the Sperm and the Pilot whale into the far reaches of the known seas. Just enough of the men were signed to sail the old tubs to their rendezvous.

On the twentieth of November, 1861, Commodore French was ordered to proceed to sea under sealed orders. At the boom of a signal gun, anchors were hoisted and the stone squadron passed down the bay at seven o'clock that Wednesday morning. The garrison at Fort Taber, now Fort Rodman in Fairhaven, saluted the departing fleet with thirty-four guns. The shores were lined with cheering citizens who waved and shouted as the fleet cleared Clarks Point under the escort of the cutter *Varina*.

The fleet's run down to Savannah was more or less uneventful except for a lively gale which sprang up on December 2nd and 3rd. But, if anything, it only helped to speed the squadron on its way to the rendezvous. In the week of sailing down the coast, one whaling skipper had his crew scour the decks daily. "The idea of going to sea," said Willis, "and not having the decks scrubbed, was too much for him." . . .

On December fourth the *Rebecca Simms,* in company with the New London ship *Phoenix* and the 425-ton *Maria Theresa,* Captain F. S. Bailey commanding, arrived off Savannah bar and dropped anchor at 4:30.

On this same day more of the fleet arrived, several getting over the bar, several striking bottom and three standing off outside with their colors in the rigging or at half-mast waiting for a gunboat to come to their assistance.

On the twelfth of December the remaining vessels were safe in port, including the flagship *Garland,* a good six days behind the swift *Simms.*

Under the convoy of a frigate and several navy steamers, this strange but heroic fleet of converted whalers sailed out of Savannah on the seventeenth bound for Charleston, arriving off the bar two days later. For the rest of that nineteenth day of December, and all the following day, the ships arrived for their final mission. The second fleet of vessels didn't leave New Bedford until the ninth of December, nineteen days after the first fleet was under sail, but they arrived in time to join the first fleet in Charleston.

A definite plan had been formulated for closing the harbor. A natural bar, or reef, ran from the mouth of the harbor paralleling Morris Island and the lighthouse to within a short distance of Fort Sumter, which lay midway between Cummings Point and Fort Moultrie. By sinking the ships on both sides of the bar in checkerboard fashion, it would create an uneven bottom, causing eddies, countercurrents and whirlpools, making it virtually impossible for the blockade runners to navigate over the bar, confining their dash straight down the harbor following the North channel, easy prey for the Northern blockade fleet.

In sight of the guns of brave old Fort Sumter, still an unconquered stronghold of the South, the vessels maneuvered into position on both sides of the bar that marked the end of the main ship channel. Though the operation was a difficult one, all the ships were sinking by ten o'clock that night.

To this day some Southern harbors are still blocked by the ships of the Great Stone Fleet. As late as 1933 a small Florida harbor was cleared of wreckage, remains of the whaler blockade, that had choked the waters for so many years. But in Charleston harbor the effect was decidedly different. The scuttled ships and the immense mass of stone formed a new jetty which changed the currents of the bay to form a much deeper and better channel than before.

And so, a heritage of New England, in one of the strangest Yankee war-time cargoes ever shipped, rests beneath fathoms of water in Southern harbors.

HE BETTERED CAPTAIN BLIGH

by Chester Howland

IN THE YEAR 1820, ON THE 28TH DAY OF MARCH, A BOY was born to the Wing family of Acushnet, Massachusetts. His name was Andrew. Andrew, although born of farmer heritage, "took to the sea" and quickly rose from a greenhand before the mast to become the master of various New Bedford whaleships.

Before he retired from the sea, and at the early age of thirty, Captain Wing performed a nautical feat that ranks him as an equal to the renowned Captain Bligh, master of the English ship *Bounty* and victim of its outraged crew of mutineers. This feat was an incident that began during the month of March.

On August 8, 1852, the Bark *Canton* sailed out of New Bedford harbor and, dropping the pilot off Hen and Chickens Lightship, began a sperm whaling voyage that would take the ship into the Pacific Ocean. Captain Wing, although in his early thirties, was known as a super whaleman. His previous voyage had brought home a cargo of oil returning a profit of $100,000.

Six months of rigorous but successful whaling had passed, every lowering a risk of lives during the chase and capture of sperm whales. Under the skillful navigating of the Captain and his ready crew, the *Canton* had sailed over 13,000 miles of deep ocean, had battled the winds of Cape Horn and on the 4th of March, 1853, was in the mid-Pacific driving before heavy winds. As the sun set in a clear sky that late afternoon, the winds increased. By nine o'clock the full sky was starlit. Captain Wing had checked his charts and gone to bed, assured there was no hidden danger lying before the ship. At noon the next day he would take his regular twenty-four hour observations and again work out his course.

Second Mate Fisher was in charge of the watch. The high hum of the half-gale through the rigging and the cut of the bow through the dark sea were the usual sounds of a ship running before a strong and steady blow.

Suddenly, out of the accustomed sounds came a roar of pounding seas upon land. Straining his eyes but seeing nothing, the young sailor standing bow watch cried out, "Hard up your helm." But before the lookout had finished his alarm, the *Canton* struck a coral reef and was driven to her beams' end.

The men below hurried to the dock and fought the sea that was sweeping the deck fore and aft.

Captain Wing, swinging a broad axe, ordered the crew to cut away fore, main and mizzen masts. The falling mast carried sails, yardarms and a tangled mass of rigging over the lee rail into the turmoil of the surf that lifted it, tumbling in confusion, onto the shore. The gale still drove it landward.

It was midnight.

When early morning came, the seas still raged but the

Guided by Andrew Wing, the crew of the Canton *traveled 3,800 miles in open boats over uncharted seas—a feat of seamanship considered by many to have been superior to that of the* Bounty's *Captain Bligh.*

wind had calmed. All thirty-three members of the ship's company had, miraculously, clung to the stumps of the masts, deck ring bolts, or the ship's stanchion and rail.

Casks of oil were heaved out of the ship's hold and poured over the side, lessening the force of the sea and lowering its flying crests.

One by one, men and officers jumped into the ugly sea, colored by the whipped-up bottom sand.

Captain Wing, the last to leave his ship, stood on the shore looking seaward. He saw a totally-wrecked, valiant craft. Her heavy planked hull still held valuable stores. But her ribs would disintegrate on the iron-hard edge of this coral-reefed island.

When evening came, Captain Wing and the first and second mates, with a boat's crew, rowed across the inland lake that lay within the coral ring of barren land. Higher land and some growth were discovered on the opposite side, but no spring or body of fresh water was located.

That night all hands gathered and were told, "There is no means of sustaining life on this island. We will repair our boats from the wreckage and fit them for an ocean voyage. There are archipelagoes in these waters. We shall hope to bear on a course that shall bring favorable land in sight. Many days and nights may pass but we cannot exist on this atoll."

The wrecked *Canton* was visited early the next morning. The day was spent procuring whatever might be useful on a long ocean voyage. But the position of the ship made it possible to obtain little of value except water and ship's bread. Planks and sections of the ship's deck had already been washed ashore.

Preparations began. Fitting the *Canton's* whaleboats for the desperate voyage required skill and time. The early American whaleboat was one of the most serviceable crafts in maritime history and the American Navy of today designates that its boats be fashioned along the lines of the whaleboat of 100 years ago. Captain Wing, nevertheless, instructed the men to add two streaks to the present gunwales of the *Canton's* boats.

Twenty-five days later the group was ready to embark on its unpredictable but forced journey. Before them lay an unknown course through 4,000 miles of Pacific Ocean perils.

On March 30 the four boats and thirty-three men pushed onto the sea and set sail.

Captain Wing had been forced to create a navigating instrument, constructing it from parts of his and the chief mate's sextants. On one of the company's trips to the wrecked *Canton*, a foremast hand had found the Captain's pocket compass in the debris scattered on the cabin floor.

The ship's biscuit and water in each boat was stringently rationed by the Captain. "Your rations must be held to one-half biscuit and one-half pint of water a day for every man of us. You will survive by the strength of your wills.

"I shall try to make the Kingsmill Group of Islands which I figure to be 800 miles to the southwest of our present position. The Ladrones are beyond."

Captain Wing had not been fortunate enough to rescue any of the several charts which had been stored in the ship's chart-closet. Because of tide movements and prevailing winds, he would sail his boats on a northerly course and then run to the westward calculating he would have a better chance to sight an island of the Gilbert Group: Byron Island, Sydenham or Drumond. No one of these was located. All were probably passed during the night hours.

Day after day went by. Once a furious gale swept the seas. At mid-afternoon the bright sun suddenly was swept from the sky by a monstrous black section of rolling clouds. In a moment of time the sea became like boiling ink, lightning flashed constantly through the entire heavens. In the flashes, one of the boats sighted a water spout whirling millions of gallons of water from the ocean to the sky. Had any of the boats been in the direct path of the spout, it and its crew would have been carried up to the low-hanging clouds. Only by frantic bailing were the crews able to keep their plunging craft from being swamped.

A lighted lantern in the Captain's boat through each night was the only beacon that kept the voyagers together.

The men began to weaken under forced rationing. A half-pint of water each twenty-four hours on an ocean that dragged the unbearable heat of the sun onto their sparsely covered bodies began to drain their tolerance. Some even plotted to attack the Captain's boat and rob his supplies of food and water, but were foiled by the stern will of Captain Wing.

Though a constant vigil was kept, with each member of the crew standing a strict lookout, relieved each half hour lest the glare of the sun and the heat blind them, the Kingsmill group of Islands were never raised. The strong trade winds drove the boats rapidly over a landless Pacific Ocean.

Captain Wing, by crude navigational calculations, reasoned that the Kingsmill Islands now lay to the windward, and he attempted to encourage the voyagers with a promise that the Ladrones were before them.

The crew of the Chief Mate's boat, suffering beyond control of their emotions, planned a second plot, a scheme that was overheard by the supposedly sleeping Mate Carroll. At dusk, as all the boats gathered around the Captain's boat for the night, the project was boldly exposed to Captain Wing. Captain Wing ordered the Mate into his boat and took command of the men in the Mate's craft. He held before them a curiously hilted ancient knife and said, "The first man who speaks or moves out of his position I will attack. There is no safety for any of us unless I remain in command. I intend to do so."

Forty-four days passed. No dot of land had been sighted. Now only a few of the men could assist at duties in the boats. The others were so famished and debilitated they

Above right. Three of the 33 men who sailed 3,800 miles in open boats, as they appeared years after the experience.

The Canton *sailing out of New Bedford on her final voyage. The date: August 8, 1852.*

Captain Andrew Wing

Thomas Braley

Alden Manter

could not stand. Under certain rays of a full moon their faces appeared like uncovered skulls.

On the 45th day, Thomas Braley, who had proved stronger than the others, spoke to the Captain. "Captain Wing, there are large birds flying over us."

Captain Wing, who had been scanning the sea in a northwesterly direction, looked upward and replied, "They are from the land. We will change our course against the direction they are flying. I have seen such birds on other voyages and in early morning they fly out away from their land retreats to catch fish in the deeper water."

It was then six o'clock in the morning. Four hours later a small island was raised and soon the outline of a larger island broke the horizon.

(The close of this remarkable small boat voyage was told to a *New Bedford Standard* special items reporter a quarter of a century ago.)

The small island was a round rock, washed all about by the sea and without a harbor. Boobies by the thousands kept up a raucous crowing. The boats edged in cautiously. Captain Wing gave orders that certain men should stand by the boats while others went ashore. A new strength came into the men. Captain Wing and Thomas Braley caught a big booby and, each taking a leg, tore the living bird apart and frantically drank the blood. Following their example, the rest ate ravenously of the still warm and uncooked flesh.

A few fish were secured also, brought in by the birds for their young—which were found in large numbers in rude nests of dry sticks and feathers. Some of the sailors built a fire and singed the crowlike birds.

With this supply of fresh meat, the boats again put to sea with a free wind for the farther island. This proved to be Anatajan, of the Ladrone Group. Here they landed in an excellent harbor and went ashore, where they found groves of coconut trees but no man dared or had the strength to climb the high trees. Each boat was provided with a hatchet, however, and they chopped down two trees. Hatchets were soon crashing into the ripe nuts and all ate ravenously of the soft, pulpy contents, and drank the refreshing milk. Indeed they drank so much that it acted as a physic, and beyond question saved their lives! There were wild hogs and fowl on this island but the men were unable to catch them. They did procure fish and what they wanted most of all—water.

The men knew that they were saved and their gratitude to Captain Wing was boundless. After supplying themselves with plenty of water and fish and coconuts, they set forth from Anatajan to Saipan and thence to Tinian.

Guam was the end of this remarkable voyage. This island they reached four days after leaving Tinian, having covered 3,800 miles in open boats under a tropical sun—during which time their only food and water for forty-five days had been half a sea biscuit and half a pint of water per man each twenty-four hours.

Sixty days after landing at Guam, where they were received with great friendship and every possible kindness by the natives and the Spanish Governor, the Swedish brig *Knut Bonde,* Captain Kollinus, put in for provisions; and on this vessel Captain Wing, the First Mate and two of the crew were taken to Hong Kong. From that port they obtained passage to Honolulu in the bark *What Cheer,* and left Honolulu as passengers on the schooner *Vaquero.* The twenty-nine men left at Guam remained for about six months, where they later found berths on whaleships bound for various oceans of the world.

Thus ended the most complete achievement of seamanship in the history of the sea—one considered by many to be an even more difficult and superior accomplishment than that of Captain Bligh in the launch of the *Bounty* in 1789.

SAVED BY
THE
BEAR

by Everett S. Allen

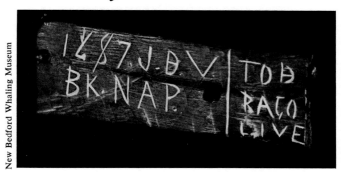

*James Vincent
sent this wooden "note"
out of the Siberian wastes by natives,
informing the arctic whaling
fleet that he was still alive.*

On the night of May 3, 1885, the bark *Napoleon* of New Bedford, Massachusetts, Captain S. P. Smith, master, was fifty miles south-southwest of Cape Navarin, which juts out from the coast of Siberia into the Bering Sea.

It was blowing harder than a full gale; it was impossible to carry a stitch of sail, and Captain Smith ordered his struggling ship hove to under bare poles.

During the next two days, the weather became steadily worse. The sea, filled with ice chunks, built up to tremendous proportions. Black and ominous, it rolled down upon the *Napoleon,* burst in icy spray which froze upon her rigging and sheathed her tossing hull.

At ten minutes before seven on the evening of Tuesday, May 5th, the *Napoleon* slammed her bow down upon a huge cake of ice with a blow that made the ship shudder through her entire length. Almost instantly, the crew, many only half-dressed, came scrambling up out of the forecastle, yelling that the ship was taking water fast, that it was already knee-deep below. They huddled on the deck, clung to the rigging in the face of wind that drove cold sheets of sea-water over them like a barrage of icy needles.

There was only one possible decision Captain Smith could make: abandon ship, even in the face of the arctic gale.

He kept the *Napoleon* off the edge of the ice floe for the few minutes during which she remained maneuverable so there would be room to lower the boats. The bark was completely unmanageable and very low in the water by the time the boats were all safely cleared away, and less than fifteen minutes from the time she struck, all hands watched grimly from the bouncing whaleboats as the *Napoleon* listed drunkenly and capsized.

There had been no opportunity to obtain food or drink. The crew was in the boats, hundreds of miles from salvation, possessing only the clothes they wore.

Ten minutes after the ship rolled over, the ice closed in around her, grinding and smashing at the crippled hull, but at the risk of losing several lives, two of the boats succeeded in getting near enough to remove the main royal.

No one knew he was the Napoleon's
only surviving castaway

This sail, the lowest and biggest on the mainmast, although crusted with ice and hard to handle, was the easiest to reach. If they had to get out onto the ice pack, it could be used to build a tent which might keep them from freezing to death.

Then darkness settled in. They spent a bleak, miserable and sleepless night bobbing around in the ice. The wind still blew a gale, accompanied by frequent snow squalls, and all hands were well soaked through within the first hour or two.

The next morning, the four boats started to work out of the ice northeasterly. The crew originally had lowered all five boats, but divided up into four and abandoned one, to make the job of hauling over the ice easier; it seemed inevitable they would eventually come across pack ice too extensive to row around and too solid to push the boats through.

By nightfall, it breezed on again, with more snow. Weary and red-eyed, the men hunched in the boats, pulled doggedly at the heavy oars. They tried to keep the boats together, yelling hoarse encouragement to each other occasionally, but the words were whipped away in the gale, and eventually they stopped trying to talk, even to those in the same boat.

At dusk, with a sudden painful awareness, they realized the boats of the third and fourth mates—for hours only vague shapes in the blizzard—had fallen behind somewhere. The boats of the skipper and the mate, Andrews, waited for them. All hands were suffering terribly from cold; few could move their toes any longer, swollen fingers were frozen in tattered mittens to the oars, and real hunger was beginning to gnaw. The sea was still very rough.

Almost an hour passed as they slatted, rolled and struggled off the ice floe, waiting and watching for the other boats.

Hoarse and wordless, a man in the skipper's boat raised his arm stiffly and pointed across the water; they looked automatically. It was the third mate's boat, half-full and laboring, but still coming. They would have cheered, but could not for lack of voice and strength.

The third mate, Peterson, thought the other missing boat was close by, but they waited another hour and it never showed, so they figured something must have happened to it. To keep from freezing, they began pulling slowly to windward again. It breezed harder, with more snow, and all the boats soon were separated.

Captain Smith gave up trying to relocate the others. The only object now was to stay alive. He looked at his weakened boat's crew to pick out the man with the most remaining strength.

"Vincent." It was young James B. Vincent, boatsteerer, of Martha's Vineyard, Massachusetts, the skipper shouted at, mittens cupped about his mouth to yell into the wind.

Vincent, always rugged and tireless, lifted his bearded chin and looked at the captain.

It was useless to continue rowing. The skipper motioned to Vincent to lash oars and mast together in a bundle, to heave them over the side attached to one end of a tub of line. Clumsy with cold, on his knees in water, Vincent went to work and moments later had the "drag" overboard and was paying out line; the drag, like a floating anchor, held the boat's head into the wind as she drifted, enabling them to lie head-on to the waves with greater safety and comfort.

Thursday, it still blew hard. Friday, it moderated a little, and in Captain Smith's boat, they made a tent of the boat's sail to keep off the sea that was breaking over her. At mid-day, the skipper felt it was calming enough to set the sail; they worked their way to a large strip of floe ice and made fast to it. This was the first chance they had to sleep since the *Napoleon* went down.

Saturday morning broke clear. Captain Smith aroused the men—all but one, who had died in the night. He parceled out the last fragments of six cakes of shipbread—all the food they had had in three days—which had been in the boat when it was lowered. Vincent, refreshed by sleep, and the strongest man aboard, volunteered to explore the ice pack in search of food; the captain granted permission, and the crew watched his plodding figure, in boots and hood, recede and finally disappear in the glittering whiteness of the floe's wastes.

Around noon, they observed two sails on the horizon, and after two hours of feverish, anxious rowing and hoarse shouting, they came close enough to be seen. In the early afternoon, they were picked up by the whaler *Fleetwing*. No man could get out of the boat unaided, and one of them died five minutes after being rescued. Most of them were badly frost-bitten, their hands and feet greatly swollen.

From the *Fleetwing*, they learned that the fourth mate and his crew had been picked up that morning at 6 o'clock, two of that boat's crew having died. This left only the boats of the first and third mates yet undiscovered. The *Fleetwing* then approached as closely to the ice pack as they dared without observing any sign of Vincent. After several hours, they concluded he had succumbed to exposure, and the *Fleetwing* sailed away to get medical attention for those she had rescued.

Vincent had walked and crawled miles across the ice, increasingly disheartened by no sight of anything edible. About to give up, he spotted two dark blobs on the floe, which proved to be seal pups. Eagerly, breathlessly, he scrambled between them and the water, to cut off their flight; with his only weapon, a piece of a broken oar, he dispatched them quickly, and started the long trek back. He

Possibly the only photograph in existence of James B. Vincent, taken at about the time of his rescue by the Bear.

An Eskimo hunter similar in appearance to those who helped Vincent. Eskimos were often employed by Yankee whalemen to furnish game. Note the parka made of mattress ticking.

Sometime prior to 1925, the Bear *assists the Corwin which was stuck in arctic ice. In 1932, Admiral Byrd paid $1,050 for the* Bear, *outbidding a junk dealer by fifty dollars.*

dragged his quarry, having to stop frequently to rest, and thus darkness overtook him.

A native islander, Vincent had been at sea all of his life. Yankee hardihood and ingenuity had taught him to take care of himself, and Arctic whaling had provided equally valuable experience. He found sparse lee against an ice hummock, ate some of the seal meat raw, and through the night, walked about, flailed his arms, kicked his legs, in an effort to stay awake and keep from freezing. With the cold light of morning, he realized with plummeting spirits that the captain's boat was gone.

He sank down on the ice next to the seal carcasses, a weary and discouraged young man, virtually resigned to die. A short time later, a shout came across the floe. He raised his head quickly, hopefully. There were the boats of the first and third mates, just off the pack!

Vincent staggered toward them; they helped him aboard, glad to have the seal meat, although several were too weak to eat it. Everybody was alive in both boats; they had found each other two days after they became separated from Captain Smith. It had been decided to stick together and try to reach the shore in the bight under Cape Navarin. Vincent's spirits rose . . . but he did not know what lay ahead.

Both boats became caught in the ice, formidable and endless, and they were four more days without food. Eventually, Vincent and two others crawled out on the floe and killed another seal, but several of the men could not eat it uncooked, for their stomachs by now were weak.

It was, in all, thirty-six days before they reached the shore, and meanwhile, nine of the eighteen men had died. They had sucked ice in their frozen hands, gnawed at stiff chunks of seal meat, and killed a couple of sea birds to stay alive. The cold was frightful and continuous; they no longer had strength to beat their bodies, or to move their toes and fingers. Vincent was the only one who could walk when they landed.

Within a few days, five more had died, huddled helplessly in the poor lee offered by ice chunks and the low terrain. The three who remained, other than Vincent, were helpless from frostbite and exhaustion; even he found it difficult to go foraging to keep them alive. On one of his expeditions, however, near exhaustion, he saw a half-dozen human figures huddled on the shore, and although at some distance, he waved and shouted until they saw him.

They were a party of Siberian Eskimos, fishing, and Vincent made them understand something of his situation with sign language. The Eskimos returned with him to the whaler's poor campsite, helped him build a shelter and a fire for the three ill men. Leaving his three comrades housed, and with fire, a supply of wood, fish and seal meat at hand,

The Bear *as she appeared later in her career. Both photos were taken during the U.S. Antarctic Expedition of 1939–1941. Directly below, she heels sharply to port under the force of a gale. Right. The* Bear *reaches the farthest point attained east of Little America.*

U.S. Coast Guard

123

Her hull dented and scarred as a result of many arctic adventures, the Bear *rests in warmer waters at Oakland, California, August 27, 1924.*

Vincent decided to return inland with the Eskimos when they returned to their homes. He was the only one of the four surviving strong enough to make the trip. It was his hope to travel around the Gulf of Anadir and reach Plover Bay, where he might come across some of the whalers and get help for his shipmates.

Once arrived at the native village—a collection of stone, hide, timber and iceblock igloos (winter houses for about 125 persons)—the impossibility of this plan became apparent. Cold weather comes early in the arctic and no natives would be traveling around the Gulf of Anadir until spring; Vincent had neither the strength nor local knowledge to go on the long journey alone—neither could he make his way unaided back to the three camped on the shore.

He did the only thing left to do, even though chafing at the passage of time; he remained with the Eskimos all winter.

The Edgartown boatsteerer was "adopted." His lonely plight, together with his natural courtesy and friendliness, won the favor of an elderly Eskimo, who received him as his son. The two men ate and worked together, gradually sur-

mounting the language barrier with a combination of basic English, Eskimo and hand signs. After several months, the old man died, but his final instructions to his wife were to care for Vincent, to keep and shelter him, to allow him to use the Eskimo's gear, hunting weapons and other equipment until he was rescued.

Weathered, bearded and shaggy-haired, Vincent came to be accepted among the Siberian Eskimos; his strength returned somewhat, and was welcome in their arduous chores, for he was a bigger man than most of them. He wore the native costume, carried his coarse-grained, shaggy tobacco as they did, in a pouch about his neck, ate their food, principally raw fish and seal meat, and shaped his daily life in their pattern.

He waited for spring with the greatest impatience, and when warming air and the arrival of new birds indicated it had come, he made the trek to the shore to fish with the Eskimos. The last few yards, he ran to the campsite where he had left his three comrades, unable to contain his eagerness to learn of their welfare.

As he approached, the significant stillness about the winter-battered shelter slowed his steps. A few feet beyond the camp rose the mounds of three rock-covered graves, recently constructed by natives of another tribe who told Vincent's Eskimo friends what had occurred. Sadly he pieced together the story. His three shipmates assumed he had gone to Plover Bay and, shortly before, they had sent a message to the whaling fleet by natives, telling of their own whereabouts and giving their names, but not mentioning his.

This message was received by the Russian trading brig *Siberia*, which searched for the *Napoleon's* survivors on her return down the coast, later learning they had died in the meantime. The Eskimos living near the shore had told the *Siberia's* master that Vincent was still alive, living inland. The Russian, however, thought they were talking about "venison." At that time, Jim Vincent was within thirteen miles of where the *Siberia* anchored.

So the summer passed, and Jim, finding his only solace in work, dared hope for nothing. After the season's fishing was over, the natives returned to the hills again for winter shelter, driving their reindeer before them. It was sometime during the middle of that winter, possibly around Jan. 1, 1887, that he carved a message for help on a piece of driftwood and gave it to some passing tribesmen who were traveling to the coast. He had little or no hope that it ever would get to anyone from the outside world, particularly after the *Siberia* episode.

As the spring opened, he started once more for the shore with the natives for the regular fishing season. One day, on the beach, he stared in disbelief at the sight of a little Eskimo girl who was eating cookies. Beside himself with eagerness, he rushed over to her, pointed to the pastry, and asked her where she had got it. The little girl smiled. They had been given to her, only a few hours before, by the wife of the captain of the Yankee whaler *Sea Breeze*.

Where was the ship? Where was the *Sea Breeze?*

Gone now. The calm that had held her over was ended, and she had sailed.

Bitterly, Jim turned back to his task, splitting the fresh-caught fish; vacant-eyed, he went through the motions automatically. Habitually, however, he now kept one eye on the horizon.

On June 8, 1887, the same kind of mild weather produced prolonged calms that held the whaleship *Hunter* off Cape Bering. From Indian Point, two to three miles distant, rising smoke was observed, and it seemed to be a signal. Consequently, no effort was made to work the ship offshore and eventually, a dozen or more of the natives, known as Masinkers, came alongside in two canoes. The *Hunter's* skipper gave each native a chew of tobacco, put a bucket of bread in each canoe, and then the visitors came aboard to trade a few furs of deer and hairseal.

Herbert L. Aldrich, who made the arctic cruise with the whaling fleet in 1887 and who made an invaluable contribution to history in his subsequent accounts of his experiences, was aboard the *Hunter* on that occasion. He recalled:

"One old deersman produced a piece of wood carefully wrapped up, on which were letters crudely carved. After some study, we read the following on one side, '1887. J.B.V. Bk. Nap. Tobacco. Live'; and on the other side, 'S.W.C. Nav. M. 10 Help. Come.'

"We interpreted the message as follows: That J.B.V. (whom we afterward found to be James B. Vincent, a boat-steerer of the *Napoleon*) was still alive in 1887, and that he wanted tobacco to be given the bearer of the message; that he was still southwest of Cape Navarin ten miles, and wanted help to come and rescue him.

"We gathered from what the old man said that several of the wrecked sailors (on boats of the first and third mates) reached the shore alive, but that all except Vincent had died. We decided that the only thing to do was to report what we had learned to the United States revenue cutter *Bear*."

The substance of Vincent's appeal for help was passed through the fleet by the *Hunter;* the first whaler to sight the *Bear* would give her the word.

The *Bear* was more than a ship and her master more than a sailor; they were arctic traditions. The renowned steam barkentine *Bear* was the first Coast Guard vessel especially designed for ice-breaking and navigating through ocean ice. Her master was Captain Michael A. Healy, to whose ability, conscientiousness and perseverance many an arctic castaway owed his life. The natives called the *Bear* "Healy's Puk Oomiak," that is, "Healy's Fire Canoe."

The *Bear* steamed out of San Francisco for the Northland regularly, with the most general orders to "aid all peoples, to assist commerce, to open lines of communication" and to carry the mails to every village not reached by the Bering Sea patrol. The farthest north of these was Point Barrow. The thin stream of smoke from her stack, and her white sails, used whenever possible to conserve coal, were beacons of hope and cheer in the frozen wastes.

The *Bear* got the word on Vincent's message, and pushed on toward Navarin. The season was getting on; pretty soon, the natives would go back to the hills for another winter and it would be too late to pick him up.

Jim Vincent himself, in typical unadorned language, told Mr. Aldrich how the story ended. Jim said, "No man can imagine how overjoyed I was when my attention was attracted by the shouting of the natives, and I looked up to see a white man, and to find myself at last rescued. The officers of the revenue cutter *Bear* were exceedingly kind to me, not only while I was on board, but particularly when I landed in San Francisco, alone and penniless."

When Vincent left the Navarin village, the widow of the old Eskimo came down to see him off; she wept at his parting, and he consoled her by reminding her how well she had fulfilled her husband's last wish by aiding him to live until his rescue could be accomplished.

So ended two years as a castaway among the Siberian Eskimos and Jim Vincent, the only survivor of eighteen men in two boats from the ill-fated *Napoleon,* returned to pick up the threads of his life among his fellow men.

Timbers creak and sea birds shriek. In Section **IV** skies darken and black seas swell . . .

. . . signaling **Disaster & Mystery** dead ahead.

This scene is a representation based on eyewitness accounts of the great gale of October, 1851. Eighty-five New England wives became widows during the storm, and many Yankee salts will tell you it was the worst gale in the history of Prince Edward Island.

THE WIND THAT MADE THEM WIDOWS

by Roland H. Sherwood

THE HARDY FISHERMEN OUT OF THE PORT OF GLOUCES-ter learned very early in their fishing experience that one of the richest fishing grounds in the world lay in the Gulf of St. Lawrence, just off the great crescent shape of Prince Edward Island, Canada.

This knowledge, while it brought them rich cargoes of fish, was of little value when hundreds of fishing vessels were caught in a freak storm. One storm was to become known as "The Yankee Gale," so called as the majority of fishing vessels, and those who lost their lives in the storm, were from New England.

No storm recorded in the long history of Prince Edward Island ever caused so much destruction and loss of life in so short a time as this Yankee Gale.

On those fatal days, the 3rd, 4th, and 5th of October, 1851, there was the greatest concentration of American fishing vessels on the Gulf fishing grounds of that year; and, although all the men on the schooners were classed as fishermen, the majority were college students, teachers, and college professors spending holidays working on the schooners.

Prior to the storm, there was no indication that one was brewing, although on October 3 the day was singularly warm for the late fall season. The morning sun came up from the sea in a blaze of splendor and during the forenoon was surrounded by a halo of peculiar color and brightness. By afternoon the halo disappeared. The sun was obscured by a thick haze, and cloud formations were of such extraordinary shape and color as to cause alarm on many of the vessels.

During the spectacle, the waters of the Gulf of St. Lawrence were as still as a millpond, the surface having a glassy appearance as if thousands of barrels of oil had been poured upon the waters. An unusual aspect of the strange calm on that Friday afternoon before the storm, was the fact

that not a single fish was taken by the hundreds of fishing vessels in the Gulf.

As night came on, a heavy swell from the east began to heave the waters. This in itself was peculiar, for there wasn't a breath of wind. Ships far out on the water, and objects at a distance on the land, seemed to float above the sea and the earth, while distant sounds could be heard with amazing distinctness. Thousands of sea birds went winging in toward the land, as if fleeing before a gale. But there was no indication of a gale.

By late afternoon, some of the fishing vessels began to make toward the harbors; but the majority stood out to sea. When night dropped over the ships, the darkness was so intense that it was later reported, "it could almost be felt."

At eight o'clock on Friday, October 3, a slight breeze began to blow from the northeast, and a fine drizzle of rain relieved the heaviness of the atmosphere. The wind and rain increased in intensity as the night hours advanced. By midnight a vicious gale was lashing the coast of Prince Edward Island, and a driving downpour of rain beat hard upon the land.

There was no let-up in the fury of the storm that night, and it continued all day Saturday and into Saturday night. By noon on Sunday the wind began to abate and gradually die away, leaving in the wake of this singular storm the wreckage of hundreds of fishing vessels, and the bodies of many men scattered along the Island shores.

Old newspapers of the time carried reports of the mountainous waves that came thundering in, to break with the sound of heavy gunfire that could be heard for miles inland. They reported that during the height of the storm on Saturday, October 4, hundreds of vessels were being pounded to pieces on the shore, and there were vivid descriptions of the destruction caused by the rain that beat in torrents, and of the gale winds that shrieked over the sea and the land.

Reports told of the vessels driven in on every shore, smashing to bits with the impact and hurling dead bodies far up on the land while watchers were powerless to aid.

A story from Rustico told how, on the Saturday afternoon of the storm, a dismantled schooner was picked up by a giant incoming wave and flung 300 feet inland from the shore and how, within a mile of that wreck, three other vessels were hurled into the pastures that skirted the shore.

Following the storm, the people of the little village of Rustico found, in one pasture alone, 36 bodies of men from the fishing fleet.

Bodies were found lashed to the rigging, fastened to stumps of masts, or half buried in the sands of the beaches.

Storm damage wasn't all with the ships, for it beat every inch of the island, with water rushing in over shore acres that never before had been under water. Buildings, bridges, milldams, fences, and trees were blown down and carried away by the wind and the water.

When the great storm was over, and the work of finding and checking the large number of wrecked vessels got under way, only 50 hulks could be identified, all the others being just so much broken timber.

From one end of Prince Edward Island to the other, the task of locating and reporting the wrecks went on. Among the fragments of dories and vessels that littered the shore, a great variety of gear and supplies were found. Barrels of flour, broken and soggy; great quantities of fish, trunks, ropes, spars, clothing, and musical instruments; books, barometers, anchors, chairs, tables, chronometers, clocks and bedding were mixed with the wreckage of the vessels and shredded sails.

It was found too that most of the bodies washed ashore were stripped of clothing by the relentless pounding of the storm-lashed sea.

Within an area of 40 miles of Savage Harbor, 32 vessels lay shattered upon the shore. At Richmond Bay, 24 fishing schooners were clusters of broken timbers along the shore, while from Richmond Bay to Cape North, another 17 vessels had been beaten to death by the storm and the sea.

A proclamation was issued asking the people of the island to salvage as much as possible for return to the rightful owners. But no such proclamation was necessary. The islanders were hard at work at the storm's end, aiding those who were injured, gathering the dead for burial, and salvaging materials. They opened their homes to survivors, fed and clothed the men, built coffins, and buried the dead.

A grim incident was reported in connection with one fishing vessel out of Gloucester. This was the *Franklin Dexter,* one of the many American vessels fishing in the Gulf at the time of the storm. She was driven ashore and totally wrecked at Cavendish. The bodies of her crew were found and buried by the residents.

A short time later, after word of the disaster reached the home port of Gloucester, the owner of the vessel arrived at Cavendish. He had the bodies exhumed and put aboard the *Seth Hal,* another New England vessel, for transport to Gloucester so the bodies of the drowned fishermen might rest in their home plots. But the gods that guard the fates of fishermen must have decreed otherwise. The *Seth Hal* sailed in the fairest of fair weather, but was caught in a brief storm of the same intensity as the Yankee Gale—and was never heard from again.

No one ever knew how many vessels were wrecked on the shores of Prince Edward Island in that storm for, in addition to American and Canadian boats, they found wreckage indicating that foreign vessels were also caught and driven ashore.

Of the hundreds of vessels that were on the fishing grounds prior to the storm, only 22 could be salvaged and used again; and of those 22, each and every one had lost all of its crew.

Eighty-five American women were made widows, and 350 children became orphans in the wake of "The Yankee Gale" that whipped out of a dead calm and beat with a terrible vengeance over the Gulf of St. Lawrence in October of the year 1851.

Out of hundreds of vessels, only twenty-two were salvaged

Many bodies were washed ashore, and most were buried in Canadian soil. In all, 160 fishermen lost their lives.

New England Vessels Lost
in the Gale of 1851

Fair Play, Portland, Maine . . . 7 lost

Traveller, Newburyport, Mass. . . . 8 lost

Statesman, Newburyport, Mass. . . . lost 10

American, Lubec, Maine . . . lost 9

Belena, Portsmouth, N.H. . . . lost 10

Skip Jack, came in with 12 bodies.

Flirt, Gloucester, Mass. . . . lost 13

Mary Moulton, Castine, Maine . . . lost 14

Franklin Dexter, Dennis, Maine . . . lost 10

Following the storm, owners of fishing vessels sent a number of trustworthy men to investigate and report on their losses. After a long and exhaustive inquiry, this delegation concluded that of the vessels hailing from Gloucester, 19 were lost or destroyed. The number stranded on the shores of P.E.I. was estimated at 74, and the number of lives lost at 160.

The Jason, *thirty-six hours after she grounded off Cape Cod on December 5, 1893. Out of a crew of 25, only one survived.*

INTO THE DEVIL'S POCKET THEY SAILED

by Asa Payne Lombard

"The waves ran high up the mast,
breaking almost to the foretop,
and shreds of the Jason's *jute cargo*
wrapped themselves like ragged garments
around the shrouds and stays."

THE *Jason*, A FULL RIGGED SHIP OF 1,512 TONS AND AN iron hull, left Calcutta, India, February 15, 1893, bound for Boston, Massachusetts; her cargo: 10,000 bales of jute to make twine, burlap bags, and furniture webbing in New England's busy factories. She was under the command of Capt. David McGin.

While crossing the Indian Ocean, a tornado swept toward the *Jason* with the speed of a demon bent on destruction. In minutes, ripples turned to white caps and the white caps to breakers. As the ship headed into the eye of the storm, the sails slackened and went limp; then, without warning, the wind renewed its forces. Spouts and tearing sheets of water tore at the rigging and dumped rivers of water onto the *Jason*. The wind in its reverse direction at an undetermined velocity convexed the sails, snapped the topsail and foremast, shredded the mizzenmast, and tore the mainmast off at the deck.

The seas, by this time 30 feet high, battered and bounced the ship about like a cork. The cargo in the hold shifted with a lurch that nearly caused the *Jason* to broach.

The squall passed as quickly as it came, and in ten minutes it was over; but the *Jason* was left without headway. Cargo loose, rigging gone, she was at the mercy of the mountainous waves in the aftermath of the storm. As the seas abated, the crew set to work, and under a "Portuguese rig," she finally worked her way into Port Louis, in those days known as belonging to Mauritius. There she was unloaded, repaired, reloaded, and made ready for sea again.

With Captain McGin laid up from injuries sustained during the tornado, she left Port Louis in the middle of September, under the command of Captain McMillan. A pleasant and uneventful voyage followed until the *Jason* neared the Bermudas. Here, the frequency of squalls increased. The captain felt it necessary to fasten the lifeboats more securely,

as well as other deck paraphernalia which might become loosened as the vessel rolled and tossed. This is mentioned because later it had an important part to play.

Bad weather made it impossible for the captain to take observations to determine his position. On the third of December, the captain intercepted a New York pilot boat from which he learned his whereabouts. After passing Georges Banks, a shoal about 100 miles to the eastward of Cape Cod, he decided to steer a course straight to the westward.

As the ship continued on that westerly course, the wind went into the northeast, the weather began to thicken, the skies darkened, and it began to rain. The day wore on; the temperature started to fall; the rain turned to sleet—and the sleet to snow. Like many a seafaring man before him, even the notorious Capt. Sam Bellamy who, with a crew of 150 pirates, lost the *Whidaw* in April 1717 on the shores of Cape Cod, and the captain of the celebrated *Somerset* (a British man-of-war) who lost his ship on these same beaches in November of 1778, Captain McMillan of the *Jason* continued on his course. He did not know about the treacherous sand bars and shoals which in those days extended several miles to sea.

It will be surprising to many to learn it was not until 1871 that the United States Coast Guard began to concern itself with rescue work. When Sumner I. Kimball, a dedicated life saver, became the General Superintendent of the United States Life Saving Service, it became a trained organization capable of carrying out its intended purpose.

In 1872, nine stations were built on Cape Cod and located at Race Point, Peaked Hill Bars in Provincetown, Highland Light in North Truro, Pamet River at Truro, Cahoon's Hollow at Wellfleet, Nauset at North Eastham, Orleans, Chatham, and Monomoy. These stations were built along the "Back Side," or the oceanside of Cape Cod from

Captain John Rich. He searched the dark, storm-lashed beach and found Evans, alive.

Samuel Evans, the only survivor. Evans hung on to a bale of jute and was washed ashore.

Surfman Richard Honey who first alerted the Pamet River Station about the Jason's *predicament.*

two to five miles apart. Besides being able seamen, capable of launching a surfboat in a raging sea if it became necessary to reach a stranded vessel, the surfmen had other duties which included nightly patrols to the half-way house. These shelters were located at equal distance from the two stations, where the surfman from one station would exchange marked keys with the surfman from the neighboring station and return to his home base. These patrols were carried out nightly, and the purpose of them was to watch for any vessel that might be in distress.

In 1893, the stations had been equipped with telephones, linking all those on the lower end of the Cape in a single communications system.

In addition to the nightly watches, daytime patrols were maintained, in fog, in heavy rain, in snow storms, and in gales.

The day of December 5, 1893 dawned dark, with that grey-black look to the eastward typical of a northeast storm. By daybreak there was a drizzling rain. Within a few hours it froze on the scrub pine trees. By noon the rain and sleet had turned to driving snow.

As the day darkened and the wind freshened, the *Jason* picked up speed, and "with a bone in her teeth" started around Cape Cod. The vessel was first sighted about 3:15 P.M. off the Nauset Station and several surfmen watched her progress. The *Jason* was last seen by the day patrol between four and five o'clock, just as darkness set in, headed to the windward with all the canvas she could carry, trying to make the end of Cape Cod. She was last seen in the daylight by No. 1 Surfman, Allen T. Gill of the Nauset Station, who said, "She's a weatherly ship but she's bound to strand unless she changes her course."

At sea, the driving, blinding snow, heavy swells, icy decks, and freezing spray hampered Captain McMillan and the *Jason*'s progress. The captain almost succeeded in making safety, because at six o'clock he had passed the Nauset Station and was below Cahoon's Hollow.

By the newly-installed telephone, Keeper Bearse of Nauset, Keeper Cole of Cahoon's Hollow, and Keeper Rich of Pamet River kept each other informed of the vessel's progress. Keeper Cole thought that the vessel would strike between his own station and Pamet River. Feeling that the responsibility for rescue rested upon him, the station was fully alerted, the horse harnessed, and the apparatus prepared for instant action. About seven o'clock both skippers agreed that, if the *Jason* should come ashore, it would be within the scope of the Pamet River Station, and the men there were readied to risk their lives in the angry storm. However, as time wore on and there had been no further news of the vessel, both skippers felt that she was still rolling and thrashing her way toward the better possibility of survival, and perhaps had a chance of standing off.

This was not to be.

About half past seven, Surfman Honey, breathless, bleeding from the stinging sand and freezing wet, burst into the station shouting, "Hopkins has just burned his signal!"

Moments later Hopkins arrived and reported that the vessel was stranded.

Aboard the *Jason*, as on land with the coming of nightfall, the snow had thickened and the seas had increased to sharp, high peaks, close together. The depth of the sea was shallowing. Salt spray was everywhere. The decks were becoming slippery with salt ice. The iron shrouds and rigging had an icy glaze. The snow sifted through the rigging, slid off the sails, and poured overboard in the howling winds. As Evans, the sole survivor, later said, "It seemed like we were sailing into the Devil's pocket."

It was then that the captain saw the breakers and shouted, "She has struck!"

The lifeboats were still on the bridge where they had originally been stowed and securely lashed for the previous storms. Their covers and lashings were intact and the tackles still hooked. The captain gave instant orders to clear them away, and together with his men set about the work. All hands rushed to the lifeboats. The freezing spray, biting snow, and lashing winds made their task almost impossible. Damp mittens froze to the lashings. Numb fingers picked at the knots made hard and frozen by the salt spray and snow. Every second was a lifetime.

To no avail. The ship lay with her starboard side to the waves. Each wave that beat her lifted her nearer the shore and came crashing inboard, swirling, beating, and upsetting the men as they struggled to clear the boats. Most of the sailors gave up this impossible task and climbed into the mizzenmast rigging and shrouds. A few continued their desperate attempt to free lifeboats. As the vessel lay, she was little more than a scoop funneling the water fore and aft as she was lifted closer and closer to shore. Those gallant sailors who continued to work on the lifeboats found themselves slipping and sliding on the icy decks. Breaking waves thrashed them about, dragging at their feet as if to carry them into the raging sea. Another towering breaker pounded the hull and flooded the deck, and with this the remaining crew were compelled to join their shipmates in the mizzenmast rigging.

It was at this point that the red glare of Surfman Hopkins' signal was seen through the darkness and snow. A cheer broke forth from the shipwrecked sailors; but within ten minutes of the time the signal on shore was seen, the *Jason* broke in half amidship. The mainmast toppled over, carrying with it the mizzenmast. The entire ship's company, except the captain, was at this time in the mizzen rigging. All were washed overboard.

The captain was last seen standing on the ladder at the quarter deck, supporting himself with a hand on each rail.

S. J. Evans, apprentice seaman, was in the lee shrouds. The next wave washed him away toward the beach. Planks, rigging, and bales of jute swirled around him. Tons of water poured over him. In desperation, he grabbed at a bale of jute which came whirling by him on the crest of a breaker, and caught it. The bale of jute kept on its crazy, swirling, bobbing course; but Evans held fast, end for end, to the top of a crest, to the hollow of the waves, for what seemed an eternity. Evans was finally deposited on the beach where, clad only in his underwear, half-frozen, he struggled toward the lantern carried by Keeper Rich.

Evans was promptly stripped of his wet, frozen clothing, wrapped in hot blankets, and taken to the Pamet River Station for further treatment.

The beach apparatus of the Pamet Station was ready, and the Lyle gun was aimed in the direction of the wreck, which appeared only as a black shadow, darker than the surrounding gloom. The line fell across the hulk. Proof that it lodged there was the firmness with which it resisted the strain to determine whether or not it was made fast. There was no pull or manipulation on the offshore end that could be detected. After waiting a considerable time, it appeared there was no hope that there might be a survivor on the wreck. The line finally parted under the heavy strain of the seas.

The only sounds that could be heard were the howling winds, the pounding surf, and to quote the official record of this disaster, the slatting of distant sails sounded "like peals of thunder and the crashing of blocks and chains as they were flung back and forth against the wire rigging and iron foremast sent out volumes of blazing sparks that seemed to some of the bystanders like signals of distress."

It was the practice of the Life Saving Service in times of such disasters to build bonfires on the beach to serve as guides to any survivor who might make the shore. But the wind blew with such force that a fire could not be maintained, and the blinding sand cut with such fury that the polished brass lantern on the beach apparatus cart was converted into a good specimen of ground glass. Other red signals were discharged to attract the attention of anyone who might have made the shore. Search patrols were maintained throughout the raging night, searching for members of the crew. None was found.

Morning found the hull broken into two pieces, about 40 yards apart, lying at right angles to each other, the bow head onto the beach with the foremast, topmast, bowsprit, and jib boom with most of the forerigging still in place. The aft section which carried the mainmast was stripped of all rigging. The waves ran high up the mast, breaking almost to the foretop, and shreds of the *Jason*'s jute cargo wrapped themselves like ragged garments around the shrouds and stays.

In the afternoon when the tide had turned, a dead body was visible, entangled in the rigging on the afterdeck. The seas were so high that the station keeper did not approach the wreck until the following morning to recover the body.

In all, there was one survivor. Twenty bodies were recovered out of a crew of 25. Whether or not any of the men would have survived if they had taken to the forerigging is impossible to say. The slatting sails and the flying blocks and the running rigging might have killed some. Some might have been washed away by the sea, and others might have perished with the cold; but the fact remains that the foremast stood throughout the storm with the foretop and crosstrees practically intact.

TRAPPED ALIVE IN A SUNKEN SCHOONER

by Edward Rowe Snow

ON SUNDAY AFTERNOON, MAY 13, 1877, THE AMER-ican schooner *Ohio* was off the shores of Nova Scotia on her route back to home port of Vinalhaven, Maine. Suddenly her lookout sighted a strange object in the sea ahead of him. Thinking that it was a whale, he shouted its position to Captain Dorr, who ordered the fifty-nine-foot schooner brought in close. Within a few minutes, all hands realized they had come upon a ship's hull, floating upside down. In order to discover the name of the unfortunate ship, two men rowed over in a dory and, as the sea was calm, boarded it. But they didn't stay long! As they began walking along the bilges, they heard a soft, tapping sound coming from beneath their feet! Believing they were hearing the ghosts of drowned men, they lost little time in scrambling back into the dory and hurrying back to the *Ohio* where they reported the noises to Captain Dorr. The Captain laughed at their "ghost story" and decided to board the derelict himself. One of the most fantastic sea stories of the last century was about to unfold.

It all began on the preceding Monday morning when the newly-built fishing schooner *Cod Seeker,* skippered by Philip Brown, sailed from Nova Scotia on her shakedown cruise.

All went well until Wednesday night when the schooner was running under foresail and jib off Baccaro Light. Suddenly, at about ten o'clock, a terrific squall hit and, without the slightest advance warning, the *Cod Seeker* capsized in ten fathoms of water. Leaping for one of the

The trouble began off Baccaro Light

dories which floated free, Captain Brown and two crew members scrambled to safety. By this time it was blowing a gale, and in the darkness Captain Brown was unable to see if anyone else was alive. He felt that all were not lost, but since his dory had no thole pins and drifted quickly away from the capsized schooner, he was helpless and could do nothing further.

Actually, two men had drowned in the cabin and another sailor, Ziba Hunt, had been sucked into one of the hatchways to his death. But there were still five others clinging to the overturned bilges. These men grabbed the lines which had been dangling over the sides at the time of the capsizing, and securing themselves to the keel as best they could, waited for rescue. Unknown to them, there were two uninjured men trapped in the forecastle with enough air to keep them alive for days!

Early the next morning the dory carrying Captain Brown and the two fishermen was swept ashore at Cape Sable Island. Here there were thirty fishing boats in the harbor, but the men were afraid to go out on account of the high gale. Captain Brown told them his story and pleaded for someone to go in search of survivors. Only one ship's master volunteered, Captain John Crowell of the schooner *Matchless*. Leaving the harbor within an hour, Crowell encountered severe winds and almost capsized his own ship, but he lashed the men to the jib-boom so that they could take in sail. In this way, he managed to navigate his vessel until they reached the vicinity of the *Cod Seeker*'s disaster.

After maneuvering in the area for over an hour, Captain Crowell decided to put back into port again, for he reasoned that no sailor exposed to such a gale could survive it. At about this time he sighted the bilges of the capsized schooner eight miles southwest of Cape Sable Island. Sailing closer, Crowell spotted five men lashed to the windward side of the vessel. With skill and daring he brought his ship in to the lee of the wreck, and began to remove the exhausted sailors, one by one, to safety aboard the *Matchless*. He managed to rescue four of the men, but when he returned for the fifth, he had slipped into the sea.

Captain Brown sailed into Barrington that afternoon with the four rescued men, and they returned to their homes in Bear Point that night. When the relatives of the sailors who were believed to be lost were notified of the situation, they began arrangements for memorial funeral services.

Unknown to either Captain Brown or the men he saved, there were still two men alive aboard the *Cod Seeker* —Samuel Atwood, and James E. Smith, adopted son of Reuben Stoddart, the ship's chief owner. These two had been in the forecastle when the schooner capsized and, to their amazement, no water had poured in to drown them. The hatchway was practically sealed off because of the storm, and at first water leaked in only gradually. The schooner floated at an angle of about forty degrees to starboard, with her head higher than her stern. The salt bins had spilled out in the hold, and this later prevented the schooner from righting herself.

Samuel and James resigned themselves to death when the water finally forced open the hatchway. It started to pour in on them in the terrible confusion of the pitch black forecastle. But a short time later, it stopped—when only about four and a half feet deep. The two realized then that they would live a while longer although the idea of rescue seemed exceedingly remote. There were cookies and bread enough for several days, but their water supply was less than a quart! They'd have to go sparingly with that. Later the following day, when their four comrades were saved, they knew nothing about it because of the violent pitching and rolling of the schooner in the gale.

In Nova Scotia the water is usually so cold most of the time that few sailors ever learned to swim. Their philosophy was that if they were going to drown it might as well be quick. Both Sam and Jim subscribed to that particular school of thought, and although they might have been able to dive through the hatch and climb upon the bottom of the hull, neither dared to take the chance, nor wished to consider it.

The next morning, the water in the forecastle began to rise, and soon it reached Smith's bunk. Still secured to the forecastle deck, the bunk was upside down and at the top of the overturned forecastle. The two men crawled on the bottom of the bunk to keep away from the rising water around them. Then, to their horror, they felt the schooner sinking. Down, down, down it went till it hit bottom with a dull thud, first at the mastheads and then at the hull. When the schooner had finally settled on the floor of the ocean, she was over on her beam ends more than before. The two men were forced to adjust themselves to the new angle at which the vessel lay. They had to leave the under side of the bunk and brace themselves as best they could by clinging to the bunk under water up to their shoulders. It was much more difficult than before, and the realization of their unhappy lot was no encouragement. They were trapped alive in a sunken schooner at the bottom of the sea!

The hours went by. Every so often the schooner shifted to a new position on the ocean floor. It was a ghastly feeling to realize that they could never escape from this ocean prison. Both men prayed to God that they would be spared; but their prayers seemed hopeless.

Some time later—neither could ever tell exactly when —the *Cod Seeker* gave a shiver, righted herself just a trifle, and then started to move, not along the ocean floor again, but up toward the surface. The men felt the schooner surge upward and they clung as best they could to the increased slant of the bunk. A few minutes later they could tell that the ship had reached the surface of the sea, for not only did she settle down to a steady, swaying movement but she went over to her original position with her bilges out of water. The men crawled back atop the bottom of the bunk. The *Cod Seeker* was drifting along on the ocean, her course guided by the wind and tide. But she was still bottom up, and it appeared that she would stay that way.

Talking it over in their old place on the bunk, James and Samuel decided correctly that the schooner had gone down because of the heavy bins of salt but that when the salt had finally dissolved into the water, the specific gravity of the schooner was altered and she was able to rise again to the surface.

Though their return to the surface was a stroke of luck, the men were still in a terrible predicament. During the next twenty-four hours it was a constant struggle to keep alive. They were still able to munch the bread and cookies, but their drinking water was completely exhausted. Adding to their troubles was a fresh gale which set the schooner tossing and twisting. At one time it seemed that the storm would send the *Cod Seeker* to the bottom again, but finally the gale subsided.

The next day was Sunday and both men prayed that the Sabbath might bring them help. They were able to recognize the sun's reflection in the water as it came up through the open hatchway. The air in the forecastle, however, was growing stale, and the two men developed violent headaches and nausea.

Noon came, and the men found themselves suffering terribly from thirst. They realized that they had been entombed in the forecastle for over eighty hours and knew that help would have to come soon or it would be too late. So cramped and uncomfortable were they on their perch in the forecastle that once they almost decided to dive down through the hatchway and attempt to kick their way out into the sunshine where they might be seen and rescued. But in their weakened condition, they felt certain that they could not reach the surface. So they remained in their cramped quarters in the forecastle.

It was late that afternoon that the schooner *Ohio,* as previously described, came upon the *Cod Seeker* in the waters west of Seal Island and dispatched the two men in a dory to investigate. Within minutes after their return to the *Ohio* with their tale of "ghosts," Captain Dorr was aboard the derelict pounding the planking with his heavy boots.

"There's someone alive down there!" Dorr exclaimed as he listened to the answering taps from below. He ordered his men to return to the ship to fetch two axes while he banged the hull again reassuringly to let the trapped men know he realized their plight and would help.

Samuel Atwood and James Smith had spent these last twenty minutes or so passing through various stages of ecstasy and despair. First they had heard, almost unbelievingly, the heavy boots of the first two crewmen over their head. They had responded by ripping a two-by-four piece of board from the bunk and pounding it against the bilges. This resulted in sounds of running steps, followed by a good ten minutes of absolute silence. Their high hopes of rescue vanished and both felt all was finally over. With help seemingly so near, and now evidently gone, the low point of their spirits was reached. Then, when they again heard feet land on the hull over their heads, they commenced once more to rap frantically with the two-by-four. A few minutes later an answering thump sounded directly above them, followed by another and then another. They pounded back frenziedly, and the next sound they heard was that of Captain Dorr's axe crashing into the bottom of the *Cod Seeker.* The men

in the forecastle realized that they had been discovered and both breathed silent thanks to God.

But there was still danger ahead. Two heavy axes descended on the new planking of the bilges in an effort to cut a hole through and release the men. The wood began to crunch, and then the tip of an axe pierced the forecastle bulkhead. The result of the next blow was a fearful whistling sound as the air in the schooner, greatly compressed by the tons of water in the forecastle, rushed through the tiny opening. Again and again the axes descended. With each blow, the hole in the planking widened. Suddenly Atwood noticed that the water was rising in the forecastle. The release of the compressed air had once more affected the stability of the schooner. She was sinking lower and lower into the sea.

Now desperate, James and Samuel tried to force themselves through the hole. It was not yet large enough for either man. James worked his head and shoulder out into the sunlight and could get no farther.

"Get in there before it's too late," cried Captain Dorr, and he pushed James back into the forecastle. The axes began again. A few minutes later the opening was large enough to allow the two survivors, imprisoned for more than ninety hours, to leave their schooner.

A physics teacher would point out that when the hull was chopped through and the air pushed out, the craft would sink again. However, there were several other air pockets in the capsized hull and, although she sank considerably lower into the water, she did not go under completely.

Within half an hour, James and Samuel were resting in bunks aboard the *Ohio.* They were taken into Shag Harbor and, two hours after, they returned to Bear Point.

Later, the derelict was found at sea still barely afloat and was towed into Port Maitland. Here it was brought up on the shore at high tide. Frank B. Goudey, who gave the first account of this story, was a boy of about thirteen, living in Port Maitland at the time. He had assisted in the pumping out of the schooner. The three dead members of the crew were found in the craft as she was being emptied of water. When the escape hole in the bilges was repaired with fresh lumber, the schooner was ready for fishing again. As the final planking was being placed over the opening, one morning about three weeks after the rescue, James Smith and Samuel Atwood, now fully recovered and rested, went over to watch the repair of what was very nearly their tomb. As they joined some of their old friends congregated around the ship, it is said that it was some ten minutes before anyone recognized either of them—and then only when Samuel Atwood began recalling their terrible experience. When the two fortunate survivors finally walked away, everyone assembled on the beach was silent. Both Smith and Atwood had, in those ninety hours inside the overturned forecastle of the *Cod Seeker,* aged in appearance from twenty to twenty-five years!

THE *LAWSON'S* FIRST AND LAST VOYAGE

by Edward L. Rowe
as told to
Capt. William P. Coughlin

Editor's Note: The only seven-masted schooner ever built, the *Thomas W. Lawson,* was launched at Quincy, Mass., in 1902. On November 27, 1907, she set sail on her first and last deep-water voyage. Her cargo never reached London. She met her end off the Scilly Islands, England, Friday, December 13, 1907. There were only two survivors. One was the late Edward L. Rowe of Annisquam, Mass. This is Rowe's detailed account of that last voyage as told to Captain William P. Coughlin of Ipswich, Mass. Captain Coughlin says Rowe was often irked at the incomplete way he was quoted by writers. This story, however, was signed by Rowe himself on March 17, 1954, as a true presentation of his harrowing experience.

It WAS HELLISH FROM START TO FINISH. I HAVE NEVER forgotten it to this day. If memory serves me, we disconnected the pipelines and cast her ropes off from the dock in Philadelphia about the 27th of November, 1907. What makes me certain of this date is a check I cashed that morning before we sailed, dated the 27th November. I'm certain of the date on the check.

The smaller harbor tugs slowly nosed her huge graceful stern downstream. Once in the middle of the river, a larger Delaware tug jockeyed under the bow, taking our hawser, running it out ahead of the ship preparatory for the long tow down the Delaware. Hawser taut, the harbor tugs tooted off. The river tug began towing. We were on our way with a cargo of lubricating oil in bulk that never made a pipeline, or lubricated anything in London, England, our port of destination.

Early next morning the river tug cast off our hawser from her after towing bitts in Liston Range, the wider reaches of Delaware Bay, a short haul below Ship John Lighthouse. We were on our own now—all lowers set but the spanker. Four more lighthouses to log in the lower Dela-ware afore we would clear the Delaware Capes, May and Henlopen, for the stretch to Overfalls Light Vessel and the open sea. Safely we left Elbow Cross, Miah Maul, and Fourteen Foot Spot astern with the last of the fair tide, only to fetch up on Brandywine Shoal (to southard of the light), luckily or unluckily on soft bottom, a preventive to serious damage to vessels grounding, unlike the rockbound coast of New England. With the coming flood tide, we floated free unassisted.

Often thought had we grounded on "Hard Water" in the landlocked Delaware that late November day, and had we damaged the hull considerable to prevent our continuing the voyage at that time, it might have saved the lives of nineteen men and the ship's cat, all of whom were lost sixteen days later on Annett Island when the breakers on Hell Weather Reef roared suddenly dead ahead on that black-clouded, thick evening of Friday, December 13, 1907. Anchors overboard! 'Twas our only chance from being wrecked on Hell Weather. We had made just to windward of Annett Island with thick weather, islands, reefs and islets to lee'ard of us.

But to get to the drift and drag of the passage. After passing out by Overfalls Light Vessel, daylight had faded beyond, the course was set. With our last glimpse of the Delaware Capes we stood off to the eastward on the port tack, the wind southwest, a comfortable sailing breeze to the southward of Five Fathom Bank. 'Twas early the next morning that our worries began. Disturbances were making up with the wind shifting to the northwest, increasing steadily to about seventy miles an hour, building up in no time a mountain of sea. The heavy sea continued rolling up on our quarter all the way across the Grand Banks and beyond, a living gale whistled by her tall steel masts and through her shrouds. Old "Tom" was making knots, as the old sailor used to say—"making steamship time." We were; we passed and showed our heels to a number of steamers that day and night.

All held. "All was well" till late that night. Soon before eight bells (midnight) every lower sail blew from the bolt ropes but the spanker. The spanker was furled to the boom. So were the head sails, never loosed from their stops. The men couldn't walk footropes to break out the head sails if

we did wish to use them. We could save them till the fine weather broke. Seas were running over her now, all along the decks from the spanker mast to the foremast were breakers, fume and spume.

Daylight the next morning our work boat, an eighteen-foot yawl lashed bottom up near the mainmast, was ripped from her fastenings. A sea smacked under her—away she whammed and banged around the iron decks like a cockleshell. That finished her into small pieces.

Running free for three days under bare poles we logged from fifteen to eighteen miles an hour in hurricane force wind from the northwest. With that wind and sea pushing us, we didn't need any sail. The seas climbing astern with the gale on our quarter looked like mountains chasing us. At the end of the third day a giant comber climbed up and over the *Lawson*'s quarter, fully boarding her, swashing tons of water on deck, breaking open No. 6 hatch. Misfortune was piling up. Water was now pouring into the open spaces between No. 6 and No. 7 hatches. Here, 300 tons of coal stored for ship's use was washing into the bilges. The mess became worse, the coal clogging our strainers and suc-

141

tions. The pumps could no longer siphon the water from the hold.

To add to misery and distress, the great weight of the tons of water flooding into and filling our after holds settled the stern to become all awash with the decks aft. Running before the gale the seas were now boiling over the after taffrail, the poop deck awash. She was a veritable ledge aft, slowing down with the tremendous weight of water on deck. She couldn't beat the heavy running sea behind her. More and more of it plumped on board.

Whang, bang, a solid sea from astern whacked fully against the starboard side of our lifeboat hung thwartship across the stern on davits, lifting it from its fastenings, smashing it on deck into a wreck against the pilot house aft. We were now without lifeboats. One thing after another hit us, seemed like no end of trouble. Our worst condition was aft. We had to do something about it.

We were faced with the problem of raising her stern. To relieve this plight, we were forced to pump the oil from No. 6 tank to bring her stern up out of the water to secure a higher load-line. This done, next job was to free the suctions and strainers; and that was a job I'll never forget. You can imagine, Captain, work, work and work! The men were tiring, no sleep, water everywhere, a long way from where we might count telegraph poles flying by.

On the fifth day the gale moderated, the sea abated some, but left a heavy ground swell which kept up for days. All hands turned to in the sail lockers, dragging out and making ready the trysails which we hoisted for steerage way to check her from wallowing aimlessly in the trough of the waves. With these storm sails we also bent a spare foresail that was stored in the locker. This done, thick weather set in; afore night it thickened into a pea-souper. It was zero observation for the next five days, with whiskers on our sidelights.

On the tenth day the glass was tumbling fast; it began to clear. The bottom was again dropping out of the glass, a forewarning of a heavy northwester in the offing. It was good observation now—first in five days. By nightfall we were shipmates once more with a howling northwester, violent, like the baby that overtook us the second day out from the Jersey Coast. All hands and the cook guessed it right, the same old gale had overhauled us to blow us and the fog back to London.

We were in for it again. It blew so hard, in order to save the foresail we were forced to try and douse it. In this operation, somehow or other the foresheet got adrift. In less time than it takes to say "Jack Robinson," the foresail in ribbons was on its way to loo'ard and "Davy Jones." With no end of trouble we were now making knots towards the British Isles under storm or trysails, our spanker and head sails still furled. The angry seas were getting their licks in once more at the *Lawson*'s fifty-foot beamy counter.

Old Hoodoo was still with us. We never did pick up Scilly Light, but, by navigation and record of courses sailed, we knew we were somewhere in the vicinity of the Scilly Islands some thirty-five miles off the Coast of Cornwall, Eng-

On board the Thomas W. Lawson *during one of her coastal runs; looking aft in a stiff breeze.*

land. It was the 16th day out, *Friday, December 13,* about 5:30 P.M. Others of the crew and myself were forward on the forecastle head, straining our eyes and ears for a sight or sound. Suddenly the roar of breakers ahead. Breakers it was! Our ears caught sound of it for position, to look, the eye getting a short hurried view through what was left of the evening dusk at what turned out to be Hell Weather Reef. No mistake. Calculations to fetch outside of Bishop Rock Lighthouse, which marks the dangerous ledges off Scilly Isle, somehow in the dead reckoning had gone askew.

With Hell Weather Reef under the bow, off St. Agnes, Annett Island, with no orders given, I let go the anchor on my own. I felt I was on that ship in the same predicament as the others on board. There was nothing else to do at that time to save her from disaster on Hell Weather Reef. Here we were, flirting with the nasty ledges of the Scilly Isles off the Coast of Cornwall, England. Lands End to lee'ard. The End. Was it? No skipper could face a more trying, difficult nautical situation to pull out of, with the largest steel schooner in the world under his feet, with seven great towering masts at the mercy of the elements, with little or no sail power to negotiate in such a tight spot. Inevitably, our bare jury rig was about as useful as the cook's dish towels. Our heavy suit of sail power had blown away.

Chain ran out, anchors hit bottom. We ran plenty more chain through the hawse-pipes to check her. The strain soon began to be felt, holding enough to swing her head around, clearing the reef. She swung clear round off Annett Head, but she kept dragging; the anchors wouldn't hold enough to spot her. The big hooks were bumping along over rocky bottom. The quivering chain spelled that. It was about

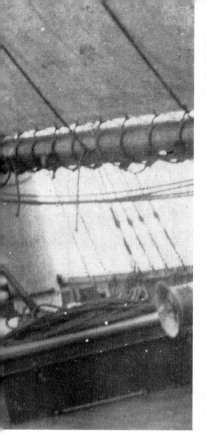

On the tenth day, the glass was tumbling fast

Above. It seems difficult to believe that a ship of the Lawson's size could be broken like matchwood, but heavy seas and gale winds tore her wide open.

The late Edward L. Rowe, one of the two survivors of the Lawson's final voyage, at approximately the time (1954) he and Captain William Coughlin wrote this account.

5:30 that we dropped anchor. We were anchored only a short time when Pilot Hicks came off in a boat from Annett Island. What was needed was a powerful English tugboat rather than a pilot. In this situation a pilot was of little or no use.

She continued to drag, steadily contiguous to Annett Island, uninterrupted by good holding bottom. From the time we anchored at sunset the *Lawson* never stopped dragging to loo'ard; the anchors couldn't get a good grip to spot herself. It was 11 P.M. the same night when she touched bottom, hard, with a falling tide. It was no sand bank we hit, but a solid rugged reef. She grounded well aft. All hands were on deck.

Things were beginning to shape up very bad now; the ship was groaning and straining. We had no lifeboats left on board to save ourselves, having lost them on the boisterous passage across. All hands took to the rigging, hoping to stay aloft to await rescue. I unlaced my shoes and took to the spanker rigging.

Captain George W. Dow, the English pilot, W. Cook Hicks (an inhabitant of Annett Island), the mate, and the cook climbed half way up, high in the spanker rigging, scattered above me. Five of us were in the spanker rigging. Captain Dow had no life belt with him.

Minutes after stranding on the reef, all seven masts went by the board. The starboard rigging let go. A heavy sea smacked the ship, she swung her head round with it heading straight for and up a cliff. With the masts gone, the big sticks toppling to port carrying the men with them, all was over now, including the hopes of the men borne to a watery grave with the steel sticks of the *Thomas W. Lawson*. It was every man for himself.

When she swung head for the cliff, the seas were lifting very high and dropping low, in one, two, three order. Seaman Allen took a long chance to hop ashore. Thinking the jib boom might touch the cliff, he scampered out along the bowsprit towards the tip end. Alas, one of those high one, two, three combers swept him from the boom, washing and tossing him seventy to eighty feet over the island. He was the first crew member to land ashore on Annett Island. It was after I got ashore on Annett Island that we got wind of what became of him. The natives on the island told me they found him with his left side ripped open, and that he lived for two hours. He was buried on the island with other crew members who were later washed ashore.

As to myself, Captain, I cut a signal halyard, tied it around my body, climbed three ratlines above the sheer pole. Apprehension or something brought me back to the sheer pole. The other men were above me, scattered in the rigging. There I stood with unlaced shoes before the masts went over the side. When the rigging let go, I found myself standing on deck with the line around my waist. At this moment I grabbed a second line which happened near. When the ship lurched and rolled heavily, both of the ropes jammed in the Coastal Doors of the pilot house aft (*Lawson* had a semi-globular-shaped room aft with those doors for steering). She was beginning to break in two now between

No. 6 and No. 7 hatches. All hands were in the water.

Temporarily, I became tangled in the snarled mass of No. 7 rigging floating beside the wreck. Somehow or other, in the turmoil I managed to get clear of the rigging. Intervention, God's divine guidance, arrived temporarily, at least. Up pops a lengthy twelve by twelve alongside of me. In the end of it was a good-sized iron spike sticking up. Letting go a hand of "B.L." tobacco I salvaged for future chewing if I did get ashore, I grabbed the spike. The stick was a piece of the center line of the ship's bulkhead. Because of it, I can tell you this story today. It had much to do with saving my life, drifting me towards terra firma. I couldn't swim a stroke. Another sailor bobbed up, catching the other end of it. He was on the end for a short time when a sea got under it, lifting his end high, my end went low, and he was tossed off. That's the last I saw of him and I cannot recall who he was.

Conditions were wild about this time. I saw the *Lawson* break in two between the 6th and 7th masts. Watching the after end float away, I hankered to be on it, feeling it would stay afloat and sooner or later drift us to safety. Alas, that didn't hold true. It blew itself to loo'ard onto one of Scilly Isles' nasty, jagged ledges, the end of the *Lawson*'s stern. I realized then my best bet was my friend, the twelve by twelve.

For some three to four hours we floated about aimlessly towards the lee shore of Annett Island. Unexpectedly my feet touched bottom. I felt I was near the shore somewhere, to find myself standing on a shoal spot nearby a ledge, or part of it. I let go the spike in the timber I had held onto so long that bleak black morning. I still have this scar in my palm from holding the spike. It bruised deeply. I grabbed the rock and hauled myself. With a little rest, I rubbed the oil from my eyes. There I stood alone, with the reef and the sea, wondering what became of the others out there in the cold, black, oily waters.

I spotted a flat, dry area about four feet wide across from me between a couple of pinnacles six or seven feet high. It was drier than where I had landed but the seas were washing between me and it. To make it was a good jump.

Rare photograph of the Thomas W. Lawson, *bottom up, on Hell Weather (also known as Helewether) Reef.*

The Lawson *in Boston Harbor shortly before her final voyage.*

I crawled along with two broken knee caps to the edge of where the water was washing across. Watching my chance between the rollers I jumped, landing head first but getting there. I hauled myself up the six or seven feet to the safe gap between the jutting rocks. This was about 3:00 A.M. the next morning. Fortunately, the tide was ebbing with more to go. The ebbing tide favored. Had it been flooded, the dry spot would have been covered well over my head, and my chances slim to climb to a safe hole higher up. I recall the *Lawson* struck about high water, and with the falling tide her great weight quickly broke her in two astride the ledge.

It was exactly daylight when I beheld Captain Dow attired in a priestly mackinaw and life belt trudging wearily into the dry spot with two broken ribs and a broken right arm. He was a heavy man, weighing 250 pounds, and after a fashion I managed to haul him up into the safe spot I had dragged myself into earlier. We were both safe now to await rescue, but cold and shivering.

It was about 4:30 A.M. when an eight-oared English gig jockeyed off the rocky terrain. Maneuvering with quite some difficulty, they finally came into where we were. I managed down into the gig first. The rescuers felt that I, being the younger, should have let the skipper be taken off first. This sentiment of the gig crew for the Captain bothered me. I explained to the rescuers that the "Old Man" was in a safe spot, was a heavy man of 250 pounds with broken ribs and arm and couldn't help himself. I wasn't much better off with two broken knee caps, which had to be lashed with two broom sticks later to walk at all. I described to the English gig crew it would be much easier getting the "Old Man" off to the lee of the island on the other side. Looking it over, they got Captain Dow off safely three hours later by coming around to the lee. The Captain and I were the only two survivors, seaman Allen, who was washed overboard from the jib boom, having died early that morning. During my stay on the island I had no medical treatment, there being no doctors available. Ashore on the island, I was cared for by a Hicks family, brother of the pilot who lost his life.

Why Pilot Hicks boarded us that night, so far from London at the western entrance to the English Channel, to lose his life in the bargain, was never understood, for we still had a long run ahead of us up to the English Channel before reaching the narrow confines where a pilot could be of help.

So ended, Captain, the day of doom for the *Thomas W. Lawson* on her only and ill-fated crossing of the Atlantic, Friday, December 13, 1907, on Annett Island, St. Agnes, some twenty-five miles from Lands End, Cornwall, England—her "Last Voyage." The elements never let up being against us. We bucked against fate from the Delaware to Hell Weather Reef—that I'm certain of—for I was there!

FEW HAVE, BUT HE SURVIVED A WATER SPOUT

by Quentin DeGrasse
as told to
Chester Howland

The New Bedford whaler, Alice Knowles.

Pardon Gifford

QUENTIN DEGRASSE ROLLED UP HIS PANTS' LEGS AND uncovered the thick parts of his feet and lower ankles. An ugly network of scar marks covered them.

"These have never left me," Quentin said. "As I grow older I do not like to look at them nor think of the fearful days and nights in the mid-Atlantic when I was helpless to prevent pilot fish from viciously biting my body. Whenever I am reminded in the day time of the details of that experience a half a century ago, I relive it all in bad dreams at night."

The story of Quentin DeGrasse is the story of the New Bedford whaleship, *Alice Knowles,* caught in the nuclear force of a giant waterspout in the Atlantic Ocean, thirty-five degrees north of the equator. The bark *Alice Knowles* was built in 1878, a good ship of 302 tons. She sailed out of New Bedford, Mass., on April 19, 1915 for an extended whaling voyage.

Twenty-one days after leaving her home port, the vessel lay off St. Vincent, one of the Cape Verde Islands. Captain Horace Haggerty was taken ashore and, as was common in the last years of whale hunting out of New Bedford, recruited supplies and men to make up a full crew. Quentin DeGrasse, a lad seventeen years old carried with him his mother's consent to ship on a New Bedford whaler, and he signed shipping papers in the cabin of the *Alice Knowles* as a foremast hand.

Five months after leaving New Bedford the vessel was hunting whales in the Atlantic's western whaling grounds, twenty-eight to thirty-six degrees north of the equator. The ship had sixteen hundred barrels of sperm oil aboard—a total cargo so great that some of the casks had to be stowed on deck, considered a risk in case of bad weather.

Quentin proved himself to be a strong, capable and willing hand. He was a skillful boatman, quick to observe and learn. He reports that the needed pig iron ballast deep in the hold of the *Alice Knowles* was removed to make room for oil that would be taken from whales captured during the six-week journey back to the home port.

I listened to the story of the wreck of the *Alice Knowles* as told to me by Quentin, the only surviving member of the crew.

"Our ship had been at sea two years and five months, when on September first, with Cape Hatteras forty miles due west, the barometer dropped rapidly. The southwestern horizon became black with a solid cloud mass, and heavy winds began to strike the *Alice Knowles* and pick up the sea.

"Captain Haggerty spoke with the Chief Mate who ordered, 'Take in all light sails and rig in studding-sail booms.'

"The squall passed off to the southeast but in spite of a brief calm Captain Haggerty sang out.

" 'Clew down topsails—haul out reef tackles and haul up courses.'

"During the next twelve hours the storm seemed to remain stationary and did not change in its intensity.

"September the third the wind suddenly increased in strength. The man at the wheel was whirled to the deck. Two men were sent to stand-by but could not hold the wheel steady. It was lashed to hold the vessel into the wind.

"About noon a huge funnel-shaped cloud even blacker

than the sky itself was sighted four or five miles from the ship. The men on the second watch paced the deck apprehensively in the threat of a hurricane. There was an uneasiness aboard. Orders were given to double reef the fore topsail and furl the mainsail.

"At midnight the sea moderated. Captain Haggerty called the ship's company aft.

" 'Men,' said the Captain, 'I cannot predict that the moderation of the weather means a favorable change in the wind. The officers are to remain on deck with me through the night; any of you who want to can remain with us or go below to the forecastle.'

"The men talked among themselves and most of the crew went down into the forecastle.

"At two o'clock a terrific roar came out of the blackness. No man could hear another's shouts. The water spout enveloped the ship, dragging her onto her beams end. She remained there a brief moment and the Captain attempted to smash in the cabin skylight to release his son in the steerage and any others of the crew. Before he had struck a half dozen blows the vessel had turned keel up—the crew was trapped below or thrown from the deck into the boiling ocean.

"Six crew members had chosen to remain on deck with the officers. I was one of these. We had climbed into a whaleboat hanging in the davits just before the waterspout struck. This boat and the crew members in it floated free but a great wave picked both men and boat fifty feet into the air and when the wave rolled on before the hurricane the boat and men dropped like a plummet, crashing onto the upturned keel of the *Alice Knowles*. The boat flew into pieces and the men disappeared into the ocean.

"I was a powerful swimmer, trained from babyhood off the ocean shores of St. Vincent Island and was not injured in the crash. I struggled to the surface of the ocean. I could not see one inch in front of me. The waterspout and gale had passed but a thundering noise still deafened me. When the light of the morning came I found myself near a half of a whaleboat that six months before had been crushed by a whale's tail and had been kept on the after upper deck (house) for repairs.

"I had hung onto it ten or fifteen minutes when I heard a cry and my name. 'Quentin, help! help!' I looked around and saw Jules Lopes, one of the ship's harpooners.

"Jules was exhausted and floating with the great ocean swells. I swam to him and helped him get on to my half boat raft. There had been no wind since sunrise.

"The weight of Jules and me in the open-ended half boat submerged it so that although it supported us, only our heads were above the surface of the sea. We feared sharks might smell us, although neither of us had been more than bruised in the smashing of the whaleboat on the keel of the wrecked and sunken ship, and not a drop of our blood had reached the water.

"The glare of the sun in a bright, clear sky was painful. Jules kept his eyes closed. He was much weaker than I. I would close mine for a few minutes at a time and then search the sea hoping to discover floating wreckage from the *Alice Knowles* or a ship on the horizon.

"Mid-afternoon of our first day in the water I sighted a cask filled with whale oil that had floated from the deck of the *Alice Knowles* when it capsized. I thought it would be more buoyant than the broken boat and swam over to it and pushed it with my head and body toward the boat. However, when Jules and I attempted to climb onto it we could not get a grip and it rolled in the water. It was a large cask, over four feet in diameter. If we could have gotten onto it we might have been able to keep our bodies out of the water. We returned to the broken half boat.

"As we drifted away from the cask, large pieces of pork floated toward us. These pieces of salt meat had been soaking in the galley aboard the *Alice Knowles* the day of the wreck.

"I again left my position in the half boat and swam out to the floating pork. Although it was soft, I was able to hold a piece between my teeth and swim back to the half boat. As I reached out to hand the pork to Jules, he shouted, 'Quentin—a shark is following you.' I turned to see his fin above the surface of the ocean. I shouted and beat the water with my arms and legs, clapping my hands in the commotion. The shark fin disappeared and I expected to feel his teeth ripping at my abdomen as I lay flat in the water. I was not attacked. Jules and I ate bites of the sea-soaked pork.

"Fighting the shark in my weakened condition robbed me of my strength and I did not recover. After the first twenty-four hours Jules and I locked our arms around each other's body and our legs under the only thwart remaining in the broken boat. This would keep us from falling into the water if the sea became rough. We had no strength for further swimming.

"We remained in this position forty-eight hours under a burning sun by day and through the damp, shivering cold nights, without food or water. Our eyes were becoming sticky and it was difficult to keep them open. The horizon was growing indistinct and blurred. It seemed that we might be blind before we died with no chance to sight and hail a passing ship. We mumbled prayers we had been taught as boys in church on the Island of St. Vincent.

"On the fourth day, September 7, we sighted a vessel coming toward us. We could not make any sounds above a gruff whisper forced from our feverish throats. As the ship approached us the Master shouted, but we could not answer him. We saw the crewmen lower a boat and row toward us. They thought us dead as we could not move or make any sound.

"We had been in the water so long we could not release our arm grips around each other nor our legs from the boat thwart. The men in the rescue boat towed us to their vessel and we were hauled aboard by tackle ropes and painfully pried apart.

"Captain Charles Gilbert, Master of the six-masted schooner, *Fred W. Thurber,* slowly nursed us and took us to Pernambuco on the Brazilian coast."

Jules Lopes died from the effects of the terrible ordeal. Quentin DeGrasse lived to tell this tale.

That much exaggeration has been mixed up with the history of sea serpents cannot be doubted. Or can it? Gloucesterman Solomon Allen and other seamen saw "The Serpent of 1817," and a similar creature was twenty minutes in sight of the Captain and crew of the British frigate Daedalus.

SERPENTS OF THE SEA

by Richard D. Estes

THE LEATHERY-SKINNED OLD FISHERMAN ON THE wharf turned to give the inquiring stranger a searching look from his watery blue eyes, and resumed his contemplation of Gloucester Harbor. He spat into the water as he mulled over the question he had been asked. Finally, deciding it was seriously put, he answered:

"I been acrost the pond many a time, but I never saw no sea serpent." He shifted his position against the piling and looked the stranger in the eye. "I don't really believe there is any such thing; of course, there's all kind of fish. I've read about it, and met people who claim they've seem them, but if there is such a thing, it's not around here."

A little earlier, at the Master Mariners' Association in Gloucester, the question received much the same, although a little less serious reaction. A group of old sea captains,

(continued on page 153)

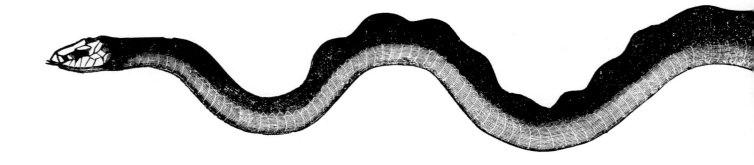

Many reports can be ignored, but some can't

A good deal of testimony concerning the sightings of sea serpents can be ignored as the undocumented vagaries of highly imaginative men. Some reports, however, cannot be ignored, such as that made in 1852 by the Captain and the crew of the British frigate **Daedalus.** When the vessel, under Captain Peter M'Quhae, was on a passage to London from the East Indies, between the Cape of Good Hope and St. Helena, Captain M'Quhae and most of the officers and crew, at four o'clock one afternoon, saw a sea serpent. They viewed the serpent for 20 minutes, until it finally passed under the vessel's quarter. Crewmen stated that the monster extended its jaws, which were full of large jagged teeth, described as "seeming sufficiently capacious to admit of a

tall man standing upright between them." The ship was sailing north at the rate of eight miles per hour.

The following is Captain M'Quhae's report to the Admiralty:

"In reply to your request that I provide information as to the truth of my statement about sighting a sea serpent of extraordinary dimensions, from Her Majesty's ship **Daedalus,** under my command, on her passage from the East Indies, I have the honor to acquaint you, for the information of my lords commissioners of the admiralty, that at 5 o'clock PM in latitude 24 degrees, 44 minutes south, and longitude 9 degrees, 22 minutes east, wind fresh from the northeast, with a long ocean swell from the southwest, the ship on the port tack heading northeast by north, something very unusual was seen by Mr. Sartoris, midshipman, rapidly approaching the ship from before the beam. The circumstance was

Head of the sea serpent seen by Captain Peter M'Quhae.

Artist's conception of the M'Quhae sea serpent as reported in Gleason's Pictorial Drawing Room Companion, *1852.*

immediately reported by him to the officer of the watch, Lieutenant Edgar Drummond, with whom, and Mr. William Barret, the master, I was at the time walking the quarter-deck. The ship's company were at supper.

"On our attention being called to the object, it was discovered to be an enormous serpent, with head and shoulders kept about four feet constantly above the surface of the sea; and as nearly as we could approximate by comparing it with the length of what our maintopsail-yard would show in the water, there was at the very least sixty feet of the animal **a fleur d'eau,** no portion of which was, to our perception, used in propelling it through the water, either by vertical or horizontal undulation. It passed rapidly, but so close under our lee quarter that had it been a man of my acquaintance I should have easily recognized the features with the naked eye; and it did not, either in approaching the ship, or after it had passed our wake, deviate in the slightest degree from its course to the southwest, which it held on at the pace of from twelve to fifteen miles per hour, apparently on some determined purpose.

"The diameter of the serpent was about fifteen or sixteen inches behind the head, which was, without any doubt, that of a snake; and it was never, during the twenty minutes that it continued in sight of our glasses, once below the surface of the water—its color a dark brown, with yellowish-white about the throat. It had no fins, but something like the mane of a horse, or rather a bunch of seaweed, washed about its back. It was seen by the quartermaster, the boatswain's mate, and the man at the wheel, in addition to myself and officers above mentioned.

"I am having drawings of the serpent made from a sketch taken immediately after it was seen, which I hope to have ready for transmission to my lords commissioners of the admiralty by to-morrow's post."

PETER M'QUHÆ, Captain.

Appearance of the sea serpent when first seen from H.B.M. Ship Daedalus.

151

American Museum of Natural History, N.Y.

American Museum of Natural History, N.Y.

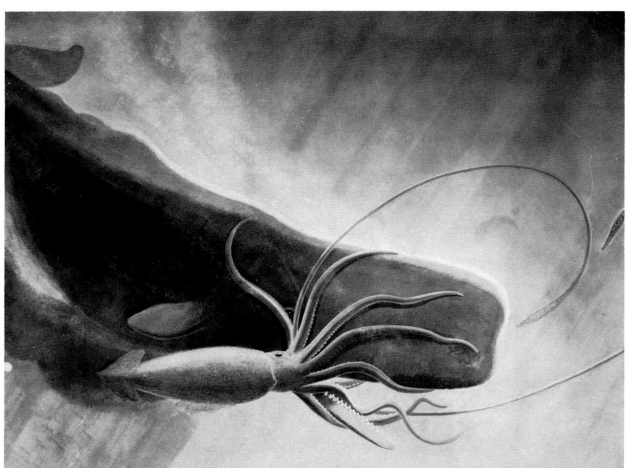

American Museum of Natural History, N.Y.

"Monsters are often seen through a haze of Scotch Whisky"

representing between them hundreds of years spent at sea, were seated in a semi-circle before the large windows looking onto the main street, watching the passersby, when the stranger came in. They invited him to take a seat, and listened to him explain that he was looking for men who had seen the sea serpent. When he had finished, and sat awaiting their reply, they regarded one another covertly. Each

Since the existence of sea serpents has never been properly documented, at least according to scientists, the Whale Shark (upper left) remains as the largest fish. Scientists do admit, however, that sea serpents did exist at one time, such as the Tylosaurus (above), which perished millions of years ago.

Left. A giant squid attacking a whale. The squid is the creature most commonly mistaken for a sea serpent.

seemed to be speculating whether his associates would let him get away with a whopper. But although considerable effort was wasted in trying to make one another begin, no one seemed willing to tell the first one.

Over in the corner next to the window, a heavy-set, rugged looking man with a pipe and humorous eyes, Capt. Archie McLeod by name, Grand Banks skipper for 43 years, spoke up: "If there are any along the coast, that's him sitting right beside you." And that little bald-headed man, Harry Clattenburg, master of 50 vessels, who had an even more droll expression, and mischievous eyes, responded with a sly grin, "Why you're supposed to be a liar if you tell about sea serpents."

The kidding went back and forth until Capt. Charles Heberle, a tow-boat master for many years, president of the Master Mariners, gave a serious opinion. "I've been all over

153

the ocean from Hatteras to Labrador and I never saw one. I don't think there are any." The other old-timers agreed; one or two thought there might be sea serpents in other latitudes. At that point a new arrival joined the group, and was quickly pounced upon. "Here's Manuel Lema," he was introduced, "he can maybe tell you something."

"I saw one before I left Portugal," the un-forewarned Mr. Lema began. "It was quite long—some are a hundred feet." The silence deepened. The stranger fixed upon him a penetrating look and inquired, "Are you sure it was a sea serpent?" Well, perhaps it wasn't at that, he couldn't be sure. Mr. Lema sat down, looking a little uncomfortable.

All up and down Cape Ann, seamen gave the same response: no one seemed to believe in sea serpents, while at the same time, no one would come out and say unequivocally that sea serpents don't exist. And yet less than a hundred years ago it would have been equally difficult to find disbelievers, because practically everybody on Cape Ann had seen or remembered hearing about the famous Gloucester sea serpent of 1817, that reappeared along the coast at intervals until 1886, and is probably the best documented of all sea serpent stories. The men who made depositions as to the reality of the serpent were, many of them, leading citizens, scientists and naturalists of Boston and the North Shore. So positive were their identifications and so unimpeachable their reputations that their testimony, on any other subject, would have convinced any jury.

The serpent made its appearance in Gloucester Harbor on a sunny, serene morning in August, 1817, gliding along in vertical undulations without paying the slightest attention to the noisy throng that quickly gathered to witness the phenomenon. It was apparently absorbed in the pursuit of a large school of herring which fled before it. For two whole weeks it disported almost daily, until practically everyone for miles around had gawked at it, and it was easily the most popular performer within a thousand miles.

Men of science and letters, their reserve finally shaken by persistent accounts, made the journey to Cape Ann to see for themselves. The staid Linnean Society undertook a scientific investigation, and in their published report, admitted it was a marine animal unknown to them, about 100 feet in length with a serpent-like head.

Irma C. Kierman, a professional writer and researcher, spent almost two years compiling her booklet, "The Sea Serpent of Gloucester," from which some of the depositions and descriptions are quoted below. Col. Thomas H. Perkins, one of Boston's leading citizens, wrote:

I went down with Joseph Lee to Gloucester . . . . and found the town alerted. There was hardly anyone who had not seen the serpent. We sat on a promontory on a point that projects into the harbor 50 or 60 feet above the water. I first saw agitation in the water like that following a small vessel. I assumed it was the serpent swimming under water in pursuit of small fish. Almost at once it appeared on the western shore. As he came along, it was easy to see its motion was not like

a common snake, but a caterpillar. Almost 40 feet of the body was visible. I had a very fine spy glass. I saw a single horn nine to 12 inches long on the front part of the head. I left Gloucester fully certain that the reports were correct.

Hard-bitten old salts made equally positive declarations:

I, Solomon Allen, of Gloucester, depose and say that I have seen a strange marine animal that I believe to be a serpent in the harbor of Gloucester. I should judge him to be between 80 and 90 feet in length, apparently having joints from his head to his tail. I was about 150 yards from him when I judged him to be the size of a half-barrel.

There are many other accounts equally convincing. But although scores of boats put out in vain attempts to harpoon, shoot or net the elusive serpent, no corpus delecti was produced. Even whalers from Nantucket, urged to bring their heavy equipment and try their luck, were com-

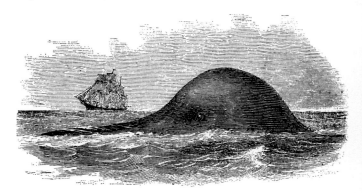

A monster that has been virtually ignored is the great Polypus, variously called colossal cuttle-fish, gigantic squid, Kraken, Krabben, Ankertrold, Soe-horven, or Haf-gufa.

pletely unsuccessful, and what was worse, entirely ignored by the cavorting beast. Finally, after two weeks of excitement the strange visitor vanished as abruptly as it came; it was last seen from a becalmed vessel off Eastern Point, headed out to sea. Robert Bragg, who pointed it out to his shipmates deposed, saying: "He made no noise. He was much swifter than a whale; his motion was up and down. It had a head like a serpent and when it passed astern of the vessel it threw out several feet of tongue, resembling a fisherman's harpoon, several times, perpendicularly, and let it fall again."

The same or similar creature was seen occasionally along the Massachusetts coast for years afterward, the last time off Rockport, in July, 1886. But the only evidence handed down to future generations were the numerous descriptions sworn to by various proper Bostonians, many of them conflicting, which however boil down to this essence; some sort of strange creature resembling a serpent was observed, with humps on its back and smooth skin, that could travel at 15 knots, turn in a U, that moved with an up-and-down caterpillar undulation. The last people who remem-

Are there creatures not yet known to science?

bered seeing it have died, and there is now apparently no one living on Cape Ann, at least among the mariners, who believes in sea serpents. But Mrs. Kierman insisted, "Never before have I encountered any fantastic tale so well documented. I am perfectly sure that something strange and monstrous was seen by many, and equally sure it's none of the things scholars describe."

Mrs. Kierman's attitude is singular in this age of scepticism and science, in which beliefs in the weird and unknown are derided as fuzzy-headed romanticism, or publicity stunts. But this is almost a complete reversal of the outlook in centuries past, when practically everybody swore by sea serpents, and it took an equal amount of moral courage to say you didn't believe in them. Isaiah and Job sang of sea serpents in the Old Testament; Aristotle described "enormous serpents" along the coast of Libya in 340 B.C., and Pliny, speaking of sea serpents in the Ganges, wrote, "They were blue, and so large that they could with the greatest ease seize and drag under water an elephant."

During the Middle Ages, peoples of the northern countries all believed in Krakens and sea serpents, and hardly any natural history was without descriptions and drawings of them. It seems that almost no self-respecting sailor could return to home port without bearing tales of new encounters which learned historians like Olaus Magnus, Archbishop of Upsala, Sweden in 1555 faithfully recorded. The Rev. Hans Egede, founder of the Greenland Missions, wrote in his "Journal of the Missions to Greenland" of his encounter in 1734 with "a very large and frightful sea monster, which raised itself so high out of the water that its head reached above our main-top."

The learned Bishop of Bergen, Norway, Pontoppidan, in his "Natural History of Norway" wrote, "In all my inquiry about these affairs I have hardly spoke with any intelligent person born in the manor of Nordland who was not able to give a pertinent answer, and strong assurances of the existence of this fish" (the sea serpent). He went on to tell how people who questioned its existence were regarded with pity, for "they think it as ridiculous as if the question was put to them whether there be such fish as eel or cod."

Call it the end of the age of ignorance, or the swan song of the romantic age, Pontoppidan was one of the last scientists to speak for the serpent. During the next hundred years a general swing away from such beliefs was spearheaded by the scientists, whose attitude of open-mouthed wonder was gradually replaced by tight-lipped skepticism. No longer would they report and lend support to the accounts of every sailor bearing tales of the weird and unknown; they were enlightened now, and wary. The new attitude about sea serpents, nearly universal today, came to be: this can probably be identified as some creature already known to science.

Nonetheless, serious and convincing, as well as fantastic encounters with supposed serpents continued, and still continue to be reported, and never cease to stir the imaginations of men. But there were these notable differences: any man so deposing was now subjected to ridicule and accusations of superstition or sensation-seeking, and the press, with no scientific standing to uphold, inherited with joy the task of publicizing such accounts.

Nor were the scientists as well informed as they believed. In the 1860s a zoological discovery was confirmed that made natural scientists appear precocious and overconfident. Specimens of giant squid, long regarded as a mythical creature in the same class as the serpent, were brought to zoologists. Aha! said the romantics. You see, next you'll be presented with a sea serpent. At the International Fisheries Exhibition in London ten years later, however, science neatly reversed the advantage gained by serpent believers by publishing a little book called "Sea Monsters Unmasked" by Henry Lee, F.L.S., F.G.S., "sometime naturalist of the

Whalemen have long known of the existence of a species of cuttle-fish which attains a monstrous size. A Nantucket whaler, it is told, was attacked by one in 1834. The tips of its arms reached to the mastheads, and the weight of the cuttle dragged the ship over, so that she lay on her beam-ends and was nearly capsized.

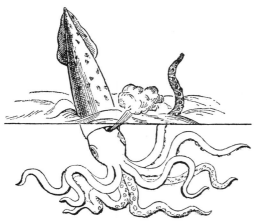

It is not unusual that giant squid have been mistaken for sea serpents. Above is the way a squid might have been viewed from the deck of a vessel. Below is an artist's conception of what the seamen couldn't see.

Aquarist and Curator C. W. Coates

Brighton Aquarium," who logically explained the great majority of reported sea serpents as so many giant squid! People, he maintained, being unaware of the existence of the rare Decapoda, and their peculiar manner of backward jet-propulsion on the surface of the water, quite naturally mistook them for the mythical sea serpent, about which they had preconceptions, and to which the partially visible squid bore close resemblance.

Lee recounted at length nearly all the famous previously unexplained stories of sea serpents, beginning with Isaiah and continuing through to his own time, and proceeded methodically to break them down and suggest the true identities. Most of them, like Egede's monster, he said were squid, a few others, porpoises playing in line. But he had no explanation to offer for the Gloucester sea serpent. Referring to its vertical undulations and "hunched protuberances" described by witnesses, Lee says, "Of this I can offer no zoological explanation." He then begs the question by casting aspersions on the credibility of the witnesses: "The testimony given was apparently sincere, but it was received with mistrust; for, as Mr. Gosse says, 'owing to a habit prevalent in the United States of supposing that there is something of wit in gross exaggeration or hoaxing invention, we do naturally look with a lurking suspicion on American statements when they describe unusual or disputed phenomena.' "

Perhaps Mr. Lee may be partially forgiven this gratu-

itous slap, since near the end of the book he softens a little and says, "I have no inclination to explain away that which others have seen, because I myself have not witnessed it." Furthermore, he admits that there may in fact be giant sea serpents. Drawing a parallel between the small squid, known to fishermen for centuries, and the giant squid, only recently proved to exist, and marine snakes, he concludes, "As marine snakes some feet in length, and having fin-like tails adapted for swimming, abound over an extensive geographical range, and are frequently met with far at sea, I cannot regard it as impossible that some of these may attain to an abnormal and colossal development." However, he points out that true marine snakes move not vertically, but like land snakes, and calls very few the instances where a giant serpent is indicated.

Since Mr. Lee's book no new evidence to support the existence of sea serpents has been produced, while of course a great amount of negative evidence has accumulated, until these days it's well-nigh impossible for serpent stories to run the gauntlet of knowledge. It seems that every time the press comes up with a truly sensational story about an alleged sea serpent being washed up on some beach, the scientists come up with a simple, or at least scientifically well-known identification. Naturally enough, being deprived of such salable copy occasionally brings embittered retorts.

For example, in 1934 at the same time as that best-known of all sea monsters, the Loch Ness Monster, was making reams of copy, and drawing thousands of tourists to Scotland, a strange animal was cast ashore on the coast of

Paleontologist Bobb Schaeffer

Dr. William K. Gregory

Normandy, with a head like a camel, long neck, huge body and flippers. Photographs were published, and even scientists scratched their heads at first and stammered out unconvincing identifications. Dr. William K. Gregory, Curator of Living and Extinct Fishes at the American Museum of Natural History, could not believe there was such an animal, the press reported with evident satisfaction. It had, Dr.Gregory summed up, the long neck of a sea lion, the square head of a manatee, and the body of an exceptionally long dugong.

But a few days later the New York Aquarium suggested an identification that infuriated the romantic instincts of one paper:

(they) now say that the Cherbourg sea monster is only a Mesoplodon. And a Mesoplodon, children, is only "a whale with teeth in the centre of its birdlike beak." How amusing to see everybody getting excited over a whale which looks like a bird and bites.

That is the enormous advantage which science always has in presence of the unusual. It can give it a long Greek name. Are you amazed by this marine creature with six legs, wings, three horns with an eye at the tip of each horn, and deep bass voice in which it recites "Sheridan's Ride?" Nothing can be simpler. It is a polymetisocradosaurus. Every scientist knows that a polymetisocradosaurus is a marine creature with six legs, wings, three horns, three eyes, and a gift for reciting popular poetry.

Finally word came from M. Petit, Assistant Professor of Comparative Anatomy at the Museum of Paris, who had taken portions of the strange animal to his laboratory for analysis, that it was no more than a mutilated basking shark, from which the huge jaws and gill arches had been torn away, leaving a long neck and "camel's head."

Setbacks in the Loch Ness Monster dispute were no less disheartening to those who wanted to believe. Roy Chapman Andrews saw a photograph of the head and neck of the monster and identified it instantly as the fin of a killer whale. As for the long lines of humps reported by hundreds of people, the *N.Y. Times* on Nov. 10, 1950, years after most of the excitement had died down, quoted a spokesman for the British Navy as saying the Loch Ness Monster was nothing more than a string of dummy mines. 320 mines, joined

Open-mouthed wonder was replaced by tight-lipped skepticism

The ocean still holds some big surprises

together eight to a string, were moored to the bottom of the Scottish loch by the minelayer Welbech as an experiment in 1918, and the strings have been popping up one at a time ever since. Quipped the unemotional *Times*, "Sceptics have asserted that the monster is most often seen through a haze of peat smoke that distorts the view, peat moss that has become suspended in Scotch Whisky."

There seems to be but small comfort for sea serpent believers in the present day and age. Public opinion as well as science are closely aligned in their attitude that the great serpent is a myth. And yet the Gloucester serpent and a few others stand out from all the fabrications, mistaken identities and "gross exaggerations." Too many people with scientific knowledge and staunch character testified too seriously to be simply shrugged off by the 20th century. So it is necessary to ask the world of science seriously about the possibilities of an enormous marine reptile still to be discovered. The inquiring stranger found himself in New York conferring with the country's leading ichthyologists and paleontologists.

At the N.Y. Zoological Park were Dr. C. W. Coates, Curator of the Aquarium, and John Teevan, Director of the zoo. It took a little explaining to convince them that this was to be a serious treatment of the subject, and more persuasion before they would permit the use of their names. Scientists it seems, have learned by bitter experience to avoid the sea serpent controversy as much as possible. They've often been quoted out of context by writers anxious to prove that serpents could exist. But once their suspicions were cleared away, all of the scientists interviewed proved to be anything but narrow-minded on the subject. Their opinions were simply deduced from known facts, and there are a great mass of them against the existence of a sea serpent.

Dr. Coates, a good-natured man who seemed amused by the idea, answered for his profession: "The point of view all reputable ichthyologists will take is that sea serpent stories are not made of whole cloth, but are mistaken identity." Turtles, he says, are the only large marine reptiles. It is easy, he said, for those unfamiliar with them to mistake such rare creatures as giant squid, oar fish (also called ribbon fish, up to 20 feet long with crests and thin, snake-like bodies), whale sharks, porpoises or basking sharks playing follow the leader, and even strings of seaweed for sea serpents. When something new to them is washed up on a beach or seen at sea, "people make the wildest surmises, but they really don't see them correctly. They see something peculiar that could easily be explained by an ichthyologist."

But what about life in the ocean depths, which is just beginning to be known to man? John Teevan readily admits that there are many new species of marine life to be discovered. Mr. Teevan, who was Dr. William Beebe's assistant and associate for 25 years, probably knows as much about the deep sea as anybody. And he says, "I never thought there was much possibility of great creatures like serpents in the

In 1830, a sea serpent was reported to have surfaced near Kennebunk, Maine. It was seen by three men who were fishing. Two of the men were so alarmed they pulled quickly for shore. The third, however, a Mr. Gooch, fired at the reptile, but to no avail.

These three drawings of the great Gloucester sea serpent of 1817 were supposedly sketched from life. Artists for top and bottom drawings are unknown, but the middle illustration is by James Prince, Esq., who claimed to have seen the serpent off Nahant, Mass., and Gloucester.

depths, because of the problem of getting food in the dark." Whales, for instance, feed on the surface. "With Dr. Beebe," he continues, "we hauled up thousands of deep sea fishes for five years. The largest creature we caught in our nets was a 54-inch eel."

Dr. Albert E. Parr, Director of the American Museum of Natural History, employed a huge net with a triangular opening 50 feet on each side, to see if there might be larger, more agile creatures that eluded conventional deep sea nets. "In one single haul," he recalls, "we got so many small new species that it took one hundred pages to write them up." Nothing big. He concludes, as Mr. Teevan did, "It is biologically unlikely that something terrifically large could sustain itself in the depths."

The findings of ichthyologists don't prove that sea serpents can't exist. Nor do these scientists say they can't. But paleontologists have really convincing evidence that they don't.

Sea reptiles did, in fact, once roam the seven seas—more than 70,000,000 years ago. It particularly annoys paleontologists, however, when it is suggested that some of these reptiles may have survived to the present. Significantly, many of the accounts of sea serpents are thinly disguised descriptions of enormous plesiosaurs and mosasaurs from the Cretaceous period. Dr. Bobb Schaeffer, Associate Curator of Vertebrate Paleontology at the American Museum, didn't attempt to disguise his impatience with survivalist theories. The rebuttal, simply put by him; "Great thicknesses of rock have been laid down in many parts of the world since the end of the Mesozoic Era. These rocks have been examined for fossils and studied intensively by paleontologists in practically all areas where they occur, and in none of them have they ever found any remains of dinosaurs or sea reptiles of the Mesozoic. . . . All scientists believe there are no dinosaurs left." He couldn't resist taking a crack at the sea serpent myth. In his dry, matter-of-fact voice, amusement in his eyes, he remarked, "For a couple of thousand years people have been seeing sea serpents, but nobody has ever produced one."

It looks very much as if it would be easier, and safer for the reputation, to come out and say you believe in ghosts. There is considerably less evidence to prove there aren't. But if you're an incurable romantic, and it is nice to have some illusions, go right ahead and believe in sea serpents. Remember, even paleontologists can be wrong. They were just as sure that the coelacanths (fish to you) had perished at the end of the Cretaceous Period. And yet only a few years ago, a five-foot specimen was captured off the coast of Africa. So the ocean still holds some rather big surprises.

However, the late Judge Sumner D. York, who was one of those who saw the Gloucester serpent in 1886, gave some good advice: "If any of you or your friends wish to preserve your peace of mind, I would suggest that if you ever see an animal of this character, unless you can produce the animal as evidence, never mention the fact."

Paleontologists and ichthyologists echo this admonition. But wait a minute. An unimpeachable scientific source has come out and admitted a first-hand acquaintance with a sea serpent off the New Jersey coast. Dr. William K. Gregory, now Curator Emeritus of Living and Extinct Fishes at the American Museum of Natural History, who has in the past written wry articles debunking the myth, tells of the time his father's partner, "an ingenious fellow," took a hobby horse, weighted it so it would float upright, made a floating tail, and towed it on a long line behind his boat off a popular resort where bathers were thronging. As he drew abreast of the beach, he suddenly dropped his fishing rod, turned and fired a gun at the beast, which, needless to say, followed after undaunted. Dr. Gregory chuckles as he describes the bathers' hurried exodus from the water, which just goes to show, people will believe what they see.

FATE
OF THE
ROYAL TAR

by Wilbert Snow

C OME TO THE WHARF AND YOU SHALL SEE
The world's most wonderful menagerie—
Elephants from Africa, lions, too,
And the greatest marsupial kangaroo
Fresh from Auster-a-li-a; wart-hogs, ounces,
And double-humped camels with fringy flounces,
Don't miss the snakes and boa-constrictors,
Slaves from the South and Roman lictors
Dressed as they were in Caesar's day;
And a uniformed band from Paraguay,
With the latest tunes of the U.S.A.
For twenty-five cents you can see it all.

Who could resist such a wonderful call?
Not we who were nourished from year to year
On Noah's Ark, why, the Ark was here!
And some who had scruples when Barnum's tent
Was pitched by the depot (of course, they went
To welcome it in at the flick of dawn)
Had no such qualms at this great hulk drawn
Up to the wharf—there was sanction wise
In Holy Writ for this enterprise.
They even expected, so well they knew
The tale, that the monsters, two by two,
Would strut as they did for Noah's crew.

I see her now as a squalid craft
Crowded with animals fore and aft,
With smelly animals pacing their cages,

Editor's Note: *One of the strangest and most grotesque
of Maine coast disasters is the now almost forgotten
burning of the* Royal Tar, *which ran from St. John to
Portland. Although the* Royal Tar *was a steamer rather
than a sailing vessel, her story is included in this
book because it was one of the most unusual disasters
of the period. It happened on October 25, 1836,
between Vinalhaven and Isle au Haut, with a traveling
circus and 93 persons on board, of whom more than
30 lost their lives.*

Venting their wrath in various rages,—
See her all too clear; but then my eyes,
Tinctured with youth's prismatic dyes,
Saw the red plush cabin, a gallery grand,
Like a room in the mansions of the Promised Land.
And the chandelier hanging, a ruby chalice,
Would have graced a hall in the Shushan palace.
The snake-charmer standing, golden haired and tall,
Was Eve in the Garden just before the Fall;
And the blindfolded wizard, adding reams on reams,
Was Joseph in Egypt unravelling dreams.
The strong man was Samson, and the lion-tamer shone
Like Daniel in the dungeon of Babylon.

We stood on the wharf when she sailed away
Out of the harbor kicking up spray,
Leaving a wake of white at her stern
That bubbled toward the dock like butter in a churn.
We heard the animals' dwindling groans,
Saw red-coated negroes rolling the bones;
And the Stars and Stripes on the Autumn air
Turned the Hebrew legends to a Down East fair.
The day being over I heaved a sigh
To know such glories could be born and die.

The boys of Vinalhaven, where the next stop came,
Saw the marvels we had witnessed, and, O grief too hard to name,
Saw the wonder ship of ocean going up in flame.
The story rose and widened, in a fortnight grew
To Biblical proportions. Was there ever such a crew?
The animal trainers set their charges free,
And shoved them off the deck in the ice-cold sea.
The Captain on the poop, ringed round with fire,
Yelled orders in vain, for a thousand times higher
Were the roars and groans of the beasts that rolled
In the fiery furnace of that vessel's hold
A negro risked his life for a pony he fed;
A dog-trainer labored till he singed his head;
The keeper of a llama that had just given birth
To a white baby llama on a handful of earth
Took the helpless thing ashore on the last boat freed,
But the mother beast was lost in that wild stampede.
These three were labelled on their very next show
As Shadrach, Meshach, and Abednego.

And some in that furnace would never feel
The up and down fortunes of another keel;
But those who came through told the weirdest tale
Of that blazing night. Our cheeks went pale
To hear how the animals swam, though spent,
Round that ball of fire, like moths intent
On a lighted lamp; how the herring, too,

162

In the harbor leaped toward the flame and flew
Till they hit the deck; how the snakes' dark skin
Turned iridescent as a minnow's fin;
And the snakes' green eyes on the purple sea
Were emeralds bedded in porphyry.
Of the beasts set free the bulk went down
By the burning ship; but a new renown
Was in wait for the few that swam ashore.
To hear a lordly lion roar
On an island nub was a thing to boast
For boys of this quiet northern coast:
But there stood one the color of sand
In the cove beside him, guarding the land.
A chestnut stallion was seen next day
On a half-tide rock far out in the bay;
And the stories of snakes in the bushes grew
Till the blackberries rotted on the vines. All through
The island ran shudders, but they really seemed slight
Compared to the jungle of our dreams at night.
In one wild nightmare I was chopping up a snake
When a lion swam toward me on the burning lake;
I tried hard to run, but heard the pound, pound
Of forty-'leven elephants beating up the ground,
Tearing through the spruces,—on the leader sat
A little baby llama in a red plush hat.
A tiger just above me in an island spruce
Made a leap for the llama, his jaws dripping juice.
He wriggled on his belly to eat me up
When an orang-outang with a moustache-cup
Full of blood, and a razor, said, 'Come, shave me,
Or pizzle-end up in the bottom of the sea
You go!' In a jiffy he put me on a plank
And shoved me in the water where I shivered and sank
Till my back hit a spike on the Royal Tar's rail
And woke me up; I could still feel the nail
In my back when I woke—some kink, I guess,
But wasn't I happy to be out of that mess!

One year later walking up the hill
Folks of Vinalhaven had a brand new thrill,—
For out on the spot where the Royal Tar lay
Red flames shot up, then faded away.
They looked at one another, 'Did you? And you?
See that flame take shape? Then it must be true.'
They remembered and believed, for many a year
On that autumn night a crowd would appear
Looking out toward Eggemoggin Reach to behold
The Royal Tar rising in a circle of gold.
And some saw a sign that the flood of Noah's warning
Would yield to fire on the Judgment Morning.
But other folks went to bask in the glow
Of the one great horror they would ever know.

They stand poised with iron harpoons aloft. Section 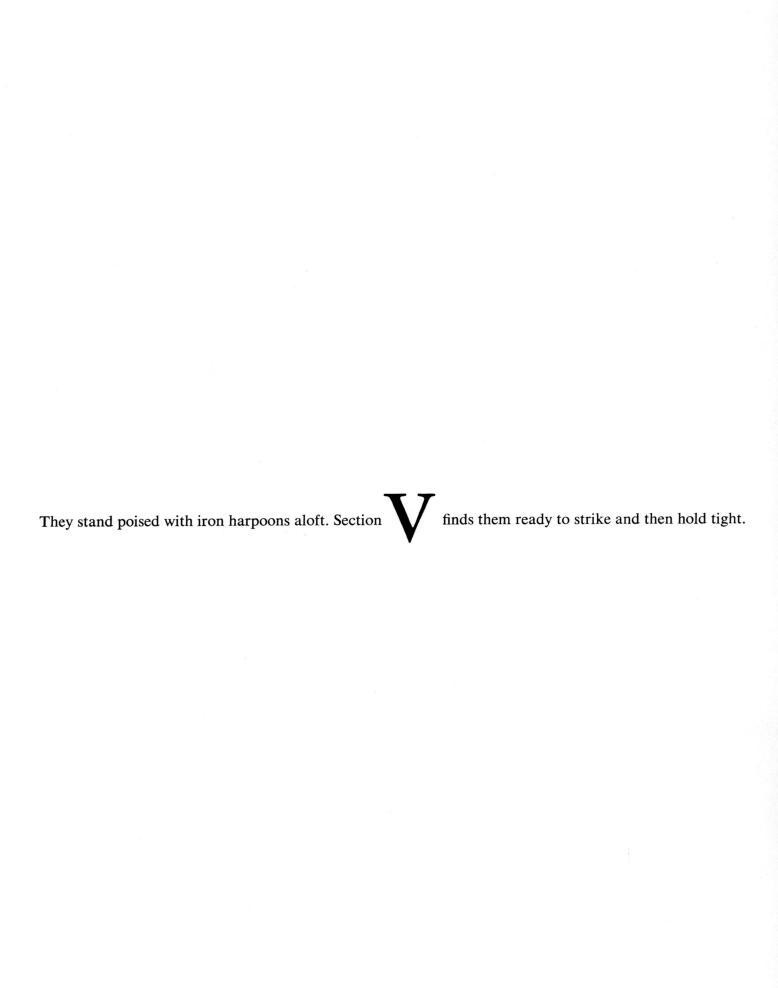 finds them ready to strike and then hold tight.

There was nothing like **Whaling** to test a man's mettle.

THE
STONINGTON
WHALERS

by Robert Sylvester

Shore crowd leaves as a Stonington whaler
departs on a two- to three-year voyage.

They live now only in myth and memory.
But this article recalls the way
it was with the Whalers of Stonington.

MY GREATGRAMMA NANCY SCOFIELD LIVED TO BE ninety-six and she never lost her eyesight or her peculiar, sharp sense of humor. Toward the end she lived a great deal in the past and used to talk much of the early Whalers. She lived to be Stonington's "oldest inhabitant" and then, one day, casually and cheerfully left us to join those other rugged figures of her own day. I have always thought that when she died she took with her the most colorful, humorous and glamorous saga of all the pioneers.

Greatgramma lived her whole life in Stonington, Connecticut, a tiny peninsula near the Rhode Island border which, while it never had the whaling fame of New Bedford, was actually the original home of the Whalers and which, for sheer color and glamor, developed a breed of seamen never surpassed on any seaboard. They live now only in myth and story, but in their day they were a rugged and often hilarious crew. A few hundred strong, they were stubbornly capable enough to twice hold off the British fleets and send them scuttling home in defeat. Also, they had, one and all, a peculiar streak of characteristic orneryness which lifts their story somewhat up from the usual dullness of mere history.

Much of my boyhood was spent in Stonington, and I remember the last of the Whalers—all Cap'ns, of course. In Stonington, the appellation of Captain was used much the same as Colonel was used later in Kentucky—you were lucky to escape it. The petroleum refineries had long since relegated whale oil to the scrapyard of useless and outdated utilities, and the whaling industry, of a consequence, had withered and was dead. But the Whalers never tired of conversationally sailing old voyages and again and again killing the bulls and sperms of another day.

They used to gather daily in front of Jim Stivers' hardware and handler's shop on Water Street. They were all old men—there were only about a dozen left in the early 1900s—and to a man they wore rubber boots and whiskers, the badges of their dead profession. The rubber boots, like the whiskers, were a permanent feature and worn in all temperatures.

The day started with the Whalers when they pulled the Stivers sidewalk bench crossways on the sidewalk. This was done so they could see *all the way down the street*. Such ladies as wished to pass the Stivers place of business could gather their skirts and step out into the gutter. The Whalers, pillars of society that they were, were busy spinning yarns and "charting" the sidewalk with carpenter's chalk. The sidewalk served as any ocean and on a good day would resemble a schoolboy's map of the seven seas.

Much of their conversation—the plain truths as well as the barefaced lies—has stuck in my memory since those days. For the rest of this yarn, you must thank Greatgramma for having such a remarkable memory and for living such a long life. Greatgramma knew them all.

The Stonington Whalers were unique in character and temperament. They had a perverse obstinacy not to be found in any other class of pioneers. As an example, let me cite the case of Cap'n Billings Burch and the mutineers.

Cap'n Burch, a veteran grown rich in the whaling trade, was taking his ship around the Horn. Idling along in the Trades, his crew, without enough work to keep them busy, got to studying up mischief. The inevitable soap-box orator in the fo'c'sle stirred them to a fever pitch, and there were murmurings of mutiny.

These murmurings were reported to Cap'n Burch by his nervous officers. That hard-fisted martinet dismissed such rumblings with a toss of his shaggy head. When the mutiny came, he announced, *he* would take care of it. Nobody would mutiny on *his* ship.

There came the day, of course, when the mutineers advanced upon the bridge, a speech demanding the surrender of the vessel fairly trembling on their lips. While his mates raced frantically for the chart room, there to procure rifles and barricade themselves against siege, Cap'n Burch calmly descended from the bridge and walked out to face his crew.

Before his baleful glance they halted in temporary confusion. It was, I should imagine, a dramatic moment. Then, with unerring judgment, Burch leveled his glance upon the ringleader. He strode slowly to this agitator, grasped him firmly by the pants and the collar, deliberately walked him to the rail and, in dead silence, lifted him high above his head and threw him into the sea.

The mutiny, as Greatgramma used to say, was abandoned.

A Stonington Whaler never, to the day of his death, lost his skill at the handling of any sort of sea craft. The rheumatisms and restraints of age might keep them shackled, for the most part, to the Stivers bench or a comfortable rocker, but they were all capable of throwing off such irksome chains and rising to an emergency as befitted heroes. An example of this was once furnished by Cap'n Joseph E. Smith, one of the more famous of the Stonington Whalers.

Cap'n Joe, having made a fortune from the whale ships, had retired to a life of pleasant ease in a fine old white house on the water's edge. No longer young, he seemed content to spend the last of his years with his memories and his pipe. There came a severe winter, however, when a heavy sea and ice floes turned the sea into a turmoil, and a schooner appeared at the mouth of Long Island Sound flying distress signals.

After desultory long-distance signalling had failed to elicit any satisfactory response, Cap'n Smith got up from his rocker and called for volunteers. As was usually the case, he got them.

With the aging whaler standing erect in the stern of a longboat (steering was a standing-up job accomplished with a long, heavy oar) the crew put their backs to the oars and started out to battle the raging seas and grinding iceblocks of the outer harbor. The twelve men were, as any seaman will tell you, entirely in the hands of the old whaler who stood grimly challenging wind, sea and iceblocks.

Seventeen hours later Smith guided the longboat back to the Stonington wharf with the sick wife and child of the schooner's captain. He had accomplished his perilous journey without even losing his hat, much less a human life.

The Whalers were, indeed, a hardy breed—and just as surely a curiously ornery breed. Schooled in the unquestioning discipline of wooden ships, these men seemed to find themselves at a loss when shipboard discipline didn't work in small-town society. In explanation, I can best quote Greatgramma's story about the retired captain and the mutinous horse.

This strict disciplinarian, whose name I have forgotten, retired with his profits and settled down to enjoy the homespun society of the small seaport. He wished to do things in the fancy manner, as befitted a man of his position, and accordingly bought a sleek horse and a handsome turnout for traveling to and from church and other social functions.

Now, while it would have been impossible to bilk this Cap'n on the sale of a ship or the character of a seaman, a horse was quite a different matter. The trader who sold the captain his horse recognized a sucker when he saw one and, consequently, the Cap'n got a handsome horse for a handsome price. The handsome horse, however, was addicted to the most annoying of equine habits. He balked.

Knowing nothing of all this, the old Viking hitched his rig and set off for church the following Sunday morning. Halfway to church, in Stonington's main thoroughfare, the nag planted four solid feet and refused to heed the call of religion—or any other call. Coaxing, sharp words, sharper words, beatings and cursings all failed to move the stubborn beast. Gradually, but surely, the Cap'n lost his temper. Accustomed to instant discipline, he was likewise accustomed to severe punitive measures.

Accordingly, he dismounted, went home, loaded his revolver, returned to the rig and *shot the mutinous animal dead in the traces.*

Greatgramma used to tell two other stories about this perverse soul which, I think, typify the attitude of the Whalers toward the namby-pamby code of shore society.

Once the old salt had an argument with one of Stonington's dignified lawyers. As he warmed to his subject, he let forth some shipboard adjectives which brought an angry red to the local Blackstone's neck.

"Sir," said this dignitary, "your language is actionable and I warn you against using it."

At this the salt fairly exploded.

"Oh, it is?" he fairly roared. "Well, it's true and I'll put it on paper if you think I don't mean every word of it."

On another occasion, after having found himself completely at odds with the local social code, he was informed that a whale ship had come into port with a live chimpanzee aboard.

"Well," he grunted sourly, "I hope they don't bring it ashore, because if they do, every first family will introduce theirselves within twenty-four hours."

There was one characteristic—or qualification—which voyaging on the whale ships never failed to develop. Any Whaler could tell lies which would bring the blush of frustration to the cheek of the late Baron Munchausen. Greatgramma was most fond, I think, of retelling Jim Stapleton's classic.

"Once we were off Hatteras," Stapleton used to relate, "and we ran right into an electric storm. Boys, I was standing at the foot of the mast, and those lightning bolts were flying around like red-hot cannon balls. Well, sir, one of them hit the mast and came right down at me. Boys, that bolt hit me and ran right down my leg into my boot. Well, sir, what do you think I did? Boys, I pulled off that boot in a hurry, ran over to the side, and poured that liquid fire right into the sea."

There are other famous Stonington lies but Stapleton's has long been acknowledged as the best of its kind.

Stonington, Connecticut, stands today much as it did a century ago. No real estate operators have invaded it with cooperative apartment houses and no car agencies flourish on either of its two thoroughfares. Twenty years ago there were between seven hundred and eight hundred houses in the town and, from all I can see, there have been few additions. For the most part, it is populated with the descendants of the early families who twice withstood the British fleets. In its tiny town square still stand the two clumsy 18-pounders which, enthusiastically manned, crippled five British warships in 1814.

It was from Stonington that Captain Nathaniel B. Palmer, a whaler and sealer of the town, sailed in *The Hero,* a mere shallop of forty-five tons, and discovered the peaks of Antarctica. This was in 1821 and, some days after the discovery, Palmer, a master in his early twenties, met a fleet of Russian fighting ships which had been sent upon an expedition of exploration by the Czar. The admiral of this fleet showed considerable amazement when the "master still in his 'teens" explained what he had already accomplished; and the land was named Palmer Land in his honor, until recently the most southerly known territory on the globe.

Another Stonington Captain, Fanning, discovered the Fanning Islands, in the Pacific, which Great Britain later annexed. Fanning, of course, was on a whaling cruise at the time of the discovery.

It was to Stonington, too, that William Kidd came so often to rest from and ruminate upon piracies but recently committed. Kidd often sailed those waters, and a store of his buried treasure was later found on Gardiner's Island. There is, also, the existing tradition that more of Kidd's loot is concealed on the shore of Lambert's Grove, in Stonington. The far-famed pirate was a frequent visitor to Stonington, and history has it that the town welcomed him in friendly fashion, albeit with its tongue in its old cheek. Kidd never preyed upon a Stonington vessel.

As a matter of fact, there are grounds for belief that the first vessel built by white men in America was built in Stonington. In 1613 Adrian Block and his Dutch crew explored the New England coast in the ship *Tiger,* from Hoorn, Holland. Block Island was named for this adventurer, and Fisher's Island for one of his crew. *Tiger* was burned and

The master was still in his teens . . .

Block built the *Onrust* (*Restless*) in Stonington, one of the first—if not actually the first, which is generally believed—ships to be built by white men in America. The *Onrust* was forty-four feet in length.

Indeed, Stonington in its glory outglamored the pioneer west. Certainly no hotel of the Wild West ever had more atmosphere than Polly Bedine's Steamboat Inn, Stonington's refuge for sea travelers. Polly tended bar with her hair done in two long braids, Indian fashion, and a bowie knife stuck through her sash. Once, when the town sent a marshal to force her to tear down an addition to the Steamboat Inn which jutted out onto the sidewalk, Polly barricaded the hotel, locking the customers in, and bombarded the law from a second story window. Drunks paid their tabs at Polly's and weren't too noisy about it, either.

"Whaling is a Wretched Business"

"It's a wretched business. I suffer more and more every cruise I make. When I was yet a young man, the matter appeared to me in a different light; but as I grow old, my desire to stay at home with my family increases, and it seems like tearing one's heart strings to depart on a cruise with the probability of being gone four long years.

"I have been on five voyages. One of those lasted forty-nine months, during which time, I heard from home but once. In 15 years of my whaling life, I have spent just 17 months at home. I have never been present at a birth or death in my family. I can never expect more than two or three letters from home in the course of a 36- or 48-month cruise. When I now look back upon the life I have lived—I consider how few and brief have been my enjoyments, and how little I have been able to contribute to the happiness of my family."

—From a letter written to a friend
by a whaling captain in 1863

Although, as I've said, Stonington twice withstood the British fleet, none of the houses was really destroyed, even if shot did come bouncing into many a dining room and parlor. In Greatgramma's house, where, of course, her parents lived, a cannon ball is still embedded in the brickwork of the sitting-room fireplace. As long as she lived, Greatgramma painted it with black enamel, each year, and it is one of the many in Stonington which is a sort of tourists' Mecca. Any Stonington lady, whose house framework or ceilings boast a British ball, spends much of her time in the summer months opening the door to strangers who want to see the historical object. No Stonington housewife ever fails to show off this mark of distinction.

It was, perhaps, quite understandable why the Whalers should so fiercely resent the British. Born of ships, lovers of the sea, and in possession of a beloved calling, they doubtless felt a special hatred for a British Navy which had, on occasion, shanghaied crews right from under the noses of outraged masters.

A whaling voyage, in those days, was no mere child's play. A voyage would last several months at the absolute minimum and frequently the ships would be away for three years. The procedure followed was, roughly, this:

The boats were owned and operated by early-day capitalists. The ship owner would sign on a captain and a crew. The officers and crew were guaranteed no salaries, but each was given a "lay" in the profits, if any. The captain, for instance, got the biggest lay—or share—of any. The mates had the next largest and so on down the line, right down to the cabin boy. Once the ship was manned, the owners stocked it with provisions.

All the provisions were packed in the hogsheads and barrels which would later hold the whale oil. If the vessel ran into a school of whales early in the voyage, the whales were immediately rendered into oil and foodstuffs and the provisions packed in the barrels were thrown into the sea—the barrels and hogsheads then utilized to store the oil. The ship, not having to cruise any farther, didn't need the provisions for a long voyage and would return to port with the precious oil, there to stock up again, and again set forth. If luck was bad the ships cruised farther and farther, gradually using up the provisions in the hold.

The Southern Pacific, the Galapagos Islands and the waters off Hawaii were good whaling grounds—the great beasts preferring the edge of cold waters. The motion pictures and adventure novels have told of the actual catching and rendering of whales far more graphically and colorfully than your author intends to do here, but the pastimes and hobbies of the whaling crews while aboard ship have too long been neglected.

The Whalers, possibly because they had time to practice great patience, were really artisans with knife, needle and pen. The Stonington homes even today have objects which might have been fashioned by the early Florentine artisans.

The-ball-in-the-ivory-cage was one of these, a popular hobby with sailors during the dull, becalmed days. The sailor would take a piece of "whale-ivory" and with a knife carve it into a solid cage, leaving one chunk of ivory fast to the floor or roof. The cage completed, this chunk was then cut away and painfully and meticulously carved into a perfect ball. Result: a ball in a solid cage. How did it get in there?

The boat-in-a-bottle is another of these gewgaws, and even today I hear landlubbers explaining to other landlubbers that the bottom of the bottle is cut off and then carefully welded on again. *Tch, tch,* such nonsense.

Greatgramma had in her home a whale's tooth on one side of which had been etched, with needle and ink, a crinoline belle who might have stepped from the pages of Godey's.

On the other side was a very accurate etching of a dancer in a Shanghai honky-tonk. Heaven only knows how many months some stubby-fingered, hard-fisted seaman chewed his tongue and perspired over that piece of craftsmanship.

My Greatgrampa Scofield was himself a Whaler, in his early days, and quite a character always. He turned to the building of small boats, in his later days, and was noted far and wide for his remarkable skill with an adze. Greatgrampa used an adze with all the finesse of a Toscanini handling a baton.

They used to tell the story of Greatgrampa's encounter with an early day kibitzer. Greatgrampa was fashioning a small boat in his shipyard, the *Lottery,* standing in the hull and with long, sure strokes bringing the craft to measurement, when the heckler appeared.

The heckler was full of ideas and criticism. He didn't like this and he didn't like that and he said so. Greatgrampa said nothing but occasionally glanced sidewise at the gentleman who, lest the point of the story be lost, was smoking a clay pipe.

"I just measured him," Greatgrampa used to relate.

When he had measured the fellow to suit his taste, Greatgrampa, without looking up, swung the adze in a side arc and *cut off the critic's pipe an inch from his mouth.*

Greatgrampa was a very reticent soul—he said as little as was humanly possible—but no one could ever accuse him of not having ideas of his own. There was the time, for instance, when he commissioned the itinerant artist to paint his portrait.

"Just make it look like Daniel Webster," Greatgrampa told the hapless Raphael, "but use my features, of course."

Of the other old Whalers whom I personally knew, one performed a feat of seamanship which, I have no doubt, is still remembered by various millionaire yachtsmen of the East as well as by me.

He was Cap'n Ben Chesebrough, descendant of Stonington's first settler and one of the great sailors of all time. When the whaling industry started to fade, Cap'n Ben took a job as captain of John E. Atwood's schooner yacht, *The Gazelle.*

Mr. Atwood, as was his custom, attended the Harvard-Yale boat races on the Thames River, New London. Cap'n Ben sailed his boss right into the thick of the traffic at the finish line. Atwood fretted a bit over this.

"It'll be hard getting out," he grouched.

"It'll be all right," opined Cap'n Ben.

The race over, Chesebrough eyed the masters of the packed craft who were tacking and hauling sail and going through other nerve-wracking maneuvers in the attempt to get their boats out of the jam and headed for the sea. Chesebrough ordered some tackle changed and then took the wheel.

Five minutes later the owners and navigators of the throng in the Thames stood aghast and watched *The Gazelle* calmly sailing out of the Thames *backwards.* There wasn't another navigator there who could tell how it was done, and Cap'n Ben preferred to keep his own navigation secrets.

In this roundabout fashion I end with the story of the good ship *Charles Phelps,* possibly the most famous of the Stonington whaling ships and certainly a true representative of a once great industry.

The *Charles Phelps* was built in 1841–42 by Silas Greenman, in Stonington. She was a fine vessel and made five long voyages from Stonington and several from other ports. During the Civil War, when (as seems to be the case in all wars) the government was offering fantastic prices for ships, she was sold to be sunk at Charleston with the rest of the "old stone fleet."

The government buyers, however, knew a good craft when they saw one, and despite the ravages she had suffered, the *Phelps* went happily (I like to think) to work as a provision ship. After the War this grand old veteran was still too healthy for the drydock cemeteries and the government sold her to New Bedford whalers for a stiff price.

Once again she reared her bow and went out to terrorize the great mammals. Into the Arctic she went on several occasions and into the Antarctic, also. Like Greatgramma, some of her most active years were those of her old age.

In 1893 she was sent to the Chicago World's Fair, there to demonstrate how the whale ships were handled and what they did.

Uniformed attendants showed off on her decks, describing and impersonating the better men of a better day. Then, the Fair concluded, she was left, a tired and sad old lady, to rot in a muddy ditch.

Shame, shame on the heartless agrarians who would let such a gallant veteran end her days in such a manner! It is too bad that these people were not more like Greatgramma.

AFTER THE GREAT WHALE STRUCK

by Marc T. Greene

CAPTAIN GEORGE POLLARD, OUT OF NANTUCKET, August 12, 1819 on the whaler *Essex*, 275 tons, was known as a lucky man. "Greasy luck," as the whalemen said, had been his lot for years. And now on November 20th, midway between the Galapagos Islands and the Marquesas in the South Pacific, when he sighted a big school of whales sporting about upon the surface in ponderous play, he headed his ship directly into it.

A daring man was Captain Pollard, so daring that now the faces of First Mate Eben Chase and Second Mate Joy blanched as they realized what he was at. For to drive into the middle of a school of eighty-foot leviathans was about as reckless as to advance armed with a .22 rifle upon a couple of lions at their kill.

The *Essex* was a small ship, with a crew of less than two-score. The Captain himself took one of the boats while the mates took the other two. After they had been manned nobody was left aboard the ship but the cook-steward and the cabin-boy.

The whales, apprehending danger, moved slowly away and two miles or so lay between the boats and the ship before Captain Pollard was able to get the first harpoon home in the side of a big sperm-whale. By this time the boats were

widely separated. First Mate Chase had come upon the biggest whale of all, more than eighty-five feet in length with an enormous head that might have weighed one hundred tons. Chase rammed a spear in its flank. The line was made fast forward and the crew got ready for what was known as a "Nantucket sleighride," a tow by a maddened whale at breakneck speed.

But to the astonishment and dismay of the *Essex*'s men the whale did not, in this case, follow the usual routine. Instead it turned and dashed directly for the small boat. As it came on, the great head looming over them like a mountain avalanche about to fall, the men of the *Essex* looked at one another "with a wild surmise."

It was a brief look, for the whale, as it tore past, gave a single flip of its tremendous tail, badly damaging the small boat. The men tore off their clothes in order to stuff the holes with them and made all speed toward the *Essex*. To their terror, they saw that the whale was also heading directly for their vessel.

Being much nearer, they gained her decks seconds before the great whale struck, a terrific head-on blow just forward of amidships.

The shock was as if a ship had hit a hidden reef run-

171

ning at a dozen knots before a strong breeze. Most of the men were flung to the deck. The stout whaler shuddered and trembled, then began slowly to list to port. The carpenter rushed below and returned to report to Mate Chase that the vessel was taking water in several places. The awful shock had opened her seams.

There was no hope of saving her, but they might keep her afloat until the other two boats, several miles away, returned. Signals were sent up for them to do so.

There was a spare boat and this was provisioned as much as possible. Compass, charts and navigational books were put aboard. As she was lowered a seaman forward gave a shout of terror.

The whale was again heading for the *Essex*.

It struck well forward and almost completely sheared off the bow and then disappeared into the sea.

Scarcely had the men got into the small boat alongside than the *Essex* turned over, and they were put to it to get clear.

Meanwhile Captain Pollard, himself engaged with a whale and not noticing the return signals, was unaware of what had happened. But one of the sailors, happening to glance in the direction of the *Essex,* cried out, "Where is the ship?"

Captain Pollard, hearing the shout, looked, too, and saw only the empty sea. This was on November 22nd.

What had happened? In Heaven's name, what *could* have happened?

What but the destruction of a ship by a whale. What but the very thing upon which Herman Melville, thirty years later, based his story of "Moby Dick."

Truly the whale had conquered. First Mate Eben Chase rowed down to join his Captain and together they awaited the arrival of the third boat in charge of Matthew Joy.

"Misters," said Captain Pollard. "We are in for it!"

The Chief handed him his sextant and, the time being hard upon noon, he took his sight. The Latitude was about eight, south, some hundreds of miles below the Equator. He did not trouble to work out his Longitude, knowing approximately what it was from the previous day.

The provisions that the Chief Mate had brought were divided among the three boats. Strict rationing would give them all about half a pint of water a day, a morsel of meat and a single ship's biscuit for a period of two months, about the least amount of time they could bank upon before reaching land—though, of course, there always was the possibility of being sighted by another vessel.

The Captain, First and Second Mates and Third Mate Hendricks consulted as to the advisable course to set. There were two possibilities, and only two. The Sandwich Islands (Hawaii) lay some two thousand miles north and by west, but the prevailing trade winds were unfavorable. The alternative was to make for the South American coast, the nearest point of which was, roughly, three thousand miles.

Captain Pollard thought of the epic voyage of Bligh with the refugees of the *Bounty,* well over three thousand miles, in a boat much more crowded than either of his trio. Perhaps if *he* could do it—.

The wind now favoring, they set their small sprit-sails. Captain Pollard fixed his course south, southeast to the Peruvian coast. For a week the boats kept together though the weather was bad and frequent heavy squalls kept them as busy bailing in order to remain afloat as the men of the *Bounty* had been in Bligh's overcrowded longboat. They made shift to raise the bulwarks by nailing along them some

t their ship was gone!

thin boards they had brought from the *Essex*.

The small lockers were insufficient to protect the supplies and the hardbread became waterlogged and almost inedible. Then, during a dark and windy night, the Captain's boat was attacked by some sort of large fish, probably a man-eating shark. With the aid of the other boats he barely kept afloat until daylight. Part of the damage was found to be a hole in the bottom of the hull. It could be repaired only from the outside, and one of the crew, Benjamin Laurence of Nantucket, went beneath the boat and managed to repair the damage.

Greatly to their relief and joy they sighted land on Christmas Day. Chief Mate Eben Chase, who kept a log throughout and was one of the few survivors, wrote that the island was five miles long and half as wide, mountainous and surrounded by reefs, and green with vegetation in Lat. 24° 40′ S., Long. 124° 40′ W.

Whether this was actually Duncie's, or Henderson Island has never been quite clear. But these have frequently been visited in later years by the people of Pitcairn Island, refuge of the mutineers of the *Bounty,* which is about five hundred miles distant. From the peculiar type of hardwood tree growing on Duncie's, the Pitcairners carve the curios they sell to passing liners. The island is almost directly in the path of ships running between New Zealand and the Panama Canal, and a few years ago an unattended light was placed here, probably the most remote light-house in the world. The supply of oil which keeps it burning is renewed every two years by the government cutter from the Fiji Islands. (Duncie's, as well as Pitcairn, is under the authority of the British High Commissioner for the Western Pacific, at Suva.) The three boats of the *Essex* landed and began a frantic search for food and water. Small success attended it.

They discovered only the merest trickle of fresh water and managed to catch but two or three fish in the lagoon, all of which they ate raw. Their lips were so cracked and swollen they could scarcely speak. "Our bodies," recorded Chase, "had wasted almost to skin and bones and we were so weak we had to help one another in the smallest endeavor."

Despairing of finding sufficient sustenance on the island to keep them alive, Captain Pollard decided on December 27th to leave. The decision was hastened by a grim and ominous discovery in a cave in the hillside—the skeletons of six men lying side by side, as if, at the point of death from thirst and starvation, they had lain down together to breathe their last. Near by them lay a piece of board on which had been carved the name "Elizabeth." But if this referred to the ship from which they had come none of the *Essex*'s company had ever heard of it.

Nevertheless, three of the men, Seth Weeks, William Wright and Thomas Clopple, decided to remain on the island. As Captain Pollard tried to reason with them they walked away into the bush until their comrades had embarked. They remained for nearly three months when, nearly at the point of death, they were taken off by the English ship *Surry,* and carried to Valparaiso.

The three boats were overtaken by a heavy gale within a week after leaving the island and blown far south of their course for Easter Island. That destination was now hopeless, so the Captain decided upon Juan Fernandez, the island of Robinson Crusoe, off the Chilean coast. The distance was more than 2,500 miles in a general southeasterly direction. It was a terrible prospect for the half-starved, weakened men, sustained only by water from occasional showers and by such fish and seabirds, eaten raw, as they could catch.

On January 10, 1821, Second Mate Matthew Joy, who had been helpless for several days, died, and the men regarded each other in grim silence, seeing in this a sure portent of what the fate of all, or at best most, would be.

And then, during a night of storm in which they barely kept themselves afloat, the Captain's boat disappeared.

"We were fast wasting away," wrote Chase, "barely able to move about at all and seeming almost to perish each day under the sun's fearful rays. Attempting to stand, we would be overcome by dizziness and fall to the bottom of the boat."

On the 20th, one of the crew, a negro named Richard Peterson, died. That very evening another storm struck them and in the morning the second boat was not in sight. Eben Chase and the half dozen men with him were alone. On the 28th, they realized their rations of 1½ oz. of bread per man per day could last but two more weeks.

Isaac Cole, a Nantucketer, died two days later, the rations now being nearly exhausted, there was only one thing to do—and it was done.

"We separated the limbs from the body," wrote Chase, "and cut the flesh from the bones. Then we opened the body, took out the heart, sewed it up again as best we could—and committed it to the sea."

On the flesh of their shipmate they subsisted for a week

"If you object," the captain said, cocking his revolver, "I'll sh

New Bedford Whaling Museum

174

...ber man who touches you!"

The Essex *being attacked by a whale. From the Benjamin Russell–Caleb Purrington "Panorama of Whaling" painted in 1848.*

and then, when the day (February 17th) had been reached at which they all lay helpless and awaiting death in the bottom of the boat, the brig *India* (Capt. Grozier) of London hove in sight at 7 A.M. Death indeed had come to all save Chase, Benjamin Lawrence, and Thomas Nickerson. A course was set for Valparaiso where they arrived on the 25th and lay long in a hospital there before recovering sufficiently to go home to Nantucket on another whaler.

Meanwhile Captain Pollard's boat had drifted a long way, after separating from Chase's, and its occupants had been too weak to attempt to shape its course. These were, besides the Captain, Georges Ramsdell and Barzilla Ray, two veteran whalers of Nantucket, the cabin-boy, the cook-steward, and three other crewmen. One by one they died and the living, half-crazed and too delirious really to know what they were about, subsisted from them. Then the remaining four men drew lots, and the fateful one fell to the young cabin-boy. "If you object," his Captain said, cocking the revolver he had brought with him, "I'll shoot either man who touches you!"

"As well this way as any other," muttered the poor lad, and Ramsdell was given the weapon to press against the boy's temple. A few days later Barzilla died, and twenty-four hours later, on February 23rd, as Captain Pollard and Ramsdell lay in the bottom of their boat too weak even to raise their heads, the New Bedford whaler *Dauphin,* Captain Zimri Coffin, bore down upon her in Lat. 37° S. off St. Mary's.

In Valparaiso the lives of these two of the nine survivors of the whale-wrecked *Essex* hung in the balance for many weeks, but at last they recovered and long afterward were back in Nantucket. The third of the whaler's boats, that which had parted from the others in the first storm, was never heard of again.

Captain Pollard from this time on seemed to be a doomed man. Soon after his return to Nantucket he secured another command, being, of course, a master mariner in high standing. But bad luck dogged him and he was again wrecked, this time about midway between the Sandwich Islands and Tahiti. Again came a long small boat voyage with the same hardships, though this time the last desperate resort was avoided. The voyage, being favored by the prevailing tradewinds, wound up in Raiatea, one of the Society Group not far from Tahiti. Captain Pollard talked with two missionaries there, and for the first time told of the details of the terrible experience after the wreck of the *Essex.* He had refused to talk of it at all in Nantucket, and it is said that none there ever knew of the desperation to which he and the survivors of his whaler had been reduced.

"No owner will ever trust me again," he told the missionaries. "I am utterly ruined."

And it was so. He returned to Nantucket and the rest of his life was spent as a dock-watchman. All the results of the might of a maddened whale.

THE LEGEND OF A LEGEND:

MELVILLE AND MOBY DICK

by Richard Merrifield

CALL YOURSELF ISHMAEL. IT IS YOUR FATE, LIKE MELville's Ishmael, the narrator in *Moby Dick,* to wander down from the New England hills, ever moving toward the sea, in quest of phantoms haunting still.

Dozens of theories, of course, exist about *Moby Dick,* like fiery segments of whale blubber in a try-works—that set of witch cauldrons for reduction to oil, between foremast and mainmast. But all agree at least on one thing—*Moby Dick* means something, perhaps many involved things, but one all-important thing. At this authorities diverge, no two agreeing.

Is the Whale devil or deity, good or evil, symbol of the subconscious run amuck or of a conscious destructiveness, a figure of blind Force or of Fate, and so on? Is Ahab, that "grand, ungodly, god-like man," is he good, bad, or what? Certainly he is sculptured like a Prometheus—"His whole high, broad form, seemed made of solid bronze, and shaped in an unalterable mould . . ." wrote Melville—and unalterable, too, was his quest of Moby Dick. Like a fallen archangel or fiend possessed he exhorts his demonic crew, passing round the great measure of grog:

Aye, Queequeg, the harpoons lie all twisted and wrenched in him; aye, Daggoo, his spout is a big one, like a whole shock of wheat, and white as a pile of our Nantucket wool after the great annual sheep-shearing; aye, Tashtego, and he fantails like a split jib in a squall. Death and devils! men, it is Moby Dick ye have seen—Moby Dick— Moby Dick!

"Was it not Moby Dick that took off thy leg?" asks Mate Starbuck, and terrible Ahab, well named after King Ahab of Kings II, shouts, "Aye, aye! and I'll chase him around Good Hope, and round the Horn, and round the Norway Maelstrom, and round perdition's flames before I give him up!"

If you come fresh to it, the language is far removed from today's realism; once full of it, you may be spurred along the road of its coming, a course running from the Berkshires to Nantucket and thence to sea.

THE ROOM

The land-voyage leads by train into Pittsfield, Massachusetts and the Berkshires. On a rainy evening, everything may seem to look like *Moby Dick.* You may even fall to reflecting on that same original Ishmael the wanderer—outcast of Genesis, son of Abraham and the Egyptian bondswoman Hagar—the archer Ishmael, ancestor of all the Arabs. Melville you may remember marked a passage in Hawthorne's *Twice Told Tales*—"they call me Ilbrahim," and his use of the idea has become one of the most famous novel-beginnings in all literature.

Hard by now is the Appalachian Trail, serpentining southwest, and your thoughts may go that way to New York where Melville, born in 1819 of a teeming family, grew up in boyhood comfort. His father had been a fancy goods importer who had failed and died. In genteel decay, the family

From the Berkshires to Nantucket and thence to sea

moved to Albany, then Lansingburgh. They were Scotch, English and Dutch, with a mixture of French Huguenot. A grandfather had been in the Boston Tea Party, boarding the Nantucketers *Dartmouth, Beaver* and *Eleanor*. The Dutch side, though, colored their life— for they had lived in Washington Irving's New York, the world of the Gansevoorts (which they were), the Van Rensselaers and Schuylers, with the legended Hudson always in their minds.

Young Herman first taught, then went to sea, first to Liverpool, then on a whaling voyage out of Fairhaven on a vessel called the *Acushnet* round the Horn, up the Chilean and Peruvian coasts and out to the Marquesas. There he jumped ship, lived among natives, signed on another ship, the *Lucy Ann* for Tahiti, then as boat steerer and perhaps harpooner on the *Charles and Henry* for Honolulu, then in the Navy for Boston.

Done with seafaring, he married, had children, and wrote several books, *Typee, Omoo, Mardi,* etc., based on his adventures. Moving to Pittsfield at 32, he wrote *Moby Dick*—in a sudden burst of colossal power. From there on his writing powers declined, as did his short fame, and he lived in such growing obscurity that at his death in 1891 a paper said ". . . even his own generation has long thought him dead, so quiet have been the later years of his life."

"Pittsfield!" sings out the conductor—the word having a sound of "Thar she blows!" Here Melville wrote his Book. You debark. A lad named George, taking you in his taxi to your hotel, will upon inquiry tell you *Moby Dick* had been required reading in his high school. In fact, you are soon to

note, in Pittsfield, a sense of pride about Melville—far inland, with never a whaler on Lakes Onota or Pontoosuc. The city has a Melville Street, a Herman Melville Memorial Room in the Berkshire Athenaeum (public library), and, besides, the very room and house in which he wrote *Moby Dick*. He bought it in 1850, and called it Arrowhead.

"I get a chartered bus to Arrowhead once in a while," says Lawrence Mackey, for 25 years driver of the cheery blue bus marked Chapman's Corner, that starts from East and North Sts. Here in the currents of automobiles the bus drivers and traffic cops banter like sea-captains. "Oliver Wendell Holmes' house is out there, too . . ." You may be the only passenger. Mr. Mackey will slow his bus to point out The Autocrat's place through the trees—and then: "Here is Arrowhead."

It is on the right, on Holmes Rd. A bronze marker rests on the lawn. It is a wide hill farm where spruces, recalling a whaling fleet at anchor, hold level their furled sails toward the broad near fields. Of that house, up in his room, Melville had written:

I have a sort of sea-feeling here in the country, now that the ground is covered with snow. I look out of my window in the morning when I rise as I would out of a port-hole of a ship in the Atlantic. My room seems

On Herman Melville's writing table (above) are his passport (1856–57), a wooden box used on voyages, and a tin cake box in which he kept manuscripts.

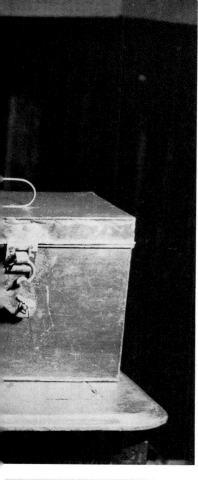

This is the present-day Arrowhead in Pittsfield, Massachusetts—the home of Herman Melville at the time he wrote "Moby Dick."

Herman Melville at age 66. Moving to Pittsfield, Mass., at age 32, he wrote "Moby Dick" in a sudden burst of colossal power.

179

like a ship's cabin; & at nights when I wake up & hear the wind shrieking, I almost fancy there is too much sail on the house, & I had better go on the roof & rig in the chimney.

Carolyn Holden, recently widowed, and her late husband Hale, a William Cullen Bryant descendant, remodeled the old house. "It badly needed attention," she remarks. "What worries me now is the chimney." She leads the way to a room, now paneled with spruce from the land and there is the chimney of the tale "I and My Chimney." It is covered with inscriptions, inside and out, and you readily see why, in the excellent biographer Newton Arvin's words, "the great spinal chimney, with its dark subterranean base, is so expressive a symbol of a man's essential self . . ." (*Melville,* William Sloane Associates, Inc., 1950). Mrs. Holden plans to seek expert advice on the chimney's preservation. Up the stairs is a door with a plaque and in script the tidings that *Moby Dick* had been written in that room.

The Melville furnishings are gone. The room has a flowered paper, a gunstock abutment up one wall, a frail little table at the window—that "port-hole of a ship in the Atlantic." Outside, there are the fields, like a sea. You harken to hear the wind in the "rigging," but hear only the creaking floorboards.

Here, then, is where the story had taken shape at first as a plain narrative. But Melville's mind, in that year, had hurtled into the empyrean. You are reminded of Handel, writing *The Messiah,* and saying, "Methought I saw the great Heaven itself." Melville had been reading Shakespeare, a large-type edition which he scored heavily (it is now at Harvard). At the same time he discovered Hawthorne's *Mosses from an Old Manse.* The two influences surcharged him, and when presently he met Hawthorne he wrote, "A man of deep & noble nature has seized me in this seclusion." It was a brief but dynamic friendship—Melville read Hawthorne "stretched out on that new-mown clover, the hill-side breeze blowing over me thro' the wide barn door," and Hawthorne read Melville, as his wife Sophia tells us, "Mr. Hawthorne has read them all (Melville's books) on the new hay in the barn, which is a delightful place for the perusal of worthy books."

Out back still stands the red barn, where the two novelists had sat smoking and talking metaphysics, during wet weather. Hawthorne had lounged on a carpenter's bench, and joked that he must write a book called *A Week on a Work-Bench in a Barn,* after Thoreau's *A Week on Concord River.*

Now *Moby Dick* began to grow, to proliferate like a gigantic tree. What Melville called "that blackness in Hawthorne" probably heightened the character of Captain Ahab to the magnitude of a tragic hero with the fatal flaw that he sees only Evil in his Whale, and enlarged the White Whale to a universal symbolism, a "grand hooded phantom," a deific force both terrible and sublime, cosmically ugly and beautiful.

The regrowth of the book contained three elements now—the original story; prose-poetic fantasy chapters inspired by Shakespeare; and the chapters about whales and whaling, designed to build one's feeling of the immensity and mythic, legendary quality of the White Whale—legendary because *Moby Dick,* as a story, grew out of two story-sources, one true, one myth.

The first was Owen Chase's true narrative of the *Essex,* a Nantucketer. A great sperm whale rammed and sunk her, and her crew, in open boats in the Pacific for 93 days, had been forced to resort to cannibalism. The *Essex* is still a touchy subject in Nantucket and along Cape Cod. You will hear there the story of the Nantucket lady who asked a survivor's daughter about the vessel: "Miss Mollie," she was told, "here we never mention the *Essex.*"

Melville heard the tale of the *Essex* in the forecastles—it was told from Fairhaven to the Antipodes. He was given a copy of Chase's memoir, and later wrote, "The reading of this wondrous story upon the landless sea, & close to the very latitude of the shipwreck had a surprising effect upon me!" The *Acushnet,* with young Melville aboard, had passed within two miles of the spot where the *Essex* lay, 3,000 fathoms deep.

Only five men finally survived, all becoming sea-captains. One, old Captain George Pollard, had bad luck, became a dock-watchman on Nantucket, and his mind slipped. They say that a reporter once asked Pollard whether he remembered a certain one of the *Essex* crew. Pollard replied, "Remember him! Hell, son, I et him!"

But that is only an island yarn.

The other Melville source was Mocha Dick. Mocha Dick was the legendary rogue whale of all whale-fishery. Year after year he stove boats, killed men and escaped with irons in him, a horrendous monster with a long scar on his huge blunt head. Whalemen would ask when a ship spoke another, "Have ye seen Mocha Dick?"

Mocha Dick had first been sighted off Mocha Island, Chile, an island visited by Sir Francis Drake, and with a piratical history. Off mid-southern Chile, it is gourd-shaped, and it shares in the unearthly feeling of the South American mainland to its immediate east, where there are such place names as Hill of Anguish, Land of Contradictions, Land of the Blue Mirrors, and Little Cones of Infidels. Some distance off lies Robinson Crusoe's island. Tales of witchcraft are part of the lore of these isles. You can, with a play of imagination, suppose Mocha Dick's lair in a craggy cove, awaiting whalers approaching the offshore grounds from the Horn.

Mocha Dick broke into print in the *Knickerbocker Magazine,* May 1839, as J. R. Reynolds related the whale's killings. This would have been about 11 years before Melville wrote *Moby Dick.*

At the Berkshire Athenaeum, in a room two stories high, painted aquamarine, with a white whale on the wall, are Melville relics, pipes, canes, letters, pictures, photos, a little furniture, sea boxes and the like. Well cared for by Librarian Robert G. Newman, the Melville room attracts everyone from scholars to children, and Mr. Newman likes best the large scrawls of the kids in the visitors' register. For kids know all about Moby Dick—there are even comic books about him.

Mr. Newman will show you a Melville desk with secret drawers. "I've found nine," he will gloat, revealing where they are, "and I'm still prospecting for more. This box has bloodstains, but I don't guarantee they're whale's blood." Nearby is Mrs. Melville's desk. The couple had known rough passages in the course of their married life, but toward the end both spoke with devotion of the other. Far within the desk are the words, seemingly burned in, "To know all is to forgive all."

Now with your visit to Pittsfield over, you recall how it was that Melville (and his Ishmael) "stuffed a shirt or two into my old carpetbag, tucked it under my arm, and started for Cape Horn and the Pacific. Quitting the good city of old Manhatto I duly arrived in New Bedford. It was on a Saturday night in December . . ."

THE MASTHEAD PULPIT

In New Bedford, the air thickens. Moby Dick characters are everywhere. There is a wildness in the atmosphere. If a car bears upon you, and misses, the driver salutes you with a mad grin. Girls look exotic and bold; in the black eyes of seamen is a curious shrewdness. A great bell booms. A piano clatters in a castled armory. Down sloping streets flows the Acushnet River—and, in your mind's eye, whalers, mast after mast. On the other shore, storied Fairhaven. Down this street, or that, had walked good Ishmael to the Spouter Inn.

"There never was a Spouter Inn," says an attendant at the Whaling Museum on Johnny Cake Hill. "But across the way is the Seamen's Bethel, the same that Melville described as the Whalemen's Chapel. You remember? Where Father Mapple preached about Jonah from the masthead pulpit?"

Who could forget the old hell-roaring seafaring preacher, Father Mapple? By all means you will see the Seamen's Bethel. Meanwhile, you may visit the Whaling Museum, board the model whaler, sister ship of the *Acushnet,* note how the attendants, some of them whaling men, call it "Curshnit," and peer at old whaling logs. Had Melville known that this sister ship, the *Lagoda,* had carried a captain named Edmund Maxfield, who like Ahab was injured by a whale, never to recover fully? Was Captain Maxfield the original of Ahab? It is an interesting thought—but by this time every harpoon, whaleline, dart and marlin spike in the museum is dancing before your eyes. And so is every musty log, beginning each day with "Commences with a fair breeze" and signing off "So ends these 24 hours"—every page teasing you to track down Ahabs and Ishmaels, Queequegs, Starbucks and Peter Coffins, Captain Pelegs, Bildads, Daggoos, Tashtegos and Little Pips, and mad Elijahs and Fedallahs and all the unholy and fascinating dramatis personae of *Moby Dick.*

Across the street you run into Father Mapple—or, that is to say, into the Rev. Charles S. Thurber, born May 22, 1864, and for 45 years Chaplain of the Seamen's Bethel.

Father Mapple in *Moby Dick* (his original was a Rev. Enoch Mudge) is a sailor, harpooner, and man of God. He preaches from a masthead pulpit, which has a prow and a "Holy Bible resting on a projecting piece of scrollwork, fashioned after a ship's fiddle-headed beak." A magnificent character, one of the best in American writing—and here stands a real present-day Father Mapple before you, the very image of the original. Chaplain Thurber, though in his 90s, is a short, bright-eyed, amazingly spry man. He stands on the porch of his Mariners' Home, over which he presides, and talks like a master on a quarter-deck. Beside the door is a marker: "Lat. 41° 38' 08" N—Long. 70° 55' 26" W."

Rev. Thurber has been on the old three-masters, then was engineer when steam came in, in coastwise and merchant marine. After 14 years of preaching, he went to sea again. The Seamen's Bethel needed a preacher. Down in his engine-room, says Rev. Thurber, "I had an apparition. It said, 'Charlie, don't let another day go by without asking for that pulpit!'" There were 62 candidates. He won. Few knew the sea as does Charlie Thurber; none knows his Lord more utterly.

All this while you are talking to him Chaplain Thurber, 90 odd or not, is up and down his porch quarter-deck, acting with zest and agility.

"Now about my masthead pulpit," he says. "One was put up in 1927, like the one in *Moby Dick* times. Yes, I'd climb her, haul up my ladder and preach on Jonah—many a time. Man named Henry J. Winslow had come in one day as I was calling 'Thar blows, sir, two points off the starboard bow!'—part of my sermon that day—and he up and gave the masthead pulpit in memory of his father and grandfather, both whalers. Aye, I loved that pulpit as Father Mapple did, and the real Father Mapple before him!"

The church board, however, voted the demolition of the Melvillean pulpit. It lies today in Peirce and Kilburn's Shipyard rigging loft, not of course Melville's original one but the fine replica made for Chaplain Thurber.

A MUSICAL QUEEQUEG

The motor ferry from New Bedford for Nantucket is the *Martha's Vineyard,* but she surely is a far cry from Melville's vessel which was listed in the New Bedford *Daily Mercury,* Jan. 4, 1841:

Sailed—Ships Accushnet, (new of Fairhaven),
Pease, Pacific Ocean; George (og do), Swift, do.

In any event, out through these same waters of Buzzards Bay had fared young Melville, 21, five feet nine and a half, of dark complexion and brown hair.

On board this and other ferry trips is a genial Queequeg (who would relish being so described) a composer, Saul Rosenberg, late of the Army and the Pacific (Saipan). A New Yorker, he has an M.A. in Musicology from Columbia.

"I've read Moby Dick many times," he muses in his strolls on the ferry deck. "I'd give anything to write music for it, a cantata or modern opera, but I know my limitations. Bernard Herrmann did it, you know, and John Barbirolli conducted it in April 1940 at the N.Y. Philharmonic—a dramatic cantata." He stands looking toward Vineyard Sound, where Melville (and Ishmael and Queequeg) had sailed toward the sea. He watches the pitching of a yawl off the Vineyard's tan-tinted shoreline, and, after a silence, concludes: "Melville's language is so complete in itself it really doesn't need anything more . . ."

THE WHALE

Leaving Woods Hole the ferry passes a buoy with a nasal note, and its companion marker which bears a light with an exotic cross. You may see a child named Jay feeding crusts to the gulls, calling upward with unconscious poetic language, "Here, sea-birds . . ." You pass Cross-Rip Lightship. And so to Nantucket, round Brant Point Light, cliffs to starboard, beach to port and Great Point Light hard aport. Five wharves point to sea, and an eerie yell arises from the *Vineyard Haven*'s engineroom.

She docks. From this same wharf had sailed the *Pequod,* in the story.

> What wonder, then, that these Nantucketers, born on a beach, should take to the sea for a livelihood! (wrote Melville in *Moby Dick*). They first caught crabs and quohogs in the sand; grown bolder, they waded out with nets for mackerel; more experienced, they pushed off in boats and captured cod; and at last, launching a navy of great ships on the sea, explored this watery world. The Nantucketer, he alone resides and riots on the sea; to and fro ploughing it as his own special plantation. *There* is his home. . . .

Once ashore there is Firechief Archibald Cartwright to tell you your way about, speak to you about Melville: "No use for him!" he will bark. "Too much made of him! Hard to read! Facts all wrong!" Facts, eh? Then perhaps, Chief Cartwright has had whaling experience? Has he! "Sailed on the *Sunbeam* out of New Bedford, South Atlantic fishery—sperm, too!" He plunges into his firehouse, a busy man . . . too busy to talk more.

That puts you in a way to visit the Whaling Museum. Owen Chase and *Essex* mementoes are here but Nantucket has no Chase descendants. Helen Winslow, the librarian, says everyone asks about *Moby Dick*. Wallace Long of the museum says he prefers Frank T. Bullen's *The Cruise of the Cachalot.* Cachalot is French for sperm whale, isn't it? Whereupon Mr. Long, a collector of whaling pictures, strokes his Stevensonian moustache and gravely speaks to you in that language, on whales.

Outdoors again, Nantucket is a town of square gray Quaker houses and cobblestoned streets. If you meet Carol Heffernan of New York, an interior decorator, leaning like Ava Gardner against her bike, she will tell you she has not read *Moby Dick* but will. And Bertha Eckert, en route to pinch-hit at the whaling museum library, may tell you of the eager interest of children in *Moby Dick* and of the library's special juvenile editions. Nantucket, you also learn, held a Melville Centennial in 1951, and a play, *Captain Ahab,* by

This old photograph of Nantucket shows the wharf from which the Pequod *sailed.*

Tyrus Hillway of The Melville Society, New London, was put on by the Barn Stages.

In 1852, about a year after finishing *Moby Dick*, Melville, you remember, had paced these streets. But the island had taken no note of him. Perhaps more exciting, just then, were notices reading, "Madame Manchester, the Independent Clairvoyant." She initiated people into the mysteries of magnetism. When in the magnetic state, Madame "could look into the human system."

But through poet Eleanor Dixon Glidden you may have arranged to meet Mrs. Grace Brown Gardner. Mrs. Gardner's grandfather was master of the *Columbus* on a four-year Pacific voyage—and here you touch fingertips with Melville. William Bunker Gardner was the master, and you can see his Log. His granddaughter now turns the

yellowed pages to find the entry of the gam with the *Acushnet,* one of the most exciting recent Melville "finds." You espy a whale description, but Mrs. Gardner reminds you like the true Nantucketer she is, "That's just the flukes," and then:

1841. Friday Nov. 19. Coms with strong breezes & clear weather at 4 p.m. saw a ship heading in latter the boats started again. Is the Ship Acushnet came to Anchor 10 months out 500 bbls.

"My grandfather finally sailed on the Bark *Hannah Thurston,*" continues Mrs. Gardner. "He died of yellow fever off Rio de Janeiro. That was 1856. He was 44. Buried at sea." With wry humor she adds: "They say the fever resulted from eating peanuts."

Of such and more is Nantucket, full of whaling memories and Melville and *Moby Dick.* Along one wharf, for example, is a quarterboard, *Charles & Henry,* on a house. An elderly gentleman suffering from gout answers the ring from the door.

"Yes, I'm the grandson of Charles G. and Henry Coffin," replies this man, George Carlisle. "That's not the original quarterboard, but it belongs. This is the old *Essex* wharf—she sailed from here. Always felt they were pretty rough on their shipmates." Mr. Carlisle can remember his grandfather and whalers at New Bedford. Himself, he had once seen a cow whale and calf from a plane over Oahu, and he identified the whale in the N.Y. Museum of Natural History as a sulphur-bottom. "But I don't see why people ask me," insists Mr. Carlisle. "It's all in the books." Yet he seems pleased that anyone has spotted the quarterboard of the whaler Melville had shipped on from Tahiti to Honolulu, "that rare old ship" as Melville called it, with its crew of "good-fellows all." She arrived 28 months out, 500 bbls. sperm. "Not many," concludes George Carlisle, "recognize that quarterboard."

Then a neighbor, lean and tanned, a Mr. William E. Chamberlain, may come by to help with the Carlisle grass.

"Have you ever heard" he queries, "of the whale that actually came to Nantucket? It died on one of the beaches, and people from here and Siasconset and Quidnet and Wauwinet and all over the island came to see it. They came in cars, afoot, on bicycles, and even horseback, and stood looking, even from housetops and widows' walks, crowds and crowds of Nantucketers. It was their whale. When I saw that whale of ours I understood Melville's description for the first time—that big old tail lashing and then coming down kerplunk. If you were under that it would be like a 10-story building falling on you. Well, a man carved his initials on the whale's side when it was dead, and the Selectmen had a special meeting. They decided the initials made it his. There was a lot of fun about it, but finally the old whale was buried."

Buried? An end to the story . . . and *Moby Dick* . . . this whale? With these fictional creations of man's imagination, Nature itself seems at times to conspire . . . to make them live forever. The thunder still rolls Rip Van Winkle's bowling balls in the hills of the Catskills, the tides still carry the echoes of King Arthur's knights off the coasts of Wales, the hurricanes of 1954 came to take away this "buried" *Moby Dick* to the sea again . . . refurbishing once more our endless store of life beyond ourselves—the nearest thing we know on earth today to immortality. Of this life, surely, *Moby Dick* is and always will be part and parcel—inscrutable, mysterious, symbolic, gigantic, diabolic, alive . . . yea, even endless.

183

THE REAL MOBY DICK?

by Chester Howland

C. S. Howland

M Y FATHER, CAPTAIN GEORGE L. HOWLAND, WAS Master of the bark *Canton* and my mother came from Australia as a bride aboard the ship to the great whaling port of New Bedford. I have known many Captains, whalemen and ships. Among them was the bark *Platina* whose master was Thomas McKenzie and listed whalemen Walter Thompson and Amos Smalley as two of her crew. Bow oarsman Walt Thompson and Gay Head Indian Smalley, harpooner, sailed as crewmen in Chief Mate West's whaleboat.

I recall meeting both of these men on different occasions to have them tell me specifically the story of the White Bull Sperm Whale that made the *Platina* famous.

Here was a real Moby Dick, a Captain Ahab, a Tashtego and an Ishmael. If you will recall, Melville named Ahab as Master of the *Pequod,* Tashtego as Mate Stubb's Gay Head Indian harpooner and Ishmael as bow oarsman in the mate's boat.

The original tale of the bark *Platina*'s catch as Thompson and Smalley told it to me was first published twenty-five years ago in the Sunday Edition of the Milwaukee *Journal.*

The story:

On the island of Martha's Vineyard, which lies off the coast of Massachusetts, there lives an old harpooner, Amos Smalley, who nearly a half century ago sent his iron straight into the "life" of a genuine "Moby Dick." He holds this unique position as the only man in history to ever "strike" an all-white cachalot.

It was in 1902 and Smalley was harpooner on the bark *Platina,* out of New Bedford.

The *Platina,* owned by the J. and W. R. Wing Company, was a typical whaler of about two hundred tons, blunt and sturdy in her lines and square at both bow and stern. Despite her lack of graceful proportions she was good to look upon, especially when her sails were set, and was a startling spectacle during the midnight trying-out of oil, when yellow flames leaped from the try-pot chimneys and the men flitted about the decks in a ghastly illumination that made them look like phantoms.

The vessel, well-fitted, sailed from New Bedford July 16, 1901, under the command of Captain Thomas McKenzie and was last reported from Fayal September 10, having taken two hundred barrels of sperm oil. The spring months of 1902 she spent in the South Atlantic and after recruiting at Barbados, north of the Venezuelan coast, came into the Western Grounds in July.

The large crew of a whaleship was not assigned to its several watches and boats until the ship was well out to sea. It was then that the captain would call the entire ship's company to the after part of the vessel to give the men general instructions and divide the crew. The first, second, and third officers headed the boats in which were four oarsmen and a harpooner. On this the most eventful of the *Platina*'s voyages, Amos Smalley was selected to row in the bow of the chief mate's boat as his harpooner.

Smalley is a Gay Head Indian, born in 1877. When he

Sixty-six years ago Amos Smalley, a Gay Head Indian, sunk his harpoon into an all-white sperm whale.

was fifteen years old he left his Island home to go to sea on the New Bedford whaling schooner, *Pearl Nelson*, sailing for a 1/150th lay on a sperm-whaling voyage to the North Atlantic Ocean. Four years later the vessel returned and the young whaleman, now nineteen years old, received $14 as his share of the cruise. In two years he shipped again, this time aboard the *Platina*.

The day the modern "Moby Dick" was sighted from the *Platina,* conditions were even more listless than usual for the vessel had been a number of days without sighting whales and was barely pushing along with all sails set to catch whatever of breeze she could in almost a dead calm.

About 5 o'clock Walter Thompson, a lad rowing an oar in the chief mate's boat, raised a spout about a mile from the ship. It was the spout of a sperm whale, low, bushy and blowing slightly forward. A spirited cry from aloft startled the crew: "Thar she blows—blows—blows, sir!"

When whales were sighted it was the usual procedure that the captain should check the sighting and verify the position of the "blowing." So Captain McKenzie went aloft and after a casual glance declared, "That's no whale, boy. That's a grampus."

The lookout replied instantly, "That is a sperm whale's spout, sir."

Captain McKenzie, looking out over the sea toward the "snowhill," called down below hailing the chief mate. "Mr. West, come up here. What do you make this spout out to be? The boy says it is a sperm whale but the body is white as snow. It must be a grampus. I never heard of a white whale."

Despite the captain the chief mate stood with Thompson in his decision. "No, sir, cap'n, it's a sperm whale."

Three boats were lowered and at once put up their sails with six men in each boat sitting along the weather gunwales paddling to hurry the boat on. In the bow of the chief mate's boat was Amos Smalley, the Gay Head harpooner, whose task it was to first strike the whale. Walter Thompson, the lad who sighted the whale, sat just behind Smalley in the bow oarsman's position. It will be recalled he had the position of Ishmael in Moby Dick, the sole survivor of that tragic encounter with Melville's great white whale.

During the time taken from the masthead sighting to the lowering of the boats, the whale had sounded. He was a mile away but long before the chief mate's boat was near him the men could see his enormous shining white body far down in the sea.

The men paddled more vigorously, closing the distance between them and the beast and as the boat veered just outside the tip of the heavy flukes into a proper position alongside the quarry the mate, Mr. West, sang out: "Ready, Smalley. Stand up there and give it to him—solid!"

In telling the story Smalley admits that he was nervous when he shipped his oar and took his harpoon. There was something fearful—almost supernatural—about a whale, all white.

The modern harpoon, with explosive bomb attached, flew from the none-too-steady grasp of Smalley and it struck

Pardon B. Gifford

The whaling bark Platina *of New Bedford on which Smalley sailed as one of the harpooners in 1901.*

fairly. The whale went down and the second mate's boats stood in position ready to "go on" as soon as the whale came to the surface again.

Presently the great white whale was seen coming up through a deep column of water and sixty feet of his body was thrown out of the sea; but the anticipation of a wild chase was turned to disappointment, for the terrific explosion of the bomb so well darted had ruptured the beast's great heart and lungs and the spotless white skin was made gory by a thick stream of clotted blood which poured out of the whale's nostril. Mr. West shot another bomb into the dying whale and "Moby Dick" rolled "fin out," a dead whale lying in a crimson ocean.

The *Platina* came into New Bedford September 11, 1903, having made history, and when she sailed again Smalley sailed with her and then retired from the sea with an accomplishment to his credit that no other harpooner can boast—the harpooning of an all-white sperm whale.

MEMENTOS OF LOVE FROM A SPERM WHALE'S JAW

by Eleanor Early

WHEN JACQUELINE KENNEDY BOUGHT A WHALE'S etched tooth for the President's collection of scrimshaw—that curious hobby of Yankee whalers—antique dealers upped their prices on scrimshaw. And women along the Yankee seacoast began looking up-attic for jagging wheels and busks—scrimshandering pieces that went out of fashion along with whales' teeth, about the time of the Civil War.

Although several New England museums have important collections of old scrimshaw (sometimes called the only art form indigenous to America), it is a pretty specialized thing. And etched whale bone was nothing, until recently, to get excited about. Just a sort of coast-town curio.

The President, a sea-loving man, bought his first scrimshaw (circa 1830) in a Cape Cod antique shop. Mrs. Kennedy bought hers, a sperm whale's tooth (9½ inches long and 4½ inches in diameter) from Milton Delano of New Bedford, Massachusetts who spent 160 hours etching the Presidential seal into the ivory and another 80 hours polishing it.

Modern scrimshaw—as, for example, the Delano piece—commissioned by the First Lady and added to the Presidential collection, has a value all its own. But it is the old-time stuff that enchants the collectors. And hardly anybody, except the experts, knows the fascinating story of this almost forgotten art of New England whalers.

Scrimshaw has been defined as an art practiced by Yankee whalers, practiced by virtually all of them, and practiced only on shipboard. Ships stayed out, chasing and killing whales, until they got a full cargo. And sometimes it took four years.

Crews were made up mostly of young men and boys. When in actual pursuit of whales, life aboard a whaler was dangerous and exciting. But most of the time there were neither whales nor wind. Then the ships floated in deadly calms, uneventfully, on silent seas and life was a complete and terrible bore.

Old logs tell the story: "We ain't whaling. We are sailing." For weeks, sometimes for months, it was like that. "Ugly faces aft today. The men have nothing to do but look at each other."

To kill the empty days, the boys made gifts for the folks at home. Gifts of whale bone, etched and carved and highly polished. Everybody—steerers, harpooners, mates, even the captains—made them. And they called them *scrimshaw*.

It is probable that the word was derived from the Dutch: *skrimshander,* meaning a lazy fellow who "just lounged around." Whaling when it was not dreadful, bloody business was pretty much "just lounging around," and the word seems appropriate.

Whalers seldom got mail. A boy from Nantucket, 3,000 miles from home, wrote in his diary:

> O Hanna P Ingalls if you and all the rest of you new how I longed to se you I think you wood rite a line to a Poor Lonsum Chap.

Scrimshaw was an outlet for lovesickness, and many lonely lads made busks for the girls they longed to see once again.

A busk was a piece of whale bone designed to thrust into an open slit in the front center of a woman's corset. A torturous thing about twelve inches long and two inches wide. Relentlessly thick and sturdy. The boys decorated the busks with hearts and flowers and, sometimes—if there was room—with a ship or whale, and etched on them such tender sentiments as these:

> This bone once in a sperm whale's jaw did rest
> 'Tis now intended for a woman's brest
> This My Love I do intend
> For you to wear and not to lend.

> Accept Dear Girl this busk from me
> Carved by my Humble Hand
> I took it from a Sperm Whale's Jaw
> One Thousand Miles from Land.

> In many a gale
> Has been the whale
> In which this bone did rest
> His time is past
> His bone at last
> Must now support thy brest.

If a girl wore a sailor's busk, it was said that she could

"Accept dear girl this busk from me, carved by my humble hand."

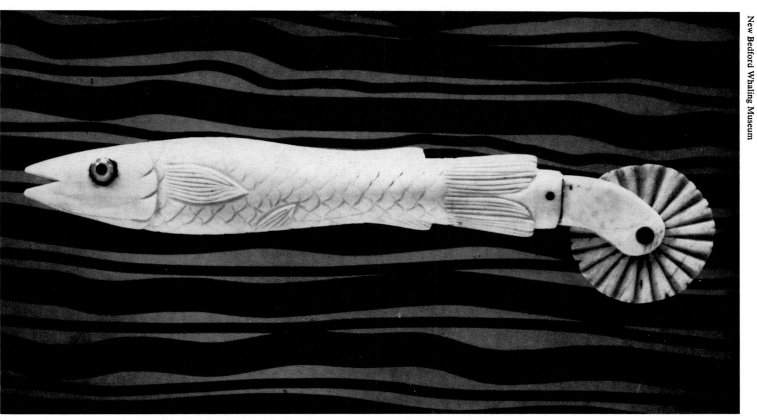

One of the most popular pieces of scrimshaw with the ladies of the day was the jagging wheel, used for trimming pastry.

If a girl wore a sailor's busk, she could not be untrue to him

Scrimshaw was useful as well as ornamental. These knickknacks and trinkets were rarely made for commercial use.

*Above. A letter-opener was one of many functional
items. The piece on the right, like many, was merely
an outlet for lovesickness; lonely lads
long away from home made scrimshaw portraits
of the girls who waited three and four years
to see them again.*

not be untrue to him. Maybe so . . . with that thing prodding
her, she certainly could not *forget* him.

Busks were made from the lower jaw bone of the sperm
whale, which sailors called the "pan bone" because of its
shape. From pan bones the whalers carved and etched
combs, brooches, earrings and necklaces, sets of chess and
checkers, and many other things—including lanterns!

After Moby Dick bit off Captain Ahab's leg, the captain had a leg made of pan bone.

Whalers are thought to have made, all together, about
sixty different articles, of which the most popular were swifts
(for winding yarn for knitting and spinning wheels) and
jagging wheels (for crimping pie crust). Every whaler's
mother, wife or sweetheart expected a jagging wheel. There
were also bodkins, ink stands, rolling pins with bone handles, and—for the men-folks—canes, the head of which
represented a girl's knee, the stick her leg.

But it was baleen—slabs of discolored bone found only
in the mouths of right and bowhead whales—that the whalers liked best to work with. Right and bowhead whales have
no teeth and swim with their mouths open, perpetually feed-

The only surviving art of the whalers

ing. And the baleen hangs down like stalactites, black and brown, in long thin strips from the roofs of their mouths, serving as gigantic sieves to strain their food.

Baleen was commercially used for buggy whips, umbrella ribs and ordinary corset bones. It was fairly pliable and could be steamed and bent into shape. The whalers made it into round trinket boxes for their mothers and girl friends, and "ditty boxes" to hold their own sewing implements. They also used it as a dark inlay on articles made of pan bone.

From the South Seas, sailors brought home parrots and many bright, tropical birds. And some of the boys made cages of whale bone for the birds. The cages were, perhaps, the largest pieces of scrimshaw made, and are now among the rarest.

Every whaler's family had a whale's tooth or two, usually a pair of them, on parlor table, mantel or what-not. And a number of the teeth are still around.

Frederick Myrick, a Nantucket boy who sailed on the *Susan* out of Nantucket, etched and signed the first teeth (1828) of which there is any record. He was a good artist and decorated the teeth with whaling scenes and mottoes:

> Success to sailors' wives
> And greasy luck to whalers
>
> Death to the living
> Long life to their killers

He did an etching on one of the teeth of the *Susan* off the coast of Japan, and on another one, the *Susan* killing and boiling sperm whales, as well as a considerable number of similar ones, all dated and bearing the name of the ship and its master, and his own signature. He gave them to friends on his island home.

The *Susan,* with all aboard, was subsequently lost in the Arctic, and it is good to know that young Myrick's friends cherished the scrimshaw he had given them. More than a century later, Everett Crosby of Nantucket acquired seven of the teeth, and wrote a delightful monograph called "Susan's Teeth."

It is only the sperm whale—the most savage fighter of them all—that has teeth. A double row in the lower jaw, from thirty to forty of them, each from five to ten inches long, thick at the bone and tapering off toward the end.

Yankee whalers chased sperm whales all around the world, because sperm whale oil was better than oil obtained from less fearsome whales. And also because sperm whales have, sometimes, a substance in their intestines called ambergris, which is formed if they get ulcers, and which perfumers use as a fixative. Since the crew shared in profits of a voyage, sperm whales were more profitable to take than other whales. And their hideous teeth were sort of velvet.

The boys loved those teeth. To get them, they often towed the jaw bone behind the ship for about a month. Then hauled it on board and left it on deck in the sun for a while, after which the teeth just naturally fell out, and were placed in a barrel of brine.

But sometimes the boys were in a hurry. They might have run out of scrimshander material and were eager for something to work on. So they pulled out the teeth with tackles, or dug them out with spades and saws. The jaw bone they sawed into pieces and distributed among the crew.

The whales' teeth were much softer when the boys handled them than they are now, and easier to work on. (Ivory becomes hard and brittle with age.) But to make the teeth softer still, scrimshaw artists dipped them in hot water, which softened the surface as they worked on it.

In their natural state, whales' teeth are rough, ribbed and discolored. The boys filed them smooth, sandpapered them and finally polished them with ashes from under the blubber try-pot. Highly polished bits were frequently used for inlays.

Some of the boys had little kits of tools that they made on shipboard, old chisels, filed-down nails and pointed bits of steel. For etching, they used sharpened sail needles. But for the most part they used what Melville called "that almost omnipotent tool of the sailor"—their jackknives.

Into the delicate furrows of etched bone they rubbed tobacco juice, which gave a lovely, warm sepia color. They also used ink, and juices from berries and lichen that they found on tropical islands.

Most of their drawings of ships and whales and palms on coral isles were original. But they were copyists too and enchanted, it seems, with the girls in *Godey's Lady's Book* and *Harper's Weekly*. A fashion picture from one of these magazines was pasted on a whale's tooth and transferred to the ivory, patiently and painstakingly, with pin pricks. Lines were then drawn between the pricks and the colors rubbed in.

One treasured old tooth depicts two girls, on one side, a voluptuous brown lass in a sarong, leaning against a palm tree, on the other, a pale Quaker girl in bustle and bonnet. The legend reads:

> To our Wives and Sweethearts
> May They Never Meet.

There were many teeth with similar designs and mottoes. A whaler's wife might not find them exactly amusing. But in the surviving art of the whalers there is nothing that is actually coarse or offensive. And there are inscriptions that are touching, among them this plea of a prayerful boy:

> O Lord look down upon us here
> And touch our hearts with humble fear
> From our vain desires O set us free
> And give us peace & unity.

*We know not who "George" was, but this piece
of scrimshaw, like most of it, was a highly
personalized gift.*

191

The wind is just for winning. Section offers a four-part chronicle of the . . .

race for the America's Cup and how far men went to win it.

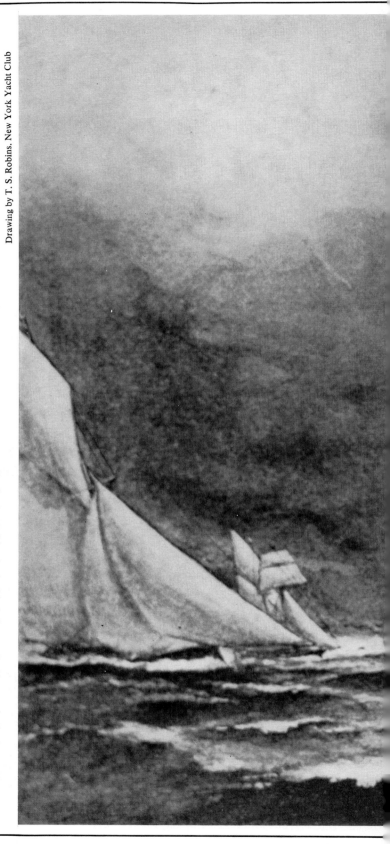

Drawing by T. S. Robins. New York Yacht Club

THE FIRST VIEW THAT BRITISH YACHTSMEN HAD OF THE
America in 1851 was when she made the trip from Havre
to take her place in the anchorage at Cowes. They were
quick to note the sheer flat trim of her sails and the sharp
cut of her bow as she sliced along through their home waters
well ahead of one of the fastest yachts under the burgee of
the Royal Yacht Squadron, the cutter *Laverock*. Although
the breeze was light the cutter showed her canvas to be well
cupped with the distinctive baggy appearance which was traditional on British sailing craft. The *America* had reached
her mooring and was lowering her sails when the *Laverock*
passed a few moments later.

There were crowds of people along the waterfront who
had come to welcome the Yankee contender to their shores
and watch the scheduled contest for the Royal Yacht Squadron Cup. What these spectators had just witnessed was an
unofficial race between the *Laverock* and the *America*. The
British cutter had been sent down the Solent channel to escort the foreign visitor to an anchorage near the yacht club.
On the way, the *Laverock* made known to her charge that

The America *as she surprised most everyone by outfoot-
ing her rivals in the race at Cowes, August 22, 1851.*

The strategy of sail design has always played an important role in the America's Cup series—but never more than in that astonishing first race.

they might just as well have a friendly little race. Captain Brown, skipper of the *America,* and never one to turn down a challenge, picked up the gauntlet and proceeded to out-foot his escort by a very comfortable margin.

The Earl of Wilton, Commodore of the R.Y.S., at the head of his welcoming committee of prominent yachtsmen, lost no time in boarding the *America* to extend their greetings. After the formalities, the group gave their full attention to the yacht and her many strange innovations, with particular interest shown in the sails. These authorities and specialists in wind force had long been schooled in the belief that the deep hollow contour of their own flaxen sails was the last and only word for maximum wind power. The baggy appearance of the *Laverock's* canvas was in sharp contrast to the stiff board-like trim that was noted in the *America's* sails. A minute inspection revealed that they were flat-cut and machine-woven of the finest quality cotton. The *London Times* of the day called them "flat boards."

This "friendly little race" and its outcome gave the British yachting hosts much to think about. Their bewilderment turned to worried concern. It shook their confidence further as they became aware of the fact that the gambling fraternity dropped their odds on a British victory and leveled them off to even money. In some quarters the betting was called off entirely.

In those days yachting regattas were usually held with a money or purse award to the victors instead of a trophy. Betting on the side lines was only natural and among them was a group of die-hards who let the odds lay as given. These were known as the "smart money" gamblers who argued that since the *Laverock* was towing her rowboat at the time, it was certainly premature to believe that her performance was a yardstick of her speed. Although the simple rigging and taut sails of the *America* puzzled them, they held to their opinion that Brittania still ruled the waves; perhaps forgetting the many logs of the past, recording the same underestimate of Yankee shipwrights and sailmakers.

In looking back over the many races for the Cup since 1851, many consider that first one to be the greatest of them all. There were fourteen English yachts, of all shapes, sizes and rigs, pitted against the trim-looking little Yankee who had fooled them all with her "flatboard" sails. The course was around the Isle of Wight, and, as the Queen watched the first yacht to sail over the finish line, she wanted to know which it was. On being told it was the *America,* she asked, "Where are the others?"

In the days of wind-driven ships, the sail loft and its artisans played a very important role. The sailmaker of that day was one of a proud breed of skilled canvas men with

Above. The America *schooner yacht under construction in Brown's Shipyard at 12th Street and East River, N.Y.C. Her overall length was 94' and she displaced 170 tons. Right. The original sail and spar plan for the* America. *It was drawn by George Steers for the R. H. Wilson Sail Loft in Port Jefferson, Long Island.*

196

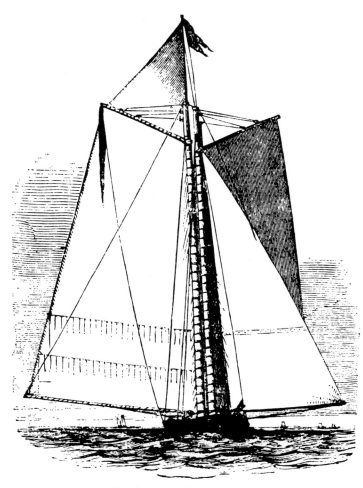

The America *booming out.*

The simple rigging *and taut* sails *of the* America *puzzled the British*

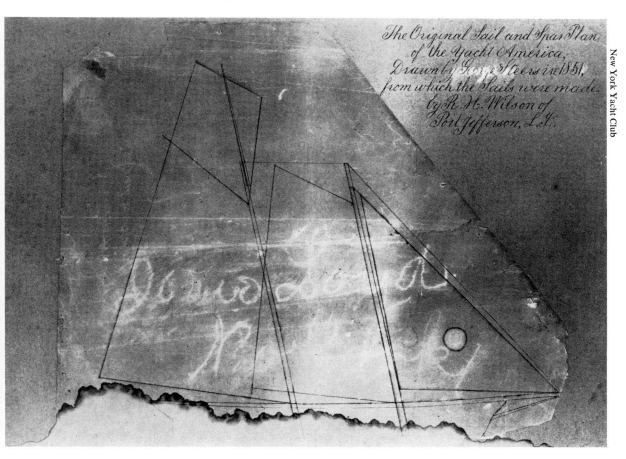

a status comparable to the engraver of fine silver. To attain this rank he had to serve an apprenticeship of seven years in a sail loft, plus a full year on a sailing vessel and a season's tour with a traveling circus as a tentmaker. The sailmaker's guild, one of the oldest in the country, seldom accepted a member of less than ten years' experience with palm and needle.

When George Steers, designer of the *America,* brought her sail plans to Brown's Yard in New York at 12th Street and the East River, he learned that a sailmakers' strike had closed down the lofts. Upon consultation with the *America*'s syndicate, it was decided to have the sails made out of town.

As a summer resident of Great Neck, Steers was familiar with the yards and lofts on the north shore of Long Island. From among these he chose the R. H. Wilson Sail Loft in Port Jefferson. The Wilsons had been in business in New York since 1836 and had an enviable reputation as masters in the trade. Many a fine clipper ship owed much of its speed to the skilled hands at Wilson's. Before a fire destroyed Wilson's loft, an important chapter in the history of sailing vessels was written in the sail plans that decorated the walls of this establishment. Among them were a host of pleasure and

Lower left. The America *in her sail trim of 1885 before she was remodeled by Edward Burgess. This photo was taken off Marblehead, Mass. Above left. A model of the* America *as it appeared in 1851.*

Scene in a sail loft during the America's *era. The sailmaker of that day was one of a proud breed of skilled canvas men with a status comparable to the engraver of fine silver. Note the stove is hung from the ceiling; this was to allow a clear area for sail cutting.*

Captain Richard Brown, first skipper of the America. *Photo courtesy of New York Yacht Club.*

199

racing yachts, such as the schooner *Irene* and the notorious *Wanderer,* a sleek yacht that had been used as a slaver. Such artifacts and records as were salvaged from the fire are lost among Wilson descendants who have long since disappeared from the area.

The original sail plan of the *America,* as she was before the changing whims of successive owners, is encased in the archives of the New York Yacht Club. Although scarred and tattered, the brittle document has survived the erosion of time and clearly shows the simple profile of the wings that took the Yankee craft to victory in the race at Cowes.

The spars and rigging of the *America* followed closely the simple lines of her prototype, the pilot boat *Mary Taylor.* The voyage across the Atlantic to Le Havre took about twenty days. The *America* used the *Mary Taylor*'s canvas as working sails, keeping her own racing sails safely stowed below, reserved for the duel with British yachts. These combat sails ran to an area of 5,263 square feet when spread over the following spars: mainmast, 81′ with a boom of 58′ and a gaff of 26′; foremast, 79½′ with a gaff of 24′ and no fore boom. Her bowsprit measured 32′, of which 17′ was outboard. Both masts were raked at 2⅞″ to the foot. These were her spar measurements originally, but over the years they were changed several times, to the extent that when the *America* was last seen under sail, in 1901, she would hardly be recognized, except perhaps by her hull.

In 1870, the champion, while under the care and ownership of the United States Naval Academy, was repaired and groomed for a challenge by the *Cambria,* which represented England's first attempt to recover The Cup she lost in 1851. The *America,* with a crew of naval cadets, came in fourth in this contest, which was won by the *Magic.* Her refurbishing at the time totaled more than her original cost, although neither her sail plan nor her rigging was disturbed. In a wave of economy, she was sold by the Secretary of the Navy and was bought at auction by General Benjamin Butler in 1873. Two years later the General, thinking she was somewhat old-fashioned, with her lug foresail and raking masts, turned her over to Donald McKay of Boston for modernizing and general overhauling. The rake in the mast was reduced to 1½″ to the foot, in place of the 2⅞″, and for the first time in her existence she was fitted with a foreboom. A new jib boom was installed as well as a new main topmast. These alterations increased the sail area, but to what extent is not recorded.

In the summer of 1880, the General again decided that, if he were to keep his status in yachting's social whirl, he would have to make further changes in the hull, among

them being the addition of six feet to the stern. As for the rigging, the first major renovation was made in 1885 when he had the single jib replaced with a double head rig. Her spar dimensions were now registered as: mainmast 78′; main topmast 33′; foremast 77′; fore topmast 28′; fore gaff 27′; bowsprit 17′; and jib boom 18′.

A year later the *America* was put in the hands of Edward Burgess for still more rejuvenations, which included some changes in the hull as well as the addition of twenty-five tons of lead in her keel. A pole bowsprit was fitted and a new sail plan brought an increase of 1,000 square feet to her canvas. Still striving for the ultimate in yachting performance, Butler sent her to the yard of William McKee of East Boston. The pole bowsprit was lengthened and the masts were stayed slightly forward of perpendicular. Again these tamperings necessitated a new sail plan and the area was increased from 12,800 to 13,545 square feet. It was the largest sail area the *America* was ever to carry, and a far cry from her original area of 5,263 square feet.

The last extensive alterations were those made by Edward Burgess in 1886. The interior arrangements of cabin and stateroom came in for their share of turn-about facilities that resulted in sumptuous appointments in decor, but in no way did they affect the vessel's performance. Her traditional black hull was painted white the following year, giving her a sleek bride-like appearance, and when the sun sparkled on her brightwork and gold leaf trimmings, she belied her thirty-five years of hard service.

These meddlings with ballast, hull and spars did little, and in some opinions nothing, to enhance her racing talents. A brief score of the fifty-one times she came to a starting line, officially, shows that she won thirteen contests and lost twenty-nine, with the remaining nine events not timed. A closer look reveals that her best days as a contestant were those before she became the victim of the whimsy of her owners.

Over the years contemporary artists have pictured the *America* in her several fashions of sail style. When serving the flag of one combatant, and later the rival in the same conflict, her canvas was grimed and patched as it shadowed the rails that bristled with cannon. In her halcyon days as a pleasure yacht, her spars and white sails gleamed in the sun and her decks knew the gaiety of champagne society. But the image more often recalled is the *America* in her garb of the simple pilot-boat rigging with the paper-flat sails, showing her heels to the elite and haughty yachts of Britain's finest, her burgee rippling a fond farewell at the finish line.

The America *was last seen under sail in 1901. This photo was taken just before she was put under cover for twenty years.*

THE GREAT NAUTICAL JAM

by Samuel Carter III

IT HAD TO BE SEEN TO BE REALIZED," WROTE VETERAN reporter Jeff Davis of the *Providence Journal.* "How many were there? It would be like counting raindrops in a summer shower . . ."

Such was the enormous fleet of spectator craft and press boats crowding the waters of Block Island Sound when the America's Cup races moved to Newport in the fall of 1930. And such is still the scene when Newport becomes the center of the greatest international yacht racing contest in the world.

As "Cup fever" takes possession of the venerable town, one can foresee history in repetition. By the orange-and-white buoy south of Brenton's Reef some 3,000 spectator craft, including half-a-dozen large excursion ships, assemble to follow the yachts along their 24-mile course. To keep them a hundred yards away, 35 Coast Guard and Navy vessels form a "diamond defense" or protective screen around the two contestants.

Ashore, tens of thousands transform Ocean Drive into a grandstand or climb the rocks of Castle Hill, armed with

The crowds watching the America's Cup races grew so large and unruly that in some instances participants actually pulled out of the contest. This scene depicting the event in 1901 shows some of the congestion.

binoculars and cameras, folding chairs and picnic lunches, to watch the races six or seven miles away. They can see little more than the peaks of white sails in the distance, and must follow the progress of the yachts on their portable radios. But at least they can say, with pardonable ambiguity, "We were there!"

Meanwhile, aboard the Coast Guard cutters, in blimps and helicopters overhead, and in the old Armory on Thames Street—wired now to all the corners of the earth—500 or more members of press, radio, and television stand by to relay millions of words and hundreds of pictures to a waiting world, to fill more newspaper space, more screen and radio time, than accorded the World Series or Olympic Games.

What is it that arouses such insatiable interest in a sport few people truly understand, and fewer still can share in? Olin Stephens, yacht designer, believes it derives from three factors: national pride in international competition, awareness that here is the ultimate climax in the age-old sport of kings, and finally the spectacle itself. While some might agree with Ring Lardner's comment that the races themselves are "as exciting as watching grass grow," few can deny that white sails bending to the wind against a background of blue water make a composition of incomparable beauty.

Whatever the reason, no international sports event in history has created such a hunger for news, such an eagerness to be at the ringside, as the America's Cup races. Established partly to promote good international relations, the contests have often strained them almost to the breaking point. And one of the great bones of contention, through the years, has concerned not the competitors but the over-enthusiastic spectators and avid reporters covering the event.

Even when the contests were being held off Sandy Hook, prior to 1930, spectators and reporters were a major problem. For yacht racing, particularly at the turn of the century, was to the American masses what big league baseball was later to become. More office boys' grandmothers died on the afternoon of a Cup race than at any other time of year. On the day of the first *Vigilant-Valkyrie* race in 1893, New York Harbor was so choked with private yachts, excursion steamers, tugs, and myriad small boats carrying reporters that Lord Dunraven, the British challenger, carried a placard on *Valkyrie*'s halyards warning this floating pressbox to "KEEP FURTHER OFF."

When, after his first defeat, Dunraven challenged again in 1897, he asked that the races be held off Marblehead, away from Sandy Hook crowds. The request was denied. Whereupon Dunraven had a sarcastic cablegram dispatched, saying that if Great Britain ever went to war he hoped American press boats wouldn't disrupt its naval operations. To which New York officials replied that it hoped Great Britain's Navy was less vulnerable than its racing yachts. "Not very funny," was Dunraven's comment.

As Anglo-American rivalry gathered momentum in this period, and the Herreshoffs of Bristol entered the arena with the first of five magnificent defenders, the interest of the public and the press centered as much on the yachts them-

Wide World Photo

60,000 *paying passengers w*

selves as on their performance in the races. Nat Herreshoff's cult of secrecy, and the tight guard thrown around his Bristol boatyards, were a challenge to reporters. Nat would give out no interviews; his answer to all questions from reporters was a simple "hmph!" after which he would tell his interviewer: "Remember, young man, print no more information than I've given you."

The war between the Herreshoffs and the press reached a climax with the launching of *Defender* in the spring of 1895. The secrecy surrounding her construction called for cloak-and-dagger methods on the part of Providence reporters. Taking up residence in Bristol, they tried to penetrate the yards by all means possible. Two enterprising newsmen hired a rowboat to reach the open shed and sketch *Defender* from the water. They were greeted by "a shower of hot spikes and other missiles."

A third reporter with a camera up his sleeve crept up by boat to the open-ended shed, and was promptly lassoed from the sail loft above, yanked from his craft, and dropped into the harbor. Others who attempted to swim to the shed

...mmed on 200 steamers . . .

ing palaces as J. P. Morgan's *Corsair*, Jay Gould's *Atalanta*, Astor's *Nourmahal* and Vanderbilt's *Valiant*. Wrote Jerome Brooks, Cup historian, "On the more than 200 steamers and other craft which crowded the course were an estimated 60,000 paying passengers. This was far beyond the common-sense bounds of safety for many of the vessels."

Conditions on the day of the second race were just as bad, although the Race Committee had hastily mobilized a patrol of 20 steam yachts to keep the course clear. These private watchdogs were hopelessly outnumbered as excursion craft and press boats blocked the starting line. One of the bigger steamers, *Yorktown*, with 500 passengers and 20 cases of champagne, stumbled squarely into the contestants' path. Both racing yachts were forced to alter course, and as they came together *Valkyrie*'s boom snapped *Defender*'s topmast shroud like an overtaut guitar string. Although *Valkyrie* won the race as the result of this damage to her rival, Lord Dunraven promptly penned a protest to the Race Committee:

> Gentlemen: It is with great reluctance that I write to inform you that I decline to sail *Valkyrie* any more under the circumstances that have prevailed in the last two races . . . To attempt to start two such large vessels in a very confined space, and among moving steamers and tugboats is, in my opinion, exceedingly dangerous, and I will not further risk the lives of my men and the ship.

Dunraven made good his threat on the day of the third race, September 12. Standing on deck with his mascot goat, he surveyed the same oppressing hordes as previously. He crossed the starting line, then lowered *Valkyrie*'s colors, and quit. He would not race under such conditions.

It is not inconceivable that at this point the America's Cup contests might have passed into oblivion, defeated partly by an overenthusiastic press and public. The incurable one-sidedness of the competition was also threatening public interest. But one man was destined to restore enthusiasm for the series, the lovable, gallant, but ever-unsuccessful challenger, Sir Thomas Lipton, with his five successive *Shamrocks*.

Lipton was a newspaper man's dream. He loved publicity, his slogan being:

> He who on his trade relies
> Must either bust or advertise.

His escorting tender *Erin*, anchored in New York harbor, played host to more members of the press than any ship in history, dispensing free tea and Scotch, and at one time providing a line of Broadway chorus girls as hostesses. Lipton's arrival not only brought an era of good feeling to the contests, but also brought about changes in the control of spectator craft and press boats on the Sandy Hook course.

in frogman style were greeted by red-hot rivets from the hand of Captain Wilcox, the night watchman.

Still they came, like a small armada, armed with box cameras, sketchpads, and indomitable newsmen's curiosity. The Bristol steamer *Archer* was standing in the harbor, and John Herreshoff asked the captain to turn his steam hoses on the invaders. With local loyalty the captain obliged. When the hoses broke down from battle fatigue, the blow-off pipe on the side of the *Archer* was turned against the press boats—a maneuver which failed for lack of steam. Driven to extremes, the Herreshoff workforce then rolled out barrels of tar, ready to be ignited and dumped on the intruders. Against this medieval threat, the press boats prudently withdrew.

It was *Defender*'s contest against Dunraven's *Valkyrie III* that created perhaps the most unpleasant situation in Cup history. On the morning of the initial race, September 6, 1895, the waters off Sandy Hook were jammed with "the hugest pleasure-boat fleet yet seen," augmented by newspaper launches with their carrier pigeons and by such float-

In the first contest between Herreshoff's defending *Columbia* and *Shamrock I* on October 16, 1899, the course was for the first time clear of press boats and excursionists. The United States Government had deemed the event important enough to send a fleet of 12 revenue cutters and torpedo boats to keep observing ships in line. As a result, one of the largest fleet of spectators ever to attend the races was obliged to follow in the yachts' wake.

One of the spectators was a young Italian genius named Guglielmo Marconi, whose invention of wireless telegraphy had brought him crank threats of assassination from those who claimed to have been poisoned by its rays. For the first time, wireless was used, from ship to shore, to report the progress of the races. Used by the more fortunate papers, that is. Those not subscribing to Marconi's service had to rely on signal balloons sent aloft from the press boats, semaphores on the Jersey shore, carrier pigeons with messages fastened to their legs, or on cans of copy hurled from launches to waiting couriers on shore.

One of the papers taking a chance on wireless was the *New York Herald* which boasted on October 1, 1899:

> Absolute demonstration of the value of the Marconi system of wireless telegraphy will be furnished the western world for the first time during the yacht race this week by Signor Marconi and a corps of assistants who will report every movement of the contending yachts to the *Herald*. This will be a feat unparalleled in the history of journalism.

News of the yachts was flashed to shore by this new invention during all three days of racing, reaching newspaper and cable offices long before other means of communication. In the final contest on October 20, fog limited visibility so that wireless became the only effective means of news transmission. Again the *Herald* was able to do some gloating, reporting that the "mist baffled land observers, and signal balloons and carrier pigeons alike failed."

The *Herald,* with its almost exclusive wireless franchise, was able to report promptly Lipton's defeat and loss of the series. Lipton lost in his second attempt to lift the Cup in 1901, also against *Columbia,* and suffered defeat again in 1903 against *Reliance,* when the final race ended with the lugubrious report on *Shamrock III*'s position: "Lost in fog." But *Shamrock IV* in 1920 was a different story.

The first four races were divided evenly with Herreshoff's defending *Resolute,* and excitement over the fifth and final race approached hysteria. Business was neglected, trading on the Stock Exchange reduced to a trickle, betting fierce. Newspaper reports of the Cox and Harding campaigns and the Sacco and Vanzetti trial were shoved aside for headlines featuring the coming battle.

The day of the first race brought out the largest spectator fleet ever assembled off Sandy Hook. The competing yachts might choose to "seek seclusion for their duel," wrote a *New York Times* reporter, but "the gallery follows along. See it pouring out of the harbor: towering Sound liners, their decks aswarm; patrician steam yachts and plebeian tugboats; little cabin cruisers, houseboats, launches, trawlers; grim gray naval vessels and sharp Coast Guard boats, marching, tumbling down to the deep, with airplanes roaring overhead; the most motley flotilla that ever leaves the land astern."

Leading the flotilla was the Ward Line's *Orizaba* with 450 enthusiasts aboard at $25 a head, and champagne selling at $9 a bottle. In the skies some 20 airplanes stunted for the floating crowd, while a passenger blimp 3,000 feet up obligingly provided excitement by plummeting nose first into the harbor. For the first time radio carried a running account of the event, and the cables stood by to carry photographs to England.

One of the fleet of destroyers assigned to keep the excursion boats in order spotted a queer-looking, hull-like object lined up with the other vessels. On investigation, it proved to be an 80-foot-long Arctic whale with abnormal curiosity, which had sailed the world for ever and aye to watch the race with unshut eye.

Beginning with 1930, and Lipton's fifth challenge for the Cup (against Starling Burgess' *Enterprise*), all matches were shifted to the waters of Block Island Sound off Newport, largely to escape the crowded conditions around Sandy Hook. The move gave some advantage to observers and the press although the large fleet of revenue cutters and torpedo boats, assigned by the government to maintain order, was commanded by a captain who would brook no nonsense. He was Robley D. Evans, the "Fighting Bob" of Spanish-American War fame and Commander of the Great White Fleet in its epoch-making round-the-world voyage 23 years earlier.

Even so, congestion took its toll. A Boston yacht named *Gay Jane* sliced into Lipton's escort *Erin*, damaging her tender and port gangway. The excursion steamer *City of Lowell* collided with the U.S. Destroyer *Wilkes* while the

The 1886 start, between the American Mayflower *on the left, and the British* Galatea, *had very few enforceable restrictions on the spectator fleet, apparent here.*

latter was maneuvering to give reporters a better view. As a result of the latter incident, the two destroyers carrying newsmen, *Wilkes* and *Porter*, played it safe and remained at the tail end of the line of spectators. Irate correspondents were a mile away when both yachts crossed the finish line. But the contest was so one-sided and dull that it hardly mattered. Wrote Jerome Brooks:

> Perhaps it was just as well that the Prince of Wales, the King of the Belgians, and Mussolini, all of whom had been invited with other notables, had prior engagements. The races were certainly not exciting to the spectators, for the Coast Guard fleet, destroyers, revenue cutters and lesser craft went to the opposite extreme of the good old bad days. Even the press boats, usually privileged, were kept far from the course.

Though the first contest off Newport had been sadly unexciting, interest revived when T. O. M. Sopwith's *Endeavour I* was pitted in 1934 against the Vanderbilt syndicate's *Rainbow*. Of the forthcoming battle the *New York Times* wrote on September 9:

> Two racing yachts, single-stickers with Marconi rigs, sailing thirty mile courses off Newport beginning next Saturday, will get more newspaper space, more screen and radio time than all the globe-girdling liners and their man-o'-war husbands on the seven seas. Not even storm-tossed ships of state, drifting toward strange social orders . . . can expect much attention while *Rainbow* and *Endeavour* race in Block Island Sound for the America's Cup.

Sopwith's *Endeavour* lost 4 to 2, before a 10,000-spectator fleet which "made the seascape look like a distant view of a big city against the skyline." There was only one minor incident—when the patrolling destroyer *Manley*, at the request of newsmen aboard, got too close to the contestants, stealing their wind. Whereupon President Roosevelt, watching the races aboard Vincent Astor's *Nourmahal*, requested the *Nourmahal*'s radio operator to send a message to the *Manley:* "Are you challenging the *Endeavour?*" It was the first time a President of the United States had intervened in the conduct of a Cup race, and the *Manley* hastily withdrew.

In 1937, Sopwith's second unsuccessful challenge with *Endeavour II*, against Vanderbilt's superlative *Ranger*, marked the end of an era in America's Cup racing. *Ranger* was the last of the J boats, magnificent machines of soaring length and towering masts, too costly and impractical for post-war competition. The class went out with a bang. On the day of the first *Endeavour-Ranger* race it took the Coast Guard three-quarters-of-an-hour to clear the starting line of a traffic jam of steamers, power yachts, fishing boats, sailing craft, "and about everything else." Noted Garrett Byrnes of the *Providence Journal:*

> No story, at any time, anywhere in the State, ever has attracted the attention from press and newsreels currently being given to the Cup races. In the number of news-writers and cameramen assembled, in the total wordage wired and radioed back to home offices, in the amount of newsreel film and still picture negative exposed, the duel of the J-boats sets a new record for news and picture coverage in Rhode Island.

Now that record is being sustained, throughout Rhode Island and the world, by the relatively new 12-Meter boats created by formula in 1956—about half the size of the Js, with a crew of 11 amateurs in place of the semi-professional crews of 22 or more who manned the Js. Less spectacular, less eye-appealing, they have nevertheless opened up Cup competition to countries whose sailing skill is stouter than their yacht-construction budget. Writes Emil ("Bus") Mosbacher, Jr., master pilot of the Twelves, "What was lost in the passing of the J boats was, at least partly, compensated for by exciting new racing techniques."

While some of the drama has gone from the races with the introduction of these smaller boats, public interest in the competition has not waned. If anything it has increased, perhaps because the more modest yachts make the sport seem less remote, less the domain of millionaires and more a prov-

ince of the people. One stood in awe of the J boats; one can love the Twelves, and even identify with them in a sort of Walter Mitty way. As a result, press coverage has become more important than ever. Using, with ingenuity, all modern methods of communication, scores of writers, announcers, and cameramen have made the America's Cup races one of the great sports stories of all time.

Until recently, broadcasters and correspondents were carried on Coast Guard cutters patrolling the spectator fleet. In 1962 (*Weatherly* versus *Gretel*) one radio announcer, who asks that he be nameless, felt that the cutter was following the gallery more closely than the racing yachts. He told the Coast Guard captain so, adding some unwise comments on the latter's handling of his craft ("His seamanship was really terrible," he still maintains). The irate captain demanded he surrender his credentials, and declared him *persona non grata* with the Coast Guard for the balance of the races.

But fortunately there is much cooperation among newsmen covering the races; the assignment is too difficult to have it otherwise. A sympathetic colleague lent the announcer his credentials, and the latter boarded another Coast Guard cutter the next morning. Minutes later he was heard broadcasting over his own name, and the censoring captain who had banned him yielded in defeat. The incident led to one remedial change. Now the Coast Guard cutter carrying the press is assigned to follow the races only, and ignore the gallery.

Seasickness has been an ever-present plague to newsmen, for there are no choppier waters than those off Brenton's Reef. But if reporters could survive the ordeal till they got ashore, they were able to write their stories on firm land. It was not until radio broadcasting came along that the threat of sickness became severe. A woozy announcer obliged to follow intricate yacht maneuvers and describe them eloquently, when he wishes he were at the bottom of the sea, is indeed performing beyond the call of duty.

Bill Robinson, veteran Cup reporter and editor of *Yachting,* recalls one of the earliest attempts at broadcasting from the course. A special ship was chartered by NBC to carry the announcer and equipment. Unfortunately, says Bill, this boat was a former fishing smack that "had a certain aura of its own to start with." The charter-owners had obligingly constructed, out of plywood, a radio cabin amidships. No air from outside could intrude; the odor of haddock was carefully preserved. What went out on the airwaves from that Black Hole of Calcutta, Bill himself has often wondered.

It was thought for a while that this problem of sickness might be solved by transferring announcers and equipment to the Goodyear blimp that generally attends the races. In its gondola, a thousand feet or more above the waves, broadcasters would surely not be seasick. They weren't; they were airsick instead.

Television coverage, which began in 1962, added a new dimension to Cup race reporting, and created an intricate procedure. Camera and tape machine, the latter about the size of a home refrigerator, were installed aboard a Coast Guard cutter. As fast as the tape came from the camera, it was processed and monitored for quality, then sealed in a watertight floating container. The container was then made fast to a line on the other end of which was a "monkey fist," or oval weight that could be hurled like a discus into an accompanying launch. With the tape aboard, the launch raced clear of the spectator fleet, and a hovering helicopter fished up the can and whirled it back to Newport. Here a light plane waited to carry the tape to Providence where it was relayed by direct line to New York, to be broadcast to the country not much more than half-an-hour after the event.

This operation proved so successful it was adopted by one of the wire photo services with reckless optimism: the still picture negatives were inserted in a watertight unsinkable can, to be rushed by launch, helicopter and plane to Providence for developing and transmission. First attempts were catastrophic. An over-zealous crewman hurled the "monkey fist" at the waiting launch with such deadly accuracy that it went through the windshield and knocked out the pilot. On a second attempt, those aboard the launch eagerly cut free the "monkey fist"—which they thought was the treasured film container—and held it up to the shocked view of those aboard the cutter, shouting reassuringly, "Okay! We've got it!"—while the film itself drifted out to sea.

The Thistle *and the* Volunteer *as they appeared below the Narrows in the first race of the 7th challenge contest for the America's Cup, Sept. 27, 1887. The picture illustrates the conditions under which races were sailed.*

THE HERRESHOFF STORY

by Samuel Carter III

It is a far cry from Minden, Prussia, to the quiet seaport towns of Narragansett Bay—from the militarism of Frederick the Great to Yankee seamanship in defense of the *America*'s Cup. But such is the background of the greatest yacht-building dynasty the world has ever seen— and a biographical preface to New England's least-known family of geniuses: The Herreshoffs of Bristol, Rhode Island.

The term "least known" is not amiss. Every yachtsman living knows the name of Herreshoff, and its role in making the *America*'s Cup a permanent fixture of the New York Yacht Club. But few know even how to pronounce it (the second "h" is silent: Hair-is-off). And fewer still connect it with inventions such as baking powder, fertilizers, motorcycles, electric furnaces, children's toys, and quite probably the outboard motor. Yet their oversight can be forgiven, for the Herreshoff name applies most ineradicably to the greatest racing yachts that ever sailed—the like of which will never sail again.

Herreshoff origins are controversial, but not obscure. In Minden on the Weser River, during the French campaign of 1763, a son was born to one Agnes Mueller and a guardsman of Frederick the Great. Rumor had it that Frederick himself was the father (not unflattering to the impotent King), and that Corporal Eschoff was being made the scapegoat. In any event, having broken a guardsman's rule of chastity, Eschoff was banished from the court, and Frederick adopted the youngster as a sort of foster-son. He brought him up in the traditions of the court, had him tutored at the aristocratic Philanthropin, and gave him his own illustrious name—eliding Herr Eschoff's into smoother-flowing syllables: Karl Friederich Herreschoff. It had a ring!

By the time the ninety-footer Columbia (*opposite*) *had beaten two of Sir Thomas Lipton's* Shamrocks *in a row, the Herreshoff Company had reached its peak of productivity and reputation. This photograph was taken in 1899 and shows the* Columbia *leading the* Shamrock.

210

Right: Nat Herreshoff, "the ivory-towered dreamer and indefatigable creator."

John Herreshoff, "the brains, manager, and driving force."

Miss Louise H. DeWolf

When Frederick died in 1787, young Herreschoff was cast adrift in Europe, wandered until his funds ran out, and eventually landed on New York's South Street, with nothing but a fluency in languages and half-a-dozen flutes. A man named Ashdour had preceded him from Germany, and parlayed some flutes into a fur-lined fortune before he changed his name to Astor. Herreschoff sought to do the same; and almost did.

His facility as an interpreter in foreign shipping circles led him to John Brown of Providence. Brown was a leading merchant of the Colonies, and took an instant liking to young Herreschoff—for his courtly manners, gracious carriage, and patrician good-looks. So did John Brown's daughter, Sarah. After nine years of accompanying Sarah's harpsichord on his companionable flutes, Karl married Sarah—and they settled at Point Pleasant Farm across from Bristol, a piece of confiscated Tory property that John had acquired in return for services to General Washington.

It was a tragic, grandeur-haunted marriage. Karl was no farmer. He preferred champagne to the milk his cows produced. And he hated the smell of Bristol onions. He poured thousands of dollars into remodelling the farm around the image of a French chateau, laying out paths and formal gardens, planting exotic shrubbery, reclaiming worthless swampland without purpose.

In nine years the family, expanded by five children, was close to bankruptcy. Just what prompted the next tragic step is hazy. But some time previous, another Brown son-in-law had witlessly bargained for 200,000 useless acres in the Adirondacks. Either through family pressure, or from a sense of humbled honor, Karl Friederich Herreschoff was banished to that wilderness. His dream of building there an empire founded upon coal and iron-smelting foundered in the pitiless forest. At the edge of one of his flooded mines, on December 19, 1819 he shot himself—or so it appeared.

Of the five surviving children in Rhode Island, only one—his namesake—left the seclusion of Point Pleasant Farm. Charles Frederick Herreshoff, having Anglicized the name, moved his family in 1856 across the bay to Bristol, to the home still well-maintained at 142 Hope Street. Two of his sons had already shown inventive promise. James, the eldest, was a high-ranking chemist at Brown University;

...the greatest yacht-building dynasty the world has ever seen

Morris Rosenfeld Photo

Left. The Herreshoff Boatyard, Bristol, Rhode Island. The year is 1903, and the colorful event is the launching of the Reliance, *hailed by critics as the finest Herreshoff creation.*

The Rainbow, *built in 1934 and photographed here June 4, 1937, marked the beginning of the "J" boat era, a still further simplification of racing craft.*

213

John, next in line, had parlayed a self-built rope walk into a yard for building small boats. Charles, the father, had set an example in small-boat design by building a succession of twenty-three-foot catboats, all named *Julia* after a devoted wife.

It was then that the first blow of a strange plague hit the family. Over the hull of the twelve-foot *Meteor* he was building, John was stricken blind. The curse of blindness returned cruelly in this generation, later afflicting Lewis, Sally Brown and Julian (all three of whom still made their marks in chosen avocations). It has since been diagnosed as probably glaucoma, checked today by simple treatment.

With Teutonic courage, John rallied from the blow. With the help of his younger brother, Nat, he not only completed the *Meteor* but expanded the boatyard by taking in a local partner. But a far more important partnership was in formation. Nathanael became not only John's apprentice, but his eyes as well. From mutual dependence and begrudging admiration they became inseparable. But it wasn't until 1878, when Nat had finished at M.I.T. and established himself as an engineer, that the brothers united to form the Herreshoff Manufacturing Company—a firm that endured for over half a century.

While one thinks of the name Herreshoff as linked primarily to sailing vessels, their first twelve years were devoted principally to steam—to remarkably light, efficient marine engines and sleek power vessels. This was partly because Nat's training had been largely in this area, and partly because the steam yacht had become the status symbol of the period. Measured in terms of commercial achievement, the Herreshoff record in steam and gasoline-powered vessels surpasses, in tonnage if not in glamor, their better-known record in sail.

Their first orders came from Spain, for gunboats to be used against the Cuban rebels, and from the United States Navy for the latter's earliest torpedo boat, *Stilleto*. *Stilleto* went down in naval history for literally running circles around the *"Happy" Mary Powell,* Queen of Hudson River Steamers, in preliminary trials. Other light naval craft, along with countless private steam yachts, followed—until delivery was due the owner on the 138-foot steamer *Say When*. To exact an extra ounce of pressure from her boiler, Nathanael tightened the safety valve. The ship exploded, killing the fireman, and Nat's steam license was revoked.

While the tragedy nearly doomed the Herreshoff's future in the field of steam, it had a silver lining. It marked the beginning, for them and for America, of the Golden Age of Sail.

The latter was spurred by reviving interest in international racing, specifically in the *America*'s Cup contests—which dated from 1851 when that Yankee schooner outsailed a squadron of British yachts off Cowes, and was

Resolute *in 1920. (Note the two men aloft.)*

awarded the bottomless silver pitcher that has since become a sacred symbol of international competition. Surely no sports event has embodied so much skill and drama—so much venom and sordid sportsmanship—as have the *America*'s Cup races, on which some $50,000,000 has been spent on both sides of the Atlantic. Even in repeated Yankee victories, the bitterness of the conflict, as Ring Lardner noted, "invariably casts a pall of gloom over the American people."

Yet on the bright side of the coin, or Cup, is the matchless beauty and breathtaking performance of the five magnificent defending sloops—more accurately seven, if we include two designed by Starling Burgess—that slid down the Herreshoff ways in Bristol in the next four decades: *Vigilant* (1893), *Defender* (1895), *Columbia* (1899, 1901), *Reliance* (1903), *Resolute* (built in 1914, defended the Cup in 1920), *Enterprise* (1930), *Rainbow* (1934). The list does not include, of course, the great ships that competed for the right to race, or made distinguished racing records under private ownership.

The story of these defenders—the intrigue and shenanigans, the valor and drama of these races—has been well recorded in still-available books by Herbert Stone and Jerome Brooks, and in Thomas Lawson's *exposé:* "The America's Cup." Of more concern here, perhaps, is the human story of the Herreshoffs themselves who colored and fostered these conflicts for a good half-century, and are unforgettably associated with their drama.

Parenthetically it might be noted (and contradicted by some readers) that that drama has been sadly watered down. True, today's twelve-meters are practical boats, and sensible in cost. But were Nat alive today, I believe he'd barely look their way. They could hardly hold a candle to those tower-

The Defender *in 1895. Note her tremendous sail area.*

ing white-winged vessels of the past, over a hundred feet in length, with thousands of square feet of sail, costing hundreds of thousands of dollars, and so supercharged with racing power that it took a crew of over seventy to control them. That was racing in the manner of the Gods!

The Herreshoff's entry into this arena dates, as nearly as one can date these things, with Nat's design in 1891 of the *Dilemma,* which introduced the fin keel, and the forty-five-foot cutter *Gloriana,* which established the overhanging clipper bow that were Herreshoff trademarks for some years to come. *Gloriana* made a clean sweep of the racing class in which Edward Burgess, designer of previous Cup defenders, had reigned unchallenged. With Burgess' death, the New York Yacht Club, custodians of the Cup, singled out Nathanael Herreshoff as his successor. There was no disputing the selection. Already, in an anxious England, he was hailed as "the greatest young designer living."

Of the two brothers, John and Nat, John was the brains and manager and driving force behind the Company. The Bristol boatyards were big business now, sprawling along Hope and Burnside Streets, and employing several hundred workmen. The latter loved the gruff and bearded John, awesome in his blindness. His sensitive hands inspected their work, his graduated walking stick measured each item with precision. It was a natural comment of newly-hired hands: "He ain't really blind—he's just pretending."

He wasn't pretending, but his affliction seemed to give him a strange sense of power, even of amusement. In financial dealings, he arranged the bills so that he appeared to make change by merely touching the numbers with his fingers. When he ordered reins for his palomino, ten stitches to the inch, he ran his thumb down the length of leather and told the harnessmaker: "Eight-and-a-half inches—start again." His feeling for different woods, so vital to hull construction, was more accurate than sight; nothing with the slightest imperfection passed his "vision." And he was the bane of antique dealers in Rhode Island. Selecting a piece of Early American furniture by touch, he would gently rebuke the proprietor: "I didn't realize they had buzz planes in those days."

In contrast to John's business acumen and facility in handling people, Nat was the ivory-towered dreamer and indefatigable creator. The designs that spiralled through his head and hands would be hailed today as a formula for "Instant Yachts." By temperament, he was once removed from the mundane operation of the yards. Not able to remember workmen's names, he called them all Charlie, and separated them by their skills: Charlie Rigging, Charlie Paint, Charlie Copper, Charlie Tool . . . of course, these were names the men, themselves, used, too.

Whether Nat's was the sole, or even the principal creative force behind the enterprise has been debated. James Brown Herreshoff, the eldest brother, was himself an inventor and perforce a draftsman, and is sometimes credited with giving Nat the idea for the fin keel, and for initiating the cross-cut stitching of today's sails. But James never

sought identity with ships; and became a millionaire inventor in his own right, creating for the public everything from garden fertilizers to tandem bicycles and ankle braces for ice skates.

As noted, too, creative genius ran through the whole generation. Lewis became a skilled musician, writer and composer; Julian an accomplished teacher; Sally a pianist of some distinction. J. B. Francis Herreshoff, who made more money than them all, created the modern electric furnaces for smelting copper, along with current methods of refining sulphur, and helped make possible much of the mobile armament hurled against the Germans in the first World War.

Yet the eyes of the world, especially from 1890 to 1920, were focused on the Bristol boatyards—and the inspired yachts which Nat first whittled out of soft white pine, and John launched literally round the world. Every gilded name in that golden era—Whitneys, Vanderbilts, Belmonts, Goulds—was linked to the name of a Yacht by Herreshoff. J. P. Morgan could not board his *Corsair,* nor Arthur Curtiss James his famed *Aloha,* without a Herreshoff tender. All the great challengers of Britain made Bristol their home port of call when the races were held off Newport.

Royalty round the world deferred to them. Victoria's Prince of Wales was barred from the Herreshoff list of clients, for having used pawky tactics in a race against the *Vigilant.* Kaiser Wilhelm had his order for a yacht hurled back at him for suggesting some alteration in the Herreshoff design. John never visited the great of Newport or Tuxedo Park; they came to him, almost as suppliants. This wasn't arrogance, but indifference towards society and wealth. When Nat was rebuked for attending a dinner in his honor at the New York Yacht Club, dressed in workaday Bristol fashion, his rebuttal was characteristic: "If they want to entertain my clothes, I'll send them down a trunkful."

Nathanael was known as the "Wizard of Bristol" from the day his first defending *Vigilant,* with himself as helmsman, defeated the British *Valkyrie* in what the soft-spoken *N.Y. Times* called: "Probably the greatest battle of sails that was ever fought." By the time the ninety-foot cutter *Columbia* had knocked off two of Sir Thomas Lipton's *Shamrocks* in a row, the Herreshoff Company had reached its peak in productivity and reputation. The maze of buildings south of

The USS Cushing *was armed with torpedo rams fore and aft, had a turtle deck with conning tower forward, was 138 feet long, and had a draft of five feet four inches. She developed a speed of 22 knots.*

Nathanael   Charles Frederick, Jr.   Francis   Lewis
John B.   Mrs. Carolina Louisa (Herreshoff) Chesebrough—Mrs. Charles Frederick H.   James and Sally B.
Julian

the elm-shaded town was a wholly self-sufficient unit. They did not just build ships, they created everything that went into their making: metal castings, rope and wire, hardware, blocks and spars, electrical equipment, paints and varnishes, upholstery and cabinets, sails and rigging. Their sail loft alone supplied more canvas to more cup-winning yachts than any shop in North America.

Every boat they produced was a little (or big) gem— so exquisitely designed, so durably built of such select materials, that many are not only still afloat, but as sound as the day that they were launched . . . and far more precious in the light of today's declining standards. When last seen, a Herreshoff Fifty, built over half a century ago, was anchored at Mystic Seaport, showing only the surface marks of idleness. Some of the Herreshoff Thirties, selling originally for $4,000, would bring easily $20,000 now, if made available.

Columbia's repeat performance—she was the only ship to twice defend the Cup—marked a dent in the Herreshoff legend of invincibility. For it was part of their unspoken creed that every ship they built should top its predecessor (else why build it?). Commissioned to build a sloop to checkmate Lipton's *Shamrock II* in 1901, they poured their heart and soul into their next proposed defender, *Constitution*. She was not only the costliest of their ships to date, but

superlative in almost everything—by far the most mechanically advanced and scientifically built, with steel spars, 16,000 square feet of sail, and all the mechanical advantages the Herreshoffs could think of. In fact, she was so super-human that the crew was frightened of her. Perhaps because of their skittish seamanship, she failed in the trials against *Columbia,* and the latter was chosen to defend the Cup a second time.

It was a crushing blow, especially to Nat. For all during his life (to paraphrase what someone said of Hemingway) he had striven to out-Herreshoff Herreshoff. It was the only victory denied him.

In the eyes of the public, however, the brothers redeemed themselves with the 1903 defender, *Reliance,* hailed by critics as the finest Herreshoff creation, and by designer W. P. Stephens as "perhaps the most wonderful and useless racing machine known to yachting." This was perhaps a proper definition. For these extreme craft were built for one purpose only: Cup defense. They were good for almost nothing afterwards. Costing nearly $200,000, *Reliance* was scrapped a few months after she defeated Lipton's *Shamrock III* in three successive races.

Reliance marked the ending of an era. Spiralling costs, and ever bigger ships, had made for "unhealthy boats"—

218

obsolescent almost at the point of launching. To their eternal credit, the Herreshoffs were first to recognize this; and were instrumental in introducing the Universal Rule which limited water-line length to roughly seventy feet, with proportionate limitations on sail area and draft.

This self-imposed restriction meant financial sacrifice, the orders would be smaller—but this irked the Herreshoffs not at all. It was not necessary to their pride to build the most expensive boats. Just the best. But interest in the *America*'s Cup was waning, due largely to the one-sided competition; and two major events, one global and one personal, cast their shadows on the boatyard. With the outbreak of World War I in Europe, the Herreshoffs might have been in line for fat Government orders for light armored craft. But in the fanaticism of the times, their Prussian ancestry worked against them . . . and the yards lay generally idle.

One unexpected bright spot in this darkness turned to ashes. John received an order from the Russian Admiralty, backed by a sizable cash deposit, for a fleet of fast torpedo boats. It could well have been the beginning of a flood of similar orders from the European allies. He showed it to Nat, who inexplicably refused to sign it—perhaps out of feeling for his Prussian homeland, perhaps out of bitterness towards a war in which the navies of the world were dying. After a painful quarrel, John went home and a few weeks later, July 20, 1915, died quite literally of a broken heart. The Twilight of the Gods had come . . .

For a lot of the heart had now gone out of Nat. Never as rugged as John, he was ailing and wracked by rheumatism. Almost reluctantly he fulfilled the N.Y.Y.C.'s commission for the next Cup defender, *Resolute*—sketching an early draft while resting in Bermuda. That was in 1914. Then, with John's holdings in the Company already sold to a syndicate of New York Yachtsmen, and the market for luxury yachts depressed (three major yacht-building enterprises folded in the post-war years), the Herreshoff Manufacturing Company went on the auction block.

Of 74,000 square feet of buildings, including all stock and equipment, the major share went to a Rhode Island brewer, R. F. Haffenreffer, who for some years continued the operation under the Herreshoff name. Greatly altered since, but still in the same location, the surviving buildings now house the Pearson Corporation, makers of light plastic boats.

Haffenreffer kept Nathanael Herreshoff on as a consultant, and the next two Cup defenders, *Enterprise* and *Rainbow,* were constructed under his quasi-supervision. They marked the beginning of the "J" boats, a still further simplification of racing craft, with sail areas reduced to half that of a vessel like *Reliance,* and crews reduced from seventy-five to twenty-five. But while Nat had promoted the Marconi rig which characterized the Js, he never regarded them as "his" ships—for the drafting board had passed to Starling Burgess, son of Edward.

In his ninetieth year, as the end approached, Nathanael had much to look back on, in his partnership with John. Between them, they had created the light steam engine, called

America's first torpedo boat, the USS Cushing, *built by the Herreshoff Company, is launched here at Bristol, Rhode Island, January 1890.*

"Herreshoff Patent Safety Coil Boiler," and supplied the first gunboats and torpedo boats to the navies of the world. They had developed nearly all the forms, and methods of construction, of light wooden hulls, along with the web-frame approach to metal vessels. Their boats were required study in the Course of Naval Architecture at the Massachusetts Institute of Technology.

They had developed the fin and fin-bulb keels for racing yachts; and the hollow steel spar—combined with scientific rigging that included the slide track for sails in use today. The extensive overhang on sloops and schooners, allowing for longer lines and greater stability, was theirs. And they had brought aerodynamic principles to yacht design that greatly promoted the use of the Marconi rig. On top of it all, Nathanael had been largely responsible for the international rules by which their ships, and their competitors, were raced.

In international racing—as well as racing in America—Herreshoff boats had won more prizes than those of all other yacht designers put together. Herreshoff sloops had defended the *America*'s Cup almost incontestably for forty years—winning twenty-six races and losing only four. Over 3,000 private sailing vessels had been built to Herreshoff specifications; and some 18,000 designs, along with over a thousand models, remain left over from their efforts, some of them now at M.I.T. Herbert L. Stone hardly needed to point out that the greatest age of yachting that the world had ever known had passed with the passing of the Herreshoffs.

Perhaps it was a kindness of fate that only after Nat's death in the summer of 1938 did a hurricane sweep from the deep Sahara across the Atlantic and up the New England coast—boiling into Narragansett Bay and reducing to rubble the docks and pilings whose barnacled remnants mark the birthplace of the Herreshoff Manufacturing Company.

Vigilant, *Cup defender of 1893, on dry-dock.*

Valkyrie, *British challenger of 1893, on dry-dock.*

Genesta, *the British challenger of 1885, on dry-dock.*

Puritan, *the America's Cup defender of 1885.*

A QUESTION FREQUENTLY ASKED, IN THE YARN-SPIN-ning gatherings of old salts is "Whatever becomes of those fine racing craft which defend or challenge for The Cup—after their debut in the nautical dueling arena?" The answer, in general, is that they are relegated to the junk yard and scrapped. Their hardware and spars are usually salvaged and their sails are recut, where practical, for smaller boats. Some of the ex-champions have been converted into family cruising yachts, only to meet the same fate as their sisters in a short span of years. New measurement rules and changing styles in hull and sail plan, as well as lengthy time lapses between matches, make these yachts obsolete for racing. The only yacht called upon twice to defend the Cup was the *Columbia*. She defeated Sir Thomas Lipton's first *Shamrock* in the match of 1899 and gave a repeat performance over his *Shamrock II* in 1901. This *Columbia* was scrapped in 1915 and is not to be confused with her namesake of the 1958 match.

The 1962 defender, *Weatherly,* is laid up at Luder's Shipyard, Stamford, Connecticut. At this writing, according to her owner, Henry Mercer, there are no plans for her return to battle; she had accomplished what she was built for —to beat the *Gretel*. The *Columbia,* victorious defender of 1958, was sold to a West Coast yachtsman who entered her as a candidate for the 1964 Cup race.

The following 20th Century defenders all met the same fate in marine junk yards: *Ranger, Rainbow, Enterprise, Resolute,* and *Reliance*.

Among the challenging yachts, *Gretel* at this time (1964) is slated for the role of pacer and trial horse for a new Australian entry if they decide to contest The Cup in the future. The *Sceptre,* Britain's lost hope of 1958, is still active and used for trial runs with the *Sovereign*. The *Endeavour,* which bowed in defeat in 1934, has been lying idle in the Hamble River, Hampshire, England, for the past eighteen years. At present there are plans to bring her to America to be enshrined as a museum ship in Newport, Rhode Island. The project is one of the Newport Historical Society's and, if their fund raising is fruitful enough, they may add the other J boat, *Shamrock V,* to their plan. She is the last of the five *Shamrocks* that Sir Thomas Lipton had built in his thirty-year effort to win the *America*'s Cup.

Outstanding among The Cup boats, in longevity as well as usefulness, is the colorful career of the yacht *America,* of 1851. She was our country's first entry in a yachting arena of international status. Her amazing record of survival, under impossible odds, reaches beyond the legendary and remains today unsurpassed in the annals of yachting history.

After the *America* outfooted England's finest fleet of yachts in a race around the Isle of Wight, the prize award (at the time known as the Royal Yacht Squadron Cup) was presented to the syndicate of men who financed the building of the speedy Yankee schooner. The sponsors, headed by John C. Stevens, were his brother Edwin, George L. Schuyler, J. Beekman Finlay and Hamilton Wilkes. The *America*

WHAT HAPPENS TO CUP DEFENDERS?

by Charles H. Jenrich

was designed by George Steers and built at a cost of $20,000.

In 1857 the trophy was turned over to the New York Yacht Club to be held in trust as a perpetual challenge award. A document known as "The Deed of Gift" went with it and specified certain rules and regulations to be observed in any competition held for The Cup as a prize. In part it stated that "any organized club of any foreign country" would be eligible to compete. From then on the award became known as The *America*'s Cup, and it rested on a pedestal in the N.Y.Y.C. awaiting the first offer to duel for its possession. This did not come until 1870. The contests that were held to win The Cup have spread over more than a century. In the meantime, what became of the schooner yacht *America,* which brought it to these shores? Let us follow her wake as she cuts through turbulent seas far beyond the peaceful waters of racing arenas.

After the *America*'s successful debut in the Mayfair of British yachting, her owners decided to sell her to Lord deBlaquiere, an Irish peer of the Royal Victoria and the Royal Western Yacht Clubs. The nobleman provisioned and fitted out his new toy and embarked on an extended Mediterranean cruise, departing from Plymouth on November 27, 1851. On the homeward voyage, the *America* rode out a hurricane off Malta, suffering no damage, and arrived at her home port in the summer of 1852, just in time for the racing season. Under the burgee of the Peer she lost the match to the *Arrow,* by less than two minutes. The British press pointed out that the *America* could have easily won this match had she been properly groomed after her long tour in southern waters. In the next race, in October, she recouped her prestige when she defeated the fast Stockholm schooner *Sverige,* by twenty-six minutes.

His lordship left no record of what he did with the *America* after the sailing bouts of 1852. Her next chapter is written in 1856 when she was sold to Viscount Templetown, who changed her name to *Camilla* and listed her with the fleet of the Royal Yacht Squadron. Her new owner seems to have had little enthusiasm for yachting and left no record of racing or cruising beyond local waters. An American tourist mentioned seeing the *Camilla* in 1858, lying on the mudflats of Cowes in a very sad state of deterioration from dry rot and neglect, her decks and appointments a shambles of disorder.

A ship builder, Henry S. Pitcher, also saw her in this condition and, in sympathy, or perhaps astuteness, bought the yacht for the proverbial "price of a song." He towed her to his yard in Northfleet and, in his off moments, replaced her frames and planking where necessary. In July 1860, fully reconditioned, she was sold to Henry Decie of Northamptonshire, a member of the Royal Western Yacht Club.

England's sympathy for the Confederate cause was no secret. The fact that a man was engaged in contraband, and turned his leisure time to yachting, was not headline news for the press. But public attention became focused on Decie because he owned the Yankee racing schooner, and yet he

Castle Hill, Newport, R.I. in the 1800s. Watching outgoing yachts prior **to** *America's Cup race.*

Most suffered a common fate, but one went on to

was seldom seen in yachting circles. He had entered but one regatta, in 1860. That fall he fitted out the *Camilla*, letting it be known that he was sailing her on a pleasure cruise to the West Indies.

Her whereabouts was unknown until the *London Times* of May 1861 reported that Captain Decie had arrived in Savannah, Georgia, and was living aboard his schooner *Camilla*, which was flying British colors and the burgee of the R.Y.S. It was further noted that he had been the honored guest in several social gatherings which included notables in banking as well as industry. According to a local pilot, Mr. A. F. Marmelstein (who left this record before he died in 1922), the yacht was guided through local waters and out to sea directly after the social whirl of her owner. On board were a number of Confederate agents bound for England to purchase war supplies. The pilot recalled that the vessel was unusually fast when he left her.

On June 28, 1861, the *Camilla* (ex-*America*) ap-

peared in the regatta of the Queenstown Yacht Club. Her masts had been shortened and she carried the loose-footed hemp sails of British fashion. In this event she beat her three opponents and sailed the course with all the dignity and grace of a sea bird. From her appearance no one could guess that a few months before she was a shadow on the horizon of the Union blockading fleet. It was all part of Decie's strategy: to be seen in races as a cover for his more questionable pursuits. On August 5 she was in a match with the *Alarm* around the Isle of Wight and was defeated. This was her last race in British waters before she disappeared from the area and her movements became only gossip to yachting's coterie.

The scene shifts to the South Atlantic coast, where Admiral DuPont of the Union Navy was mopping up after seizing all the Confederate ports. He detailed Lieutenant Thomas H. Stevens to take the gunboat *Ottawa*, and a few light-draft vessels, on a search up the St. Johns River for

T. O. M. Sopwith's Endeavour 2nd *sails under racing rig for the first time.*

ctacular career

hidden Confederate shipping above the captured city of Jacksonville. With information obtained from a native farmer and a letter found in a rowboat abandoned by the hastily retreating rebels, the naval detachment proceeded seventy miles up the river to Dunn's Creek.

The finding of the renowned yacht is probably best described in a paragraph from *The Aquatic Monthly,* Washington, D.C.:

Where the boughs of the old forest trees on either side of the creek arched over, leaving but a small strip of blue sky, where the silence was seldom broken except by the crane, or the plunge of an alligator, and where the boats from the fleet were never likely to penetrate, the champion *America* was found. She was scuttled and sunk, in a bend in the creek, and but for her masts would have been well concealed, as there was about four feet of water above her deck.

Included in the official report of Lieutenant Stevens to Admiral DuPont, on April 23, 1862, he noted that "The *America* was brought to Jacksonville by a Lord Dacy (Decie), and, I am well informed, was sold to the Confederate government some four months ago, at which time she ran the blockade, for the sum of $60,000. It is generally believed she was bought by the rebels for the purpose of carrying Slidell and Mason to England."

Added rumors at the time of her discovery claimed that the Confederate States Navy had changed the name of the yacht to the *Memphis*. Although a vessel by that name appears in the the records of the C.S.N., she does not fit the description of the *America*. On the other hand, a supplement of the Confederate Naval Records, published in 1921, lists without details; "C.S.S. Yacht *America*." Despite the lack of clear records, it had been firmly established that the schooner yacht *America* was the one found in Dunn's Creek.

By devious use of three-anchored tackle, hoists and two large jackscrews, the yacht was raised in about a week. Three scuttle holes were plugged and she was pumped dry enough to be floated and then towed to the captured naval base at Port Royal, South Carolina. Aside from tackle abrasions to her paint work, she was in good condition. Fitted with new canvas and armed with three cannons, the Federal Navy put her in service in May 1862. Her first assignment was carrying mail and dispatches to the fleet that lay off the Florida coast.

On July 23, the *America* joined the armada of blockading vessels in the Charleston area. She received her baptism under fire the next night off Rattlesnake Shoals when she gave chase to a blockade runner. Her prey succeeded in getting through only because the *America* was too deep-drafted to follow in the shallows.

Throughout the year of 1862 and the spring of 1863 the *America* served with the South Atlantic Blockade Squadron. The constant patrol in an area known for its rough seas and stormy skies was a hard service that took its toll of ships as well as men in the effort to strangle Confederate shipping. In a short period this vessel that had been a sleek and well-groomed racing yacht now took on the image of a battle-scarred warrior. Her brightwork of brass and polished wood had been dulled and her cloud-white sails were dark-stained to hide her movements. Her spotless decks, that once knew the step of royalty, now echoed to the harsh rollings of cannon carriage while her bulwarks were charred from the flame of thundering guns.

The speed and ease of maneuvering of the *America* became legend among the crews of the squadron blockaders. Reference to her brilliant performance may be found in the letters and private diaries extant today, as well as in the record of naval archives. Admiral DuPont was well pleased that he had placed this salvaged schooner as a first-line chaser in his blockading armada. In his reports to the Secretary of Naval Affairs, he was high in his praise of her accomplishments. When he was ordered to send the *America* to the United States Naval Academy, in March 1863, he delayed her departure as long as he could. In the interim she had chased and captured the British schooner *Antelope*, which was to be her last fling with the squadron before leaving for Newport, Rhode Island, where the Academy had its wartime quarters.

Her status legally was that of a prize of war taken from the Confederate States Navy. The captors who had confiscated the yacht at Dunn's Creek, were awarded $700 prize money. Historians have recorded (but not documented) that the claimants waived their rights on condition that the *America* be turned over to the Academy for use as a training vessel for midshipmen. During her service as a school ship, the Academy was moved back to Annapolis. In 1865, in company with the *Constitution*, the *America* sailed back to the old quarters where she continued her role as a training ship and made her last cruise for the Academy in 1866.

For the next three years the *America* was out of commission and tied up at a wharf, where she joined the flotilla of several other retired vessels, including "Old Ironsides." In the fall of 1869 Admiral David Porter, Superintendent of the Academy, ordered her to the Washington Navy Yard where she was repaired and refurbished at a cost of $3,000.

Sentiment and pride for the *America* were high in the feelings of Navy personnel; from apple-cheeked neophyte sailors to hard-faced admirals—they all loved her. When the challenge came for The *America*'s Cup, the first in nineteen years, nothing would do but that she had to be entered in the international race. This time she was taken to the New York Navy Yard where she was groomed and recanvased to put her in proper condition for the contest. The cost was $10,342, not including the sails.

The challenger in this race, scheduled for August 8, 1870, was the schooner yacht *Cambria* of the Royal Thames Yacht Club. Twenty-three yachts were entered to defend The Cup. Of these only fifteen ever reached the finish line. The match was won by the *Magic*, with the *America* coming in fourth place and the *Cambria* a poor tenth. In yachting circles the *America*'s failure to win was said to be due to her "Navy rig" as well as to the inexperienced racing crew of Navy personnel. It was to be the last time that the *America* competed for The Cup that she brought to this country.

In 1873, the Secretary of the Navy saw no further use for the famous yacht, pointing out that she had already cost the government in repairs and upkeep more than her original price. She was put up for auction and, after much political haggling, was sold to General Benjamin F. Butler, of Boston, for $5,000.

The Butler family owned the *America* for forty-four years, during which time she had undergone many changes in hull, rigging and sail plan. She was entered in the regattas of the Marblehead, Boston and New York areas, winning and losing her share of the honors. As a cruising yacht she was the rendezvous for many notables in the political circuit of the General, as well as in Mayfair society. During the Spanish-American War she served her country by taking officers and soldiers at the Montauk, Long Island camp for a day's sailing picnic. The last time she was seen under sail was in July 1901 with the New York Yacht Club cruise to Vineyard Haven. In October of that year she was decommissioned and lay under cover at Chelsea Bridge in Boston. The Butlers had no plans for her future and left her in storage awaiting the first good offer.

A trading company made the offer in 1917, but before negotiations were completed, a group of yachtsmen, headed by Charles Foster of Boston took over the aging yacht. They raised the funds for her restoration and presented her to the United States Naval Academy to be put on display as a museum ship. To make it all legal, the sum of $1.00 was paid. In September of 1921, she made her last voyage, in tow of Sub Chaser #408, from Boston to Annapolis. Shoresides along the route were crowded with cheering spectators, brass bands, and fluttering banners paying spirited homage to this prima donna of sailing craft. At 12th Street and the East River, her ensign was dipped in a salute to her birthplace of seventy years ago.

For the next twenty years she lay at her berth in the Dewey Basin, a museum and shrine for visiting tourists. In 1940 she was hauled ashore and blocked, her aging hull no longer able to stand the rigors of time and the elements. A sympathetic group of workmen, on their own time, covered her with a protecting shed. In the spring of 1944 an unexpected snowstorm piled two feet of heavy snow atop the shed, which collapsed and smashed the old dowager to splinters. The debris, and what was left of the ninety-three-year-old champion, was burned in a funeral pyre, remindful of the legendary rituals in Viking traditions.

One of the few surviving relics of the *America* is her rudder, which may be seen at Mystic Seaport in Connecticut. Another piece of artifact is the beautifully-carved spread-eagle escutcheon that graced her transom until 1859. At that time it was removed as she lay neglected on the mudflats near Cowes. It was later found over the doorway of a pub at the Ryde. Rescued by a group of yachting enthusiasts, it was presented to the New York Yacht Club in 1912 by their traditional rival for The Cup, the Royal Yacht Squadron. It is now in the lobby of the N.Y.Y.C. on 44th Street. But whatever its pedestal may be, The *America*'s Cup will stand as a symbol of man's endeavour for the ultimate in wind-driven craft, its very title a lasting tribute to the schooner yacht that brought it to these shores.

The 12-meter Constellation *drives to windward in the 1964 Cup race. The English* Sovereign *was far astern.*

From large clipper to small dory, Section **VII** recalls Yankee craftsmanship at its best.

was a time of many skills, when **Shipbuilding** was truly a high calling.

HE BUILT
THE FASTEST
OF THEM ALL

by Edward Rowe Snow

At eight o'clock in the morning of Friday, March 18, 1853, a spectacularly beautiful clipper ship was slipping her way through enormous breaking waves far out on the ocean. The mighty *Sovereign of the Seas,* cutting into the surface of the South Pacific Ocean at a rate never achieved before anywhere, was making sailing ship history.

Donald McKay's brother, Captain Laughlin McKay, was her master. This craft was actually a new development in the world, for the faster she went, the steadier she sailed and the drier she stayed!

The night before had been a time of terror for all. The splendid new clipper, roaring along "under her royals," had ignored rain squalls and gusts of wind alike. The new sailors on board were almost frantic with fear, but with the coming of dawn, they began to take heart.

Even five years earlier any sane sea captain would have been extremely nervous sailing at such speed, in fear that his vessel might dive forever beneath the waves; but Captain McKay had no such worries. He knew that his brother Donald had planned and built the *Sovereign of the Seas* in such a way that this could never happen.

Instead Laughlin had other troubles. Far above him the awesome power of the wind was splitting apart the *Sovereign's* topmasts. Already the foretopmast had cracked open in two locations, while the main topmast was starting to go. But Captain McKay was determined to keep her royals on, at least for the time.

About ten o'clock that morning the master ordered the royals taken in, and little more than ninety minutes later it was recorded that for three hours the great clipper had sailed at a speed of nineteen knots! This was the swiftest sailing recorded up to that time. Secure in the knowledge that his clipper was the fastest craft afloat, Captain Laughlin McKay ordered the furling of the royals.

What led to such an amazing achievement? Who was this genius named Donald McKay whose radical ideas were showing the rest of the shipbuilders how to construct clipper ships?

Let us look back to September 4, 1810, when Donald McKay was born on a Nova Scotian farm in the old loyalist town of Shelburne. This infant was destined to grow up and become the world's greatest builder of clipper ships.

The second of sixteen children, Donald was the son of Mr. and Mrs. Hugh McKay. One day when he was seven he rode down to the waterfront on top of a wagon load of potatoes from his father's farm, and for the first time he saw a Grand Banks fishing schooner. Then and there he made up his mind that he would enjoy being associated with the building of ships.

His schooling was meager, but what he learned he retained. Hugh, his father, who had migrated to Nova Scotia after serving with the British during the American Revolution, told Donald that he should study hard while he could. Donald remembered those words for the remainder of his life!

At sixteen Donald left Nova Scotia to seek a career in New York. Finding employment in Isaac Webb's shipyard there, he began to learn the shipwright trade as an apprentice. I quote excerpts from the indenture he signed on March 24, 1827:

> This Indenture Witnesseth, that Donald McKay, now aged sixteen years, five months and twenty days, and with the consent of Hugh McKay, his father,

Donald McKay posed for this old photograph in the office of his East Boston Shipyard at the foot of Border Street. There he built the most beautiful thing ever constructed by the hand of man, the clipper ship.

McKay's residence at 80 White Street, East Boston, which still stands. Designed by him, the house reflects his classical architectural ability.

hath put himself, and by these presents doth voluntarily and of his own free will and accord put himself, apprentice to Isaac Webb, of the City of New York, ship-carpenter, to learn the art, trade and mystery of a ship-carpenter, and after the manner of an apprentice to serve from the day of the date hereof, for and during and until the full end and term of four years, six months and eleven days next ensuing; during all of which time the said apprentice his master faithfully shall serve, his secrets keep, his lawful commands everywhere readily obey; he shall do no damage to his said master, nor see it done by others without telling or giving notice thereof to his said master; he shall not waste his master's goods, nor lend them unlawfully to any: he shall not contract matrimony within the said term: at cards, dice or any other unlawful game he shall not play, whereby his said master may have damage; with his own goods nor the goods of others without license from his said master he shall neither buy nor sell; he shall not absent himself day or night from his master's service without his leave; nor haunt ale-houses, taverns, dance-houses or play-houses; but in all things behave himself as a faithful apprentice ought to do during the said term.

After working five long years at $2.50 a week, receiving a sum of $40.00 annually for meat, drink, and other necessities of life, young Donald graduated to become a shipwright. This allowed him at twenty-one years of age to work fifteen hours a day for the princely sum of $1.25 per diem, and to marry if he wished.

Before long he attracted attention at the Brown and Bell shipyard by his outstanding ability and deep interest in his work.

During this period he fell in love with Albenia Martha Boole of the local New York shipbuilding family of John Boole. They were married and soon settled down. Their first son, Cornelius Whitworth, was born February 1, 1834.

Donald obtained employment at the Brooklyn Navy Yard, but unfortunately there was a strong feeling of nationalism at the Navy Yard, and as Richard McKay later wrote, Donald, from Nova Scotia, was "bullied" out of the yard.

When Mr. Bell heard of McKay's trouble he sent him to Wiscasset, Maine, where the young man soon was drafting and building vessels for New York shipping offices. Here he discovered that New England shipwrights were far behind those of New York in the mechanics of ship-building.

One day he received a call to visit Newburyport. After inspecting the shipyards and talking with the Newburyport shipbuilders he agreed to work on the building of the ship *Delia Walker* for John Currier, Jr., on a temporary basis. The *Delia Walker* was finished in 1840. Owner Dennis Condry was much impressed with McKay's own ability and the amount of work he had been able to get out of his men. Condry praised Donald so highly that it brought about a turn in McKay's career which eventually led to fame and commercial success.

The builder, John Currier, wished to hire McKay on contract for five years, but the young man had already decided on a future of his own and would not tie himself down in such a way. He had saved a little money, and when William Currier offered him a partnership, he moved his family from Wiscasset to Newburyport and settled down as a member of the firm of Currier & McKay.

The third ship they produced, the *Courier,* was built for New York merchants to sail in the coffee trade. Shipping men in those days refused to believe that such vessels could be built outside New York or Baltimore. The success of the *Courier* was amazing, and since quick passages meant additional money, the builder was brought prominently before the maritime public. Captain Charles Porter Low, in his biography, had high praise for the beautiful handling and speed of the *Courier,* on which he was a passenger.

McKay reached the parting of the ways with Currier, and the firm of Currier and McKay was dissolved. The models and moulds were divided in two equal parts with a saw, and the association ended. McKay then went into business with William Pickett, and built the New York packet ship *St. George,* pioneer ship of the Red Cross Line, also called the St. George's Cross Line.

The shipbuilding families of Newburyport in the early forties were refined and reserved, and the charming qualities of McKay's talented wife fascinated his associates. His own unusual mechanical knowledge and ability impressed the outstanding shipbuilders, and the young couple soon became favorites of those in the best social circles.

Donald McKay had a very high ideal of womanhood, and because of this he was always drawn to cultivated and refined people. He appreciated education all the more because he had received so little schooling himself. Possessing a fine ear for music, in his younger years he played the violin.

Among the prominent men of Newburyport was Orlando B. Merrill. He it was who first conceived, in 1794, the water-line model which practically revolutionized the science of shipbuilding. The long and intimate friendship of Merrill and McKay contributed to the outstanding models made by McKay, masterpieces of the art and science of shipbuilding.

McKay and Pickett built the packet ship *John R. Skiddy*, 930 tons, in 1844. Her performance was so satisfactory that Captains William and Francis Skiddy of New York employed McKay in building other ships at their yard in East Boston.

Mr. Condry had spoken to Enoch Train about Donald McKay, and Train visited Newburyport. The contract to build the ship *Joshua Bates* was made in an hour. Upon the day when this splendid vessel was launched and floated safely upon the Merrimac River, Enoch Train grasped Donald McKay by the hand and said to him, "Come to Boston for I must have you!"

Because of this Donald McKay moved to Boston in 1844. He was then thirty-four years of age. At once he began the construction of a shipyard at the foot of Border Street, East Boston, at the same time living in a house on Princeton Street there.

Shortly afterward he built the residence which still stands at 80 White Street, East Boston, and was able to put some of his own architectural ability into the edifice. Actually, with every one of his great clipper ships gone forever, his house stands as the only remaining object of his unusual genius.

Over at the shipyards, Donald McKay was hearing reports of his Newburyport vessels. The *John R. Skiddy* had reached Liverpool from New York in fourteen days, while two other craft which he built were sailing faster than any other ships between America and England.

In 1850 Donald McKay built the *Staghound*, the first clipper ship of more than 200 feet in length.*

There were many small clippers built in England. The first was the *Scottish Maid*, launched in 1839. Three years later the *Fairy, Rapid* and *Monarch* were built. These four craft were known as the Aberdeen clippers.

In 1846 Alexander Hall built the clipper schooner *Torrington*, which was followed by the *Wanderer* and the *Gazelle*.

However, no one ever attempted to produce the lines of a small, swift vessel in a large craft until 1832, when the *Ann McKim* was built at Fell's Point, Baltimore.

One hundred and forty-three feet long, the *McKim* was the first real clipper ship. It cannot be said, however, that she founded or even began the clipper ship era, *since*

---

* Incidentally, the origin of the word "clipper" may go back to the days of Dryden, who in 1667 stated that
>   Some falcon stoops at what her eye designed,
>   And, with her eagerness the quarry missed,
>   Straight flies at check, and clips it down the wind.

By 1800, the word clip was used to indicate that a vessel was "going at a good clip," when vessels of newer models apparently clipped over the waves rather than ploughed through them.

McKay's home in Hamilton, Massachusetts. He died here, in 1880 and was buried near the sea in Newburyport, Massachusetts.

she was never copied. It more truthfully could be stated that Donald McKay's *Courier* dominated the design of the crafts which followed, and eventually influenced the production of the extreme clippers.

The *Flying Cloud,* launched in 1851, sailed from New York to San Francisco in eighty-nine days, shattering all previous marks.

The *Sovereign of the Seas* was built so large that no one else dared accept the financial responsibility of a ship of such gigantic proportions. Two hundred and fifty-eight feet long, she was the largest in the world!

Leaving from New York on August 4, 1852, she crossed the equator twenty-five days out from Sandy Hook, making an August run which was never bettered.

After rounding Cape Horn, she carried away her fore and main topmasts and also her foreyard, and fourteen days later she was rerigged. She arrived in San Francisco one hundred and three days out.

Later on February 13, 1853, she left Honolulu for New York, but sprung her fore-topmast on March 4. Two days later the mast was fished, or repaired, so that it could last the voyage.

On March 15 the first strong westerly gales were experienced and a series of remarkable day's runs began. Up to noon on March 16 she sailed 396 miles. In the next twenty-four hours she sailed 311 miles. On the 18th, she ran 411 miles, and on the 19th, 360 miles, a total of 1,478 miles in four days.

During her great run of 411 miles on the 18th, she actually had a sea day of only twenty-two hours, eighteen minutes, as she made ten degrees of longitude during this time. Nineteen miles per hour was chalked up three times on that morning of Friday, March 18, 1853.

By now East Boston, South Boston and Medford were all turning out clipper ships and Boston was easily the clipper ship center of the world. The important question was that with so many competing clipper ships, why did Donald McKay hold most of the records?

I think that the answer lies in the fact that McKay always tried to improve on what he had done before. "With all my care, I never yet built a vessel that came up to my own ideal; I saw something in each ship which I desired to improve," were his words.

All of Donald McKay's ideals were combined in the majestic craft which slipped into the waters of Boston Harbor on October 4, 1853.

The largest clipper ever designed, the *Great Republic* attracted universal attention from the very beginning. Of 4,555 tons register, she was 335 feet long, in breadth fifty-five feet and thirty-eight feet in depth. She had four decks, and carried a fifteen-horsepower engine to hoist the yards and work the pumps.

The *Great Republic* had four masts, with Forbes' rig on the fore, main and mizzen, but the spanker was bark-rigged.

October 4, the date of her launching, was a holiday. All over coastal Massachusetts business was suspended and schools were closed. At least 30,000 people crossed by ferry alone from Boston to watch the launching. Chelsea Bridge, the Navy Yard, and the wharves at North End were crowded. No less than 50,000 people were in attendance.

The moment came for the launching. All the staging around the ship was removed, and her long black hull with the giant eagle's head figurehead made a wonderful impression on the massed thousands.

Moving slowly down the ways at first, she then began to gather momentum. Faster and faster she went, accompanied by the roar of artillery, the music of bands, and the cheers of the multitudes. No such moment had ever occurred in Boston history, possibly no similar moment will ever occur again.

During the afternoon following her launching she was towed across under the great shears at the Navy Yard to receive her masts. Their gigantic dimensions even today appear incredible.

Her mainmast at the base had a diameter of forty-four inches, while the mainmast itself was 131 feet long. Next above the mainmast the topmast and the top-gallant added another 104 feet, while the royal and skysail each towered twenty feet more into the sky. Technically, if extended, the complete mainmast would soar about 275 feet above the deck, but whether or not the entire assembly ever was in place in elongated fashion will never be known.

The greatest tragedy in Donald McKay's shipbuilding career now occurred. At her pier in New York on December 26, 1853, the *Great Republic* caught fire from flying embers from a blaze at nearby Front Street, and she burned to the water's edge.

Cut down later and rebuilt, the *Great Republic* still was able to reach the equator from New York in less than sixteen days and to sail to San Francisco in 92. But McKay never really recovered from the shock of the fire which destroyed the extreme effectiveness of his dream craft.

Donald McKay Memorial, Castle Island, Boston.

Kay's last effort, as well as the final work at his great shipyard

Donald McKay then built the *Lightning* for the Australian run, and on March 1, 1854, she logged 436 miles, thus becoming the world's fastest ship. Not for thirty years did any other craft of any type exceed her speed, and for sailing craft the *Lightning* was the swiftest ship which ever sailed the seas!

A tribute to Daniel Webster, the "defender of the Constitution," was made on July 28, 1855, when the *Defender,* a combination clipper ship and packet was launched. Webster's son Fletcher attended the launching, as did Edward Everett, along with former Boston Mayors Seaver and Bigelow, Colonel Adams, and Enoch Train.

The figurehead of Daniel Webster ornamented the bow of the *Defender.* After the launching, open house was held at Donald McKay's home on White Street. Edward Everett spoke during the feast, during which time the former mayor of Boston, Benjamin Seaver, and Colonel Train, added their own remarks.

The *Defender* sailed from Boston for San Francisco on September 1, 1855, but on February 27, 1859, she was wrecked and lost on Elizabeth Reef, South Pacific Ocean.

Back at his home at 80 White Street, East Boston, McKay received the news of the disaster the following fall. In the house where he had entertained Daniel Webster, he thought back to the moments when the statesman had told him of the country's future. Other great men later graced his East Boston parlors, among them Garrison, Longfellow, Farragut, Ericsson and Matthew F. Maury.

The last great clipper ship was launched in November, 1869, the *Glory of the Seas.* She was one of the most satisfying vessels ever produced at the McKay yard.

When seen broadside, she had all the majesty of a ship of war, but still resembled a clipper. She was 250 feet long, had three full decks, and carried double topsails. On January 18, 1874, she sailed into San Francisco ninety-six days out from New York, having completed the ninth best record in history.

After a long career, she was burned at Endolyne in Washington on May 13, 1923, the last sailing vessel built by McKay for the American Merchant Marine.

During the Civil War, McKay had been turning out iron-clad gunboats and monitors. Some of the craft built by him for the government include the *Trefoil,* the *Yucca,* the *Nausett,* the *Ashuelot,* and the *Aftermath.*

When the war ended, the Navy suffered decay. Finally in 1873, eight warships were authorized, and McKay successfully bid for the sloops of war *Adams* and *Essex.* The *Adams* was placed in commission on July 21, 1876, and the *Essex* followed her into the Navy on October 3, 1876.

In 1851, McKay, with the rest of the shipping and yachting world, was thrilled when the *America* won the Queen's Cup in Great Britain. Sold to John Stevens in England, the *America* was later sent to the bottom by the Confederates in the Southern river so that the Northern forces could not capture her. Later she was raised and brought to Boston Harbor, where she served as a governmental school ship for a time.

General B. F. Butler purchased her in 1873 at auction and then asked McKay to put her back in the condition which would represent her former maritime glory.

The renovation of the *America* proved to be McKay's last effort, and also the last work at the great Donald McKay shipyard. By June 15, 1875, the *America* had been restored to the original condition of 1851 and lawyer-soldier-politician Ben Butler could really enjoy cruising up and down the Atlantic coast.

By 1875 Donald McKay knew that he had incipient consumption, and realized that he would have to retire. Moving his family to a house which is still standing in Hamilton, Massachusetts, McKay became a farmer.

Early in 1880 it was seen that his condition was so advanced that no longer could he work in the fields of his farm, and from April in that year he was restricted to a passive existence. On September 20, 1880, McKay died at his Hamilton home.

His remains were taken to Oak Hill Cemetery, Newburyport, where he lies buried on the slope of a small hill. His two wives, Albenia Martha, who died in 1848, and Mary Cressy Litchfield, who lived until 1923, lie buried with him.

About eight years after the death of the widow of Donald McKay, a movement was started to erect somewhere in Boston, or along the waterfront, a memorial to the man who was responsible for making the clipper ship famous.

Funds were raised to construct a granite monument fifty-two feet high, on which the names of all McKay's ships were recorded. Finished in 1933, this memorial on Castle Island is visited annually by thousands of people, who can either walk or drive out to the island which is also the oldest actively fortified area in America.

In 1967 Donald McKay's homeland honored him by dedicating a monument to his memory in Nova Scotia.

The finest creation of American genius, the clipper ship, has gone forever. Even those children who watched the beautiful sails as they disappeared off Boston Light during the '50s and early '60s have passed on, but the thoughts inspired by Donald McKay's *Sovereign of the Seas, Flying Cloud,* and *Lightning* will never die.

Over a century and a half ago, the American frigate Constitution*, already a hero of the Tripolitan War, reduced the British vessel* Guerriere *to, in the words of her commander, a "perfect wreck." This was not unusual. "Old Ironsides" never lost a fight. In 1927, however, she nearly struck her colors to Father Time. In fact, she was literally falling apart.*

236

THE *U.S.S. CONSTITUTION* *by T. M. Prudden*

TIME DOES NOT TREAT WOODEN VESSELS KINDLY FOR, unless they are continuously maintained, deterioration sets in quickly. So it was with our frigate *Constitution*. In 1923 she was badly disintegrating and distorted, being eleven inches wider in the port side than on the starboard, and her stem was twisted eight inches to port. She has been drastically repaired many times, including two almost complete rebuildings; once in 1833 at the time that Oliver Wendell Holmes' poem "Old Ironsides" sparked the work, and again in 1927–1931. In 1954, President Eisenhower signed a bill that would guarantee the *Constitution* maintenance for life. Such authorization permitted the Navy to spend $890,000 for the vessel's preservation and, in 1957, she was hauled up onto the same drydock, opened in 1833, first used by the *Constitution*. But it is with the gigantic rebuilding task undertaken in 1927 that this article is concerned.

Her rotted condition at that time was appalling. The problems involved were:

1. The cost would be far greater than her original cost of $93,000. Actually, the expense of rebuilding was $923,000, of which $271,000 was donated by school children, the rest being appropriated by Congress, and by the sale of souvenirs such as her copper bolts made by Paul Revere.

2. There were no authentic plans of the frigate, and a confusion of different and contradictory lines required extensive research. A tracing in the Bureau of Construction and Repair in Washington had been considered as correct. But an examination of the drawing showed that the dimensions did not correspond with those of the actual ship, she being fifteen inches deeper and nearly eleven feet longer than the plans depicted. The experts decided that the Navy tracing was probably only cribbed from some French design —a plausible theory since Mr. Humphreys, her designer, leaned toward French ideas for his plans.

Three of Mr. Humphreys' plans were available, the original sheer plan, the half-breadth, and the body plan. But the value of these original plans was lessened because many changes were made during the actual building.

Other plans in the Boston Navy Yard were largely incorrect and probably sketchily represented the ship prior to various overhaul or restoration work.

In the end, working drawings were made by applying half-breadths lifted from the decks of the ship herself, and comparing them with Humphreys' drawings which were on a different scale. When the rebuilding was finished, an accurate plan of her offsets was made. Thus, the plans we have today are considered reasonably accurate.

3. There were few records of any wooden vessel so old as the *Constitution* being safely dry-docked. Even a very decrepit ship can hold herself together in the water where she is evenly supported all around. But to mount the same ship in dry dock on keel blocks puts uneven strains on her which can readily cause her to fall apart. With the *Constitution* this meant 2,000 tons (about the weight of a World War II destroyer) had to be transferred by rotten frames to a weakened keel. (She's been drydocked since, of course, but in better condition.)

The *Victory,* Nelson's flagship at the battle of Trafalgar, is contemporary with our *Constitution,* and she is still in existence. But she is so far gone and tender that our British cousins have not dared to dry dock her, except to set her in concrete.

It was a great challenge to the Navy constructor who was placed in charge of rebuilding. If he succeeded, he would be honored, but if the ship fell apart in dry dock (as she very well might if much skill and good engineering were not used), then his name would be infamous.

His name was Lieutenant John A. Lord (C.C.) USN; and he was born in Bath, Maine, in 1872. He entered the Navy as a carpenter, and as a "mustang" rose to commissioned rank. He served for several years on the China station in charge of maintenance of our river gun boats.

It is reported that he requested the assignment to rebuild the *Constitution*. He was all wrapped up in the work, rather stern, and strictly business. He was indefatigable and would work all day at his job, then often put in evenings lecturing about the ship in the interest of raising funds.

The docking of the *Constitution* was quite a ceremony. The Secretary of the Navy, numerous admirals, and the Governor of Massachusetts were present. She was warped into the same old dry dock which had received her as its first client nearly ninety-four years before.

The first step was to remove her guns, her masts, her bowsprit, her ballast, and all her interior fittings to lighten the hull. Then, a heavy timber cribwork was built on the spar (upper) deck. Over this, as a fulcrum, were passed two heavy cables running fore and aft, one on each side of the masts. They were carried through the hawse holes in the bow and secured to a huge timber outside the hull at her stern and just above the rudder. They were hauled well taut.

This bracing formed a truss to support her ends, since the whole hull was so weak, distorted and hogged that there was danger of the ends falling away. The truss was hauled taut by turnbuckles.

This view of one of the Constitution's *channels and decayed outer oak planking clearly demonstrates the rotted condition she was in before the delicate task of restoration began in 1927.*

To supplement the truss, a cable was run all around the ship at the level of the gun ports. Cross-ship cables were passed through every third gun port and drawn up with turnbuckles.

Internally she was supported by over two hundred shores set in a fore and aft plane and having slip-joints to permit adjustment as the hull worked during settlement on the keel blocks. In this well-trussed condition, the *Constitution* was successfully docked, blocked and shored for her restoration.

The most delicate operation was settling her on the keel blocks as the dock was slowly pumped out. The *Constitution* had been "hogged" during her original launching, i.e., her keel arched upwards fourteen inches. The injury had never been repaired, and does not seem to have hurt her, for she carried it all her life. The keel blocks were of uniform height, and the ship was lowered till her bow and stern rested on them. Meanwhile, the butt ends of the planking on both gun and berth decks had been cut slightly short, leaving a ¾-inch gap between the ends of each plank, and making her somewhat limber. It would have been simpler to have stripped the planking from these two decks since it had to be replaced anyway, but apparently Lieutenant Lord felt the ship was too decayed to be without some support from the deck planking. The *Constitution* was further lowered until her weight straightened out the keel on the keel blocks, so that new keelsons could be installed. It must have fearfully wracked the hull, but she stood it. She was more rotten than anyone realized and it was possible to wrench her as it would not have been possible with a stiffer ship.

The distortion of her port side and her twisted stem

were corrected by tackle attached to bollards on shore, and her shores held her from being dragged sideways.

A forest of shores were placed outside the hull. It was even necessary to support with shores the overhanging part of the stem which carries the billet head.

Obtaining the right lumber, particularly white oak, was a real problem. Fortunately the Navy, prior to the Civil War when ships were wooden, had cut white oak in Pensacola, Florida, and had kept it stored underwater. It still was excellent and was described as "alive" and neither waterlogged nor brittle, since it had been placed underwater when green, and the sap had never wholly dried out. Besides the 1,500 tons of oak lumber it was necessary to procure some two hundred white oak knees. It took two years to get them.

The Douglas fir for deck beams, deck planking and ceiling came from Oregon, and practically every state contributed something. Many firms gave material, from copper to marine glue, and those firms and their gifts are listed on a scroll on the berth deck.

The problem of finding experienced shipwrights was great, although many yacht yards today employ skilled adzmen. Boatswains mates familiar with the heavy rope of the shrouds were even scarcer. We have little shroud-laid rope

The Constitution *in action with the* Levant *and the* Cyane. *On the right is seen the upper deck gangway carrying carronades.*

today (the reverse twist to usual rope) and four-strand rope at that.

Each step in replacement of old timber was carefully worked out, so that at all times the ship would be safely supported.

In rebuilding, the 7-inch outside white oak planking was removed down below the waterline—there was less decay below this point. Thus, the upper ends of the frames (ribs) were exposed and templates (patterns) were made on thin boards to copy the curve of that part of the frames which had to be replaced. Her frames were made of several sections of timber (9 inches to 12 inches square), perhaps twelve sections, called futtocks, each carefully scarfed and bolted together. They were not one piece, steamed and bent into shape, as is done with smaller vessels. It was the upper sections which were renewed. The decayed futtocks were carefully cut away at the scarf, using hacksaws to cut through the bolts, and new sections installed. Galvanized bolts were used, rather than using copper bolts as originally furnished.

The amount of metal required in the original building is evidenced by a section of oak removed from her keel in 1833—"A piece of timber 9 feet long, 27 inches wide, 14 inches thick, and weighing 1,460 pounds was removed from her. On breaking it up, in it were found 364 pounds of iron and 163 pounds of copper."

The spar and gun decks were stripped of their planking to expose the deck beams whose ends were decayed. New beams were installed, and the new lumber was brush-treated with creosote. This would give an estimated life of twenty-seven years. Compare this figure with a shipbuilder's estimate of seven years' life for untreated wood on a ship built in the open air or 15 years if she were built under cover.

The *Constitution*'s keel was found to be in good shape (oak stored continuously underwater, even fresh water, decays very little and hardly at all in salt water). But the keelson (the supplementary keel inside the ship and on top of the keel) was in bad condition since an inferior oak had been used in her previous rebuilding. It was decided not to replace this keelson but to build two new keelsons on either side of the old one, so the oak ordered for a new keel, and not needed, was used for these members.

Many of the lignum-vitae deadeyes and some of the blocks were found fit for reuse, but some 1,300 new blocks were needed. For new heart-blocks on the forestay a 20-inch diameter lignum-vitae log was required, which is a rare piece of wood.

All new spars were made, mostly in the Navy Yard spar shop. The mainmast was built up in four sections and secured with iron bands. (The *Constitution*'s original mast was a solid stick but in 1811 this was replaced by a four-piece stick.) There is much doubt if the *Constitution* carried

If he failed, the young lieutenant's name would be infamous

Firmly trussed to support her ends (which, it was feared, would fall away due to the weak and distorted condition of her hull) and with cables around and across her, the Constitution *is readied for dry-dock.*

The Constitution *as she is today, tied up at her home port, Boston, Massachusetts.*

Gordon N. Converse

To this day, she remains a commissioned warship

sky-sails on these upper masts, but each captain introduced variations in her rig to suit his whims, and no one can be certain.

All her standing rigging was made in the Charlestown Navy Yard ropewalk, much of it being four-strand and shroud-laid. The Navy Yard ropewalk had been in use for over a century, and had the old-time equipment and long walk for twisting the rope. Today it still operates, but with modern and compact machinery.

She was recoppered up to her waterline, using sixty-five tons of copper, including eight tons of old copper fastening left in the ship.

Only 15 per cent of the old vessel was re-used, and 10 per cent of this is estimated to be material built into the original ship. This old material included the outer keel, lower futtocks or transverse frames, floor timbers, lower part of the stem, lower section of the stern post, about 30 per cent of the outside planking below the waterline, some large oak stern knees, about 50 per cent of the breast hooks and 35 per cent of the oak knees. The greatest decay was under the waterways. Waterways are the planks on the upper deck next to the bulwarks. They carry any sea which has splashed aboard, guiding it down the edge of the deck to the scuppers. In any wooden vessel, even modern yachts, there is difficulty keeping the waterways tight. As a result, moisture reaches the planking and timbers underneath, and in the *Constitution* the result was the rotting of the ends of the deck beams and the upper ends of the frames. But the knees for the deck beams were usable.

Many of her fittings were reinstalled, including the wood-burning galley (a shipmate, and not the original one), some of the stanchions, the large oak bitts for hawsers, cable compressors, her wooden-stocked anchors, hawse-pipes, wooden rudder, capstans, bilge pumps, steering wheels and binnacle. She now has a second double steering wheel on her gun deck. It was not there in 1812.

The story of the guns on the *Constitution* is quite involved. It comes from Mr. Charles S. Adams, who was the designer of them.

The last guns on the ship prior to her rebuilding were phony. They were copied from a French Naval Ordnance book, and were purposely made light-weight to lessen the load on an old vessel. The thickness of the wall in the barrels was only ½-inch thick. Unfortunately, these are the guns which have been distributed around the country as "guns from the frigate, *Constitution*."

The present 24-pounders were carefully copied from guns of 1812, and were cast in the yard. Some of these guns carry, cast on the barrel, the royal monogram GR, which is correct, as the *Constitution*'s original armament came from England.

The present guns are accurate as far as research can determine, except that the touch holes have not been drilled completely through the barrel. This was a concession to prevent tampering by visitors. If a woman visitor will attempt to walk off the ship with a 24-pound cannon ball hidden under her coat—as actually happened—there is no telling what someone might try, even to a 5,000-pound gun!

When her masts were stepped, the traditional gold piece was placed under her foremast. In addition, a silver coin went under her main and a copper coin under her mizzen.

She received back her ballast of 103 tons of grapefruit-sized round stones. These were old cobblestones which had been presented to the ship by the City of Boston and were formerly the paving stones from Revere Street. They had been the actual paving there for many years.

Her spar deck is armored with carronades, a shorter and lighter cannon, and these the *Constitution* actually carried. In 1907, someone had furnished 24-pounders for the spar deck, but although they were her armament before 1812 they proved to be too heavy for even a vessel of the stiffness of the *Constitution,* and also made her top-heavy.

As a concession to safety, the *Constitution* is equipped with electric lights and a sprinkler system, and water pressure is maintained aboard. In each of her stern galleries (the glassed-in bulges at either corner of her stern) are installed a modern toilet and a tiny bathtub. These galleries were originally the heads for the captain and the commodore. Of course, she must be well lighted for the many visitors, but it would be interesting if it were possible to use her whale-oil lights to show how dim was her below-decks, or to sling a few hammocks to give an idea of her crowded quarters—four hundred men sleeping on her berth deck—or to indicate the stifling temperature on the gun deck in bad weather when the ports were closed and her large galley was in use, all this in the warm, sticky climate off the coast of Algiers.

After her rebuilding, the *Constitution* visited (under tow) some ninety-one ports on both our east and west coasts. Over 4,700,000 people visited her from July 1, 1931 to May 7, 1934.

She now lies at her home port, Boston, tied up in the Charlestown Navy Yard. In 1953—twenty-seven years since her complete rebuilding—much of her planking and decking had to be replaced and perhaps 60 per cent of her rigging. Her sails have perished and are worthless. Today all her running rigging is missing, as is her flying jibboom. She is towed into the stream once a year and turned around so that each side will weather equally. The operation seems to be more of ceremony rather than shipkeeping.

She is a commissioned warship and is the flagship of the Admiral commanding the Boston Navy Yard. Her captain is a reserve lieutenant, and she has a complement of forty-two sailors, many of them apprentice seamen.

There is no more worth-while historical exhibit in Boston than this ship.

THE DUTIFUL DORY

by Samuel T. Williamson

Ralph Lowell of Amesbury, Massachusetts, the seventh generation of Lowells to carry on the family's business. The Lowells made their first dory in 1793.

ONE OF THE FINEST SEABOATS DEVISED BY MAN IS THE dory, rugged rowboat of North Atlantic fishermen and as essential for artists' seascapes and downeast fiction as a rock-bound coast, lobstermen's weatherbeaten shacks and nets drying in the sun.

From twelve to eighteen feet long, a dory has sloping sides, overhanging bow and V-shaped stern, and a broad, flat bottom. This inward flare at all points offers less resistance to waves than a hull with straight-rising sides and is the secret of the dory's extraordinary seaworthiness. Recent America's Cup contenders performed better because they had inward sloping sides. Using test tanks and electronic computers, their designers arrived at the same principle that dory makers of more than two centuries ago figured out by guess and by gosh.

An empty dory draws about three inches of water and won't capsize even when a hefty boy teeters on its gunnel. Its carrying capacity is greater than any craft its size: two tons of flopping fish without being awash. With a landlubber at the oars, the direction is as unpredictable as an unhitched mule's. Husky college crewmen, trying to row with the long, sweeping strokes they use in racing shells, become gasping wrecks in a few minutes. A dory must be rowed with short, round-shouldered, chopping strokes which inch it as steadily through rough water as if motor-driven. This is the "fishermen's stroke," not pretty but it gets there.

The ugly duckling dory is a maritime poor relation. Nautical historians barely give it a nod. Lushly illustrated books about America's romantic seagoing past ignore it. One or two marine reference books mention "dory" not as a boat but as a fish in the English Channel, and Nova Scotians call redfish "John Dory fish." Some dictionaries attribute the boat's name to "duri," a Central American Indian dugout, which is like crediting grass skirts to the Eskimos. After more than two centuries of its known existence, this victim of neglectful history deserves an authentic story—as well as a monument.

It is a story of sturdy people who built it and of hardy men who used it, and it begins with the Lowell family of

Editor's Note: *No book dealing with the era of wind-driven ships would be complete without a tribute to that unsung hero requiring elbow-grease—the dory. Whether used on the high seas for setting and picking up trawls, or on calmer waters for tending lobster traps, fishermen knew that she was built in such a way that no matter what, "if you stay with it, you won't go down." The photographs on this page were taken at Annisquam, Mass., during the 1890s.*

Amesbury, Massachusetts. Here, in a pleasing bend of the Merrimack River six miles above the old seaport of Newburyport, is the boatshop of Hiram Lowell & Sons. And in this shavings-cluttered shop where dories have been turned out since the 1790s, Ralph Lowell of the seventh generation of boat-builders carries on the family business. On the wharf below is the paint shop with a rough, bumpy floor of what looks like six-inch plastic. "More than a hundred and sixty years of paint drippings," Ralph explains.

Ralph went to work for his grandfather when he was thirteen and later bought out that hard-driving old man. Now in his early fifties, he is slow-spoken and staid, a trait he sheds at square dances Friday nights. He selects all the stock, and watches with a pair of appraising blue eyes every board that goes into his boats—dories, skiffs and outboards —and he has developed such a "feel" for wood that he can go into his loft in the dark and pick just the quality board he wants.

The first Lowells came to this country in the 1630s, settled in Newbury, a few miles from Amesbury, then branched out. One branch moved to Boston and acquired such affluence and exclusiveness that it was reputed to speak only to God, although there is no report of a two-way conversation. Besides judges, bankers and mill-owners, it produced a Harvard president, A. Lawrence Lowell, and such poets as James Russell Lowell, who wrote in rhyme, and cigar-smoking Amy Lowell, whose free verse was sometimes baffling.

These were *The* Lowells. Their admiring biographer dismisses the other branch as "worthy citizens" and attributes their lesser eminence to the lack of driving power of an ancestor who remained in Newbury. He, it seems, was sickly and didn't live beyond eighty. His descendants were farmers, country parsons, mariners and soldiers in ten wars from King Philip's to Korea. "We belong to the Other Lowells," Ralph says of his people. "They didn't write poems, just built ships and boats."

Their biggest ship, the *Alliance,* was one of the first frigates authorized by the Continental Congress and sailed with John Paul Jones. Commanded by a renegade Frenchman when the *Bon Homme Richard* met the *Serapis,* she fired broadside into Jones' flagship instead of at the Britisher. After the Revolution, Hiram Lowell moved his boatshop a bit down the river where it is today. According to family tradition, it was his grandfather Simeon who built and named the first dory in 1793. If so, neither Ralph nor existing town and Lowell documents explain how he made it or why he named it. But there is no serious dispute of the Lowell's claim to priority. They were building dories before there is any record of others doing so, they are still building them and, at least, are entitled to squatter's rights to the claim.

Until well into the last century, the dory was a coastal fisherman's craft, and the Lowell dory-building business didn't flourish until the offshore banks fishermen gave up handlining for the trawl. Before that, chin-whiskered cod and galumphing halibut were caught on the Grand Banks

Ralph Lowell, above, personally selects every board that goes into his dories. He has developed such an "educated feel" for lumber, he can actually pick out in the dark the quality board he wants.

Sam Smith, upper right, uses a wooden plane—an old tool still in use at Lowell & Sons—to shape planking.

Contrary to popular belief, all dories are not alike; the distinctive difference in a Lowell dory begins here with the initial shaping.

off Newfoundland with single hook and line from a vessel's deck, the same way Portuguese fished there fifty years before Columbus saw the New World. Around the 1840s, some innovator sank a long line along the bottom with hoops every six feet. This was the trawl, sometimes more than a mile long and with a thousand hooks. It was a fussy thing to bait and handle; lines had to be coiled in tubs just so, or there'd be a hurrah's nest of tangled hooks and twine—and outraged fisherman language beside which some fiction dialogue would be pure Louisa May Alcott.

Gloucester skippers of the world's biggest fishing port took to the trawl as eagerly as cod take squid bait. If they sent crews out in rowboats, they figured, the combined catch would be greater than from one trawl. The problem was how to get the boats to the banks: mustn't clutter up a schooner's deck and couldn't be towed in a string astern like a mother duck with a brood of young ones.

The Amesbury Lowells had the answer. Their dories were built to a single pattern, one fitted into another as neatly as saucers in a china closet, and a nest of six occupied the deck space of one. So began a close relationship between dory-building Lowells and Gloucester fishermen of Cape Ann that continues to this day. The "Lowell dory" became the "Cape Ann dory," and use of it spread to the rest of the North Atlantic fishing fleet. French and Portuguese adopted

it, so did State of Mainers and boatshops from Newfoundland to Cape Cod.

"To most eyes, all dories are alike, but they aren't," says Ralph Lowell. "Out of a whole harbor with dories from different builders, I can spot one of ours every time. I can't explain it; there's something about the way our dory sets in the water. Maybe it's the stock we use. Sides and skillets— bottoms, I mean— are seasoned white pine; stem, stern and ribs and rails are oak. Some dory builders use spruce instead of pine and applewood instead of oak; a few don't wait for the wood to season. But even when our design is copied exactly, the balance differs.

"A few years ago, the Coast Guard people came to me and said that every time it was in the market for dories, they told builders to copy a 'Hiram Lowell dory,' but they didn't have plans and specifications. So I drew up a set, and what did the Coast Guard do but put it out for competitive bidding and another builder got the contract. I was kicking myself for giving away our plans, but after the boats were delivered, the government condemned them, and we ended by building the dories anyway."

When Glo'stermen took to dory trawling, the North Atlantic fisheries were already the most perilous of all occupations. Mountainous seas swept decks and washed men overboard. Schooners foundered or were cast ashore by fe-

Production of the more contemporary outboard far outnumbers the old dory at the Lowell's shop today.

They rounded her sides and squared off her stern

rocious gales, and a man was safer going to war than fishing; while the Civil War took 142 Gloucester lives, the sea claimed 307. At the height of banks trawling, 100 Gloucester men lost their lives in dories in five years—starved or died from thirst in summer, froze to death in winter or pitched overboard in storms. A dory put overboard in a high-running sea rode high above a schooner's rail one moment and down in the trough of a wave the next; a man had to know to the split second when to hop in. In winter he'd be bundled as snug as a sound-barrier-busting aviator in two layers of thick outer and inner clothing, two suits of oilskins, and a pair of heavy seaboots. If he missed his footing, down he went like a lead sinker, and the next August there would be one more name to call and one more bouquet of flowers for little girls in starched white dresses to toss into Gloucester Harbor on Fishermen's Memorial Sunday.

The trawling fleet sent out two men in each dory; they could set and pick trawls quicker, and one spelled the other at the oars or bailing when trouble came. High praise for a fisherman was "He's a good dorymate," but "He's a damn' good dorymate" was accolade.

The Lowell boatbuilding business was as rugged as banks dorymen. And more frugal. "Winter mornings," Ralph recalls, "my first job was to light the stove at 6:30, then lug buckets of water from my great-grandfather's place across the street. One bucket always stood exactly six feet from the stove, and by ten o'clock on coldest days the water was froze solid."

Ralph made the indisputable assertion that "it was no fun working when it was that cold." But he added, "We've gone modern now with a furnace. Of course, we still burn wood." Electricity was another innovation. "We had none when I first went to work here. Not even lanterns; just worked by feel when it grew dark, and from one end we could barely see a dory's other end. But the workmanship was as perfect as if we'd had all the light in the world."

Fred E. Lowell, Ralph's grandfather who taught him the business, saw both the height of dory building and its decline after World War I. During the early 1900s, he turned out 4,000 dories a year for the Danes, Germans and Portuguese, as well as the Gloucester fishing fleet. In those days a dory cost a dollar an over-all foot, delivery extra. A 14-footer was $14; today, the stock alone costs $90. Sometimes grandfather Lowell made extra money by delivering dories in person. When the tide was right, he would row a string of a half dozen boats six miles down the Merrimack, then seventeen miles across Ipswich Bay to Cape Ann and Gloucester. "Grandfather often told me," says his descendant, "he didn't think my generation was quite so rugged as his."

When he was a young man, Fred Lowell made newspaper headlines by launching a 60-ton schooner single-handed. A crowd gathered on launching day to watch and lap up the customary free rum. The chocks were knocked away, a young woman in her best bustle and basque stood with the christening bottle at the ready, but the vessel didn't move. The boss builder carried on like a wild man until up stepped Freddie Lowell to put shoulders and heft against the keel at a certain point, and the schooner whooshed down the ways.

"He wasn't a big man," his grandson explains, "but he always knew where to put leverage to move things. In 1941 he had a stroke which did quite a job on him and left one arm useless. After he was able to walk again, he'd come to the shop with a wheelbarrow and load up firewood. He held one handle with his good hand and the other handle was in a sling hanging over his neck. Just before I entered war service we were shoving a big motor boat across the floor not as fast as he would like it, so he joined us and put his good shoulder against the boat and moved it at least five feet with one shove, whereas six of us hadn't been doing so well."

By this time, the dory output of Hiram Lowell & Sons had shrunk to a mere handful. Another revolution hit the banks fisheries. Replacing the once revolutionary trawl and the graceful schooner, came the diesel-powered dragger or beam trawler which draws a tough-fibered net, shaped like a woman's snood, along bottom and brings up every living thing on the ocean floor. After more than a century of tending trawls by dory, the Yankee banks fisherman is back where he started: on a vessel's deck. But when things go wrong, the Cape Ann dory still brings him back to safety.

Instead of 4,000 fishermen's dories a year, the Lowell boatshop turns out less than a hundred. Possibly grandfather Lowell anticipated the change, for years ago he cut the dory in size, slightly rounded the sides and squared off the stern for a boat a small boy or a nervous woman could handle. He called it a skiff, but yachtsmen, duck hunters and imitators over the country knew it as the "Amesbury dory." It was a natural craft for the new-fangled outboard motor, and now that the outboard craze prevails wherever there is a stretch of water more than knee-deep, its basic hull can be recognized in hundreds of adaptations.

In this multi-million-dollar business, the Hiram Lowell boatshop has only a microscopic share. All its boats—dories and outboards—are still hand-built. With more than two centuries of wooden boat-building behind him, the seventh generation of the Amesbury Lowells cocks a skeptic eye at such materials as aluminum, plastic and fiber glass. All right in nice weather with Mae West life preservers handy, he says, but "a wooden boat doesn't sink and if for any reason it should capsize, stay with it and you won't go down."

BENEATH THE BOWSPRIT

by Oliver Bank

SHIPS' FIGUREHEADS WERE LOVELY LADIES WHO WENT to sea with stern clipper captains and salty sailors; they lived beneath the ship's slender bowsprit.

When a sea captain walked his quarter-deck on sunny days, he could see coquettish curls tossed back over bare white shoulders, and glimpse a gown of blue and gold. At night when the moon was high, he could watch the lovely lady turn to silver over the shining water. When his ship was tossed in the fury of Atlantic storms he saw his lady plunge beneath the waves to rise sea-drenched.

Such was the figurehead of clipper ship days when Yankees went to sea. The lady figurehead was coy, she was prim, she was entrancing; she was wife, she was sweetheart, she was maiden, she was understanding woman, she was romance, during endless days at sea. She kept hope and

Figureheads in Mystic Seaport Museum, Mystic, Conn. The fine craftsmen who carved figureheads largely disappeared from the scene at the turn of the century.

affection and desire alive in men who were usually cold and hungry and often exhausted by the unbelievable hardships of those times. The lady figurehead was usually seductive even when her proportions were heroic. But the fancy of either the owner of the ship or perhaps the carver of the figurehead produced various forms of ladies.

For example, there was the lady figurehead that sailed the seven seas clad in a hat and veil and with a rolled umbrella in her hands.

One was a sailor girl—a roguish, wicked looking lass with her hat on the back of her head and a real come-hither look in her eye. Another was an Apostle with a mermaid's arms around him. Many American ships carried figures of Indians, both warriors and princesses. There was Dolores, the Spanish girl with beautiful long black curls and flowers in her hair.

Once a Yankee ship adorned with a beautiful lady figurehead sailed to a South Sea port. When the natives came out on their boats to meet the Yankees, the ship

Most are now under sea grass on the ocean's floor

lurched and the figurehead hit a dusky chieftain on the head. Instead of being angry, the chieftain was so pleased by the delicate loveliness of the lady that he commissioned the captain to have the New England ship-carver make him a collection of similar beautiful figureheads. This was done. The next time the ship came to the islands, they were delivered, and the chieftain and his subjects worshiped the figureheads as idols the rest of their lives.

Believe it or not, the ship *Santa Claus* sailed from Boston with the figurehead of Santa Claus at its prow! Her master was Captain Bailey Foster of Brewster, Cape Cod. The *Santa Claus* was built by Donald McKay, creator of the clipper ships that revolutionized American sailing.

The *Saint Paul,* built in 1833, had as its figurehead a white bust of the Apostle Paul. The ship's large square stern with cabin windows was embellished with a superb carving, representing the Apostle Paul shaking the viper from his hand into the fire when he was shipwrecked on the Isle of Malta.

When the *U.S.S. Constitution* was built it was announced that she would typify the dignity of the Union and it was thought proper, therefore, that her figurehead should suggest strength and power. *Old Ironsides* had three figureheads; first a Hercules that did not wear very well and disappeared from the ship in about 1807. The second figurehead was a Neptune. This was removed, and in the War of 1812 the ship carried only a carved scroll.

On June 7, 1866, the whaling schooner, *A. L. Putnam,* commanded by a Cape Cod Captain, was in the Indian Ocean. The look-out, thinking he saw the body of a woman in the water, stopped the ship and sent a boat out to get her. It was a woman, but a wooden one—a beautiful figurehead apparently torn from a ship. Too large, it had to be cut in half to get it into the ship's hold. This derelict figurehead now rests safely on top of a house on Commercial Street at Provincetown, Cape Cod.

No longer, of course, do winsome lady figureheads and brave captains put out to sea together. Most of the captains sleep peacefully in quiet New England graveyards. Some of the figureheads stand disconsolately in seaside gardens. Others stand alone in airless museums where they seem out of place so far from sea and sky. And a few you will never see for they lie, where perhaps they belong, under waving sea grass on the ocean's floor.

Bow of the Downeaster Great Admiral, *showing her figurehead.*

Index